LION WITHIN

LION WITHIN

P.D. WORKMAN

ISBN: 9781926500980 (IS Hardcover)

ISBN: 9781926500973 (IS Paperback)

ISBN: 9781774680360 (Large Print)

ISBN: 9781926500454 (KDP Paperback)

ISBN: 9781926500461 (Kindle)

ISBN: 9781926500478 (ePub)

pdworkman

ALSO BY P.D. WORKMAN

MYSTERY/SUSPENSE:

Reg Rawlins, Psychic Detective

What the Cat Knew

A Psychic with Catitude

A Catastrophic Theft

Night of Nine Tails

Telepathy of Gardens

Delusions of the Past

Fairy Blade Unmade

Web of Nightmares

A Whisker's Breadth

Skunk Man Swamp (Coming Soon)

Magic Ain't A Game (Coming Soon)

Without Foresight (Coming Soon)

Auntie Clem's Bakery

Gluten-Free Murder

Dairy-Free Death

Allergen-Free Assignation

Witch-Free Halloween (Halloween Short)

Dog-Free Dinner (Christmas Short)

Stirring Up Murder

Brewing Death

Coup de Glace

Sour Cherry Turnover

Apple-achian Treasure

Vegan Baked Alaska

Muffins Masks Murder

Tai Chi and Chai Tea

Santa Shortbread

Zachary Goldman Mysteries

She Wore Mourning

His Hands Were Quiet

She Was Dying Anyway

He Was Walking Alone

They Thought He was Safe

He Was Not There

Her Work Was Everything

She Told a Lie

He Never Forgot

She Was At Risk

Kenzie Kirsch Medical Thrillers

Unlawful Harvest

Doctored Death (Coming soon)

Stand Alone Suspense Novels

Looking Over Your Shoulder

Lion Within

Pursued by the Past

In the Tick of Time

Loose the Dogs

AND MORE AT PDWORKMAN.COM

To all of the Stormys, and the Phils, and even the Leos

LEO. THE LION. SOMETIMES I wonder if I am the only one walking around with a lion inside me. I try to suppress it, to bury the lion, to keep it deep, deep down inside me. But it doesn't seem to matter. It is still there, barely beneath the surface, showing its snarling face at the least provocation.

I see other people walking around without a care in the world. I see people who ignore insults and slights. I see people who ignore it when they see wrong and injustice around them, who are able to turn their backs on neglect and abuse, who seem to go through life with a sort of peace and apathy incomprehensible to me.

Do I feed the lion? I mean, I must, for it to live on and be so strong. I don't try to. I don't mean to. I try to starve it out, but it feasts on everything I try to thrust down inside me. Someone cuts me off on the freeway, I swallow the anger and the lion feasts. I find a dog someone has beaten and tied up for three days without food, and I push it down. Try to suppress the rage and the lion feasts and grows. Then something happens at the gym… someone doesn't put equipment away or one of the kids doesn't show up for practice or I hear one of them is in trouble, and the lion comes out. He roars, he rages, he is uncontrollable. I say and do things I know I shouldn't and I will regret later, but it doesn't matter. It doesn't matter I know it is wrong, because I can't stop it any more than I could stop a hurricane in its path. It is simply against nature. Can't be done.

But that's me, and maybe everybody else doesn't have a lion inside them. Maybe everybody has a different animal. This one a soft rabbit or puppy. That one a sly ferret. Him a stallion that makes him want to run free. Maybe normal people have quiet, domestic animals, and those of us who rage, who can't seem to get the beast under control, we're the ones with lions, tigers, gorillas, or man-eating-sharks.

I know what anger and rage can do to a person. To a family. To friendships and freedom. It isn't like I want to be this way. But I can't overcome my own nature. Whether I inherited my lion from Him or whether I learned behavior from Him, it doesn't really matter. It is a part of who I am. This lion couldn't be removed even by surgery. They've tried all of the drugs. Drugs that made me tired. Drugs that made me foggy. Drugs that gave me hallucinations and let a whole host of other wild animals out. But even though drugs may put the lion to sleep for a while, at the expense of the rest of my self, they can't remove him. They can't completely bury him. And one day, after feeding him a steady diet of suppressed rage, he is going to come out again. It is inevitable.

I am Leo. The lion is in me. I am part of him.

CHAPTER ONE

LEO WALKED ALONG THE aisle of the parking lot, looking in car windows as he went. It was a hard habit to break. Not because of his past delinquency, when he might have broken into a car to get something that attracted his attention. Or to get back at someone who had angered him. But because of his work. Too many hours spent rescuing poor creatures from overheated cars.

He hated how people would leave their dogs in the car, window cracked slightly, and go into the store 'just for a minute,' leaving the animal suffering as the indoor temperatures soared to one hundred and thirty degrees. So many animals died. And how many more that he never knew about; their guilt-ridden owners just quietly burying them in their back yards?

So even now, off duty, Leo couldn't help but check the cabin of each vehicle he walked past, looking for any animals in distress. It wasn't as hot as it could be. Cabin temperatures probably wouldn't be over one hundred, but that was still pretty hot for any critter, especially one who couldn't sweat.

He glimpsed his reflection in the windows as he walked between the cars. His face was too young. When he was with the after-school kids, people would mistake him for a teenager instead of the coach. Dark hair, cut military short. And even in the hazy reflections, you could still see the scars on his face.

Passing one car, Leo heard a noise. A sort of crying, choking sound. He stopped, frowning, and peered in the window trying to see. A dog? Sounded more like a cat. Which was less usual for people to leave in their cars, but that isn't to say it was never done.

People were stupid! They should leave their pets at home, where they were safe and comfortable, not bring them to the mall and leave them suffering and dying in the car. Leo looked around. No one was watching him. No one was purposefully heading toward the car. Wherever the owner was, they didn't see him hanging around their vehicle.

He looked in the window again. He couldn't see any animal, but there was definitely a noise inside. Maybe a litter of puppies? It didn't sound like an adult dog. He wasn't sure it sounded like a cat, either. It was muffled like there was something pulled over top. An animal in the trunk? Owners usually at least pretended to themselves they were kind to their furry babies. Leo's chest was tight, his breathing getting faster.

How could someone do something so stupid and thoughtless?

Leo focused on a gym bag tucked between the back seat and the front passenger seat. Listening carefully, he was sure that was the direction the noise was coming from. Who would stow an animal in a gym bag in the back seat?

Leo looked around the parking lot again. Still no one interested in what he was doing. Still no one caring that he was looking in their car. No one else heard or cared about the noise.

He didn't bother calling the police or fire department. His anger peaked without even hearing their response. 'We don't break into cars.' 'We don't provide that service.' 'You'll have to do what you think is best, we can't be involved.'

No one wanted to get involved.

The emergency services were overworked and didn't need stupid animal calls.

And they certainly didn't want to have to take responsibility for breaking into someone's car.

Leo took a breath, and without stopping to think about it—which might make him stop and not take action—he slammed his elbow into the front passenger window. It took a couple of bone-bruising blows before it shattered. He was always too hesitant, hit a window too lightly the first time around. Glass was less fragile than it looked and car windows were designed to withstand a certain amount of impact in a crash.

Leo reached in and unlocked the front door. He opened it and then unlocked the back door and opened it. He delicately lifted the gym bag from where it had been jammed. He didn't want to hurt the puppies. Leo set the bag on the back seat and carefully unzipped the zipper, then grasped the flannel blankets and pushed them to the side.

"Aaah!" The startled exclamation left his mouth before he could check it.

Expecting a litter of puppies, he was totally unprepared for what he saw. It was something he couldn't have imagined or braced himself for. A baby. Not puppies, a human baby. Discarded in a gym bag and stowed in the back seat of the hot car like a pair of dirty sneakers. What kind of creep would do such a thing?

Was it a kidnapping?

An unprepared mother who had the baby in a washroom somewhere and didn't know what to do? It was so mind boggling he couldn't take in the sight at first.

A baby. In a gym bag. In the back seat of a car.

He looked into the back seat. No baby car seat. This wasn't someone who was used to transporting a baby.

After a few deep breaths, Leo forced himself to really look at the baby. Evaluate it.

This was no premature newborn delivered in a toilet. He wasn't an expert on babies, but it was too clean, its face and head too round, to be a newborn. But it was still tiny and very young. The heavy, dark hair around its head, looked out of place like someone had tried to glue a wig or toupee on it. Open, gulping mouth, eyes squinted closed in a cry.

Its cries were quiet. Thin, choking sobs. Not a screamer, this one. How long had it been in the car? He touched its skin. Very warm to the touch. Too warm? How could he tell? It certainly seemed that way. Its skin was dry, not sweaty.

If it had been a dog, he would have checked to see if its nose was dry and how badly it was panting.

He unswaddled the baby from the flannel blankets into the cooler air. The sobs hitched for a moment and then started up again.

"Shhh, it's okay," he comforted the best he could. Wondering if it really was okay. Now he really did have a medical emergency on his hand. Now it was time to call nine-one-one.

What kind of idiot left a baby in a car?

"What are you doing?" a strident female voice interrupted his thoughts. "Get away from my car! What are you doing?"

Leo looked around. A young woman. Blond, with pretty, delicate features. Coming toward him too fast; any young woman by herself should know better than to approach some man who was breaking into her car, but she didn't seem to be afraid. She was scowling at him.

"What are you doing?" she repeated. She took in the broken passenger window, the glass on the pavement and on the seat. "Did you break my window? Who do you think you are? Get out of here before I call the police!"

It was interesting she didn't just call the police. But she didn't take him on tooth and nail either, for which he supposed he should be thankful.

"Is this your baby?" Leo demanded, showing her the infant.

Her eyes widened in shock and he was reassured that she had no idea where the baby had come from.

Maybe this wasn't her car?

Maybe she had stolen it without knowing what was in the bag in the back seat?

Maybe her boyfriend had stolen it and she had borrowed it without knowing what he was up to? Her eyes went to the gym bag on the back seat in confusion.

"That's my bag," she said. "What are you doing with my bag? Did you do this?"

"Lady," Leo growled. "There was a baby smothering to death in this car. Why don't you tell me what's going on here, instead of making accusations?"

Her brows drawing down in puzzlement, she looked back at him, and then looked back at her car, the broken window, and the gym bag. She slumped, the anger leaving her face, replaced with defeat and sadness.

"That's my baby," she said.

It completely threw Leo for a loop, as he had decided by now it wasn't her baby and she had no idea there was a baby in the back seat.

"What happened here? This doesn't make any sense."

She took the baby out of his arms and Leo let her. She leaned against the car, looking exhausted. She ran a finger down the baby's cheek.

"Are you okay, Juleen?" she whispered. "What happened to you? How did you get in that bag in my car?"

The woman rocked the baby, calming her, whispering softly to her. Leo just watched in stunned amazement, the adrenaline starting to drain away.

"So what happened?" he asked. "Where did you leave the baby? Who was supposed to be looking after her?"

"I don't know," she looked totally spaced out and Leo wondered what she was on. She must be high as a kite. "Did you put her there?" she accused.

"No, I saved her! I took her out of the car. You know she could have died in there?"

"Yes. I know. Thank you. I don't know how this happened. I don't know what I would have done if you hadn't found her."

Leo shook his head. "Who was supposed to be looking after the baby?" he repeated, trying to get to the bottom of the mystery.

"No one. Just me."

"No one? Well, how did she get in the bag? Did you put her there?"

She looked at the bag vaguely. "I don't know. I guess I must have. I don't remember."

"You don't remember?" Leo repeated, his voice rising.

He wanted to grab her and shake some sense into her.

"You were shopping, and you forgot you put your baby in a bag and left her in the car? Where's your baby seat?"

His fists clenched and he tried to maintain control of himself.

"What the hell were you thinking?"

There were tears in the corners of her eyes. "I don't know. I can't remember anything that happened before I came here. I don't remember."

"Where is your baby seat?"

"I don't have one."

"Well then, how are you supposed to get around with her in the car? You need a baby seat!"

"Yes," she agreed. She looked toward the Wal-Mart. "I should go get one. Maybe that's why I came here. I couldn't remember when I got into the store what I was supposed to be getting."

"Holy crap!" he blew up. "Should I call an ambulance for you or something? Are you having a stroke or are you always this stupid?"

"I—I've been having kind of a tough time lately." She rocked Juleen, humming very quietly. "Will you help me find one?"

"A car seat?"

She nodded. Leo looked at her, looked at the store, and looked at the baby.

He certainly couldn't leave her to fend for herself right now. If he could keep an eye on her and the baby for a while, he could better evaluate what he should do. Whether he should call an ambulance, or the police, or Child Services.

"Yeah, I'll help you," he agreed in a more subdued tone. He shut the door of the car. He just left the gym bag on the seat and the glass all over. She didn't seem to notice. She just turned around and headed back toward the store. Leo followed her.

"So what's your name?" he asked, falling into step beside her.

"Elizabeth," she said. "Hi."

"Hi. I'm Leo."

"You can call me Lizzie," Elizabeth told him.

"Okay. Lizzie. So how old is Juleen?"

She stared at him without comprehension.

"Your baby. How old is your baby?" Leo pointed to her.

"Oh." She looked down at the baby in her arms. "Just a few days. I don't remember the date… what day is it today?"

"Thursday."

"Oh," she nodded, "okay."

Inside the store, she looked around. "So… what was I here for?" she asked.

"A baby seat. For the car."

"Right," she nodded and seemed to take hold of this thought more firmly now. "A baby seat. For Juleen."

They walked toward the baby department.

"Are you on any medication?" Leo guessed.

She nodded vaguely. "Yeah."

"Are you having memory problems a lot? Because you should probably have your doctor change it. You can't be forgetting you even have a baby. That's not good."

An understatement, but he wasn't sure how to reach her. Surely she understood something was wrong!

"I'll talk to my doctor," she agreed. "Once I get settled."

"Oh? Are you new in town? Just moved to a new place?"

"Yeah. I've been overseas."

"Overseas. Someplace they don't have baby seats?" Leo asked with a bit of a laugh.

"Iraq," she said. "They don't."

"Oh. What were you doing there? Are you… a reporter?" He tried to think of what profession this flaky young blond might have that would take her to Iraq so close to her baby's birth. It didn't make sense.

"No. A soldier. I am—I was—in the army."

Leo looked at her face to see if she was joking. Her? This petite, air-headed blond bombshell? But she seemed to be completely serious. The two of them stood and looked silently at the baby seats on display.

"You were in the army," Leo repeated after a few minutes of silence, browsing over the baffling assortment of seats. "Right up until the baby was born? I wouldn't think… was your husband in the army? Was he in the army, and you were there with him?"

"No. I was a soldier."

"But, you can't serve in the army while you're pregnant."

"No, of course not," Elizabeth agreed.

Leo stared at her, baffled. Of course not. But she had.

"How about this one?" Elizabeth suggested, pointing to a frothy pink seat. Leo shrugged, looking it over.

"It says newborn," he agreed, "so I guess that should work."

"Yeah. I like that one."

He picked up a box. "Okay. You'll get that one," he agreed. "Now what else do you need? Do you have all of the clothes and diapers and blankets and supplies you need? Formula and bottles?"

"Yes, they bought me a bunch of stuff," she agreed vaguely. "I think I've got everything now. I just needed to get a car seat."

"Okay. Let's go check out, then."

Leo half-guided, half-followed Elizabeth to the checkouts and watched her make her way through the line. Amazingly, she managed to pay for the car seat without any apparent difficulty. He went with her to the car and immediately inserted himself into the situation, ripping open the cardboard box and glancing at instructions that looked as detailed as engineering blue-prints. He set the seat on the back bench of the car, in the middle and used the seatbelt to strap it in.

"There," he said. "I guess that's it, then."

"Thank you for your help," she said sweetly. She bent over to put Juleen into the car seat.

"Umm… do you want to go for a coffee or something?" Leo suggested. He felt the need to keep an eye on her for a little while longer, to see if she managed to take care of Juleen without forgetting her on the restroom counter or something. "Can I buy you something to eat? Juleen still looks pretty warm. We should probably sit where it is air conditioned and make sure she gets rehydrated." Elizabeth was nodding. "You should feed her," Leo said firmly. "Are you—you know—breastfeeding?"

"Oh, yes," she agreed.

"Good," said Leo, having noted she didn't have a bottle or diaper bag. "And that's okay? With you on medication?"

"Yeah, they changed my meds all around, to find stuff that's supposed to be safe for nursing. But it takes time to find combinations and doses that will work… figure out the side effects…"

Side effects like forgetting your baby in the car?

"Should we take this bag, then, so you have a blanket to cover you up?"

She consented to him taking the gym bag with them, back into the mall. Leo lingered by the car for a moment, wondering just how smart it was to leave the car with its broken window and brand new baby seat in the parking lot. But he shrugged and escorted the mother and baby back into the mall, leaving the car as it was.

Soon they were settled at the food fair, each with a cup of coffee and a cookie. Juleen was making eager sucking noises under the blanket. Leo tried again to figure out Elizabeth and the situation she was in.

"So where's the father?" he asked.

"What father?"

"Juleen's father. Is he back in Iraq or here?"

"In Iraq, I guess," she said with a shrug.

Leo shook his head, frowning. "So was he someone you met in the army?" he persisted. "I didn't think you were allowed to… what do they say? Fraternize?"

"Yeah, they have strict rules about that kind of thing. You can't get together with a commanding officer, or with someone else in your squadron. And you're not supposed to… you're really not supposed to hang with the locals, either. They don't want soldiers getting pregnant or picking up some disease, or getting a local pregnant if it's a man."

"So how did it happen, then? Were you pregnant before you shipped out?"

"I'm not sure."

"Well, how long ago did you ship out?"

"About nine months."

Leo nodded slowly. "I guess that could be a problem, then. She's pretty small. Was she premature?"

"She was under five pounds. But her lungs were okay. They kept her warm but they didn't have to put her on a ventilator. Then we came back here."

"And you've just been here for a few days?"

She nodded in agreement.

"And you don't know whether the baby's father was someone here or someone in the army?"

"No," she agreed.

"Okay…"

She didn't seem bothered by him poking his nose in what was definitely none of his business. His queries about her sex life seemed to have no effect on her. But then, how much of what he was saying was just going straight over her head? He didn't know what the IQ requirements were to join the army, but she seemed to be a little bit dim, to be kind.

"Why didn't they send you home before Juleen was born?" Leo asked with brows drawn down. Was this all just a big lie? He couldn't imagine her tottering around on the front lines in Iraq, her baby belly sticking out, and the army not sending her home. She had to have been home longer than she was letting on.

"Well… no one knew until she was born," Elizabeth explained.

"No one knew?" Leo demanded, his voice rising again. "How did you manage to hide that?"

"Well, some people really don't show." At Leo's look of disbelief, she leaned forward, seeming for the first time to enjoy his consternation and really appreciate how flummoxed he was by the whole scenario. "I hid it really well. I did have to wear a bigger uniform, but I thought I was just putting on weight because of the mess. A lot of soldiers do, you know. It's like the 'freshman fifteen.' Lots of people gain weight. So I just got bigger clothes and tried to watch what I was eating so I wouldn't get any heavier," she smiled. "No one knew. Not even me."

"How could you not know?"

"Well, I was on the pill so I wasn't getting my period anyway. I just put on weight… you know, got back aches, sore feet, that kind of thing. What soldier doesn't get sore feet?"

"So when did you figure it out? Why didn't you tell someone?"

Elizabeth raised her eyebrows, laughing.

"I was in the trenches. Started getting these horrible, ripping pains in my belly. At first I thought I'd caught shrapnel, but there was no wound. Then I thought, maybe food poisoning or chemical warfare. Maybe I had appendicitis. I was doubled up, couldn't move, and was screaming in pain. Nobody knew what was going on. They took me in a truck with some of the wounded, back to the hospital tent. That's when they examined me and told me I was in labor. I couldn't believe it. It didn't make any sense at all. They gave me a stethoscope and let me listen to the baby's heart." Elizabeth beamed. "That was the most amazing experience. Can you imagine finding out you have a little person growing inside of you? A whole new life, in your own body that you knew nothing about?"

"And then having her make an appearance ten minutes later?" Leo said dryly.

"Oh no, it was a lot longer than that. I was in labor for… hours… days… I don't know how long. And then she came out and they put her in my arms." Elizabeth shook her head in amazement, eyes sparkling. "I love the idea of being a mommy."

Leo analyzed the words. She loved the idea of being a mommy. Not she loved being a mommy. Not she loved Juleen. She loved the idea of being a mommy.

And until she figured out she was a mommy and had responsibilities, there were going to be problems.

He should call Child Services. He couldn't live with himself if he let her hurt or neglect Juleen. If he saw it in the papers; they had found an infant in a garbage can, in a locked car, or lying rotting in her crib. He just couldn't let that happen. Someone had to be told.

"So you like being a mom?" he asked.

"Sure. It's like having my own living doll. What little girl doesn't wish for a baby of her own?"

"But you're not a little girl."

Her face changed, taking on a pout, a six-year-old who'd just been told to give back the kitten she'd been playing with, after having set her mind on taking it home.

"Elizabeth…"

"Lisbet," she suggested. "I like Lisbet better than Elizabeth."

He remembered she'd asked him to call her Lizzie earlier. Now she was Lisbet.

"Lisbet," he obliged, "I'm really worried about you and Juleen. Are you really okay taking care of her?"

"I do just fine," she insisted, fluttering her eyes at him. "I'm good at being a mommy."

"You said you were on medication," Leo said, as Elizabeth took a nibble of her cookie.

She nodded. "Yes. But that doesn't stop me from being a good mommy."

"It does if it makes you forget you have her or you put her in a bag in the back seat of your car!"

She rolled her eyes, flushing a little, and shook her head. "Madame used to say I was such a flibbertigibbet," she acknowledged.

"Who's Madame?"

"One of my foster moms. She said I was always flitting from one thing to another, losing track of things. I'd leave the laundry in the washer to get mildewed, forget my homework at home or at school, start things and never finish them…"

"But this isn't a science project. This is a baby. She could have died in that car."

"But you saved her," Elizabeth protested. "You're like a superhero! My superhero. How did you know she was in there?"

It was his turn to flush. He felt his cheeks and ears get hot. "I'm an animal control officer," he explained. "So I notice when people leave their animals in their cars. I just heard her and I reacted."

"You're a dog catcher?" she asked, in not quite the same tone as she had declared him a superhero. Sort of a far-away, thoughtful voice.

"Well, yeah."

Leo knew it wasn't a romantic job. Dog catcher. People thought of him as a villain more often than a hero. Taking dogs to the pound where they had to be bailed back out again. Costing people money in fines, telling them how they should take care of their own property. He got a lot of people who thought him the lowest kind of low.

"Well," she said in a bright tone, "you heard her, and you saved her. So no harm was done. Everything is okay."

"You're going to go to your doctor to get a new prescription, right? To get your medication adjusted? Because it's important. You can't just forget big things like this."

"Yeah, I will."

"Maybe I'd better go with you," he suggested. "Just to make sure you don't forget to do it."

Elizabeth ducked under the blanket for a moment to shift Juleen from one breast to the other. Then she reappeared.

"Can I come with you?" Leo persisted.

"Come with me where?"

"To your doctor!"

"Sure," she agreed easily.

Leo breathed a sigh of relief. He had been sure she would freak out about him suggesting he see her doctor. About her privacy, and him thinking she was stupid and unreliable. But it was the truth, and she'd better be able to take the truth.

They talked idly then, moving away from the topics of babies and doctors and just moving to general topics. The news, the weather, incidental things about the two of them. Eventually, Elizabeth swallowed the last of her coffee, removed Juleen from her breast, and did up her shirt.

"This was nice," she said. "Thank you."

"Sure. So are you ready to go to your doctor's now?"

She looked at him with a surprised expression for a moment, then seemed to remember, and nodded. "Yeah. I guess we can do that now."

"What's your doctor's name? Where is his office, do you remember?"

"Yeah. Doctor Marvin. He's down in the valley."

Leo nodded. "Okay. Let's go."

CHAPTER TWO

LEO LOOKED AWKWARDLY AROUND the psychiatrist's office and chose a seat. His muscles were tight and his heart pounded. Elizabeth walked up to the receptionist. "I need to see Doctor Marvin."

"Um, remind me your name. It's… Peterson?"

"Elizabeth Peterson."

The receptionist nodded and typed it into her computer. "Lisa?" she asked.

"Yes."

"Okay. The doctor is in with someone right now. If you'll have a seat, I'll get you in to see him as soon as I can. Okay?"

Elizabeth nodded and went back to sit down next to Leo.

"Can I hold her?" Leo nodded at Juleen.

"Sure."

Elizabeth handed Juleen over to Leo rather sloppily, making him jump to catch the baby's heavy head and support it.

Leo gazed down at Juleen. Contented now instead of squalling.

"I love babies," he commented, stroking Juleen's silky soft cheek.

"Do you have any of your own?" Elizabeth—or was it Lisa now?—asked.

"No," Leo laughed. "None of my own. I don't have a girlfriend, let alone one close enough to have kids with."

"Why not?"

"I… well, I don't make friends really easily. Especially girlfriends."

"You seem okay to me."

"Well… I don't always handle things as well as I have today. I grew up kind of rough and I'm a bit… awkward sometimes." Not to mention he had a lion inside which got out at inopportune times and tended to scare decent people away.

"Oh. Well, sooner or later you'll find someone."

"I hope so," Leo admitted. "I'd like a family of my own. But I don't know if it is in the cards."

"So, no babies for you."

Leo gazed down at Juleen. "No," he said. "I have brothers and sisters. They're not babies anymore, but I remember when they were. I helped raise them."

"Really? How many brothers and sisters?"

"Three sisters and two brothers."

"All younger?"

"Yeah. I did have an older sister, but she died."

"Oh, I'm sorry." She searched his face. "Recently?"

"No. Years ago."

"Oh. Okay," she amended her expression accordingly. "Sorry to hear that."

Leo looked down at Juleen, vividly remembering Stormy at that age. Stormy had wild curls even as a newborn. And red cheeks. Dancing dark eyes, always full of mischief.

"I hope we don't have to wait too long," Elizabeth sighed.

"I don't know that I've ever been at a doctor's office when I didn't. You always wait. And then they take you into the other room where you wait again. Then they see you for two minutes and you're out the door. It's so frustrating."

Elizabeth nodded. "Dr. Marvin is good, though. He'll give me more than two minutes. He listens good. Even when I don't have an appointment."

"Do you show up without an appointment very often?"

"No. Not a lot. Sometimes."

Leo nodded. He sat there, looking into at Juleen's eyes. Covertly, he was keeping an eye on Elizabeth. She was restless. She looked through magazines. She got up and paced. She looked at her watch.

"I think I'm just going to go," Elizabeth told the receptionist, who looked alarmed.

"No, no. Don't go. Let me see if I can interrupt him for you, okay? Just stay here for a minute."

Elizabeth shrugged. The receptionist got up and walked through a door behind her, disappearing from sight. Leo was surprised. They actually cared about taking care of Elizabeth. That was a nice idea. Pretty rare for a doctor.

A couple of minutes later, the receptionist returned to her seat. She nodded toward the closed door to the waiting room. A moment later, a doctor walked through the door. He was short, dark complexioned, with black rimmed glasses. He had a clipboard in his hand. He glanced around the waiting room.

"Elizabeth? Come on in and tell me how you're doing."

Elizabeth headed into the hallway behind him. Leo stood up and sidled over to try to talk to the doctor. Dr. Marvin looked at him, eyebrows raised.

"And you are…?"

"I'm… just a friend. But I kind of wanted to talk to you. I'm concerned…" he trailed off, glancing around at the other patients in the waiting room.

"Okay, why don't you come into my office?"

"Separate from Elizabeth?" Leo suggested.

Dr. Marvin nodded. Leo followed him not to an examining room, but to an office with a desk. Leo saw Elizabeth disappear into another room further down the hall.

"I'll be with you in a few moments," Dr. Marvin called to Elizabeth.

Leo waited in the office nervously. He jiggled Juleen. He'd forgotten how much he hated doctors' offices. The anxiety was starting to build. Why had he bothered to come here? Let Elizabeth deal with things on her own. Let her talk to her doctor and sort things out. Leo had enough of his own problems to worry about, without babysitting some dumb blonde.

"How can I help you, Mr…?"

"Leo. I, um… I just met Elizabeth… but I'm a bit worried…"

Dr. Marvin nodded, looking Leo in the eye and waiting for more information.

"I'm worried she can't take care of Juleen properly. I don't know if it is just whatever medications she is on or something deeper…"

"I can't tell you anything about Elizabeth's case or her care."

"No, I guess not. Do you think she can take care of Juleen?"

"Why don't you tell me what happened?"

"I don't know if I should. But I think she… she's having problems concentrating, focusing. Remembering she needs to take care of Juleen."

Dr. Marvin tapped his pen on the clipboard, thinking.

"I'll talk to her," he said finally. "And see what's up. But if you think there's an immediate danger, I should know…"

Leo clenched his fists at his side and held his breath, wrestling with the problem. He hated to make trouble for Elizabeth. Or to overreact. Who would take care of Juleen if Elizabeth couldn't? But he couldn't leave her to abandon Juleen again.

"Well, yeah. I think there is. She didn't even remember she had a baby…"

"If she needs it, I can take her into care on a seventy-two hour evaluation. That would give the baby immediate protection. Then we can see if Elizabeth is focused enough to take care of Juleen."

Leo let his breath go. "Yeah, you know, that might be a good idea. Just to make sure… you know… she can handle it."

Dr. Marvin nodded. "Are you going to take care of the baby while she is in the hospital?"

Leo shook his head quickly. "No—I don't really know her. And I have a job. I couldn't."

"Okay. Why don't you leave her with me and you can go home?"

Leo reluctantly handed Juleen over. "Do you mind if I go say goodbye to Elizabeth?" he asked.

"Go ahead. I'll give you a couple of minutes to wrap it up and get on your way before I let her know I'm ordering a fifty-one fifty. Then you'll be out of the way if she blows."

Leo nodded his thanks. He backtracked to the hallway and went down to the examination room he had seen Elizabeth go into. He tapped on the door and went in. She looked up and cocked her head to the side, apparently surprised to see him again.

"Hi," she said. "Is he coming?"

"Yeah, he'll be just a minute."

Leo thought he should apologize for not having Juleen in his arms anymore. Or he should explain he had passed her off to the doctor. But Elizabeth didn't even seem to notice the missing baby and Leo decided there wasn't any point causing more awkwardness by pointing it out to her. He shrugged.

"I'd like to see you again…" he ventured.

"Oh, sure. I guess that would be okay. Do you want to give me your phone number?"

Leo pulled out his phone. "Yeah. Could I get yours too?"

She could, after all, simply forget they had ever met. But he wanted to keep in touch, to see how she was doing and make sure Juleen was doing all right.

"Sure," Elizabeth agreed. She waited while he tapped her name into the phone, then recited her number for him. Leo nodded.

"Got it. Can I take a picture of you to go on the contact card?" he suggested.

She didn't answer, but gave him a bright camera-smile and waited for him to snap the picture.

"Where do you live?" Leo ventured. He kept waiting for the push-back, for the woman to decide she didn't want him sniffing around. She should be afraid of a stranger who wanted to know all of her personal information. But Elizabeth just gave him the address as if it was the most natural thing in the world. Did she trust him just because he had saved her baby and that made her feel safe? Or because he had taken her out for coffee and cookies and not made any moves on her? Or did she just trust everyone?

And how was she going to feel about him when she found out he had gotten her put on a seventy-two hour hold? He might encounter a whole different Elizabeth in three days. Maybe he could visit her at the hospital before that.

Could you visit someone who was on a psychiatric hold? He somehow doubted it.

Leo started to give Elizabeth his contact information, but she just handed him her phone. "You put it in," she suggested.

"Okay," Leo agreed. Trying to shield his deformed hand from her as he did so, he tapped his own information into her contacts app. "You know, I'm really glad we met. I'll call you, okay?"

"Yeah, call me," Elizabeth agreed. She bounced forward and gave him a brief hug. It was quick and not intimate, over before Leo knew what she was doing. It was a friendly, almost childlike hug.

She was so uninhibited. He wasn't used to that in a girl. With his scarred face, his intensity, and his temper, he tended to scare girls away.

Nodding, Leo backed out of the room and down the hallway, sighing as he went. Dr. Marvin passed him going the other way but didn't say anything. He was apparently already focused on the next task at hand, which Leo imagined was not a pleasant one.

Leo didn't see Juleen and didn't know who the doctor had passed her on to. He felt guilty about not taking the baby himself. But how could he take care of a baby right now? He had his job, his volunteer work, and his dying father. He couldn't commit to taking care of a baby too. But he still felt guilty.

He felt angry for feeling guilty.

The lion was stirring. Leo had been able to distract himself for a while, to forget about his own troubles by focusing on Elizabeth, but as he nodded to the receptionist and walked out of the doctor's office, the anger and the worry started to gnaw at him.

He had troubles of his own, and they were not so easily managed as dropping Elizabeth and Juleen at the doctor's office.

Not that easy at all.

CHAPTER THREE

IT HAD BEEN A long day, but looking at his watch, Leo decided he'd better stop at the hospital, just for a few minutes. He really didn't feel like it, but when he thought about not going, there was a knot in his gut. No matter what his father had done, Leo couldn't neglect him. He couldn't just ignore Lyall or leave him there by himself, helpless in the hospital bed.

He paused in the doorway to see if anyone was there. Not that there was ever anyone there but Shayla. Maybe there would be a nurse checking Lyall's vital signs, but Shayla and Leo were his only visitors.

The room was empty. Maybe Shayla had gone for supper or a book. Leo walked into the room and sat down beside the bed.

"Hi, Dad," he said awkwardly. He didn't like to talk to Lyall, but he didn't feel right just sitting there without at least announcing himself. It probably didn't make any difference to Lyall. What did he care? The doctors said he was brain dead. But Shayla said sometimes the doctors were wrong. You heard those stories sometimes; people with locked-in syndrome. They could hear and maybe even see everything going on around them, they just couldn't respond. Doctors said there was no brain activity, but the patient could recount everything that had happened while they had been 'asleep.'

Lyall looked so strange to Leo. He'd always been a giant in Leo's life, and to see him lying there now, completely helpless, was bizarre. Once tall, now constantly below eye level, supine. His eyes were dark and sunken bruises. His head was bandaged, his hair shaved or hidden, and he had all manner of sensors and tubes and drains attached and flowing in and out of him, making him look more borg than human. The tattoos on his arms stood out starkly as his tan continued to fade and his pallor turned sickly white. This man who had been a force in Leo's life was merely a shadow now and Leo felt unbalanced looking at him.

"Nice day out there today," Leo said, watching out the window instead of staring at the tubes and machines connected to his father's body. "A bit hot, but it's cooling down now. I like it when it's a bit cooler. Better for running. Better for the animals."

Leo never talked to his father about running or the animals when Lyall was conscious. He never talked to Lyall about anything that mattered when he was conscious. Too many years of being belittled for every thought, for every mention of his own interests, for everything his father perceived he was doing wrong. If Leo said he liked something, it was more likely to be taken away than encouraged.

Why had Lyall done that? Was he trying to reduce his children's reliance on the outside world? On anyone other than him? It must have been a way to keep control over them, but it baffled Leo. Couldn't the man encourage them in something? Anything?

Did putting everyone else down make Lyall feel better? Was it his way of raising himself up over the people around him? It made Leo feel low, that was for sure.

He learned to hide everything he cared about. Brag about nothing. Show interest in nothing. Just keep his head down and get out as quickly as he could.

Eventually, Leo was forced to pull his gaze away from the window and take another look at his father. Was there any difference today? Did he look any better? The bruises were still dark and ugly. He still had more tubes coming out of him than Leo could figure out the use for. He looked ugly and helpless. He'd always been the monster, the giant, with the strength of ten men.

Leo had always been inclined to help the helpless: to protect the younger children, to rescue animals, others who appeared to need him. He had never anticipated his father becoming one of the helpless.

He heard footsteps and looked up to see Shayla framed in the doorway. She was a petite blonde, like Elizabeth, but not nearly as appealing. Where Elizabeth had those big twisting curls, Shayla's hair hung limp and straight. She hadn't been taking care of herself while Lyall was in the hospital; her hair was clean and combed, but it hung lank and lifeless along her face. She had on red lipstick, but it looked unnatural on her pale face; like she had picked something out in the dark that didn't really suit her. Maybe the hospital lighting made her washed out. She looked frail and tired.

"Oh, hi Leo. How's it going?"

"Okay, I guess," Leo said. "It ended up being a pretty busy day."

"All quiet here," she said, looking over Lyall, her forehead wrinkled and eyes tired. She bent over him and kissed Lyall on the forehead in a spot bare of any bandages, tape, or tubes. "No change."

"Did you expect there to be?"

"No. I just hope and pray… I light a candle for him every day."

"He doesn't even believe in God," Leo said. "Why would God do anything for him?"

"God blesses all of us, whether we believe in him or not. It doesn't matter if Lyall isn't a Christian or if he's an atheist. That doesn't mean God's not there. God loves all of his children."

Leo rolled his eyes and turned away from Shayla to look out the window. She didn't need to see his expression. God. How could Lyall be together with someone who believed in what you couldn't see? He'd never encouraged any kind of faith in his family. Lyall was God in his family.

Leo supposed it was easier for someone who had been raised in a loving home to imagine a loving God, a loving Heavenly Father. But still, Leo couldn't understand her naiveté.

"Have any doctors been around today?" he asked.

"Just one. Becker. Said the same as they all keep saying… He's brain dead and we should just donate his organs. Recycle him."

Leo nodded, looking at the blinking beat of the heart monitor hooked up to Lyall. Every doctor who came in said the same thing. Donate him. Unplug him, unzip him, and gut him. Just reuse those parts for someone else who needed them.

Leo understood it was good business. Transplants brought the hospital lots of money. They were huge. And they made a big impact on the public's perception of the miracles their doctors were performing.

But Lyall was as helpless as a baby. Leo couldn't let the doctors hurt him.

"I was reading some articles about organ donation today," Shayla said. "My mom did a search and sent me some of them. Did you know they sedate organ donors and give them huge amounts of painkillers before removing their organs? Because they groan and react when you cut into them. The doctors say they are brain dead, but they react! There have even been cases where the donors have woken up on the table, come out of it, and started talking. That's why they have to sedate them. So they don't wake up when the doctors start cutting into them."

Leo swallowed the bile that rose in his throat.

What a sickening thought. He didn't know if it was true or not, but he could envision it.

He could just see his father on the operating table, in his last few moments, crying out as they cut into him. Screaming. Sitting up and looking around at them wild-eyed, horrified to see what they were doing.

It was the stuff nightmares were made of.

"They just see people in vegetative states as incubators for donatable organs," Shayla said pedantically. "They don't see them as people, as patients. Just… warm-blooded machines."

Leo knew Shayla didn't want Lyall's machines to be shut off. Every time Leo showed up, the doctors and nurses tried to persuade him he should pull the plug on his father. They knew Shayla didn't have any say on it. Lyall and Shayla weren't married. She had no legal standing to make decisions for him.

That was up to Leo. Up to him to decide what to do with his father's life. Was Lyall dead, and this was simply a corpse being kept alive by machines? Or was he still in there, somewhere?

Last week Shayla was telling him about how long some of these 'corpses' lived after their machines were shut off. Breathing, heart beating, bodies continuing to function long after. Hours, days even. He couldn't imagine sitting, watching his father die by inches that way.

Lyall was every bit as fragile and vulnerable as Juleen. Worse than an infant, even incapable of crying out if he was hungry or in pain. Locked inside his own body, or outside it, depending on what your beliefs were.

Did Lyall have a soul that would carry on after he died? And if he did, where would that soul go when they pulled the plug? Leo knew the life Lyall had lived. He knew little about religion, but he knew Lyall had violated all of those moral rules religion set out. If there was a hell, and if Lyall had a soul, that's where Lyall's soul was going.

Was Leo going to be forced to consign his father's soul to hell? Could he accept that responsibility?

Shayla was still talking, going on and on about those gruesome articles her mother had sent her. Leo nodded and made noises like he was listening, but he had stopped long ago. Now he tried to push away all thoughts of Lyall altogether. To remove himself mentally from this room and go somewhere else.

He thought about Elizabeth. How was she doing in hospital tonight? Was she upset about being put on a psychiatric hold? About having her child removed from her? Or did she not even care? Did she take it calmly in stride like everything else today? Was she drugged? Straitjacketed? Or just peacefully asleep on clean white sheets, unconcerned about the rest of the world?

Leo looked at Shayla.

"I really have to go, Shay. I'm sorry."

She cut off her elucidation of the truths of organ donation. "You're so good to keep coming here, Leo. You're not going to… do anything, are you?"

"I'm not pulling the plug on him yet," Leo agreed. "Nothing is going to change."

"You're so good to him. I know he was a pretty tough father on you kids. It's so generous of you to be forgiving and take care of him, and keep visiting him. You're a good son, Leo."

Leo looked at her and shook his head slowly.

"My dad never told me I was a good son," he said. "He told me plenty of times I was a horrible son. Worthless. An embarrassment. He never once told me I was a good son."

Shayla looked at him with her mouth open, looking for something to say. Leo left the room before she could find it.

After work the next day, Leo headed over to the gym. First he had to take care of the boys, and then he had his own training regime to worry about. If he wanted to make anything of himself, it was going to take hard work. And the harder the work, the better the distraction from his father, his past, and his anger.

At the gym, Leo saw some of the boys playing basketball outside while they waited for him. He waved to them and darted in to grab the ball and shoot a few hoops himself before going in.

"Is this everyone?" he asked, looking around at the young teens.

Flipping his head to get the shaggy blonde hair out of his eyes, Chase looked at him mournfully.

"Bubblegum is in jail," he advised.

"In jail?" Leo repeated. "Why, what happened?"

"Drugs in his locker at school."

"Drugs!" Leo looked around at the other faces. "If I ever catch any of you guys with drugs…!"

They all shook their heads quickly.

"We don't do drugs," Chase assured him. "I don't think Bubblegum did either. It was probably his locker partner's. We gotta keep our bodies clean," he declared, with a proud lift to his head.

"That's right," Leo agreed. "An athlete can't pollute his body with junk. It will never make you better. And it will just cause you trouble. Like jail."

They all nodded in agreement.

"Except roids," Reggie commented. "Roids make you buff."

Leo studied him. "Don't be fooled," he said. "Steroids do harm to your body. Yeah, they might give you stronger muscles, might make you stronger or faster for a while, but they'll kill you in the end."

"Roids don't kill you," Reggie scoffed. "Look at all the athletes taking them. They're okay. They're strong, healthy."

"And you don't hear about the others?" Leo snapped. "The ones who die from heart problems, or hang themselves, or kill their families? Or drive their stupid shiny cars off the cliff? Steroids mess with your mind. With your mind and your heart. You don't want anything messing you up."

Reggie shook his head, looking sullen and assured. His dark hair, narrow face, and small stature made him look wolfish. Or maybe an urban coyote, skinny and wary.

"Besides," Chase inserted, "roids make your balls shrink."

Stunned, everybody went silent, the atmosphere awkward. Reggie looked at Chase, frowning. "Is that true?" he asked tentatively. "Do they really?"

Chase nodded. So did Leo.

"Ask anyone on them," Chase said with certainty.

Leo laughed and everyone looked at him, not sure what was so funny. Leo just shook his head.

"You think it's a good idea if Reggie here goes up to some super-buff weight lifter or boxer, to ask him about the size of his balls?"

They all burst into laughter. Leo herded them into the gym as everyone tittered and nudged Reggie and Chase.

Jaime looked up as they came into the gym, his dark eyebrows raised. Jaime's name had thrown Leo at first. It wasn't pronounced like it looked at all. He'd been embarrassed to ask for 'Jamie' and then find out this stocky, dark man actually pronounced it 'High-me'. He still had to always correct himself when he saw Jaime's name written out or had to write it down himself. 'High-me.' Not 'Jamie.'

"You don't want to know," Leo told Jaime at his questioning look, wiping a tear from the corner of his eye. "Really, you don't want to know."

The boys laughed and nodded in agreement. Jaime shrugged heavily. He looked over the boys.

"Is this it today?"

"Billy is apparently in jail," Leo explained. "And you know Jose, he'll be late if he makes it at all. So yeah, just these guys today."

Jaime pulled out a clipboard and checked their names off. He glared at each one of them in turn.

"You know the government doesn't pay me if you don't show up?" he demanded. "You skip out on me, the gym loses money. It's hard enough to keep it going without losing my after-school money. Okay? So you come. Drag your butts in the door every day and don't wimp out on me."

They all nodded.

"We're the ones who are here," Reggie pointed out, pissed off. "You don't gotta give us a lecture!"

"Just make sure you do," Jaime reiterated. He nodded to the ring. "All yours for the next hour," he told Leo.

"Great, thanks, Jaime." Leo motioned to the small group of boys. "Well? You know what to do, right? I don't gotta tell you."

"Man," Chase protested, "I hate the calisthenics."

"You gotta get warmed up and you gotta keep in shape. Otherwise, you're gonna get injured. Now I wanna see some sweat. Grab a rope."

Each of the boys dragged themselves over to the wall rack to grab jump ropes.

"Chase, toss one here," Leo called out.

Chase obeyed. He skipped slowly across the floor, falling into rhythm beside Leo. Leo went slow for a couple of minutes to warm up and then started to jump double-time, as quickly as he could without losing the rhythm. Chase watched him, trying to match his speed to Leo's. The other boys were scattered around the ring, but all of them were busy with their warm-ups, so Chase was the only one who would hear their murmured conversation.

"So what's up with you, Chase?" Leo asked.

Chase looked at him, stumbling and then getting his rhythm back again.

"Whadya mean, Coach?" he asked.

"You get that black eye falling out of bed this morning?"

Chase was fair-haired. His mane was a bit wavy and kept long, so it tended to hide most of his eyes and face from onlookers. But it wasn't that good of a camouflage. Anyone who really looked at him could see the painful, puffy black eye under the fringe of hair. Whenever Chase shook it out of the way to see, it was plain to all.

"Nothin'," Chase said. "I just got in a fight."

"You come here to fight. And you wear a helmet to protect yourself. What are you doing fighting anywhere else?"

Chase looked at him. "Sometimes you don't really got a choice," he pointed out. "Sometimes you don't go to the fight. Sometimes the fight comes to you."

Leo had to chuckle at that one. His experience was the same. No matter how he tried to structure his life so he stayed out of trouble, the fights still came to him. Or they started inside him and burst out with a snarl, fangs, and claws. He just couldn't help it.

"You stay out of trouble," he advised, "I don't want to hear *you're* in jail, you know?"

Chase nodded but didn't look too confident of himself.

Leo nodded encouragingly. "You can do it," he said. "I believe in you."

There was silence for a few minutes, just the boys' ropes hitting the floor and Chase's panting breath beside him.

"You're the only one who believes in me," Chase said with a shake of his head. "You stupid or something?"

"No. I just believe in you."

A few more minutes and Leo called to them to put their ropes up. Jose burst in the door and ran over.

"Sorry Coach, sorry, I had to stay after," the slight, Hispanic boy puffed. "I got here as quick as I could, okay? I'm sorry."

Leo cast a glance at him. Although Jose was out of breath, he wasn't sweating. He obviously hadn't run far. And even with a detention, he should have had enough time to get there on time.

Leo loved the boys, but he had to be fair to everyone.

"You're late. Everybody else is warmed up and you're gonna miss out because you still have to do your warm up."

Jose groaned. "Aw, come on, Coach. Just today. It's not gonna kill me not to warm up just this one day."

"No way, Jose. Go warm up. A full fifteen minutes, not just two minutes. Everybody else was here on time."

Grumbling, Jose walked away and went to get a rope. Leo gathered the other boys around him and started giving them instructions on what they were going to be doing. Jose started jumping by himself, a lonely sound in the gym, just one boy jumping while the rest of them listened to Leo and got ready for their drills and matches.

But he'd been late. Leo couldn't give in even once, or they would all think they could get a walk if they had a good enough excuse.

There was only one way to maintain discipline, and that was by having tough rules.

Rules that didn't bend for anyone.

Looking back at the faces of the boys who were waiting for him, Leo continued his instructions.

"Reggie!" Leo yelled, watching the boys sparring in the ring. "What are you doing? Did I tell you to stand around and pick your nose? Pay attention! Focus and get in close. You can't have a good match leaning on the ropes on the other side of the ring. Close in, get tight, make your opponent uncomfortable. He doesn't want to chase you in circles around the ring."

"Lemme alone," Reggie retorted, still standing back of the bigger boy, looking for an opening. Was he hoping Big Joe was going to tire himself out swinging like a windmill and then Reggie could knock him down?

"Reggie—" Leo started again.

"Shut up, Coach!" Reggie snapped.

There was a collective gasp, followed by stillness. Everyone who had been standing around talking while the match went on was suddenly silent. They all looked at Leo to see what he was going to do. Leo blew his whistle, a snarl twisting his face. The fighters kept circling, ignoring the signal. Leo approached the ring, blowing another blast on the whistle.

"That means stop!" he said furiously. "Break it up and come down here!"

He already knew they weren't going to. Reggie was committed to the fight and he wasn't coming out until he was dragged out.

Leo climbed into the ring and grabbed him by the shirt collar, pulling him back. Reggie turned around wildly, his face bright red, swinging at Leo. Leo kept pulling on the collar, twisting it around quickly, making Reggie tumble down to the canvas. There were hoots from the other boys. Reggie got back up, his temper clearly out of his control.

"Don't touch me!" he screamed. "You can't touch me! I'll tell my parents! I'll call the cops! You can't lay a hand on me!"

"Watch me," Leo challenged. The lion was sharpening its claws. Leo was still in control of himself, but the beast was barely beneath the surface, begging to be released.

How much he wanted to just smack this kid in the head.

Really show him who was boss. That Reggie wasn't a tough guy just because he did a boxing program after school two times a week.

Leo was in charge, not Reggie.

"Gear off," Leo ordered.

Reggie's lip was in a sneer. "Make me!" he goaded.

Leo grabbed him and pinned him to the floor of the ring. He forced Reggie to submit and tore the gloves and the mask off of him. Reggie pounded the canvas impotently with his bare fists. Lifting him to his feet, Leo gave him a shove, accompanied by the command: "Go home."

"I'm not going—"

Leo caught him by the arm and pushed him through the ropes to the gym floor. Reggie started to move his feet to obey, to be compliant now, but it was too late.

"I'll go—" Reggie tried. "Just let go of me!"

Leo wasn't about to give in. Fire burning in his gut, he dragged Reggie to the gym door, opened it, and shoved Reggie out into the basketball court so hard that he almost fell down.

Leo slammed the door.

Swallowing, clenching and unclenching his hands, trying to stay in control, Leo walked back to the group. They whispered and nudged each other, quiet, nervous. Leo blew out his breath a couple of times.

"Chase," he said finally, his voice strangled.

"Yeah, Coach?"

"Lead the boys through some drills. Just give me a minute."

Chase nodded, looking at Leo worriedly. He jumped at Leo's every move like he was afraid he might be hit. Leo breathed out again, and retreated to the equipment room, and then out the back door.

He breathed the fresher air for a few minutes, trying to tame the lion, get it to lie down again, to release its hold on his gut.

Everything was okay.

Reggie was just being a brat. Being a kid. It wasn't like Leo didn't remember what it was like. What it was like to have everyone else in charge, telling you what to do, and not to be able to make a single move by yourself.

What it was like to have to put up with adults ordering you around, yelling at you, manhandling you.

One of the problems Leo had with Reggie was that the boy was just too much like Leo himself. He didn't want him having to go through everything Leo had.

Yeah, Reggie was a problem. But Leo didn't see him the way the cops saw him, the way the teachers at school saw him. He saw promise… the boy could be something if he could just listen and keep himself under control.

Leo didn't want him to be a failure, still hanging around here in ten years, maybe with his own group of after-school kids by that time…

After the boys were all gone, Leo started his run. He knew his pace was too fast. There was no way he was going to be able to keep it up the whole time. But he felt the lion burning and coiling inside of him, stretching out and unsheathing its claws.

He had to try to outrun it. He couldn't let his anger get the best of him.

He had to try to push it back down, to keep it buried.

He knew he shouldn't let the situation with Reggie get to him. The boys were always going to be a challenge. You couldn't expect kids to act like adults and stay under control. Had he been able to control himself at that age? Leo knew very well he hadn't.

He'd been the worst offender of all.

Leo remembered one day in particular. He was fourteen or so and he'd had a rough morning before school. Nothing had gone right at home; his father raging, his siblings wound up, Stormy crying.

Phil was hurt; Leo couldn't remember how anymore. A broken finger? A bloody nose?

Going to school was escaping his prison, escaping bedlam, but when he arrived there, he was still uptight. He hadn't had time to relax, to talk to his friends or have a quiet smoke and get his head on straight before class.

He had taken too long on his chores, on getting everything done just right, and then taking the car to school instead of the bus, got there late. Not late enough that it was quiet and everyone was in their classes and he could take his time. Just late enough to be stuck in the middle of the chaos of students racing to their classes, a bottleneck in front of his locker, confusion over what day it was and what was on his schedule.

Leo realized he had left his math books at home. Had he even done his homework? He couldn't remember from one day to the next what he had finished and what he hadn't. Leo tried frantically to get his other books together, to get everything he needed and get to class to sit down and close his eyes and just relax for a few minutes. But it wasn't in the cards.

The second bell rang and he was officially tardy.

"Bakerfield, get to class!" Mr. Giles yelled at him.

Leo's stomach clenched. He dropped his books, his hands curling into fists. He was already in fight-or-flight mode. Now Mr. Giles was going to come down on him? Leo's face was hot, a mask of anger. He faced Mr. Giles head on. "Leave me the hell alone!"

"You're late for class. Pick up your books and get going. You want a detention for language?"

"I wasn't doing anything. Just trying to get to class. Why don't you let me be!"

"Who do you think is in charge here, Mr. Bakerfield? Think it's you? Because I've got news for you. It isn't. You do what you're told and don't talk back, or I'll have you in detention faster than you can go crying to your mama."

"Go to hell!" Leo immediately reacted to the mention of his mother. Mr. Giles had no right to talk to him about his mother.

"Okay, you got it. Detention for language. Detention for talking back. Detention for tardy. Are you going to stop there?"

Leo clenched his teeth, anger boiling inside him.

He felt nauseated as the cat sharpened its claws on his insides. He felt like he was filled with hot flames. Like the white gas used in a camping lantern. Those flames were licking up his insides and erupting out of his mouth.

Leo couldn't remember what happened then. Had there been more provocation? Had Mr. Giles said more? Goaded him into it? Shoved his shoulder?

All Leo remembered now, years later, was that he had let go. He launched himself at the teacher, a retired fullback two or three times Leo's size.

Leo just let the lion out, pulled back all the stops, and went after the teacher tooth and nail. He punched and bit and kicked and no one could pull him back.

Students filled the hallway to see what was going on.

Teachers tried to get closer and to pull him off, but Leo was determined.

He couldn't fight his father. He couldn't fight the unfairness of his life. He couldn't fight all the things that kept happening to him. But he could hit Mr. Giles, and he did.

The fight even made it to the local papers. Not Leo's rage and the way he had beaten a man three times his size to a sobbing, begging pile of pink, bloody flesh. No, that might have made a good story, but not as good as the story about poor misunderstood Leo and how when the police had arrived, they had tasered him.

Leo wasn't proud of the fact. He was embarrassed he had lost control so completely, that he had continued to beat a man who was already down and gave no sign of getting back up or fighting back.

He was grateful the police had come to pull him off before he did any more damage.

But he kind of wished they'd just shot him. Why not just shoot him and let the whole nightmare end?

No more family, no more home, no more school, no more Leo the lion.

Just the cold, final peace of the grave.

But the police had a fantastic new tool. Conductive energy weapons. Of course, Leo and the other boys had heard of them, had maybe even seen them used on TV, maybe seen the cops carrying them around. But none of them had actually been shot with one.

"Freeze!" one of the cops shouted before deploying the weapon. "Just stop where you are, son, and let us sort things out."

Leo barely heard him. He barely heard or saw anything. The rage was just pouring out of him, frothing out of his person like the white foam of a baking-soda-and-vinegar volcano.

"Get down on the ground!" It was the same cop, or a different one, Leo didn't know or care.

He wasn't freezing and he wasn't getting down on the ground. He was just going to continue to vent his anger, the endless, overflowing rage, until he died. Until they shot and killed him, because nobody was going to stop him now.

"I'm going to tase you! Get down on the floor!"

Last shout. Last warning. Leo ignored it too.

Would they tase him? What would it feel like when they did? Could he keep fighting through it?

If he hit Mr. Giles again while the electricity was flowing through his body, would Mr. Giles feel it too? Could it really stop Leo, when he was so wild, the cat free to rage and rip and unwilling to be recalled?

Then the blast hit him. There was no more thought of hitting Mr. Giles again to see if he felt the electricity. There was no thought of fighting in spite of the pain.

The electricity stiffened all his muscles, like one huge body cramp.

He felt pain all over and was as stiff as a board.

Boom, he was on the floor, his muscles convulsing, pants soaking wet, his red brain turning to black as all the rage drained away, to be replaced by pain, panic, and relief.

The electricity stopped. He had read since then that the pulse only lasted a second or two, but it had seemed like an eternity to his screaming, convulsing body.

The electricity stopped, and he lay limp as Jell-O on the floor, muscles no longer stiff, but some of them still twitching, like a muscle tic after you've been leaning on your arm the wrong way for a while.

He lay there like a puddle on the floor, in a pool of his own piss, sobbing in relief that it was over.

It was all over.

They removed the Taser claws. They put handcuffs on his wrists and they pulled him to his feet. Leo's legs were wobbly and would not support him. One of the big cops had to hold him up. Not just steady him, but hold Leo's whole weight as he struggled to get control of his legs again.

Almost immediately, there were whispers and murmurs amongst the cops.

"Did you realize how young he was?" one of the cops said nearby, in a worried voice. "What if you had given him a heart attack? These things are meant for adults, not kids."

"What else were we to do?" someone else replied with a note of self-justification. "Would you look at what he did? There was no way to get him under control otherwise. He was warned. He was causing harm to someone else. There was an imminent threat."

"I'm sorry," Leo babbled. "I didn't mean to hurt anyone. I just lost it…"

"It's all right now," one of them reassured him. "It's all over. We're just going to take you out to the car now. Can you walk?"

Leo tried to nod, but his head seemed to bob every which way, like his neck was spaghetti or he had cerebral palsy.

"I can walk," he assured them.

Hands let go of him tentatively and Leo almost hit the floor again. His legs wobbled and shook.

"I didn't mean to hurt anyone," Leo protested, as if they were arguing with him. As if he could apologize and make everything right.

Hadn't he learned yet that saying sorry doesn't mean anything?

"You hurt your teacher pretty bad," a woman cop said to Leo, a snap in her voice. And Leo knew he deserved it. He didn't deserve to be treated gently like these other cops were doing, acting like he should be protected like an innocent child.

He wasn't innocent. He'd attacked a teacher.

And attacked with such force, the only way to stop him was by tasering him.

There was an incredible uproar over this poor young boy being tasered in the school. Too young. Too much of an overreaction. Leo put on bravado for the other boys when it hit the papers over the next few days, but he was both embarrassed and grateful. Embarrassed he couldn't be controlled by any other method and that the newspapers made out he was a victim.

And grateful. Because Leo knew he was out of control and he was glad to be taken out of the fight, to hit the floor and have no choice but to lie there, groaning and crying, while the police removed the claws of the Taser from his shirt, handcuffed his wrists, and hauled him to his feet.

Gasping, Leo slowed, starting to lose his vision as oxygen deprivation reached his brain. He held onto a street sign, breathing hard and waiting for the vertigo to pass. When he got angry, it all came back. All the monsters he was running from. They were all still there. As much as he might try to run from his past, to dismiss his childhood, to forget the whole history and start fresh, he was still that kid inside. That young kid who couldn't control the lion and who attacked a teacher. He would always be that kid, no matter how much Leo tried to insist he had overcome it. Just like Lyall.

Gradually, his breathing calmed down and Leo turned around and headed back toward the gym. He was surprised to see how far he had run. He'd really been moving! He was tired when he got back to the gym, but moved immediately to the heavy bag and started throwing punches.

This for all the teachers who had ever mocked or belittled him. *This* for people who left their dogs in their cars. *This* for Elizabeth, leaving her baby in a bag in her back seat and then looking at him with wide, innocent eyes, empty of any guilt for what she had done. *This* for all the cops who had ever looked at Leo with suspicion.

This for his father. His father... now lying senseless in a hospital bed.

How could Leo stay angry at the man when he was unconscious? When he might never wake up? It didn't make sense to stay angry at him, but Leo was. Furious at the shell of a body that no longer held any spark of life.

"Tough day, Leo?" asked Hakim, a middle-eastern man, father of two, who tried to squeeze his workouts between work and going home to the family. He was jumping rope at a slow, steady pace, watching Leo.

"It's fine," Leo lied. "You know. Just Reggie, one of the after-school kids."

"I hear you had a bit of a problem."

"No problem. I can handle it. He was just giving me attitude. Just wouldn't stop fighting when I told him to."

Leo didn't fail to see the irony of the situation. That he, who had more than one time had to be pulled out of a fight, tasered, or beaten senseless before he would stop. That he was the one who censured Reggie and ejected him from the gym?

"You should kick him out of the program. No way you should have to put up with that crap," Hakim declared.

"And then where would he go? He comes here so we can help him to work out his aggression and learn how to control himself. If we kick him out, where is he going to go?"

"To jail," Hakim said philosophically.

"I still think I can help him. I really do. I see a lot of myself in him. I should be able to reach him."

"You were like that? I doubt it. You're a good guy. He's just so full of attitude and anger. You're never going to reach him."

"I was too. I still am, deeper down. If I can overcome it… he can too. He just needs a little help. A little direction."

Leo continued to hit the bag, slower now, making each power punch count. His muscles protested. He'd worked hard the day before, and it should have been a light day. His muscles were still a pulp.

"Billy's in jail," he informed Hakim.

"Billy! For fighting?"

"No. Drugs in his locker."

"Oh, drugs?" Hakim cast his eyes around the room, then looked back at Leo, shaking his head. "I don't think Billy's into drugs."

Leo frowned at the bag. "I don't know. Do you think we would know if he was into drugs? How?"

"You can tell," Hakim said off-handedly. "It's just a mistake. He'll be out in a day or two."

Leo shook his head. "I hope so. I don't want to lose another kid. We need enough boys to keep the program running. I hate it when we lose one."

"You can't save everyone, Leo. They have to want to change themselves. They have to be in charge of their own change."

"Easy to say," Leo sighed. "I just can't watch him fail."

CHAPTER FOUR

L EO ARRIVED AT WORK. He nodded to the receptionist and coordinator, Melanie, who always smiled at the drivers and other workers, cheerfully pushing through mounds of work like it was nothing. She was a pretty redhead who didn't look old enough to hold down a job, let alone do the amount of work she did. She was tall and slim, with an angular nose too sharp for her face.

"Morning, Melanie. Anything exciting?"

She shook her head and handed him a half-page printout. "Just the usual," she advised.

Leo ran his eyes down the page. A couple of dogs-at-large. A sighting of a large snake in an apartment building downtown. Overnight, some kittens had been brought in, after having been dumped on the freeway. Leo clenched his fists, feeling the anger rising inside him. He never understood how people could do that; just dump helpless animals, in a box where they could be flattened.

How could you have any respect for life and do that?

Leo folded the page and took a few deep breaths to try to calm himself back down, to sedate the lion and try to relax. Just another day on the job. He couldn't let it get to him. He was doing what he loved, helping the helpless. He couldn't let his emotions get away from him and take over.

Leo went out into the parking lot to his truck. He did a walk around like he was supposed to, looking for any damage to the truck, flat tires, any other issues. Everything looked fine, just like usual. He climbed inside and turned the truck on. Looking at the first address on his list, he pulled out. Didn't need the GPS for that one.

The first was a dog-at-large. If he was lucky, he would be able to find it and bring it in. If not, he would drive around aimlessly for half an hour and then go to the next one on the list. It was supposed to be a German shepherd. Big dog, easy to see. And usually expensive, people didn't like to let them just run free. Someone was walking down alleys opening gates or the dog had dug underneath. Probably he was close to home. Quite likely, the owner would already have noticed the animal was missing, called it home, and locked it back in its kennel. Leo drove around, watching under trees, in fields with flocks of crows or gulls on the ground, against the sides of buildings where it was shadowed and sheltered. Nothing. He drove down a few back lanes, keeping a sharp eye out. Then he did the whole circuit again another time. Eventually he shrugged, reported in, and looked at the next entries on the list.

Leo was tempted to take the boa next. A snake call was slightly more tempting than a dog call. Chances were, he still wouldn't find it. It would be in a pipe or wall somewhere, or it would be sunning itself on top of a warm light. But they were more interesting to track down and easy to catch. But the next entry on the list was another dog-a- large and Leo knew he really should take that one next. He checked the address and wasn't sure where it was, so he keyed it into the GPS and headed out again.

He was driving around the neighborhood looking for the small dog, a cockapoo this time, when the emergency call came in. Leo's heart raced. Finally, some excitement!

"All cars respond," the voice came over the CB. "We've got a cat lady. All units report to Five Fifty Eleventh Avenue to help with trapping and removal."

Leo turned off the GPS and headed over. Cat ladies were interesting folks. They professed to love their animals and yet they kept so many of them, it was impossible to take care of them properly. So, starving and sick, living in horrible crowded, dirty conditions, the poor pussies lived and died horrible lives.

It was a mental condition. Leo felt sorry for the cat ladies, but he felt anger too.

How could they put animals through this? How could they watch them suffering and dying each day, and yet take more in, let them have litters of miserable kittens, and not find a way out?

Why not take in one or two cats. Try to find homes for the others. Take them to the Humane Society! Get the ones you kept neutered. If they were sensible, they could do more good than they could by just trying to save all the cats in the city single-handedly.

Leo gripped the steering wheel tightly, trying to stay focused on his driving and not to let his anger break out.

He arrived at the destination. There were police cars, an ambulance, a couple of fire trucks, and a couple of bylaw workers who had arrived ahead of him. Leo got out, collected some equipment, and looked for who was in charge.

"Over here." A policeman gestured to him.

"What do you want me to do?" Leo asked.

"Just go in and catch whatever you can. There's no organized plan. Just get what you can."

Leo looked at the little, dilapidated house. It was impossible to mistake. Even ignoring the little cat decorations outside and in the windows, you couldn't fail to smell the place. The neighbors had probably been complaining for years, and every time, the cops just said, 'nothing we can do about it.' Or maybe they had been here before, had cleaned out the animals, condemned the place even, and yet the cat lady stayed. Stayed and collected more cats to replace the furry babies she had lost. Started over again and just collected, and collected, and collected, trying to save all the cats in the city.

As he walked past the ambulance, he saw her. Smelled her too. In a gurney behind the ambulance. Maybe she'd fallen and broken her hip, or maybe she'd gotten sick from the ammonia in the air, the fecal contamination, worms or toxoplasmosis. Who knew how much of that crap she was ingesting every day. She sobbed and cried to the paramedic who was beside her, to the policeman who was trying to talk to her.

"My poor babies—you can't take my poor babies away. I need to take care of them. Please, don't take me away. Let me just stay here and take care of my poor kitties."

"We'll take care of them for you, ma'am," the cop reassured her. "We'll have people who can take care of them. You have too many to take care of yourself. You have to let us help."

"You won't take them all away, will you? Just the ones that are sick? I'll be back later today, or tomorrow. I'll be able to take care of them still."

"I'm sorry ma'am. They've all got to go. The house has to be sanitized. Or you'll get sick again."

"I'm not sick because of them!" she protested indignantly. "It's pneumonia. I've had it before. It isn't from the poor pussies!"

Leo shook his head, pulled a mask over his mouth and nose, and entered the house. He slipped in the door as quickly as he could, watching his feet for any animals trying to get out at the first opportunity. It was dark. Electricity out? Had it been shut off for failure to pay her bills? Or had the fire department shut it off, worried about methane gas build-up in the house?

All the windows had been opened. Luckily they had screens over them or they wouldn't have been able to open them without escapees.

As expected, the place smelled worse than an outhouse. Leo breathed shallowly through his mouth, trying to avoid smelling it, trying to ignore the burning feeling in his throat. Trying not to gag. He'd get used to it after a few minutes.

He turned into the first room, which happened to be the kitchen. Bowls lined the walls like one massive feeding trough. But most of them were empty. There was way too little food here to keep the woman's babies fed. Leo stood still, quiet, and looked around. Most of the cats were hiding, trying to avoid him. They were crouched in the chairs, behind the curtains, up on top of the cabinets against the ceiling. There was a hole in the ceiling by the light fixture and Leo could see eyes reflecting up there too. They would be everywhere. In the attic, the basement, the crawlspaces, the walls themselves. Would they ever be able to find and catch them all? Leo murmured quietly, soothingly, and approached the nearest cat. A white long-haired cat. At least, he assumed the natural color of the long, muddy fur was white. It opened its mouth in a silent mew.

"I know," Leo said softly. "I know, little one. Let's get you somewhere you can have a nice meal now, hey?"

He reached out slowly and let the cat smell his hand. It wrinkled its nose at the smell of his gloves and he slid a finger behind its head, giving it a little rub behind the ears. It stayed there, looking at him, trusting. Leo grabbed it by the scruff of the neck and put it in a cage. That it didn't like, and it yowled and scrambled, but Leo was persistent and in it went. One down, two hundred to go.

Leo made numerous trips back and forth between the truck and the house. More cages. More felines. Some were too thin and weak to fight. Emaciated mothers trying to nurse kittens with wasted bodies. Too weak even to get up and run away. Some of the toms still had a good amount of fight in them and tried to take his hand off.

Leo walked past a few of the police officers who were being treated at the ambulance, having scratches and bites cleaned up and bandaged. He heard a paramedic giving one cop a lecture about trying to do animal control's job and picking up animals without proper protection. These officers would probably end up having to go through a round of rabies shots, antibiotics, and whatever else amused their doctors. Next time, they wouldn't be so quick to do the job of animal control. Next time they would wear gloves or wait until the proper authorities got there to do it the right way.

In and out, in and out. The cats were getting harder to find. The more obvious ones had been caught and removed. Leo walked past his comrades, his brother animal control officers, without saying much. They were all too intent on their work. This wasn't the time to socialize. Some of them had loops or nets. Others, like Leo, preferred to just use their hands until they got down to the last few stragglers; the most accomplished fighters and runners.

Leo moved the table under the light fixture in the kitchen and stood on top of it to peer up into the dark hole. He used his flashlight, making a complete circle.

"Lots of them still up there," Leo said, as he stepped back down. "Need a ladder and a couple of nets over here."

Gordon nodded. "We'll get set up in here in a few minutes," he agreed.

"Has anyone taken the first few batches in?" he asked.

"Yes, they've made a few trips."

The fire engines were gone. The police were gone except for one who stood by to seal up the house when they were done. The ambulance was gone. There would be no more injuries. It was just the professionals now.

They moved in with ladders, with axes to break open portions of the wall, with infrared machines to check the walls for heat signatures. While some of the others worked on dragging the cats from the ceiling over the kitchen, Leo started a slow circuit around the house with the infrared machine. There were actually fewer in the wall than he would have expected. But there were still some there. Leo broke open the wall in a few places. He tried to get in above the animals but had to be quick enough they couldn't squirm and scale the walls up into the ceiling. Working quickly, he would break open the wall, grab what he could, cage them, and then tape a screen over the hole and move on to the next portion.

It was late. He knew they were long beyond quitting time now. His body ached. It was getting darker and the sweltering house was starting to cool down, a quiet breeze blowing in through the windows. Leo paused to take a few breaths of the sweet smelling air and then got back to work again. Gordon was looking over his shoulder as Leo found another nest within the wall.

"Cats or rats?" Gordon asked, frowning at the image.

"Cats," Leo said.

"Can you actually tell that?" Gordon asked, studying the shapes on the infrared machine.

Leo shook his head. "I really *want* them to be cats," he explained. "Besides, you think rats could survive in this house? They'd be dinner in two minutes."

"True." Gordon made a face. "…You don't suppose the cats ever eat each other, do they? Or the kittens?"

Leo sighed, putting down the machine and getting out his axe.

"You've seen the corpses," he said. "You tell me."

Gordon shuddered. He stood by, ready to help Leo once the wall was opened up. With a deep breath, Leo attacked the wall. He allowed his anger to vent for just a few seconds, putting it behind the swing of his arms and the blow of the axe to do something constructive. *This* was for the people who couldn't take care of their animals. For the cat ladies. *This*, and *this*, and *this*!

No cats squirmed up and out of the nest, so he bent over and looked. Mama cat was not here. Only the kittens. With the gentlest possible hands, Leo reached in and took them out, sliding them all together in one cage, where they mewed and huddled together, shivering and weak. Had they already caught the mother? Had she escaped? Or had she died a day or two ago, leaving these little ones dehydrated and on the edge of death? Leo closed up the cage and left it to Gordon to transfer it to the truck.

He couldn't allow himself to stop and think about it for too long. He would just get too angry. He'd be too paralyzed to actually get his job done. So he picked up the infrared machine, and just kept going.

Finally, they were done. They had gone over all of the walls, all of the ceilings, all of the nooks and crannies where they thought a tiny kitten could have secreted itself. There were none left. The house was still.

Leo and Gordon sat on the steps of the house while the cop closed up all of the windows and sealed the door, putting up a health hazard sign to keep everyone out. Leo pulled out a cigarette and smoked it, trying to get the taste of cat piss out of his mouth.

"Will they sanitize it?" he asked. "Or knock it down?"

"Knock it down, I hope," the cop said. "I don't think a place like that can be cleaned up properly. Best to tear it out and build a new one. You wouldn't want to live in a house like that after this, would you?"

"Not me," Leo agreed.

It was late and Leo realized he was hungry. He hadn't stopped for either lunch or supper all day. Only a few swigs from his water bottle when he went back to his truck. He'd felt too sick to eat anything. But now that it was over, and he was out in the fresh air, his stomach reminded him he needed to eat.

"Go for a beer?" Gordon suggested.

"No." Leo turned him down. "I need to get something solid in me. And more than pretzels or peanuts. I've got some errands to run."

Leo looked at his watch to see if he had any time to do any of the things he had planned. Shopping would have to wait for another day. He was too exhausted to clean or cook. There was no after-school program, and even if there was, the time was long past. All he had time to do was to see Stormy. And he could do that and get a meal at the same time.

CHAPTER FIVE

LEO HATED GOING TO the club Stormy worked at. He hated to see her putting her body on display for men. Who knew what else she was doing to earn a few extra dollars for crack. He didn't know and he didn't want to know.

He still hadn't managed to save Stormy.

Leo sat himself down at an empty booth and motioned for a menu. One of the skimpily dressed waitresses brought it over to him, slinking sexily toward him. Then she got close enough to see who it was in the dimness of the place, and her shoulders slumped.

"Oh, hi Leo."

"Hi, Marie," Leo greeted politely.

"Here you go. She should be on in about twenty minutes."

"Okay. Thanks."

"Just wave when you're ready to order."

Leo prided himself in the fact he didn't have a regular order. Each time he came, he made the effort to carefully peruse the menu, weigh his options, and decide what it was he really wanted. There wasn't any: 'I'll have the usual,' or 'That's Leo, he'll have a cheeseburger and fries.' His diet was varied.

He was careful not to fall into a routine. He didn't know why it was important to him, but it was.

Maybe because he had grown up in a home where predictability was dangerous.

Leo avoided looking at the stage. He wasn't there to see the girls. He just wanted to talk to Stormy. He looked studiously at the menu in front of him. Eventually, he waved for Marie. She came up to him.

"What's your pleasure?" she asked.

Leo squirmed at the phrasing of the question. Still looking at the menu rather than Marie, he ordered a club sandwich with a side of fries, and a Coke. Marie nodded, taking the menu from him.

"Sounds good. I'll have that to you in a few minutes."

Leo nodded. "Thanks."

He gazed around the club, trying to find a place to focus without staring at the girls. But looking around the club too much was bad too. The other patrons would think he was a cop and get uptight about it. It smelled like sweat and smoke and beer. The lighting was dim and the room was packed to capacity.

Leo took out his phone and thumbed through his e-mails, looking for anything important. There wasn't anything there. It wasn't like he was going to get anything important by e-mail. He might get a phone call if Stormy or one of the other siblings was hurt or in trouble. Or from the hospital if Lyall's condition changed for the worse. But he didn't really have a lot of friends on the internet. Mostly just subscriptions to various e-mail newsletters and magazines. He didn't read them. He just thought he should have an e-mail address and some kind of community… but it didn't really turn out that way.

It was just a reminder his life didn't really matter.

Leo wondered how Elizabeth was doing and sent a short text message to her. She was probably still in hospital, but it was always possible she got home sooner than expected. There was no response. Even if she wasn't in hospital, what were the chances she was sitting around waiting for his text? Or that she cared enough to text him back?

He got his sandwich just as Stormy was getting up on stage. Leo ventured a glance at her. It sickened him how much she had changed since she was a little girl. He remembered when she was just little, four or five, and she had those wild curls, like the little girl from the movie 'Curly Sue.' She'd been a firecracker even back then. He was always having to jump in and get her out of trouble. He tried to keep her from catching Lyall's attention.

He'd gone to the school and talked to school teachers about her when they called home to talk to a parent. He'd done everything he could to keep her from having to take the consequences of her actions. She was so impulsive; she never thought ahead to what was going to happen after she acted.

Now she was a woman. He couldn't deny that, even though he still saw that little girl when he looked at her. That wasn't really what bothered him. It was her blatant exhibitionism that made him uncomfortable. But now there was nothing he could do to protect her. She had to take the consequences of her own actions. And the things she chose to do... earning money by stripping, taking drugs, getting involved with all the wrong guys... It was like she was set on a course for self-destruction. She was determined to try everything he'd ever told her to stay away from.

Some kids just couldn't be told. You tell them what to do and they do the opposite. Stormy was one of those kids. Leo's other siblings were different. They were more cautious. They learned from their mistakes, even learned from others'. They listened to Leo's advice, and mostly they were better than he was about staying out of trouble. He was proud of the way they had succeeded.

But Stormy... Stormy by name and stormy by nature. She wasn't going to change. He always hoped he could keep talking, keep chipping away at her, and some day she would start to listen. It would all start to make sense to her. She'd start connecting the dots. Like him, she had learning disabilities. It was harder for her to learn. Harder to learn how to avoid making those stupid mistakes in the first place, to avoid doing the first thing that popped into her head. But if Leo repeated himself enough times, maybe it would make sense sometime. Sooner or later.

Stormy finished her song and the curtain closed. He imagined her picking up her clothes behind the closed curtain, and he headed back to her dressing room, the last couple of bites of his sandwich in hand. He knocked on the open door and poked his head in to see if it was okay to enter.

"I saw you," Stormy commented, dressing behind a screen.

"I wasn't exactly hiding."

"Why do you even come here? If you hate it so much, why bother?"

"Because it's the only place I can catch you. If you would meet me for coffee or something, it would be a lot easier."

"Yeah, well, that's not really my thing, is it? You work all day, you're only free when I'm sleeping or working. So what am I supposed to do?"

"I could help you find a better job. One where you didn't have to work at night like this."

"What, flipping burgers at McDonalds? Do you know how little money they make doing that? I wouldn't have enough for anything."

"People make a living at it," Leo countered. "And that's not the only thing you could do. I make pretty good money working for the City."

"The people who make a living at it don't live the kind of lifestyle I want. Besides, I don't want to flip burgers. And I don't want to work at the City. I want to be a star. I want to make a splash. I like being in the entertainment business; it makes me feel good. So why should I settle for something else?"

"You want to be a singer," Leo said. "How is stripping getting you any closer to that?"

She scowled at him and ducked down behind the screen for a few moments, saying nothing. He wasn't sure whether she was getting on her shoes or if she just didn't have a good answer.

"I'm in the entertainment field," she reiterated. "I get to know people, who the players are. I know the clubs and who performs at them. I figure out who the agents are and stuff. You don't think I'm getting anywhere, but I am. I'm moving forward. I'm moving the way I want to go. So just quit ragging on me, okay?"

"Maybe I could find someone who could help you out…"

"Any time you want to make introductions for me, big brother, you're welcome to it. I'm still waiting on that one."

"I'll try to make some connections," Leo promised.

"Yeah, well I'm not holding my breath. Who do you have connections with? Dog catchers? School kids? You're not exactly in my field, Leo."

She came out from behind the screen. She tugged down her mini skirt, but it still didn't cover anything. She offered to hug Leo, and he awkwardly put and patted her briefly on the back. Stormy gave him an air kiss.

"Now," she said. "You want a drink?"

Leo nodded. "Sure, let's go have one."

She led the way back to the main room and looked around at the crowds. She waved to another girl.

"Hey Crystal. There any private rooms free?"

Crystal looked Leo over. "This one doesn't bring in any money," she disapproved.

"No. We just want to have a drink where it's a bit quieter. If there's a room not being used. If it's not being used, then it's not making any money anyway."

Crystal sighed, rolling her eyes. "Yeah, the red room is open. Just don't spend too long there. I want it free if we have someone who's willing to pay."

"Sure," Stormy agreed. She led Leo to one of the private entertainment rooms. They sat down, and Stormy poured out a couple of glasses of wine. Leo looked at his.

"Oh, just drink it," Stormy snapped.

Leo shook his head. "A soft drink or a tomato juice or something," he countered. "I don't want alcohol."

"There's nothing wrong with a glass of wine now and then. They even say it's healthy, you know, good for your heart."

"Well, it's not good for me," Leo said. "I don't want to end up like Him."

"You're not like Him. You never have been. And taking one drink isn't going to make you like Him."

"It could," Leo maintained. "I'm not taking any chances. I already know how easily I lose control if I've had a few drinks."

"A few? I'm saying one. One glass. Why are you acting like you're so much better than me?"

"I'm not. I just don't want to drink."

"Be a friend and drink with me."

"I'll drink with you. As long as it's virgin."

"Oh, you are hopeless." She got up and went to the mini fridge, pouring him a tomato juice and garnishing it with a celery stalk. "There, how's that?" she demanded. "Nice and healthy for you."

"Maybe this will counteract the fries," Leo said, trying to lighten her mood.

"So what's new in your life?" Stormy asked, changing the subject.

"We had a cat lady today."

"Eww. How many?"

"I didn't hear what the final count was," Leo said. "There must have been at least sixty. Maybe a hundred."

"Holy cow. And was the house full of crap?"

"Of course. Pretty nasty place."

"I'm never going to grow up to be a cat lady," she said seriously.

Leo grinned. "No. Just two cats to keep you company when you're an old lady," he suggested.

"I dunno. I don't really even like cats. I wish I had a dog."

"I could get you one. You just say the word."

"You know I can't have one where I'm living right now. Maybe someday, when I've got a house."

"When you're rich and famous."

"Yeah, that's right. And if I'm rich and famous, I'm going to buy my own dog. Something really expensive. Purebred. Maybe one of those dogs you can carry in your purse."

Leo shook his head.

"High strung. And more likely to have some kind of genetic defect that will end up with it getting a broken back or some disease. And those purse dogs are just so yappy and annoying. People decide they can't stand them anymore and we get them at the pound. Poor things."

Stormy rolled her eyes. "I don't care. I'll get what kind of dog I like, and I'll take care of it. You know I will."

Leo smiled at her. "I know you will," he agreed. "Not like some of the people I run into on the job."

Stormy nodded, taking a sip of her wine. "You see the worst of the worst," she pointed out. "That's not the way the whole world is. Probably not even the majority. But you think that's how everyone is."

"I suppose."

Thinking about people who couldn't take care of their animals made him think about Elizabeth and Juleen. Juleen wasn't just a dog she couldn't take care of. She was a baby. And that was much worse. You didn't just take a baby to the pound when you decided you couldn't care for any more. Even safe haven laws only covered babies younger than seventy-two hours. He wondered if it was better in the countries overseas where they had broader abandonment laws. Places where you could just take a baby, and put it in a special crib, and ring the doorbell, and they would come take the baby and put it in an orphanage. Not that he thought orphanages were good. They were bad. Worse than foster homes. But the abandonment laws… being able to just take a baby and drop it off, and not have to worry about what people thought, or if the police were going to come after you for neglect…

"Where are you?" Stormy coaxed. She was looking at him, her eyes laughing.

"Oh. Sorry. I was just thinking about this woman I met yesterday."

"A woman. At work or socially?"

"Umm, socially. Sort of. Not at work."

"Oooh, Leo's got a girlfriend," Stormy teased.

"No. Just met her once."

"You get her phone number?"

"Yeah. I got her phone number. She said I could call her."

"And did you call her today?"

"No, not today."

"Why not? You playing hard to get? I'm not sure you can afford to."

"No. I just know she is busy today and tomorrow," Leo explained. "I'll call her when she gets home again."

"You'd better. Don't let this one get away."

"I texted her today. Just in case."

"Well, that's good. Something, at least. So what's this girl's name?"

"Elizabeth."

"Elizabeth. That's nice. A bit formal, though."

"She seems to have plenty of nicknames."

"A lot of nicknames?"

"Lizzie, Lisbet, Lisa. I don't know, I lost track after a while."

"Huh. So what's she like?"

"I don't really know yet. She's friendly, but she seems like she might be a little bit flaky. Just… I don't know if she really is, or if she just comes off that way, or it could just be one of the medications she's on."

"Medications?" Stormy made alarm sounds. "Woot, woot, woot! Danger, Will Robinson, danger!"

"I know. I'm not jumping into anything. I'm waiting to see how it all turns out. I don't know if I want to get involved with her or not."

"You can't save everyone."

"I'm not trying to save her," Leo objected. Though he knew it was a lie. Of course he wanted to save her. And Juleen.

"Who do you think you're kidding? Of course you do. All the animals, all the children, everyone you think needs to be fixed! Now that even includes Dad. How sick is *that?*"

"I know I can't save everyone," Leo said steadily, looking her in the eye. "Just you."

Stormy looked away. "You don't need to fix me," she said. "There's nothing wrong with me. I'm not broken. I may not be where I want to be yet, but there's nothing wrong with me."

"I worry about you so much, Stormy. I wish I could help you to see what I see. I want you to be happy. I don't want you to keep putting yourself in danger, to keep doing things that are just going to end up hurting you. I want you to be happy and safe."

"I am happy and I am safe. Nothing to fix."

"Are you still doing crack?" Leo asked, trying to meet her eyes to analyze whether she told him the truth or not.

"I'm… just smoking a little now and then. I'm not snorting and I'm not shooting. Just relaxing with a bit, now and then. Not even every day. Just a little now and then."

Leo shook his head. "It's bad for your body. It can give you heart problems, all kinds of things."

"I could say the same about your cigarettes."

"You know crack is worse for you than cigarettes. And I'm not going to get arrested for carrying a pack of cigarettes. It's not the same."

"I'm weaning myself off. I can't do it cold turkey. I'm not that strong."

"We could find a program for you."

"Oh puh-lease! I don't need a stupid program. I'm not an addict. I'm not in trouble. I'm not going to get myself arrested."

"I hope not. Please think about it. Take care of yourself. I worry about you so much."

"You don't need to worry about me. Everything's fine." Stormy looked at her watch. "Well, we've been in here long enough. Crystal will be having kittens. Come on."

Leo stood up. "You didn't ask how Dad is doing."

"Do I care how he is doing? He's dead, Leo. We're all just waiting for you to unplug the machines. And even if he was alive, I wouldn't care. Unplug him anyway. Do the world a favor."

Leo followed her out of the private room. He gave her another hug and received an air kiss before leaving, and went home to put his weary bones to bed. Another work day tomorrow. He'd better get some rest and be ready for it.

Leo peeked in the door. Shayla wasn't there yet. He tiptoed into the room and sat down next to the bed looking Lyall over. Everything seemed the same. Leo was starting to accept now that he might be dead. Maybe Lyall really was dead and gone.

Leo sighed. He looked out the window, listening to the hum and huff of the machines. He heard a rustling and looked back at the bed, startled. Lyall was still, motionless.

Leo's heart thumped.

He was imagining things. There was no one else in the room. And Lyall was brain dead. He couldn't move. He couldn't even breathe on his own.

He looked at Lyall's face, looking for any change.

Lyall's eyes were open.

Leo startled violently.

He looked around the room, looking for someone to give him an explanation. To tell him he was just tired and was imagining things.

The nurses had warned him. They had said Lyall might make an involuntary movement, or breathe, or open his eyes, but he was still brain dead. It was just random nerves firing.

Leo breathed out, trying to settle his heart. Relax. Just relax.

Lyall started to make a noise, a sort of low humming, a groan.

Leo hit the nurse call button. And hit it a few more times for good measure, panicked by these new developments.

Where were they? They had to tell him what was going on.

Was Lyall waking up? Was he not brain dead after all? Had they all been wrong?

Lyall's hands started moving in an odd swimming gesture, nightmarish, like he was waking up from a dream.

"Help! Hello? Help me!" Leo called out, rushing to the corridor. It was usually busy, but now as silent as a crypt. "Hello? Nurse! He's waking up! Help me!"

There was no answer. There was no one manning the nursing station. Leo rushed back to the bedside.

"Shhh," he said weakly. "Everything is okay." He tried to explain "You were in an accident."

Lyall's open eyes sought him out.

The humming, growling noise became louder.

Lyall reached up with his hands and pulled the various tubes and lines away from his face.

"You," he said in a deep, hoarse voice. "*You* did this!"

Leo tried to scream, but nothing came out.

He tried to run, but his legs were paralyzed his feet were super-glued to the floor.

With a crash, Leo fell out of bed.

He dug his fingers into the carpet, feeling the coarse texture of the loops, using all his senses to persuade himself that this was reality, and the other was a dream.

It had seemed so real, he had a hard time convincing himself. He lay there on the rug gasping for breath, his heart pounding, the vision of Lyall still bright in his head.

It was a long time before he managed to crawl up off of the floor and back into his bed.

He lay there thinking, not wanting to fall back asleep again.

CHAPTER SIX

NOTHING BIG OR EXCITING at work. Lost or at-large dogs, a cat in a tree. One of the other animal control officers had managed to find the albino boa Leo had seen the report on earlier. He got his picture in the paper, boa wrapped around his shoulders, the owner of the apartment grimacing beside him.

At the end of the day, Leo parked his truck and checked out with Melanie.

"What was the total count at cat lady's house?" he asked.

"One hundred and five."

"Ugh." Leo shook his head, a lead weight in his stomach. "That's crazy. How many do you think we saved?"

Melanie looked at him, shaking her head, her eyes shiny with tears and the corners of her mouth pulling down. It looked unnatural on her usual cheerful visage.

"There were a half dozen newborn kittens we gave to Sadie. I think they'll be okay. But most of them… too sick or unsocialized to ever adopt out. We've got a few that might be adoptable, but we probably won't save more than ten, including the kittens. Morton was working overtime putting them down last night."

Leo felt like throwing up. The lion raged inside him.

A hundred cats dead. Put to sleep.

A hundred cats dead because some crazy lady was so off her head she didn't understand she was killing them with her love.

Someone should put *her* out of her misery to prevent her from ever doing such an evil thing again. Someone should throttle her. Bash her head in.

Someone should fix it.

He shook his head and staggered out, nearly blind to his surroundings.

He seethed in the car all the way home. The lion was sharpening its claws and Leo kept biting the inside of his cheek, trying to stay in control.

He didn't want to explode if someone cut him off on the freeway.

He had to stay in control.

He had to stay in control until he could get home.

It was a tense trip; it seemed like it took four times what it usually did to get through the highway traffic and pull into his parking space.

Leo walked in through the door, shut it behind him, and bellowed in wordless rage.

He rushed downstairs and propped a couple of exercise mats up against the concrete walls, and started hitting them furiously.

His nose started bleeding spontaneously, his blood pressure was so high and his breathing so harsh.

He slammed and slammed and slammed his fists into the thick exercise mats over and over again, until he finally collapsed on the floor, sobbing, out of breath, exhausted.

He lay there for a while, just breathing and trying to regain control, until the bleeding nose really started to irritate him.

He had the choice to either lie there with the blood trickling down the back of his throat or trickling down his face into a puddle he would have to clean up. He didn't like either option. So Leo forced himself to his feet and went back upstairs to tear off a paper towel and pinch his nostrils shut until the bleeding stopped.

Once it stopped, he went outside to the yard and opened up the kennel.

Rascal rushed out, barking, prancing around him, happily seeking out his hands to nuzzle Leo and get him to scratch Rascal's ears.

Leo breathed deeply. Rascal was one of the few things that could break his mood when he boiled over. He rubbed Rascal's face and ears with both hands.

"Who's a good boy?" he asked.

Rascal squirmed before him, so excited and happy to have his attention.

"Shall we go for a run?" Leo asked.

Rascal yipped happily, running to the back door, and back to Leo, and to the back door, and back to Leo; each circuit slightly shorter as Leo approached the house and got out the leash. Then Rascal sat politely when commanded, his tail thumping hard, and Leo hooked the leash onto his collar.

"Okay, let's go!"

He and Rascal took off down the street at a quick lope. Leo knew he wouldn't be able to keep up the speed he began with, but it didn't matter. He needed to exhaust himself. Rascal wouldn't care. He was happy to be out with Leo, however fast or slow they went.

Leo pounded out the miles.

He started to slow down. He stopped for a break, walking and stretching his calves.

Leo looked around the neighborhood, frowning. Something tweaked in his memory. He pulled out his phone and checked to see what Elizabeth's address was. He was right. He was on her street.

Leo walked along, rolling his shoulders, aching from punching the wall. He looked down at his knuckles, badly bruised and split. He must look a sight.

Looking at the numbers on the sides of the buildings, he found Elizabeth's building. It was an old building of red brick. He went into the alcove between the doors, where he dialed her number on the keypad beside the speaker. He wasn't sure if she would be home yet. He'd lost track of the number of hours and days since she'd been committed.

"Hello?" Elizabeth's voice floated back.

"Oh, hey. This is Leo. We met the other day? Had coffee?"

"At the mall?" Elizabeth queried.

"Yeah," Leo was relieved she remembered. It would be awkward if she didn't even know who he was.

"Come in," Elizabeth said. The lock buzzed to let him know she had unlocked it for him.

Leo looked down at Rascal. "Past the first barrier," he said.

Rascal looked up at him and made a snuffling noise in agreement. Leo rubbed Rascal's head and Rascal wagged his whole backside. Leo went up the elevator to Elizabeth's floor and looked up and down the hall. She stuck her head out into the hallway.

"Over here."

Leo went into her apartment. Elizabeth looked down at Rascal.

"That's the most butt-ugly dog I've ever seen!" she exclaimed.

Leo was used to this reaction. People just didn't see Rascal for how beautiful he was on the inside. They only saw the scarred outside. But it was his scars and deformity that made Leo feel a kinship with him.

"This is Rascal," Leo introduced. "He's very friendly if you want to pat him."

She looked like she didn't want to, but to be polite, she bent over and offered her hand for him to smell. Rascal shoved his snout under her hand, sliding her hand up to the top of his head. Elizabeth laughed and scratched his head and ears. She giggled at the way Rascal's hindquarters bounced around as he wagged his tail so hard you'd swear it was going to fall off.

"He likes you," Leo said.

"Well, he may be ugly, but he seems like an awfully nice dog."

"He is," Leo agreed. "He lost his leg and his eye in a building fire. Saved a little girl. Even got his face in the paper. They wanted to put him down, but I wouldn't let them. He's such a nice boy."

"Yeah, he seems like it. I guess you talked them out of it."

"It wasn't easy."

"So, are you on the job?" Elizabeth asked, looking Leo over.

Leo opened his mouth to scoff at the idea. Obviously he wasn't on the job. They'd never let him take Rascal in his truck. He was out running, which should have been obvious from… Leo looked down at his clothes and realized he hadn't even stopped to change into his running gear when he got home. He'd gone out running in his city worker uniform. And, looking down at it, he realized he'd spattered blood on it during his blow-up.

"Umm—no. See what happened was… I was upset after work, and I went running in my uniform. I forgot to change first. Looks pretty weird, I know. But I am actually off duty."

"What were you upset about?" Elizabeth asked.

She headed to the living room and sat down on the couch, motioning to him to pick a seat. Juleen was in the middle of the floor on a blanket, looking like she'd been marooned on a desert island.

"Hey, pooky," Leo greeted her. He stooped down and picked the baby up. "How are you doing today?"

Rascal nosed at Juleen, snuffling the baby and trying to figure out whether the little one would play with him or not. Leo turned Juleen toward Rascal and let them examine one another. Rascal let the baby smack his face and grasp his ear, and licked her face happily.

"Is that okay?" Elizabeth asked worriedly. "What if he bites her?"

"Rascal loves kids. He's not going to hurt her."

But Leo motioned Rascal down. Rascal sat back on his haunches, panting, watching his master and the baby with adoring eyes.

"So what were you upset about?" Elizabeth asked again. "After work?"

"Yeah. Well, yesterday, we had this really big job. A cat lady."

Elizabeth considered. "Does that mean she thought her cats were her children, or she had a whole bunch of them?"

"Well… she had one hundred and five of them."

"One hundred and five?" Elizabeth repeated, her jaw dropping. "How could you fit that many cats in one house?"

"Yeah. One house. Poor things. They were all starving, covered in… crap… living in the ceilings and the walls… it was the worst I've ever seen."

"I bet," she agreed. "But if this was yesterday, then why were you upset about it after work today? It just took that long to hit you?"

"No. I found out at the end of work today they had to put most of them down. There won't be any more than ten to adopt out."

Elizabeth shook her head, her face flushing red. Leo was comforted that she felt just as angry about it as he did.

"They shouldn't use the word *adopt*," Elizabeth said petulantly.

Leo looked at her, floored. "What?"

"You don't adopt animals like you adopt kids. When you get a pet, they're not part of your family. They don't become your kids. They're chattels. You just own them. It's not the same."

Leo tried to pick his jaw up off the floor.

"Well, yeah," he agreed weakly. "It's not exactly the same, I know. But what else would you say?"

"Sell. You sell cats to people. You don't adopt them out."

"I guess. People don't like you to say that, though. And the Humane Society people say you can't own an animal, you just agree to share your home with it, to give it a good life. The animal itself cannot be owned."

"Ridiculous," Elizabeth snapped. "Of course it can."

She was right. You could go to the pet store and buy an animal. When you licensed it with the city, they agreed you owned the animal, not that you were its mother or father. You didn't have to go to court to have it declared part of your family. You didn't have to provide child support if you ever gave it to someone else to take care of. You could turn around and sell it to the next door neighbor, or a dealer, or a Chinese restaurant. Nobody laid down rules saying you had to provide for it for the rest of its life.

"I guess," he agreed. "I never really thought about it that way. No one ever objected to the word adoption before."

"I know all about adoption," Elizabeth said with the wave of a hand. "And it's not like buying a dog."

"Oh. Were you adopted?" Obviously she hadn't adopted Juleen; he'd already heard how Juleen was born on the front lines of the war. Assuming Elizabeth was telling the truth.

"I was once," Elizabeth said stoically, "but it didn't work out. They… dissolved it. Gave me back."

Leo was puzzled. "How do you give a baby back?" he asked with a frown.

"Well, I wasn't a baby. I was three or four or something at the time. As for how do you give it back… they put me on a plane, with a one-way ticket and a note in my pocket."

Leo felt his eyes widen. "What kind of creep would do that?" he demanded.

"They decided they couldn't handle me. Didn't want me in the house anymore. So they just shipped me back. Like I was a bowl they ordered that arrived broken or something. Thirty day money back guarantee."

"They can't do that!"

"Yeah, it all went to court and that's what the judge said too. But it wasn't like they were going to take me back. The judge couldn't force them. He imposed some fines, made them pay child support, but he couldn't make them take me back if they didn't want me."

Leo shook his head in amazement. "I don't understand how anyone could do that."

"Me neither."

"You must have been so traumatized! Did you understand what was going on?"

Elizabeth shrugged. "I knew they were supposed to be my parents and then they changed their minds and wouldn't. I knew they sent me away and didn't want me back."

Leo thought of his own life, his own family, his own past. What he wouldn't have given to be taken away from his own family. To just be able to leave there, and start over again with someone else. But where was the guarantee he'd be treated any better at someone else's house? You heard all the time about foster families being abusive, of kids being removed from horrific situations, much like the cats he'd removed from the crazy cat lady's home.

"That must have been really hard."

Elizabeth didn't look sad or upset about it. She shrugged, her expression blank, impassive. "I don't need anyone else to survive. I learned that. You gotta just look out for yourself. Learn how to manage on your own. Be a grown up. Just like you," she pointed out.

Leo stared out her window. It looked across the street at another brick apartment building. Not very inspiring scenery. He smiled and cooed at Juleen. He looked down at Rascal, lying politely at his side.

"I'm sorry you had to go through all that," he said. "I know what it's like… not to be loved."

Elizabeth tossed her head. "Love. Who needs it? You grew up with a family, didn't you?"

"Yes. But they weren't loving. I mean, I love my siblings, but…"

"There you go. You grew up in a nice home."

"It really… wasn't so nice," Leo protested.

"But you had one. And I didn't. And I'm fine, just like you."

Just fine. Couldn't acknowledge she was pregnant. Couldn't remember to take care of her own baby. But she was just fine.

"Maybe if you admitted what it was like," he said slowly, "you'd be able to come to terms with it better. Feel better about yourself. Be a better mom to Juleen."

"I am a good mom. It doesn't affect me."

Leo just looked at her steadily. Did she really believe that?

"Well, okay, I could be a better mom," she acknowledged, rolling her eyes. "But mostly that's just the meds, not because I had a rough childhood."

Leo nodded. "Did you get it all straightened out?" he asked, happy to segue to a safer topic. "Did the doctor help you to adjust your meds?"

"Yeah. I'm feeling a lot clearer now. I'm not going to forget about Juleen anymore. I know I have to take care of her. And she has a social worker assigned to keep checking in, making sure I'm doing all right."

CHAPTER SEVEN

SOCIAL WORKERS. LEO HOPED Juleen had one of the good ones. But social workers became jaded so fast, he wasn't sure there were any good ones left.

Leo resolved he would keep an eye on Juleen too. He wasn't relying on any social worker to do it.

How many social workers had Leo and his siblings seen? Social workers who just made phone calls instead of coming to the little farmhouse? Who smiled and nodded at the children playing in the front yard and didn't insist on seeing the one sick in bed?

Who acted like everything was okay when really the children needed her protection so badly?

There was a knock at the door, and Leo looked up, wondering what was going on. He heard Margaret answer it and talk to the unexpected visitor in a quiet, respectful voice. Leo cocked his head to try to catch some of the words.

Lyall came into the bedroom, his face flushed red, glowering at Leo sitting on the bed and Lewis in his wheelchair.

"Which one of you little morons talked at school?" he demanded in a low growl.

Leo and Lewis exchanged looks. Lewis's dark eyes were frightened. Leo gulped. It was bound to be him. Things always leaked out when he was talking, before he had thought things through. He was the one that made mistakes like that.

"Talked about what?" Leo said nervously.

"Talked about Michelle and her punishment."

Leo felt a heavy weight in the pit of his stomach. He *had* talked. Not to a teacher or a cop; he hadn't called Child Services. But he had talked to a friend at school, upset and worried about Michelle. He knew afterward he shouldn't have, that it was bound to come back to him. But sometimes he just couldn't seem to keep stuff from coming out. David had looked at him with big eyes. Leo quickly warned him not to tell anyone, or Leo would get in trouble. But David had gone to a parent or teacher anyway, and they had made a report.

"I—I didn't *mean* to," he told Lyall, eyes down, trembling all over.

There was no point in trying to hide it. Lyall would just punish them all if he couldn't figure out who had said what. By confessing, Leo at least protected his siblings from a punishment they didn't deserve.

He was the one who had talked.

He was the one who should be punished.

Lyall shook his head slowly, the veins on the sides of his temples swelling. But his voice was quiet, to keep from being overheard by their visitor.

"You come out here and both of you tell the social worker nothing happened. It was just Leo telling stories to impress his friend. You say Joyce is Michelle, and she'll see she is fine and go away."

The two boys nodded obediently. Leo followed on Lyall's heels, with Lewis behind him, buffered by Leo's presence. They all assembled in the living room, where their very pregnant mother, Margaret, was sitting down with the social worker. Her face was red from the heat of the stove in the kitchen, her dark hair sticking in tendrils on her cheek and neck. She fanned herself with her hand.

"Here are the boys," Lyall said. "I'll just go find Michelle."

Leo and Lewis looked with terror at the social worker. She smiled pleasantly. Blue blazer, plaid skirt, hair coiffed neatly. Not part of their world. Not familiar with the nightmare they lived in.

"Hello, boys. Now, which of you is which?"

Leo said nothing, his voice frozen. Lewis looked at him, then spoke, sitting up taller in his wheelchair, trying to sound grown up. He patted his thin, sandy hair to make himself look respectable.

"I'm Lewis. This is Leo."

"It's good to meet you. I'm Mrs. Frobisher. I'm just checking to see how everything is." She blinked, looking from one to the other, her eyes probing. Exuding confidence and reassurance. Leo could almost have trusted her if he didn't already know all about social workers. He knew they just made trouble. Took kids away from their parents, put parents in jail, and caused all kinds of trouble if someone said the wrong thing.

Leo kept his eyes away from her, scuffing the toe of his shoe on the carpet, waiting for Lyall to return with Joyce. Lyall carried Joyce into the room and sat down with her on his lap. Joyce was dark-haired like Margaret though her hair was kept very short. She was thin and pale and she looked around the room with wide, anxious eyes. Lyall had not had much time to talk to her, and she was only four. Leo wasn't sure if she would be able to go along with it and follow the script Lyall had set out. She was still so little. She hadn't learned how to play along like the others had.

"This is Michelle," Lyall said.

"Hi, Michelle," Mrs. Frobisher said in a syrupy sweet voice, smiling steadily. "How are you today?"

Joyce pulled back, pressing herself against Lyall and turning her head away shyly, hiding her face against his chest.

"Say hi," Lyall encouraged, his voice quiet and even. But his face still was red with suppressed anger.

Joyce's face was pressed against Lyall and her answer wasn't clear, but it was obvious she answered.

"How are you?" Mrs. Frobisher asked.

Again, there was no reply from Joyce.

Lyall nudged her. "Tell Mrs. Frobisher you're fine," he ordered.

Again, Joyce said something into Lyall's chest.

"If you could just let her answer me herself," the social worker instructed.

The room was silent. Everyone exchanged looks, waiting for an explosion. Mrs. Frobisher continued to smile at Joyce.

"Why don't you come over here, Michelle, and tell me about how you like school?" she suggested.

Luckily, Joyce had started preschool already, so she didn't protest that she didn't go to school. She didn't move from Lyall's lap.

"Go on, Michelle," Lyall encouraged, prodding her.

Joyce still refused to move from her place. Leo made a small motion toward her, eyebrows raised at Lyall.

Lyall gestured for Leo to go ahead and take Joyce. Leo went over and picked her up, and went over to sit beside the social worker. Joyce looked for a moment at the woman, eyes wide, then she hid her face against Leo. He rubbed her back soothingly.

"It's all right, Michelle," he soothed. "Just look at Mrs. Frobisher. She's not going to hurt you." He shrugged at Mrs. Frobisher. "She's a little shy sometimes," he apologized.

"Oh, that's fine." Mrs. Frobisher stroked Joyce's short hair. "She missed school today?"

"She had a bit of a fever," Margaret contributed. "I don't think she was really sick. But I didn't want to infect the classroom if she was coming down with something. She's fine now."

"Yes, she seems to be, doesn't she?"

Then Mrs. Frobisher's eyes moved to Leo. If Leo hadn't already confessed to Lyall, that look would have sunk him. She studied him.

"How about you, Leo? How do you enjoy school?"

"School is good," Leo said, too quickly, almost before she was done asking the question. "I—I'm not very good at it, but I don't mind."

"Uh-huh. It can be pretty hard sometimes, can't it? And kids who don't get good marks sometimes try to find other ways to impress their friends."

He could have heard a pin drop. All these years later, Leo still wondered how she could have been so careless or so cruel. Reports to Child Services were supposed to be confidential. But she made it very clear who had blabbed with just a look and a few words. Even if she didn't think there was anything to worry about here, she had to know there was still a chance her words would make things difficult, even dangerous, for Leo. Even if she thought there was only a slight chance of actual abuse, she still should have protected him.

"I…" Leo didn't know what to say. He looked at Lyall, who was glaring at him fiercely, and tried to figure out how to fix it. "I might have… told a story," he said. "Because… cause I wanted David to… think I was tough…"

"So you lied to David?" Mrs. Frobisher questioned. "You told him a story about Michelle that was untrue?"

Leo gestured at Joyce.

"You can see Michelle's okay," he said with a hopeless shrug. "It was just a made-up story."

He tried to hold back the tears. But he didn't need to. The tears were a good way to convince Mrs. Frobisher of his sincerity, of his remorse for having done the wrong thing and gotten into trouble. Leo sniffled loudly, trying to keep the sobs silent. Joyce could feel Leo's stomach jumping convulsively, and she looked up at him, pulling her head away from his chest. She put her hand on his cheek, then kissed him.

"Okay, Leo," she whispered.

"Yeah," he agreed. "Okay."

He gave her an extra squeeze. Mrs. Frobisher looked touched at the little scene of tenderness between the two children. She smiled; less forced this time, her eyes softer.

"And you have another daughter?" she said to Lyall and Margaret.

"Yes, Joyce," Lyall agreed. "She's at a friend's house this afternoon. And one more boy, a two-year-old. He's sleeping."

"All right. Well, I'm going to go back to the office and write this up, close the file. I don't see anything I'm concerned about at this point. The children all seem to be fine. Michelle, in particular, seems to be well and safe. If I could just take a quick look around?"

Lyall shrugged. "Help yourself," he said.

Mrs. Frobisher got up, tousled Joyce's hair, and took a quick walk around the house. She checked out the kitchen, the fridge, Phil sleeping in the crib, and each of the bedrooms. She returned to the living room.

"Everything seems to be in order. You don't need to worry about this any further."

Lyall and Margaret both nodded.

"Good," Lyall agreed. He glanced at Leo. "Sometimes children just don't understand the consequences of their actions. How a made-up story could be taken seriously and cause real problems for a family. I appreciate you being sensible about this."

"Oh, no problem. That's why we're here. If we believed every report that came into our office…" She shook her head and rolled her eyes. "It's not just kids making up stories to impress their friends. Sometimes it's neighbors or relatives who feel they have been wronged, trying to get revenge. You wouldn't believe some of the things we hear."

Lyall stood up and ushered her to the door as she chattered on. Leo was left in the room with the rest of the family. He hid his face in Joyce's hair, closing his eyes to try to prepare himself. There was real trouble coming now. He waited, still and silent, listening to Mrs. Frobisher's car engine and tires fade into the distance. His heart was thumping hard and fast, like a train engine. Leo pushed Joyce off his lap, onto the couch beside Margaret.

Lyall's fist caught him in the ear before Leo could bring himself to look up.

It knocked him to the floor.

Leo howled and held onto his ear. He bit back the cry, holding his breath and trying to stay quiet, knowing it would only aggravate Lyall and encourage him to continue the beating.

Lyall kicked him in the stomach.

"Where the hell's your head, boy? What do you think you're doing, telling stories at school? You know better! How many times do you have to be told?"

Leo held one arm over his stomach and one over his face, trying to keep the blows from landing in the most vital places.

He cried out when Lyall's blows caught him off guard or hit a particularly tender spot. Lyall reached down and grabbed his wrist, dragging him to his feet.

"Stand up! On your feet, like a man!"

Leo wobbled and tried to keep his balance.

"Put up your fists!"

Leo raised them uncertainly.

Lyall swung, and Leo raised both forearms in front of his face, trying to block him.

Lyall knocked Leo down, and again kicked him, again and again, hard crunching blows that flashed white light across Leo's brain.

Leo sobbed, crying for Lyall to stop.

The beating seemed to go on forever, but finally Lyall backed off and walked away, muttering to himself.

Leo scrubbed at his eyes, gasping for breath and trying to stop his sobs. The house was as quiet as a tomb, aside from Leo's crying. Everyone had fled the scene.

Leo moved slowly, painfully. He tried to get to his feet but was too weak and his belly hurt too much. He crawled along the floor. He heard the quiet tread of Lewis's wheelchair approaching. Lewis bent down and grasped him by the arm, trying to pull him up. Leo tried to get to his feet.

With Lewis's strong arms assisting him, he managed to pull himself up into Lewis's withered lap, panting. Lewis hugged him close for a minute and tried to settle him so he wouldn't fall out again.

"Just stay still," Lewis whispered. "Hang on."

Leo hung on while Lewis wheeled back to their bedroom. He shifted Leo carefully onto his bed.

Lewis brushed Leo's hair back from his face. "You okay?" he whispered.

Leo gulped and couldn't answer. Lewis stroked his hair for a few minutes. As Leo's body started to relax, Lewis moved him into a more comfortable position, pulling his bruised, aching limbs straight. He pulled Leo's shirt up and gently felt Leo's ribs and belly.

Leo gasped and pulled back, which caused even more pain. "Ahhh," he groaned.

Lewis withdrew his hand and continued to stroke his hair.

"Just go to sleep," he murmured. "You'll feel better in the morning."

They both knew it was a lie. He'd be stiff and sore as hell in the morning. And he wouldn't be able to go to school or help with the chores.

"Okay," Leo agreed anyway.

He closed his eyes and let Lewis's gentle fingers comfort him, helping him relax his grip on consciousness and fade away.

CHAPTER EIGHT

LEO SHOOK HIS HEAD clear of memories. He knew he shouldn't go back there, obsess over the past. Too many dark places.

Elizabeth was watching him, her eyes half-closed.

"So, were you in a lot of different homes?" Leo asked her, trying to distract himself. "Or just a couple? Did they try to keep you in one place?"

Elizabeth stared off into space. "A few different places. I didn't have very good luck staying anywhere for long."

"Yeah. That's too bad. Were they usually pretty nice? Or abusive? I know there can be lots of abuse in foster homes."

"No, I was never abused. Had some weird parents, sometimes, but that's not abuse."

"Yeah? Like what?"

Elizabeth looked at him briefly, weighing her response. "I had one old lady," she said slowly. "She kept her husband's corpse in her sitting room."

Leo gaped. "What?" he demanded.

Elizabeth nodded serenely. "She loved him too much to let him go. And she was still collecting his pension. So she just left him there, dead, and I was supposed to pretend he was alive and, you know, a part of the family."

Leo shook his head. "That doesn't make any sense. Really?"

"Since when do people have to make sense? You think your cat lady made sense?"

"No. Well, I can sort of understand it because I know how some people want to save all the animals. On the other hand, it's crazy, because letting them live in filth, starving to death, cannibalizing each other, that's not saving them. That's torturing them."

"Well, same with Mrs. Ogilvy. You could understand she didn't want to give up her husband and his check, but on the other hand…"

"Bonkers," Leo summed up.

She laughed. "Yeah."

"So you just pretended he was still alive? What about the smell?"

Elizabeth thought back. "I don't remember a lot about it," she admitted. "I remember coming down to breakfast one day. Seeing him still sitting in his easy chair. He was never up at that time of day, so I knew something was weird. I went over to him… called his name…"

"Mr. Ogilvy…? Mr. Ogilvy, are you okay?" Elizabeth asked tentatively, getting a little closer.

The old man was white, waxen, and still. Elizabeth didn't have a good feeling. He was a crabby, crotchety old man and never missed the opportunity to criticize her or get after her. Here she was, dawdling instead of getting breakfast on, staring at him, interrupting his nap, but he didn't stir or say anything.

"Mr. Ogilvy?" Elizabeth took one more frightened step forward and grasped his thin arm, giving him a little shake.

His body was stiff and cold. Elizabeth shrieked. "Missus! Mrs. Ogilvy! Mrs. Ogilvy, Mister—he's dead!"

"What are you going on about, child?" Mrs. Ogilvy demanded, upstairs in the bathroom. "Go and make some breakfast."

"But Missus! He's dead! He's dead!"

"Just leave him be and go make breakfast."

Elizabeth stood there, stunned, trying to figure out what to do. Just ignore it and go make breakfast? Just pretend he wasn't sitting there in the sitting room, stiff as a board and cold as death? Shouldn't she call nine-one-one or the hospital? Who did you call when someone was dead?

"But—" she started, trying to put her argument into words.

"Breakfast. Now," Mrs. Ogilvy ordered in a hard tone.

Elizabeth dragged her feet into the kitchen. She felt creepy, turning her back on Mr. Ogilvy's body. She knew what she was doing was wrong. She needed to do something. She needed to report this. To make Mrs. Ogilvy understand something was really wrong. But she was afraid to do anything other than what she was told: ignore the body and make breakfast. So Elizabeth moved around the kitchen in a trance, pulling together a meal by sheer muscle memory, her brain paralyzed and disengaged. Eventually, Mrs. Ogilvy finished getting herself dressed and came down the stairs. She cooed a cheerful "Good morning, Oliver," at her dead husband and entered the kitchen.

"That's a good girl," she told Elizabeth. Under any other circumstances, Elizabeth would have been overjoyed at the compliment. But as it was, she just stood, bowl in hand, looking at Mrs. Ogilvy.

"Sit down, and let's eat," Mrs. Ogilvy instructed.

Elizabeth sat down, served Mrs. Ogilvy, and reached to put a spoonful of the oatmeal in her own dish.

"No!" Mrs. Ogilvy snapped.

"What is it?" Elizabeth asked wildly, spoon frozen over her bowl.

"Serve Mr. Ogilvy first," Mrs. Ogilvy instructed.

"But… he's—" Elizabeth stammered.

"He's having a nap, but then he's going to want to have something when he wakes up. Serve him next."

"He's dead," Elizabeth protested, afraid Mrs. Ogilvy somehow hadn't heard or understood her when she'd called up the stairs. That she'd somehow missed Mr. Ogilvy's waxen pallor when she came down. But Mrs. Ogilvy just looked at her steadily.

"Serve him next," she insisted.

Elizabeth spooned oatmeal into Mr. Ogilvy's dish. She put a piece of toast on each plate. She looked at the apricot preserves.

"Do you want me to…?"

"Yes, that would be nice. Put some preserves on Mr. Ogilvy's toast for him."

"Okay," Elizabeth agreed weakly and obeyed. Then she gestured toward her own bowl. "Now can I…?"

"If you don't get a move on it, you're going to be late for school. Dish yours up and get eating. I'll just take Mr. Ogilvy his."

Elizabeth watched as Mrs. Ogilvy took her husband his bowl and plate. She waited for the screech of understanding when Mrs. Ogilvy realized her husband was, in fact, deceased. But she simply carried on, chattering to her husband about some inane thing, clinking the dishes as she set them beside him and eventually returning to the kitchen.

"Lizzie," she said, "I told you to eat your breakfast."

"I'm… I'm not feeling well," Elizabeth said, staring down at her toast and oatmeal. She couldn't imagine eating right now. Her stomach was a dead weight. Her mouth was dry as a bone. The only thing she felt like doing was running away.

"Are you sick?" Mrs. Ogilvy asked. "Can you still go to school?"

"Yes—yes, I can go to school. Maybe I'll just take an extra apple in my bag, in case I get feeling better and want a bite to eat. Just in case."

Mrs. Ogilvy nodded. "That would be fine. You'd better get everything ready. The bus will be here in ten minutes."

"Yes, ma'am," Elizabeth agreed. She quickly stood up and disposed of her toast and oatmeal. She grabbed an apple from the fruit basket and put it into her backpack. She collected the sandwich she had made and some baby carrots and put them in her lunch bag. She threw a juice box on top of the sandwich, even though she knew the food would get smushed. What difference did one smushed sandwich make when there was a corpse to be dealt with in the sitting room?

She went obediently off to school, but she didn't know what to do or say about the situation at home. She tried to tell Mrs. Skinner, her second grade teacher, but the woman just looked at her with amusement.

"You're such as silly girl, Lizzie. What an imagination you have!"

"No, it's not just a story," Elizabeth protested. "Really, he died—"

"It's time to sit down and do math. Go back to your seat and don't interrupt with your stories."

Elizabeth went desolately back to her seat.

What else was she supposed to do? Nine-one-one was only for emergencies. She knew there was nothing they could do about Mr. Ogilvy. He was already dead and the paramedics couldn't do anything for him. There was nothing else she could do about it.

When she went home, he was still there.

When she got up the next morning, he was still there.

Elizabeth obediently reported on school proceedings to him, made him his meals, asked him what he wanted to watch on TV, and all the other things she was supposed to do normally.

Within a couple of days, there was a heavy, acrid smell in the sitting room. Elizabeth tried to stay out of the room and away from the smell. Mrs. Ogilvy sprayed air freshener and burned candles, complaining there must be mold in the carpet.

Neither one of them said anything about Mr. Ogilvy and his deceased state. Within a few weeks, the smell had started to dissipate. Or maybe Elizabeth just didn't notice it anymore. Either way, it was easier to walk by the sitting room without holding her breath.

A couple of times, she studied Mr. Ogilvy's face as it turned more gray, and grew more deeply wrinkled and cadaverous as it dried out.

She tried not to stare. Mrs. Ogilvy wouldn't like that. But the process was macabrely fascinating. She couldn't help but look.

It was a long time before anyone else found out. The social worker merely checked in at the door, commenting on the weather and asking Mrs. Ogilvy if Elizabeth was behaving.

Mrs. Ogilvy had given positive reports on Elizabeth's behavior, which had made the social worker happy. She was so pleased Elizabeth had settled down and was fitting in somewhere.

Then she finally had longer to visit one day and wasn't in such a hurry to get away.

"Maybe I could come in?" she suggested to Mrs. Ogilvy. Mrs. Ogilvy shrugged and motioned for her to come in. Elizabeth continued to cower behind Mrs. Ogilvy, hiding behind her skirts.

She couldn't believe Mrs. Ogilvy was letting someone else come into the house. It was an event. So few people came to visit, and no one had been allowed to come in since Mr. Ogilvy's death.

She always protested he was sleeping and couldn't be disturbed.

Miss Shaefer came into the house. Her nose wrinkled a little as she walked in and she looked around.

"Oh, good morning Mr. Ogilvy," she said cheerfully. Mr. Ogilvy's chair was turned away from the door, so she couldn't see his desiccated face.

Elizabeth looked at Mr. Ogilvy, looked at Mrs. Ogilvy, and looked back at the social worker.

"Mr. Ogilvy says hello," she said helpfully.

She and Mrs. Ogilvy often played that Mr. Ogilvy was carrying on a conversation with them, so Elizabeth was happy to comply now. Miss Shaefer gave her an odd look, a slight frown on her face and seated herself on the couch.

"So how have things been going, Lizzie?" she asked primly.

Elizabeth shrugged. "School is good," she suggested.

"Are you getting good marks?"

Elizabeth screwed up her face. "My report card is okay," she hedged.

"What's your favorite subject?"

Elizabeth looked at her blankly.

"What do you like to do at school?" Miss Shaefer encouraged.

"Oh… I like to draw," she said.

"Art. Good for you. How are you doing at reading and math?"

"Oh… okay," Elizabeth said.

"Hmm, we don't sound too sure."

"Her teachers haven't complained," Mrs. Ogilvy contributed. "Lizzie's been a good girl. And she's very helpful around the house."

"Good for you," Miss Shaefer said. "What do you help out with?"

Elizabeth looked around, trying to figure out what to say. "I help with breakfast, and the laundry," she said slowly. "And talking to Mr. Ogilvy."

"Talking to Mr. Ogilvy?" Miss Shaefer laughed. "Is that a chore?"

There was only silence in response to the question. Miss Shaefer looked at Mrs. Ogilvy and Elizabeth, and then glanced toward Mr. Ogilvy, waiting for him to laugh or to explain the joke further.

"He says Lizzie is a good girl," Elizabeth offered in a small voice.

She wanted so much for Miss Shaefer to just join in the game. This is what Mrs. Ogilvy wanted her to do. She was a good girl. She did was she was told. Mr. Ogilvy was dead, but the game was to pretend he was alive, to say what he would say if he was part of the conversation.

"Mr. Ogilvy?" Miss Shaefer said tentatively. "What's going on here?"

Mrs. Ogilvy stood abruptly. "I think it's time for you to go now," she said. "Mr. Ogilvy is having a nap. He cannot be disturbed."

Miss Shaefer stood up. She got closer to Mr. Ogilvy.

Mrs. Ogilvy darted in between them, trying to keep Miss Shaefer away. "He's sleeping," she insisted. "You should go now."

Elizabeth went up to Miss Shaefer and took her by the hand, trying to lead her back to the door. "Bye-bye, we'll see you again next time," she piped up, tugging on Miss Shaefer's hand. "Bye-bye."

Miss Shaefer pulled away and wouldn't let Elizabeth catch her hand again. "What's going on?" Miss Shaefer asked, looking back and forth at them. "Mr. Ogilvy? Is everything all right?"

Mrs. Ogilvy tried to keep her from seeing, but she just wasn't big enough or fast enough to keep Miss Shaefer from seeing the body. Miss Shaefer shrieked. She started to swear or to pray. "What happened here? This is awful!"

Elizabeth shrank away from her. Why was she screaming? They were supposed to be quiet to keep from waking Mr. Ogilvy up.

Mrs. Ogilvy shook her head, distressed. "No, no, it's all right," she protested. "It's all right. He's just having a nap. You'll wake him up!"

"He's not sleeping!" Miss Shaefer screamed. "He's dead! He's a skeleton! How long has he been dead?"

Mrs. Ogilvy made calming motions with her hands, trying to get Miss Shaefer to settle down.

But there was no turning around now.

Miss Shaefer immediately picked up the phone and called nine-one-one, screaming for the police and an ambulance and the fire department and anyone else that would come to the house. She was hysterical, but that didn't keep the police department from showing up within a couple of minutes.

They took Miss Shaefer out first, then came in and looked at Mr. Ogilvy's body and took Mrs. Ogilvy out while she screamed and cried for her husband, terrified about what they were going to do.

Police swarmed over the place. Elizabeth sat crouched in the corner, trying to stay out of the way. But eventually, an officer noticed her and bent down to pick her up.

"What are you doing, honey? We need to get you out of here now, okay? I'm sorry, you shouldn't be in here."

Elizabeth allowed herself to be picked up.

"What's your name, sweetie?" the policeman asked, carrying her out of the house.

"Lizzie," she murmured, putting a finger in her mouth and sucking on it.

"Lizzie. Do you live here?"

She nodded her head.

"Is Mrs. Ogilvy your grandma, Lizzie?"

"No. My foster mom."

"Oh, your foster mom. Can you tell me what happened here?"

They sat down on the front steps and Elizabeth leaned her head in the policeman's lap. "I was good," she said softly.

"I bet you are a good girl," he assured her. "What happened to Mr. Ogilvy?"

"He's having a nap," Elizabeth said.

"Having a nap?" the policeman chuckled. "And when did this nap start?"

That made Elizabeth giggle. She liked this policeman. He would play the game with her, but he knew it was a game and how silly it was.

"A loooong time ago," she told him.

"Yes, it looks like a long time. How long? Christmas?"

"Before Christmas."

"Are you sure?"

Elizabeth thought back to the tree, her stocking, the exchange of presents—presents for all of them, including Mr. Ogilvy. She remembered how popcorn from the garlands had fallen in Mr. Ogilvy's hair, and she had carefully picked all the bits out.

"Yes," she agreed, "before Christmas."

"Before school started?"

"No. After school started."

"Hmm… what about Halloween?"

Elizabeth nodded. "Before Halloween."

"Before?"

Elizabeth nodded. "At Halloween… we moved him over by the door. He helped to pass out candy."

The policeman looked down into Elizabeth's face, going pale, slightly green. "He helped to pass out candy? After he started his nap?"

Elizabeth buried her face in her arms, in the policeman's lap. "He looked scary," she said earnestly.

"I'll bet he did. Okay. Between school starting and Halloween."

"Uh-huh."

"Okay. That helps. Thank you. Do you know how it happened? How Mr. Ogilvy died? What happened before he took his nap?"

"I don't know. He was still in his chair in the morning. He didn't go to bed, he just stayed in his chair."

"Okay. And you just found him there like that in the morning?"

Elizabeth nodded.

"What did Mrs. Ogilvy say? Was she upset?"

Elizabeth shrugged. She shook her head. "No… she just said he was sleeping… we played a game."

"What was the game?"

"Play that he's still alive. Play that he talks to us and eats dinner with us."

"That must have been confusing. I'm going to need you to go with Miss Shaefer. You know Miss Shaefer? Is she your social worker?"

"Uh-huh."

"Okay. Let's see if we can get her to take you somewhere safe."

Elizabeth looked over her shoulder, back into the house. "I can't go… I need my things."

"We'll bring your things to you. You can't go back in."

"But if I go without my things… I'll lose them. I want my things."

"Miss Shaefer will bring them to you later."

He took Elizabeth by the hand and led her into the front yard, to where Miss Shaefer was sitting on the seat of one of the police cars, looking shaken and sick.

"Miss Shaefer. How are you doing?"

She looked at him and looked at Elizabeth. "Come here, Lizzie," she said, holding out her arms for Elizabeth. The police man handed Elizabeth to her. Miss Shaefer held her close, uncomfortably tight, and kissed her hair. "Lizzie, are you okay? You must have been so scared!"

Lizzie sighed. She squirmed a little and Miss Shaefer loosened her grip.

"Where will I go now?" Elizabeth asked.

"I don't know. I'll find you a place. Don't worry about it. Are you okay? Are you scared?"

"No."

"Let me make a few phone calls and we'll figure out what to do. Okay?"

"Not stay with Mrs. Ogilvy?"

"No. You can't stay here."

"I need my things," Elizabeth insisted. "I need to get my things."

"We'll get them later."

Elizabeth scowled. She'd been moved enough times to know if you didn't have your things when you left your house, they wouldn't follow you. You'd be left with nothing.

She knew Miss Shaefer wasn't going to get her things.

Miss Shaefer wasn't ever going back in that house again.

Leo rocked Juleen, whose eyes were closing. She was nearly asleep. Leo was mesmerized by Elizabeth's story.

"And did you get your things?" he asked.

"No. Went to my next family with nothing."

"That must have been hard. And you never saw Mrs. Ogilvy again?"

"Why would I go back there? Crazy old bat."

Leo shifted. "She must have been ill," he agreed. "Normal people don't do that."

"Duh," Elizabeth said, shaking her head. "Here, let me show you something."

Elizabeth got up and went to the window. Leo stood slowly, trying not to wake Juleen up. He stood beside Elizabeth and looked out the window. She scanned the street below and after a moment pointed out a woman down the street.

"See her?"

Leo nodded. "Who is she?"

"We call her Lady Bathrobe. Can't remember her real name."

The reason for the nickname was clear. She had a tattered pink bathrobe and slippers, and she walked down the street, stopped and turned, and paced back again. Her face was vague, expressionless.

"She's the landlady!" Elizabeth said. "You can't get her arrested as a vagrant; she owns the place! But she walks up and down the street all day long in her bathrobe, spying on everybody, watching everything around here. Gossiping about what she thinks everyone is doing."

"Another Mrs. Ogilvy?"

"Yeah. Crazy old cat lady. We're surrounded by them. You just can't get away from the crazies."

"So you learned from Mrs. Ogilvy to recognize and stay away from the crazies?" Leo suggested.

Elizabeth looked at Leo intensely, making him squirm. "No. From her I learned to always bury the bodies."

"What?"

"Always bury the bodies. Or the body parts. Don't leave them in the sitting room for everyone else to see!"

CHAPTER NINE

LEO SWALLOWED.

HIS HEART had started to beat extra fast and he felt the blood drain from his face.

"What?" Elizabeth said with a laugh. "I'm just kidding."

Leo stared out the window to avoid looking at her. "I grew up in a home," he said slowly, "where we did bury the bodies. Or the body parts."

"What do you mean?" Elizabeth asked, looking interested and not at all shocked or horrified.

Leo wasn't sure he could talk to her about it. Not with her looking at him like this was just a curiosity at the state fair.

Leo went back to where he had been sitting, settling Juleen in his lap again. She fit against him, warm and limp and asleep.

"My family… my dad was really… abusive. Very… cruel and cunning."

"What did he do?" Elizabeth said with interest, sitting back down and picking at her nails while she waited for him to relate his story. She had, after all, obligingly told him her worst moments.

Leo cleared his throat uncomfortably. "Maybe a glass of water?" he suggested.

Elizabeth rolled her eyes. Sighing, she got to her feet again. She went into the kitchenette and ran him a glass of water. She handed it to him. Leo took a sip. It was lukewarm. But it irrigated his throat.

"We had a jar buried in the back yard," Leo said. "A big old pickle jar. He... if we did something really bad... defied him... he would..."

Leo couldn't find the words. But he held his hand up. The left hand, which was missing one finger completely, and another past the first knuckle.

Elizabeth's eyes widened. "No way! He cut off your fingers?"

Leo nodded wordlessly. Elizabeth just looked at him with wide, horrified eyes.

"And we'd have to dig up the jar, and... and add..."

"Add your own finger to the jar," Elizabeth breathed.

Feeling nauseated, Leo nodded.

Once again, the horror of it struck him. When his dad would look at one of them, with that cruel glint in his eye, Leo just wanted to run.

To get out of there before Lyall could get his pruning shears and do that awful thing.

The pain of losing a finger... sometimes not even one swift clip, but one joint at a time, until he was screaming, hollering, fainting from the agony of it.

Leo closed his eyes, trying to block out the flashbacks.

How could a man do such a horrible, evil thing to an innocent little child? Even if a child was being intentionally willful or disobedient, how did he jump to 'cut their fingers off'?

They had been tortured, the enemies in some bizarre war.

Lyall thought he was justified in whatever he did to them. They were his property, his chattels, and they would obey him absolutely.

"How many of you?" Elizabeth asked morbidly. "Have all of you...?"

"Not Stormy," Leo said. "I did everything I could to protect the kids. Stormy was the baby. We all tried to keep her safe, to intercede for her. She's the only one with all her digits and other body parts."

Elizabeth swallowed visibly. She got up and poured herself a drink, not from the faucet, but from the liquor cabinet.

"You want something stronger?" she asked.

Of course he did.

But Leo knew he couldn't.

Start drinking and he was in danger of becoming his father. He would let out the lion. Become a monster.

"What other body parts?" Elizabeth asked doggedly. She had to know it all, get it all out in the open and watch him squirm.

"Toes. Ears." Leo shrugged hopelessly. "Pulled out fingernails."

Elizabeth shook her head. "Talk about crazy," she breathed.

"He wasn't crazy," Leo said. "He was evil. There's a difference."

"Really?" she raised her eyebrows. "What's the difference?"

Elizabeth was crazy, Leo thought, but not evil. Not like Lyall.

"I know my dad… he was sane. He thought things through. He knew exactly what he was doing. He did things to hurt us… Even when we weren't doing anything wrong… he would think up things to do to torture us. He wasn't out of his head. He was just… a demon. A monster."

"Why didn't you guys call Child Services? Get taken out of there? Foster care may not be nice, but at least no one ever cut off my fingers!"

"We called or asked for help plenty of times," Leo said. "He'd just convince them we were lying and just attention-seekers. Enough of us were in trouble he could just say: 'They are in trouble at school and don't want to be punished. It's a prank call.' And they'd believe him."

"But you weren't okay. They could see that."

"If we weren't… he'd put us in the back room. In the basement in chains. Take us out in the woods to the shack. We wouldn't be around when the social worker got there. Only the other kids, who all looked fine. The social workers would just sign off."

Elizabeth nodded slowly. She'd seen it herself. She'd seen social workers who just stood at the door and glanced around. Those who were in too much of a hurry to get to the next appointment, the one that might really be an emergency.

"So we stopped calling," Leo said. "It only got us in more trouble. You just suck it up, take the bad stuff, because it could always get worse. Always."

"Where is he now?" Elizabeth asked. "Is he dead?"

"No… well… maybe."

"You don't know?"

"He was shot in a hunting accident. They say he's brain dead. But we haven't taken him off of the machines yet."

"Why not? I'd unplug that monster in a second," she said viciously.

"I know… I just can't. He lays there in the hospital bed, helpless, and I can't kill a helpless creature. I've always had a soft spot for… anyone who couldn't help themselves."

"But…" Elizabeth sputtered. "After all he did to you? Don't you look at him and see the brutal monster he is? I wouldn't look at him and see a help-less creature. I'd see the monster who beat and tortured me. I'd just as soon slit his throat as pull out the plug. Maybe chop *his* fingers off one at a time, just to see if it still hurt."

Leo recoiled at the image. He shook his head. "No. I could never do that. You don't know what it's like, you haven't been there."

"Nope," Elizabeth agreed. "And don't ever hope to be. No folks, no attachments, no one who can hurt me ever again."

Leo frowned. "But you still need people. You need to talk to people and have friends and family. You can't just live alone and never open yourself up to someone else."

"No? Cause I'm thinkin' I can."

"What about Juleen? You're not going to open your heart up to your baby?"

"*She* won't hurt me," Elizabeth said dismissively.

"Not physically, maybe. But when she gets older and she doesn't listen to everything you tell her…? Or when she moves out, maybe starts getting in trouble with drugs or the wrong guy? You think that won't hurt you?"

"How did this get back to me?" Elizabeth retorted. "We were talking about *your* horrible father and your impotence to get rid of him."

Leo felt anger snarling at his insides.

How could she talk to him like that?

Impotent was exactly how he felt, and her words pricked him to the core.

He was impotent.

Unable to sign a paper to allow his father's life to end. Just to let nature take its course. Except for the part about keeping his heart beating so they could harvest his organs.

Harvest. What a gruesome word! He couldn't think about it without thinking of those various operations over the years.

The lost fingers, toes, nails ripped out of their beds, earlobes cut off… His father had tried to reduce them, demean them, take parts away from them.

How humiliating and horrifying to have your finger or another body part savagely removed.

No anesthetic. No sympathy.

Just 'crack' with the shears and it was gone, separated, ready to be put into the pickle jar buried in the yard.

None of them would ever be whole again. Even Stormy, who had all of her fingers and toes, would never be the happy, carefree girl she might have been if they had been able to protect her from seeing their father's horrific acts.

His hands trembled, the fury bubbling up in his chest. Leo got up and put Juleen down on the blanket on the floor.

"You don't know what you're talking about!" he shouted at Elizabeth.

White-hot fury burned his eyes and his throat.

"You don't know what it was like. You're not inside my head and you don't know how I feel about… about any of this. Who are you to be telling me how to take care of my family? You can't even take care of Juleen!"

She cowered before him.

She didn't just draw back worried he might shout some more or wake up the baby; she recognized that rage, the snarling wildcat raging and ripping inside him. And she was afraid.

Leo tried to breathe away the fury that blinded him. Tried to regain control again.

But he couldn't talk. Couldn't do anything.

He patted his leg to call Rascal, who bounded over to him, and he swept out the door, down the hall, down the stairs instead of waiting for the elevator, and down into the street.

He had been tired and thirsty after his earlier workout and run.

But he ran home anyway, the cat chasing him all the way.

Leo poked his head into the hospital room, like he always did and saw Shayla was not there. But there were a couple of police officers. Leo swallowed and stepped in.

"Hey," he greeted. "What's up?"

"You must be Leo," one of them said, standing up to greet him, shaking his hand firmly. Leo looked at his name badge. His name was Jones. Big and broad, built like a truck.

"Yeah, I'm Leo."

"Why don't you have a seat, Leo?"

"What's going on?" Leo asked.

He sat down on the chair but didn't like looking at the two officers as they stood over him. He got back up. After standing awkwardly for a moment, he perched on the edge of the window sill, where he could rest himself but still look at the policemen eye-to-eye.

"We wanted to talk to you about what happened, Leo," the other officer, Harkness, explained.

"What happened? I already explained all that when I first got here."

"Well, we've been assigned to the case now and we want to hear it directly from you. Why don't you tell us what happened the day your dad got shot?"

Leo shrugged. He assumed a casual attitude and recited the story once more.

"We went on a hunting trip. He always wears camo. He won't wear an orange vest. He went off to my right, and I thought that's where he was. I saw something big moving in the trees. I saw antlers. I fired. And when I went down to see… it was him."

"How could you mistake him for a deer?"

"Accidents happen. I guess he bumped a tree and made the branches wave, and I thought the branches were antlers. Something like that. I was sure I saw a buck. Maybe there was a buck. He might have been driving it toward me. And maybe I shot past the buck and got him."

"Do you think that is what happened?" Harkness questioned

"Yeah."

"Had your dad been going through a hard time lately?"

Leo was startled by the question. "Um, no… I think things were going pretty good for him."

"You don't think he was depressed?"

"No. He had a new girlfriend. He got his face in the paper. Everyone thought he was a hero. What did he have to be depressed about?"

"People can get depressed without a reason. Clinical depression can happen to anyone, it's a brain thing, not necessarily an emotions thing."

Leo shook his head. "No, I think he was fine. I don't think he was depressed. Ask Shayla; she could tell you better than I could. I don't live with him."

"No, but you have more experience with his moods, with how he might act. Other people might not notice the nuances."

"No. I don't think so. He seemed fine to me."

"And how about you? Have you been all right lately? Not depressed or upset?"

"No," Leo said, shifting. "I'm just fine."

"How do you and your dad get along? Do you go hunting together a lot?"

"No. We don't get along really well. I don't do very much with him."

"You don't get along well?" Jones demanded.

Leo shook his head. "No," he said. He breathed. "He was pretty tough on us as kids. I don't spend much time with him."

"So why did you decide to go on a hunting trip with him?"

"I don't know. Things were going good for him. He's been happy. So I thought maybe we should try to make up. He suggested the hunting trip and I said okay."

"It was Lyall's idea?"

"Yeah. He's the hunter, not me."

"You don't shoot?" Harkness questioned sharply. "You're not an experienced hunter?"

Leo swallowed and tried to keep his face and voice calm and casual.

"I don't choose to go hunting, but I can. I hunted plenty when I was younger. I'm a good shot. I didn't just accidentally shoot him in the head. I mean, I did. But it wasn't like I was being careless. He wasn't supposed to be in front of me, where he was. He was supposed to be off to my right."

Leo felt his neck and face flush. Sweat trickled down his back.

"How much target practice do you get?"

"I don't go to the range. I don't go hunting now. But I did plenty as a kid, I can hit a target. I can hit a deer or a rabbit. It was just an accident. I saw a deer… but it wasn't."

"Hmm. So it was Lyall's idea."

"Yeah. He asked me. I said yes. We went together. And then he got shot."

"You said everyone thought he was a hero. What's that about?"

"You didn't know?" Leo asked. "He was all over the papers. I thought you would have at least Googled him."

"Well?"

Leo breathed out in a long sigh. "He was illiterate, never could read when we were growing up. And then, last year, he went to a tutor, and he learned how to read. Sixty years old, and he learns to read for the first time. He talked about how he pulled himself up by his bootstraps and was doing a great thing. He wore a suit and tie for his picture. I've never seen him wear a suit before. Made him look respectable. Lots of quotes about how wonderful it was… everybody knew him, pointed him out, this great example for kids. For everyone."

"Sounds like a little jealousy there," Jones said.

Leo's anger flared. The cat growled. Jealous of Lyall? That wasn't it.

He clenched his teeth.

"No. I'm not jealous. I just don't like… didn't like him showing off how wonderful he was when he was… a monster."

"A monster?" Jones repeated.

"He was! He wasn't a good man, but the papers and everyone else was treating him like he was something special!"

"If he wasn't a good man, why did you go hunting with him?"

"I told you why," Leo said, exasperated. "Because he was trying. And I thought I should try to reconcile. People can change, right?"

His fists clenched, and he fought with the lion, trying to wrestle it down.

He'd like to sock one of the stupid cops. Both of them. Right in the teeth.

Why were they blaming him for this? What made them think it was intentional?

"Why don't you leave Leo alone?"

They all jumped, turning to look at Shayla. Leo hadn't heard her come in and wondered how much she had heard.

"This isn't Leo's fault, and he already feels bad enough about it," Shayla declared. "You just leave him alone! Leo saved his dad's life. You're acting like he did this on purpose. Leo would never do that. He's been so good helping me out, being here by his dad."

"Maybe he has a guilty conscience."

"Of course he does, wouldn't you? You'd feel awful. But he's the only one who's been here by his dad's side. None of the other kids have been here. None of those people who wrote about him in the paper have been here. No one else. Just me and Leo. So leave him alone!"

The officers looked at each other awkwardly. After a couple of murmured words to each other, they nodded their goodbyes and left the room.

Leo breathed out, trying to relax.

"Thanks," he told Shayla.

"It's true, Leo. You're the only one who has been there for me. I don't know how I would have gotten through this without you."

"Yeah. Well. I do what I can. Thanks for helping me."

"Lyall did love you," Shayla said. "I don't know all the details about what happened between you guys, but he really did love you and your brothers and sisters."

Leo looked at her. She had no clue about Lyall's past life, so how could he blame her? Lyall had kept that part of himself hidden from her, the past few months they had been together.

"Lyall didn't have any idea how to love," Leo objected. "Love isn't just having regrets now and then, or thinking about someone now and then. There's a lot more to it than that."

"You don't know how much he regretted the way he treated you kids. He really did. He wanted the chance to be a better dad. We were going to try to get pregnant."

Leo breathed deeply. He had sensed it. Neither of them had ever told him, but they had gotten so close, so fast. Leo had known Shayla was young enough she would want kids of her own.

"Shay… I know you're trying to make me feel better, but… you just don't know how it was."

"I wish you could forgive him. Maybe that's why he's still alive. So you can find a way to forgive him and move on."

"I'm never going to forgive him," Leo said. "So you can give up on that."

"Leo. When you don't forgive someone, it doesn't hurt them, it hurts you."

Leo shook his head. "I gotta go," he muttered to her, and he walked out.

CHAPTER TEN

ORGIVE HIM?

SHAYLA SAID forgive Lyall, and Elizabeth said slit his throat, or at least unplug him. Two beautiful blondes with two very different viewpoints. And while they both seemed sure their way was the right one, Leo couldn't reconcile himself entirely to either course. How could either one of them be right?

Leo thought back to the abuse.

Thinking again about the fingers.

He was about fourteen the first time. Sick of the abuse. Sick of the pain and of the little kids being in danger.

He knew there was something wrong with Lyall. Other kids at school didn't have to go through what they did. But this time he had gone too far.

Leo could never have imagined Lyall would actually start cutting off body parts.

Even thinking about it now made him sick.

In spite of Lyall's threats and in spite of what he had done in the past, Leo didn't really believe he would do it. Clenching his jaw and putting his lips together tightly, he had laid his hand down on the counter.

Looked challengingly at Lyall, daring him to follow through on the threat. Knowing this time, Lyall would back down and Leo would be the victor.

Equally certain, Lyall painstakingly washed the pruning shears under the kitchen tap and positioned them around Leo's finger.

Both of them stared each other down in a sick game of chicken.

And then Lyall quickly snapped the shears together.

In shock, Leo screamed. He stared down at his hand before the pain hit, not believing it had really happened.

He saw his dismembered finger, saw his hand start to bleed.

Holding his other fist over his mouth he tried to hold in the screams of pain and horror. Then he switched his hold to his wrist and to his hand, trying to stop the pain.

Trying to stop the bleeding and figure out what to do.

Lyall just stood there, looking at him with a triumphant gleam in his eye.

"Didn't think I'd do it, did you boy?" he gloated. "You think your old man is a softie? What do you think now?"

Lyall picked up the finger from the counter and waved it in front of Leo, who gagged over the sink in a fit of nausea, just about blacking out.

He didn't remember what the other kids had been doing. Most of them disappeared when Leo started screaming. They knew better than to stick around when Lyall was in a mood.

Lewis was there, hanging back, looking at Leo with wide, terrified eyes. Lewis wanted to go to him but was too afraid of Lyall to approach.

Lyall laughed gloatingly and dumped an almost-empty jar of pickles into the sink, then tossed the finger into it and filled it halfway with vinegar.

"There, how about that? Maybe now you'll learn not to challenge me!"

Lyall left it there on the counter and went out to the garage to drink or to grab the car and go into town to drink.

Leo was left gasping at the counter, black blotches blocking out his vision, hardly able to breathe.

He swore over and over, and couldn't look down at his hand.

He couldn't look at what his father had done.

Lewis pulled Leo over to the table to sit him down on a chair.

Leo put his head down, dangerously nauseated and faint.

"It's okay, it's okay. I'll fix it," Lewis promised in a hoarse whisper. "I'll bandage it up. It will be good as new."

"He cut it off!" Leo cried. "He cut it off, Lew! It will never be the same again! Oh man, he cut it right off!"

"Shh, shh," Lewis told him, trying to calm him down and keep him quiet. "It's okay, Leo. Hold still."

He started to wrap Leo's hand with a bandage. It didn't bleed as much as Leo would have expected, but it was still bloody.

Lewis wrapped it tightly and wrapped the bandage around the outside of his hand like a mitten, hiding the damage.

Hiding the fact the finger was missing.

"It's okay, Leo," Lewis repeated. He was gone for a minute, then back with a glass and a pill. "Drink. Here. Drink it down. It'll make you feel better."

Leo washed down the big pill with a glass of burning whiskey.

One of Lewis's narcotic painkillers, for when his legs were hurting him.

Leo didn't know what was worse; the physical pain, or the shock and the mental pain. It hurt just as much to think about what had happened to him as the pulsating pain in his missing finger.

His stomach heaved.

"Keep it down," Lewis advised. "Don't throw it back up; those pills are expensive."

And Lewis couldn't do without them.

Leo focused on settling his stomach down, on slowing his breathing to try to calm down.

"It's okay," he said, echoing Lewis's words.

"Yeah. It'll be okay," Lewis agreed. "It will heal. You'll be fine."

Leo looked at his bandaged hand.

"I hate him. He shouldn't a done that. He should *not* have done that."

"Why did you have to make him mad?" Lewis complained. "You always gotta get in his face!"

"Gimme the phone."

"The phone?" Lewis rolled his wheelchair across the room and fetched the wireless handset, taking it back and handing it to Leo uncertainly. "Why? What are you going to do?"

Leo held it in his uninjured hand and carefully punched in the numbers he had memorized.

Lewis watched him, forehead wrinkled, his eyes worried. "Are you calling a doctor?" he said tentatively.

Leo shook his head. There was an answer on the line, and he spoke, trying to keep his voice steady. "I need help," he said, trying to talk around the lump in his throat; to keep his breathing even. "My dad hurt me, and I need help. And my brothers and sisters too."

Lewis's eyes got big. He reached over to push the 'end' button. Leo pulled it away, turning and holding it up out of Lewis's limited reach. A dirty move.

"No," Lewis protested. "Don't do that. Don't call Child Services!"

The woman on the other end kept asking questions, and Leo tried to answer as best he could, avoiding Lewis and trying to keep him quiet. She promised to send someone out to see them.

Leo hung up. Would they come that night? The next day? How long did he have?

"Leo!" Lewis railed. "How can you do that! Didn't you learn from him cutting off your finger? Now you're going to make it worse!"

"He hurt me bad," Leo said angrily. "I ain't gonna let him do that again. To me or to you, or any of the others. If we don't get help, he's never gonna stop. He's just going to keep getting worse and worse."

"No, Leo. Please don't," Lewis begged.

Leo shook his head. He held his hand against his stomach with the other hand.

"He's not going to do this again," Leo promised.

<hr>

But he was wrong. That's not the way it had turned out. Leo went to school the next day, in spite of his injury.

He had to make sure the other kids got there safely.

They all had to be safe. School was the only safe place.

But Lewis had been terrified of the consequences of Leo calling Child Services and he had warned Lyall.

Leo knew it immediately. All he had to do was look at Lewis to see the guilt pouring off of him like sweat.

But the kids were all safely at school and Child Services was coming. Lewis couldn't stop that. Neither could Lyall.

After school, Leo looked for the other kids at the bus stop after picking Stormy up from preschool. He couldn't see Joyce. He looked for her friends.

"Karla. Karla! Come here!"

She looked at him and raised her eyebrows, not coming over and not saying anything.

"Where's Joy?" Leo demanded.

"I don't know," she shrugged. "Your dad came and picked her up."

Leo's heart dropped to his stomach. "No!"

Karla just looked at him. Leo went into the school, to Joyce's classroom. The teacher was cleaning up.

"Miss Patton…?"

She turned around to look at him. "Oh, Leo. Did you come to pick up Joyce's work?" she asked.

"No, I… I didn't know she was leaving. Someone picked her up?"

"Your dad came by this afternoon. Just after lunch."

"What for?"

It was bad. Very bad. He could only hope there was an innocent explanation.

"Was she sick?"

"He said she had an appointment."

Leo groaned. He knew Joyce didn't have any appointments.

"Are you okay, Leo?" Miss Patton asked, frowning with concern.

"Oh, no. No, it's not okay!" Leo choked out. He hurried out of the room, back to the bus before he missed it. He had to get home before something happened. Even though in his heart, he knew it was already too late.

Lewis had talked and Lyall had devised a plan. He had Joyce already.

It was too late for Leo to solve anything now.

The bus went slower than it had ever gone before. It was late leaving the school. The bus driver missed one kid's stop and had to go back to drop him off. He was driving slowly for no reason at all. They finally got home and all got off the bus.

"Where's Joy?" Stormy asked, taking Leo's uninjured hand.

"Already home," Leo said.

She didn't like his answer, looking up at him with dark, worried eyes.

"It's okay," Leo said.

They both knew it wasn't true.

Leo was the first one into the house. He looked around quickly for Joyce. She wasn't in her room.

Lyall came into the house as Leo was looking for her, smirking.

"Where's Joyce?" Leo demanded. "What did you do with her?"

Lyall stood, arms crossed, looking pleased with himself. It obviously wasn't going to be good for them.

"Joyce isn't here," Lyall said. "And you don't know where she is. Nobody knows where she is except me."

Leo opened his mouth, then closed it, thinking this through.

"You called Child Services," Lyall said. "And you're going to make them feel better when they get here, or something's going to happen to your sister. And if you don't, and if they take me away from here… nobody knows where she is. And she's going to die a long, slow, painful death."

Leo stared at the evil man, his stomach roiling with anger, nausea, and fear.

He took a step forward, furious, his fists clenching, and a bolt of pain in his hand made him stop.

He gasped and looked down at his injured, bandaged hand. It screamed with pain. The agony forced him to stop and take stock before launching into an attack.

Lyall could beat him at the best of times. Now was not the time to try.

Now he had to keep himself under control.

For Joyce.

And for the others.

He looked down at his feet, defeated. He tried desperately to keep his temper under wraps and to look beaten and submissive.

Lyall chuckled darkly. "Yeah, how about that, boy?" he sneered.

"Okay," Leo agreed sullenly. "I'll get rid of them. Okay?"

Lyall nodded, pursing his lips. "You tell them you were mad cause you got punished for a bad report card. That you were just making up stories."

Leo nodded.

"They wanna see your hand, you tell them you burned it and the doctor says it can't be exposed to air," Lyall continued inexorably.

Leo nodded again.

He swallowed a hot lump of anger that threatened to make his eyes tear up.

Lyall would not see him cry over this.

"You tell 'em Joyce is over at a friend's," Lyall ordered.

"Okay."

Lyall nodded, satisfied. He walked away laughing.

For a few moments, none of them said anything. Leo stood there frozen, watching his father walk back out to the garage.

Lewis was at his side.

"I'm sorry, Leo," he whispered brokenly. "I'm sorry… I couldn't…"

"I wouldn't care if it was just me. But now you put Joyce in danger too," Leo told him harshly. "We woulda been okay. It woulda gone all right. But now she's locked up somewhere. Somewhere no one can help her!"

Now the tears spilled out. He felt so furious and so helpless.

"Nothing will happen if you listen to him," Lewis protested hurriedly. "It'll be okay if you just get rid of Child Services. Just tell them you made it all up and Joyce will be okay."

Leo clenched his fists.

He wanted so bad to hit something. Someone. To hurt someone. The way he had been hurt.

But today he couldn't so much as hit a pillow without reopening the wound where his finger used to be.

Between his injured hand and the sister held hostage, he was as helpless as a baby.

He couldn't do a thing.

Leo slammed his uninjured hand down on the table with a crash, swearing furiously.

Lewis withdrew, his eyes big and scared. The others scampered away to their rooms or safe places.

Leo sat down at the table. He put his head down on his folded arms and sobbed.

They weren't very long. Leo was still at the table in the kitchen when they came. Not just Child Services, but a couple of cops as well. The social worker could see him through the screen door and tapped on it to get his attention without alerting anyone else.

Leo wiped his still damp face, though he had stopped crying by now. He got up and opened the door for them.

The social worker was short, dumpy. Dressed like social workers were always dressed. She glanced around the room, eyes alert. "Are you Leo?"

"Yeah. I shouldn't have called you. I was just mad—"

"I'm Mrs. Finnley. Why don't we sit down and have a little chat?"

"No, you should just go—"

"Is your father here, son?" one of the cops questioned, towering over him.

Leo backed away. "He's in the garage," he said, gesturing to the back. "But he didn't really do anything. He just made me mad, and I—"

The two cops started to withdraw, to go to the garage.

"No, don't!" Leo cried out. "It's all my fault. Don't…"

"There's no need to be scared, Leo," Mrs. Finnley soothed. "Have a seat. You and I will chat while the officers go talk to your dad."

"Oh…" Leo sat down uncomfortably. He bit his lip, trying to keep it from trembling.

He was more scared now than he had been when Lyall had faced him down.

He was at the crux now, the part where he had to convince them, or Joyce would be hurt or killed.

"Now. Why don't you tell me what happened?"

"No. It was nothing. I just… I got a bad report card. And he was mad. He… he grounded me, and… I was really mad he did that," Leo said lamely.

He didn't know how to make it believable. He'd been mad about getting grounded? Who got mad over something so silly?

But Mrs. Finnley nodded, her eyes narrowing slightly, studying his face for the truth. Was she dealing with a hurt, abused child, or a sullen, angry delinquent?

"Why were you so mad?" she asked.

Leo was at a loss.

"Did you have a party you wanted to go to or something?" she suggested.

"Yeah," Leo said with relief. "I was—one of my friends was having a party. Is. Is having one this weekend. But Dad says I'm grounded and now I can't go." Leo tried to look sulky.

"That must have been pretty disappointing."

"Yeah. Yeah, I'm real disappointed about it," Leo echoed back.

"Are you telling me the truth, Leo? It's pretty serious, you getting us all the way out here. Taking us away from other calls that might really be emergencies."

"Yeah." Leo dropped his eyes to the table, trying to look ashamed. "I'm telling the truth. I know I shouldn't have. I was just mad... and disappointed, like you said. I thought if I got him in trouble... I don't know what. I just was mad."

Mrs. Finnley sighed, leaning back in her chair and studying him, shaking her head.

"I was really scared for you, Leo. Out here where we can't get out to help right away. I was worried what might happen to you before we could get here. And now, here's two police officers, who should be out enforcing the law, protecting the public. And they're busy talking to your dad in the garage instead of helping someone else."

"I'm sorry. I am."

Her voice changed. "You know, you're getting quite the reputation of a troublemaker, Leo."

Leo looked up at her, surprised.

"This isn't the first time you've made false allegations. And there has been trouble with the school. And some issues over illegal substances?"

Leo set his jaw. So she'd made the leap. He wasn't the victim anymore.

Maybe she'd never thought he was. If she'd looked at his file before coming out here... Maybe she'd come knowing he was going to recant, knowing it would be a wasted trip.

The cat shredded his insides, making Leo tense up and squirm in his seat.

She should *know*. She should be able to see through all of it.

She should be able to look at Leo's face and know he was the injured party.

Not a criminal. Not a false accuser.

That was her job.

Leo bit his lip, trying to keep the anger under control. Just a few minutes more and she would be gone. And the cops would be gone. And Joyce would be safe. He just had to hold it together a little bit longer.

Mrs. Finnley saw the cops returning through the window and got up to meet them. They shook their heads. She talked to them in a low voice, glancing back in Leo's direction a couple of times.

One of the cops folded his arms and stared hard at Leo.

Leo tipped his head back, banging it on the wall behind him, and closed his eyes. If he'd done his job properly, he was now in the bad books of the town cops.

If he hadn't already been.

They'd be watching him now, branding him a delinquent, trying to catch him at something to punish him for wasting their time.

The other cop put his hand on the doorknob to come in. Mrs. Finnley put her hand on his, shaking her head and saying something, but he shook her off and came the rest of the way in to talk to Leo anyway.

"Hey, stupid," he thundered. "Are you serious? I come all the way out here because Daddy grounded you? You're wasting my time to whine over a blasted report card? What a moron! You think that's what Child Services is for? You think that's what I'm here for? We come out here to 'save' you while you mewl over the consequences of your own stupidity? Shape up! We've got enough work to do without you making up stupid accusations about your hard-working father!"

He was big and heavyset. He towered over Leo.

Leo nodded, biting his lip hard, trying to hold back tears. Trying to keep on the mask of indifference, the tough attitude he practiced so hard at.

He flipped his head slightly and put his head down, making his long bangs slide down over his eyes, shielding him, protecting him from the cop's scrutiny.

"You tell us he cut off the end of your finger?" the cop demanded, nodding at Leo's bandaged hand. "And you think we won't even look, won't even verify it?"

Leo slid his hands under the table, out of sight.

"What did you do to your hand?" the officer demanded.

"I burned it," Leo said in a low voice.

"What?"

"I burned it. That's all."

"Your dad figures you burned it on a crack pipe."

Leo's surprise at this new development must have been obvious. Now he was not only a bad student making malicious abuse calls about his hard-working father, he was on drugs too?

"You didn't think he knew, huh?" the cop observed. "Parents know a lot more than you think. A lot more. You'd better clean up your act, Leo, or you're going to be in a heap of trouble. A heap!"

Leo nodded quickly.

The officer seemed to be running out of steam. Not getting any attitude back from Leo, he was winding back down.

He shook his head in disgust. "Don't call again," he warned.

"No, sir," Leo agreed.

They left. Leo sat at the table, slumped over, his heart pounding and his finger hurting so bad he wanted to scream. He swallowed the lump in his throat. He tried to get up the energy to stand up and check on the kids; to start making dinner; to do something to show Lyall he was being the compliant, obedient son.

He felt weak as a kitten.

The screen door banged open and Lyall stood there looking at him. Lyall chuckled, shaking his head at his son. "That cop tear a strip off you?" he asked. "Boy, he was not happy about being dragged all the way out here for a stupid kid just trying to get attention."

Leo nodded.

"You think you can get one over on me," Lyall goaded. "You think you can go behind my back and try to get me into trouble, and I'm just a stupid truck driver who doesn't know how to handle it. But I can handle you, Leo. I *own* you."

Leo nodded, waiting for Lyall to leave him alone.

"Get off your butt and get some supper on the table," Lyall snapped.

Leo's butt was up off the seat in an instant, despite his inertia of moments before.

He pulled out a couple of pots and put them on the stove. He glanced over his shoulder at Lyall, wondering why he wasn't leaving yet. Why wasn't he headed for the TV or back out to the garage to work on his latest project?

"Get me a beer," Lyall ordered.

Leo opened the fridge door. There, on the nearly-empty shelf, was the pickle jar, Leo's finger still floating in it. Leo rushed over to the sink, retching. Lyall laughed uproariously like it was the funniest thing he'd ever seen.

Leo gagged and retched.

He couldn't believe Lyall had the guts to just leave the finger there, knowing Child Services was on their way over.

Who did that?

Leo breathed, trying to get his body under control.

He was shaking like a leaf. His legs were Jell-O. He hung onto the edge of the counter, head down. He wished he could just go to his room and black out.

"Where is Joyce?" Leo asked weakly.

"I'll get Joyce later. When I'm sure you've learned your lesson."

"Please. I've learned. I won't ever do that again."

"You behave yourself. Do what you're told. We'll see."

"You'll get her today, won't you?" Leo begged. "She'll be scared."

"I'll get her when I've decided you're going to listen," Lyall repeated.

Leo didn't argue. He gritted his teeth. "Yes, sir," he agreed. "I'll… I'll get you your beer and start on supper."

Lyall waited.

Leo pushed himself away from the sink, went to the fridge again, and pulled out a can of beer. He handed it to his father without looking at him.

Lyall patted Leo on the cheek. "Good boy," he mocked. He went into the living room and sat down in front of the TV.

Late in the evening, Lyall walked out without a word and got into the truck. Leo and the others watched him.

Stormy tugged on Leo's uninjured hand.

"Is he going to pick up Joyce from her friend's?" she demanded.

"Yeah," Leo said, "I think so." Under his breath: "I hope so." He tousled her wild, curly hair. "Come on, time for you to get to bed."

"Awww! I want to stay up. I want to see Joy."

"You'll see her in the morning. Go on. Brush teeth and into bed. You too, Phil. Come on."

Phil grumbled too. But he was yawning and rubbing his eyes, and they had learned obedience under an iron hand.

Phil and Stormy fought over the sink to brush their teeth, pulled on their pajamas, and headed off to bed. Leo went to check on them and tuck them in.

"Night guys," he said. "You stay in bed. No matter what, okay?"

They both nodded. Leo went back out to the kitchen to finish cleaning up. He knew he should be doing his homework. But his hand was hurting.

He didn't want to take another of Lewis' pills, but without it he could barely function. It hurt so bad.

Leo was used to pain. He'd dealt with plenty of pain. But this was beyond him.

"You guys should go to bed too," he told Lewis and Michelle shakily.

They shook their heads. Lewis was watching Leo closely, his eyes dark hollows.

"You should go to bed," he told Leo. "You're sick."

"Can't. I gotta make sure Joyce is okay. You guys go ahead."

They both refused. So much for learning obedience. Lewis wheeled himself in front of the TV and settled in to watch. Michelle sat on the couch, leaning her head on Lewis' shoulder.

Leo sat back down at the table, cradling his pounding head in his good arm. He didn't know how much time passed before the door opened and his father was home.

Leo dragged himself to his feet, rubbing his eyes.

"Hey Joy," he greeted softly.

She had been crying. Her face was tear tracked and smudged with dirt. She shivered and clung to Lyall's hand, looking anxiously at Leo for permission to run to him.

"Should I get her some supper?" Leo asked Lyall.

"First you gotta take your punishment for calling Child Services.."

Leo gulped. He thought he had already taken enough punishment. How much more could Lyall expect him to take?

Leo took an involuntary step back from Lyall, but he nodded compliantly, not looking Lyall in the eye.

"Put your hand on the table," Lyall told him.

Leo put his hand slowly onto the table. He looked up at Lyall, his heart beating hard and fast. Lyall let go of Joyce's hand and put his hand into his pocket. He pulled out the pruning shears. Leo gasped, pulling his hand back off the table in a reflex reaction.

Lyall caught Joyce's small hand again, making a motion toward it with the shears.

Leo shook his head, barely able to breathe, let alone speak.

Shuddering, he put his hand back on the table.

"Other one," Lyall told him.

Leo put his already-injured hand on the table. He had to hold it there with the other hand. It seemed to have a mind of its own and would not stay put.

Leo pinned it and held it still, gasping for breath, feeling like he'd just sprinted a mile.

His chest hurt.

Tears started running down his face.

"Leo?" Joyce said, her eyes wide and scared. She looked at Lyall, with the shears, not understanding what was going on.

Lyall let go of Joyce's hand and went over to the table. He unwrapped the bandage around Leo's hand. He pulled away the gauze packing the empty space, pulling painfully at the clotted blood. He looked with satisfaction at the wound left by the missing digit.

He grinned at Leo, a wild, crazy light in his eye. He placed the shears above the first knuckle of Leo's index finger. Leo felt the cold metal against his skin. He braced himself, the tears squeezing their way out of his eyes.

Lyall snapped the shears shut.

It didn't matter that Leo was braced for it.

He thought with the pain he was already in, it wouldn't make much of a difference. But he was wrong.

His legs crumpled.

His head dipped down like his neck was spaghetti.

He screamed and hollered when he got breath enough back to do so.

Joyce burst into tears. The rest of the house was silent. Leo couldn't help waking the others up with his screams. They would all be listening now, cowering in their beds.

Lyall grabbed Leo when his legs buckled, and lowered him into the chair, chuckling maliciously.

He held Leo's hand pinned to the table.

Leo didn't look at it.

Didn't look at the dismembered digit this time. Didn't look at the mangled hand.

He let the world swim before his eyes, blurred, dark, and distant.

Lyall shook Leo by the shoulder, trying to keep him conscious. Leo struggled to sit upright. With Leo supported by his own spine once more, Lyall released his shoulder.

Leo felt Lyall move the shears down to the next joint on the same finger. Leo swore desperately.

The clip of the shears.

The blinding, unbearable pain.

Leo let go.

It was just too much, and he was gone, swirled away down into a whirlpool of unconsciousness.

Leo awoke in the gray hours of the next morning.

His whole hand pulsated with pain.

His whole body hurt, but it was focused on his hand, all pointed toward that one white-hot point.

When he moved, he bumped into someone and realized Lewis was sitting in his wheelchair next to the bed, having laid down his own head beside Leo's and fallen asleep.

"Shh, stay still," Lewis murmured.

He picked something up off of the bedside table.

Leo felt Lewis press a pill into his mouth. Leo wanted to protest, but he couldn't. He swallowed the pill and Lewis held a glass to his mouth to help wash it down.

Leo moved his head back and forth feverishly.

"Is she okay?" he asked. "Is Joyce okay?"

"Sure. Joyce is gonna be fine. You'll both be fine," Lewis reassured him. "Go back to sleep. You gotta get some rest."

"Gotta do chores before school," Leo mumbled.

"No. No school today. Go back to sleep."

Leo closed his eyes and once again swirled down that hole.

When Leo awoke next, light streamed in the window.

Lewis was asleep again, his head lying on the pillow next to Leo's while he sat beside the bed in his chair. He was going to be sore from the awkward position when he woke up.

Leo eased slowly out of the bed, trying not to disturb Lewis' sleep. The glass was empty, and Leo was parched. All of the moisture had bled out of him during the long, fevered night.

He tiptoed into the kitchen, glancing at the girl's closed bedroom door, checking the easy chair in the living room, trying to stay silent.

He got himself a cup from the cupboard and put it down on the counter to open the fridge door.

He was braced for the sight of the pickle jar. He looked studiously away from it, checking to see how many cans of beer were left, whether he could steal one without Lyall noticing it. The more alcohol he drank, the fewer of Lewis's painkillers he would need. So it was a good thing, he was doing everyone a favor by not incurring the expense of extra painkillers.

As he took a can of beer, his eyes slid unwillingly to the pickle jar.

Now the first finger was no longer alone.

It had been joined by two other pieces… and by a smaller, more delicately-shaped finger with a few chips of red nail polish still clinging to the nail.

"No!" Leo screamed, holding onto the fridge for support, swearing. "No, no, no!"

The house stirred. Lewis wheeled himself swiftly out of his bedroom to intercept Leo before he could get to the girl's bedroom door.

Leo heard Michelle's soothing voice on the other side, Joyce's muffled cries.

"We're trying to keep her asleep," Lewis said lowly, trying to block him. "Don't go in. Let Michelle put her back to sleep."

"No! No, how *could* he? She didn't do anything to him! She didn't do anything wrong! I took my punishment!"

Tears streamed down Leo's cheeks.

Lewis shook his head grimly. "You think he doesn't know you'd rather lose your whole hand than see her get hurt? He's making sure. Making sure you never do anything like that again."

Leo fell to his knees, sobbing.

"I wouldn't have," he promised. "I already wouldn't have. He didn't need to do that!"

Lewis rubbed Leo's shoulder. Tried to reach him to give him a hug. "I know," he agreed.

"He didn't need to do that," Leo repeated.

"I know. Come on. Let's get you back to bed. You need it too."

CHAPTER ELEVEN

LEO FOUND HIMSELF BACK at the gym. Sometimes he didn't know how he managed to drag himself there after work. Some days he just wanted to go home and go to bed.

But after rescuing the animals, he had to go rescue the kids. And then he had to try to rescue his family. That was his life.

He listened to the grunts of the other men as they worked out. The tinny music from the stereo in the corner. He inhaled the familiar smell of sweat and hard work.

As he ran through his own calisthenics, Leo started to relax. The stress started to recede. The cat that had been writhing around his stomach started to calm down.

It stopped sharpening its claws on his insides and curled up.

Leo wanted to be totally relaxed and chilled for the class. He didn't want any fights.

No one was going to get under his skin.

He would just run the class, see if there was anything else he could do for the kids, and then go home. Nothing else. Just take care of himself for once. Curl up in front of the TV with Rascal, and maybe even fall asleep right there on the couch.

The boys started to arrive and Leo greeted them in a friendly voice. They seemed a little hyped up.

Then Reggie arrived. He dawdled and dragged his feet. He approached Leo, his face down, eyes on his shoes.

"Um… Coach…"

"Hey, Reg."

"I'm sorry about the other day. Being so disrespectful. I was just mad. I shoulda listened to you."

"Yeah. It's okay," Leo assured him. "We all good now?"

Reggie looked up at his face hopefully.

How many times had he burned his bridges, ticking people off so badly they wouldn't let him come back again? It was hard for kids who were impulsive, easily upset. People didn't really stick around for long. They didn't understand how hard it was to fight the demons inside.

"Yeah," he said warmly. "We're good."

"Good."

Leo slapped him on the shoulder.

It was easy for him to forgive a few words or blows exchanged in a fit of anger. A lifetime of abuse… that was a whole 'nother ball game. Leo called the boys together to get started.

"Let's go, boys. You all warmed up?"

They grumbled a little, as most of them had been messing around and hadn't done their warm-ups yet. A couple had been diligent and came over to spar with Leo while the others were completing their routines. Leo looked down at them.

"What's up, Bubblegum?"

"Hey, Coach."

"What's this I hear about you being in jail? Drugs in your locker?"

"Oh, yo!" Billy immediately put on a tough-guy attitude, folding his arms across his thick chest. "I didn't do nothin', man. You know I don't do drugs! What, pollute this temple?" He gestured to his ragged but trendy clothing.

"You better not," Leo warned. "You do drugs, you're off my crew."

"Drugs are stupid, man. I'd never do that!"

"You'd better not." Leo was going to leave it at that, then he frowned at Billy. "You'd better not be selling that crap either."

For a moment, Billy's eyes flashed guilt, but he quickly covered it up. "My boys here all know better than to use, don't you?" he asked, bobbing his head at the other boys. "None of us are doing drugs, boss."

"You'd better not. Selling drugs will land you in prison, you know, and you don't want to end up on the receiving end of that action."

"No sir!" Billy agreed, grinning widely, sweeping his wavy long bangs back out of the way.

Leo shook his head. "Okay, come show me what you've got. Did you forget everything, missing a day?"

"No way!" Billy protested.

He got on his protective gear and bounced over to Leo, making him laugh by bounding all over the ring like a kangaroo.

"Slow down, Bubblegum! This is a fight, not a dance!"

"If you can't catch me, you can't beat me," Billy teased.

Leo stepped quickly, cornering him and cuffing him across the head.

"Quit dancing and be serious!" he instructed. "You'll end up flat on your back before you even know what hit you. Be alert, not silly."

Billy slowed down and assumed the correct fighting posture, focusing in on his coach obediently. They sparred for a few minutes, and then Leo called Chase up. Each of them got a few minutes with Leo, and then he broke them into pairs and gave them some more instruction.

Class went well, and when the boys broke up and said their goodbyes, Leo watched them go affectionately.

They were good boys. If he could just keep them away from the drugs and other bad influences. He couldn't be with them all the time. The best he could do was a few afternoons a week. But if he could interest them in something constructive, teach them some self-control… that had to be enough. Sometimes he wanted to take one of them home with him, fearing abusive situations at home, feeling them slipping away from him and gravitating toward the gangs… If he could just keep them fighting in the ring instead of at school, or at home, or with each other…

"You think you're so wonderful," a voice harangued. "You're hardly any older than they are and you think you're all grown up and mature. This wonderful coach, this great influence on their lives. What a crock!"

Leo looked at the other man. Not that he was much older than Leo was. Leo didn't know where he got off acting so much older and wiser.

"What's up, Texaco?" he asked with forced cheer.

Lex hated the nickname. Leo knew it grated on him and took delight in seeing him cringe.

"It's not Texaco," he growled. "It's Lex. I don't call you some stupid nickname, do I, moron?"

Leo shook his head. The lion within him stirred, but he was happy and calm after his workout and training with the boys and he breathed slowly to try to soothe it. To keep it nice and calm and warm.

The man didn't look like a 'Lex'. Lex should be some big blonde Russian dude, and Texaco was a middle-height, slightly heavy black man. Leo thought the nickname suited him better.

He tried not to let Lex's words rankle. Lex wasn't his father. He barely even knew Leo. Lex couldn't hurt Leo.

"You got a problem?" Leo demanded. "I have the equipment booked for the after-school program. You know they're here until five-thirty."

"It isn't them that bother me. It's you."

"What'd I ever do to you? You're always getting in my face. Just chill, huh? You do your thing and let me do mine."

"I see you're booked to fight Heartbrake next week," Texaco observed.

So that was what was bothering him? Leo had a better gig than he did?

"Yeah, so what?"

"He is *so* going to school you. You're nowhere near his league."

"Well, that's why I fight people who are better than me. If you only fight people who are below you," Leo fixed Texaco with a knowing look, "then you're not going to get any better, are you?"

"Oh, you *wish* you could take me. What an idiot. You're a lightweight, Leo. You're never going to be anything but a lightweight."

"Then I'll be the best damn lightweight in town," Leo shot back. "Better than being a fat—old—man!"

Texaco put down his dumbbells.

"You wanna say that again?" he growled.

"What's the matter, you deaf too?" Leo mocked.

"Put on your gloves," Texaco ordered, nodding to the ring. "I'll show you how old I am!"

Some of the other guys were watching the argument now. Hakim shook his head at Leo. "Don't let him bait you."

"He wants to fight, I'll give him a fight."

He said it calmly, but the cat was roused, waiting for its chance. Ready to escape.

Leo put on his gloves and climbed into the ring.

Texaco jumped in on the other side.

They didn't ring the bell. It wasn't a real match. It was a street fight; it just happened to be inside a ring.

They both went at it, throwing punches, watching for an opportunity to show off their skills, to get in tight and hurt the other.

Leo's cat was thirsty for a fight. His vision turned red, focused on nothing but Texaco, anticipating his movements, trying to avoid the enormous fists that jarred Leo from head to foot whenever they landed a blow. He tried to find some way to get beneath Texaco's guard and do some damage.

Then the bell was ringing. Leo backed up before looking to see what was going on. He wasn't going to let Texaco hit him again just because Leo had gotten distracted.

He looked at the bell. It was Jaime.

"Get out of my ring!" Jaime ordered. "Is that how you behave here? Show some respect!"

Leo let his gloves drop after making sure Texaco was far enough away not to be a danger. Texaco slipped out through the ropes. The last one left in the ring was the one who was going to get the most of Jaime's attention.

"Leo, you know better!" Jaime railed. "We're not animals here that have no sense and just fight whatever they can! We are men. We think, and we follow the rules, and we don't enter uneven matches. You know I don't put up with that nonsense here."

Leo climbed slowly out between the ropes. Jaime gave him a hand down.

"He was bugging me," Leo whined, even though he recognized he sounded like one of the boys instead of like a man. "He wanted to fight me, so I did."

"Not on my watch. You follow the rules, or you won't be fighting here. Not on your own, not in a league, and not coaching the boys. I'll tell them to kick you out of the program. *Comprende?*"

Leo nodded.

"Yeah, I get it," he agreed. "I'm sorry. I shouldn't have let him get my goat."

"That's right," Jaime agreed. "Be a man, not an animal. Fight in arranged matches. Matches that are even."

"I did okay, though," Leo protested.

"You're going to be wondering tomorrow. Go get some ice and clean yourself up."

"I'm okay."

"You're bleeding. You've got to get some ice on your face, keep the swelling down."

Leo felt his face with careful fingers. "I've got a high pain threshold. I've had a lot worse."

"As someone who has seen your X-rays, I can't argue with that. But you still need to take care of yourself. The faster you heal, the sooner you'll be ready for the next match."

Leo meekly went to the small fridge and took out an ice pack, and got a couple of rags to clean up at the sink. Texaco walked by him, snickering. Leo avoided looking at him or responding.

Be a man, he repeated to himself. Just like Jaime says. Be a man, not an animal.

Not that animals were bad, but they didn't have the choice like Leo did. Just like his dad could have chosen not to hit them, Leo had to make the choice not to get into stupid fights just because someone felt like jerking him around.

Breathing steadily, he refused to look at Texaco and continued to clean up. He overheard Jaime getting after Texaco, and kicking him out of the gym, and smiled slightly to himself. If nothing else, he'd at least succeeded in getting rid of Texaco for one evening.

"Sorry again," he told Jaime when he was finished cleaning up. "I'll do better."

"Yeah. You'd better. I don't want to have to find a new coach for the after-school program. And I don't have the patience to do it myself. Just don't let people get to you."

Leo nodded. "I know. I'm sorry. It won't happen again."

"Well, not for a couple more weeks anyway," Jaime said with a sigh.

He knew Leo too well.

"Let me see," Jaime ordered, motioning to Leo.

Leo stepped closer to Jaime, lowering the ice and angling his face so that

Jaime could get a close look at the worst of the damage. Jaime's fingers were gentle but firm as he felt the boney structure of Leo's face.

"You know Texaco—Lex—is out of your weight class. He could do real damage. It's dangerous enough boxing *in* your class with all of these old breaks."

"Yeah." Leo strove not to move his face when he answered, or to flinch away from Jaime's touch when he hit a tender spot.

"All it takes is one splinter in your brain and you're toast. You sure as hell don't fight without a helmet!"

"Uh-huh."

"That's not even talking about TBI. Are you concussed?"

He moved on to Leo's neck. His fingers were cold as he lifted Leo's shirt and probed his ribs and belly.

Jaime paused. "Are you?" he demanded.

"No. Don't think so."

Jaime continued with the amateur examination. "You've got a brain. Use it."

———

Leo never took much thought for his own injuries. But he worried constantly about the other children's.

They had been sitting eating supper, and in spite of everyone else's moods, Michelle and Joyce were chattering away about school and their friends and the teen dramas of their day.

Leo mostly kept his eyes on his plate, trying to just get finished and hoping Lyall would go sit down in front of the TV with a beer and leave Leo alone. Leo had a headache from the pot he'd smoked earlier in the day, and just wanted to go stretch out in bed and doze off.

It wasn't bedtime yet, but morning was coming too soon. The sooner he could get safely away to bed, the better.

"Michelle," Lyall's voice snapped out.

The girls went quiet. Everybody froze, only their eyes moving to see what was bothering Lyall. Sliding around the room to look for the quickest escape route.

Leo looked at Michelle, who had turned sheet white.

"Yes, sir?"

"What did you do to your ears?"

Leo hadn't even noticed the tiny studs in the center of Michelle's earlobes, mostly covered by her dark hair.

Michelle touched her ears self-consciously, looking like she wished she could hide them.

"I… I got them pierced," she explained.

"Who said you could get your ears pierced?"

"Well, no one… but mom had hers pierced. I didn't have to pay for it…"

"Why didn't you have to pay for it?" Lyall demanded.

"Margot's sister does it, so she just did it for free. She had all the proper equipment, so everything was clean and all…" Michelle trailed off.

"You didn't have permission," Lyall asserted.

"I'm… I'm sorry. If you don't want me to have pierced ears, I can just take the earrings out and let the holes close back up. That's all I have to do."

"No, I don't think that's gonna do it for me," Lyall said thoughtfully.

They all looked at him in terror. They didn't like his cold, cruel tone any more than his rage when he'd been drinking. He was going to do something, and it wasn't going to be good.

"Go to the bathroom," Lyall ordered.

Michelle got up, holding onto her chair for support for a moment.

Leo wanted to intervene, to say something that would distract Lyall or persuade him not to hurt her.

But he couldn't think of anything.

His brain was paralyzed.

Even if he'd been able to think, even if he'd been smart like Lewis and hadn't been smoking, he doubted he could have done anything.

But Lewis wasn't home anymore to prove him right or wrong. All of them just sat there frozen.

Lyall followed Michelle out of the kitchen, into the bathroom. He stopped at the junk drawer, pulling something out.

Leo didn't see what it was and was afraid to look.

Lyall went into the bathroom and shut the door. Michelle's begging voice was indistinct.

Leo got up and walked a few steps toward them, but couldn't make himself go any further.

Joyce shook her head at him, even though she and Michelle were as close as twins. She knew it was hopeless.

Michelle started screaming shrilly and without any thought, Leo was there, opening the door, pushing through to save his sister, to get in between Lyall and Michelle.

"Go get her the shovel," Lyall said to Leo, throwing two little flaps of skin adorned with stud earrings onto the side of the sink.

Michelle was sitting down on the toilet, hands over her ears, half anguished, half fainting.

Leo wanted to throw up.

He avoided looking at the bits on the counter. Avoided looking at Lyall.

"Go on," Lyall ordered. "Or do you want me to clip yours too?"

Leo turned on his heel and headed for the door.

Michelle's sobs followed him out and then were cut off abruptly when he left the house and shut the door behind him.

Leo grabbed the shovel from its place inside the shed, and he started to drive it into the ground in the corner under the oak tree, loosening up the ground.

It was a breach of the rules, but he had to do something to help Michelle. To make it easier for her somehow.

Then Leo headed back into the house and stood inside the front door, waiting for Michelle.

Joyce was crying as she followed Michelle out of the bathroom toward the door.

She had bandaged Michelle's ears as well as she could, but the bandages were already red with blood, and there were rivulets down Michelle's neck and into her collar.

Leo would have to be sure to soak it right away, or the blood wouldn't come out in the wash.

Sobbing, Michelle took the shovel from Leo's hand and marched out to the spot where he'd loosened the ground for her.

Lyall appeared and Leo got out of the way as quickly as he could.

He didn't need to see this. He knew how it would play out.

Lyall would watch her dig up the jar. He would examine it, turning it around to look at all the gruesome body parts that had been added, in their various stages of preservation or decay.

Then he would show it to Michelle and make her add her earlobes to it, and re-bury it again.

Leo went to the kitchen to clean up and found out that was where Joyce had retreated to.

"What the hell is his cover story going to be for this one?" Joyce demanded. Furious tears coursed down her cheeks. "How is he going to explain this away? You think people aren't going to notice *he cut off her ears?*"

"I know," Leo agreed, "but he always manages."

Lyall always came up with an ingenious story. He had said that their fingers had to be amputated because of a genetic disorder, some circulatory thing that obstructed the blood flow and ended up leaving them with gangrene.

But even that story had only gone so far. Too many fingers missing too quickly had started raising suspicious questions amongst the teachers and administrators. They had started to ask for more information about this rare genetic disease the children all had. Lyall had had to dispense with cutting fingers off as a punishment.

He had cut off some toes—not enough to prevent them from walking or doing chores—and had switched to pulling out fingernails. Easier to cover up with a few Band-Aids. Less likely to be noticed.

Lyall would come up with a story. He always did.

CHAPTER TWELVE

LEO WAS SITTING IN front of the TV, with Rascal cuddled up with him when Elizabeth called. It had been such a busy week, Leo didn't feel like doing anything. Just cocooning and hiding from the real world for a while.

But when he saw it was Elizabeth on the caller ID, he answered.

"Hi, Elizabeth," he greeted.

"Why don't you call me Lu," she said. "Just for today."

"Just for today?" Leo repeated, trying to sort out the strange request. He'd never met anyone who cycled through nicknames as quickly as Elizabeth. "Okay then, Lu. How are you?"

"I'm going crazy being cooped up. You want to go out for a walk or something? Juleen is driving me nuts. Maybe she'll quiet down if I take her out in the stroller."

"Sure. Right now, or…?"

"Yeah, now if you're free. I'll understand if you have something else to do; but, you know, I'm jonesing to get out of here now."

"Sure. I'm not doing anything. Just give me a few minutes… you want to meet over there? At the merry-go-round? Or do you want me to come to your place first?"

"Merry-go-round sounds perfect," she agreed. "Let's do that."

After Leo had hung up, he pushed Rascal from his lap. "Sorry boy. But

I've got to go out for a walk. How'd you like to see Elizabeth—or Lu, today? Do you want to see her again?"

Rascal's tail thumped.

In a few more minutes, they were out the door and on their way to the park.

It wasn't too hard to spot Elizabeth. She was walking along the trail, pushing Juleen up and down a long, straight stretch near the merry-go-round. Leo waved at her and approached.

"Hey—Lu! Here we are!"

"Yay," Elizabeth said without much enthusiasm. "I really needed this. Thanks."

"What do you want to do? Walk for a while and see if Juleen goes to sleep?"

"Yeah. That would be nice."

Leo went around the stroller to check on Juleen, surreptitiously checking whether she was dressed properly, had a dry diaper, and was clean. Juleen was crying, but he couldn't see anything wrong.

"So what's wrong today?" Leo asked. "Is she eating good?"

"Drinking," Elizabeth corrected. "She's not on solid food yet. I don't know. She's always hungry or grumpy. I can't tell if she's getting enough milk. I'm wondering about starting her on a bottle."

Leo nodded. "Then you'd at least know how much she was getting."

"It's just so frustrating, listening to her cry, day and night."

"I'll bet," Leo agreed. He looked at Elizabeth. Her eyes were dark shadows. She looked like she hadn't slept in a week, even though a day ago she had looked fresh as a daisy. It was amazing how quickly she could turn around.

"You look tired," he said. "Are you still getting your meds?"

"I'm taking them. I'd sleep fine if it wasn't for this little monster!"

They started to walk. Juleen quieted down a little bit once they got started, lowering her cries to a low complaining grumble as they moved along.

"She's settling down. Maybe she'll go to sleep," Leo said.

"Man, I hope so. Sometimes I hate kids, you know?"

Leo looked at her. "No… I like kids."

"Well, you wouldn't if you had a crab around all the time. Kids are fine in small doses, especially when they're bigger and more like real people. But when they can't even tell you what they're bawling about? I hate it."

"They grow out of it," Leo said. "Maybe she's just colicky."

"Maybe you should try taking care of her for a while?"

"Calm down," Leo soothed. "It's going to be okay. If you're all uptight, she will be too. Just give both of you a chance to settle down."

They were silent for a little while.

"You know," Leo said, "if you can't take care of her, you could call Child Services."

"Yeah, you think I don't know that? That's what my doctor and everybody says. But they haven't been in foster care themselves. Or adopted and then returned. It isn't all roses."

"No," Leo agreed. "You've had some pretty tough experiences."

Elizabeth shrugged it off. "I was pretty lucky. But I know from other foster kids, foster brothers and sisters at different houses I was at; I know how bad some of them had it in other places. Me, I was always taken care of pretty well."

"Well, that's lucky. I know some people really play the system. They just want the extra money and don't give a dang about the kids."

Elizabeth nodded. "Sure," she agreed. "There was this one house I was in… I don't really know how it worked because they had way too many kids. You're not supposed to have that many. It was just… kids upon kids. She was nice, very loving and everything. She wanted to help all the little guys out… Like your cat lady, I guess. I know we couldn't all have been her foster kids, officially. I don't know if she took care of other people's kids casually, or babysat, or what. But there were always new kids coming and going. Never enough beds, or food for everyone. You scrounged what you could. And clothes… everyone was half-naked. There were never enough clothes to go around."

"How could a social worker see that and still approve them?"

Elizabeth shook her head. "I don't know. She was such a nice lady, maybe they didn't care if she was breaking a few rules. When the social worker would come, a lot of us would get told to go to the park, so there weren't so many at the house. But it was still… you know, no electricity half the time, everything untidy because nobody could ever clean up after that many kids. Everybody just dropped things where they were. Went to sleep anywhere they could curl up."

"Wow. That must have been really hard."

Elizabeth shook her head insistently. "No, it sounds worse than it was. I was fine there. She didn't hit us or anything. She was always looking out for us. She loved everybody. More than you can say for a lot of families."

"So would you have stayed with her if you could?"

She nodded. "Sure, why not? I woulda stayed there."

"Why did you have to go? Did she get shut down?"

"I don't remember. I just remember it was dark so much, and I was hungry, and never had any panties." She laughed brightly, belying the seriousness of the words, making a joke of it. "But it's hazy. I don't remember much about any of the families I was with. They all blend together after a while."

Leo was silent. He studied her as they walked.

Elizabeth smiled sideways at him. "It's not polite to stare."

"No. Sorry. It's just… You're pretty. I like you. I like being with you."

"Well, don't be wishy washy. Pick one and go with it!"

Leo laughed. "I just like being with you. You're sounding better now, not so tired."

Elizabeth looked at Juleen. She peeked over the edge of the stroller. "She's gone to sleep. We can stop and relax for a while."

Leo gestured to the green lawn. They parked the stroller under a tree and sat down.

"Hang on," Leo said. He took off his backpack and dug out a checked plastic tablecloth.

"There, how's that?" he said, spreading it out.

Elizabeth sat on the edge, looking delighted. "Now all we need is some food and we can have a picnic," she said.

"Well, I don't have much, but…"

Leo pulled out the various bags and bowls he'd put hurriedly together.

Elizabeth laughed. "You thought of everything, didn't you? How did you get all of this together so fast? I barely beat you here."

"I can be quick," Leo said. "It's not a real meal. It doesn't all go together; it's just a bunch of snack stuff. But I thought it would be fun."

"It is," Elizabeth agreed. "What a great idea. I feel like I just got out of prison!"

"Good. I want you to be happy. Dig in."

And dig in, they did. Leo was a little taken aback by how Elizabeth attacked the food. She acted like she hadn't eaten in a week.

"Slow down there, you're going to choke," he warned, unable to keep quiet at the display.

Looking up at him with a chicken leg in one hand and a spoonful of fruit salad in the other, Elizabeth flushed and looked sheepish.

"I'm sorry. What a pig. A lovely way to show you what a lady I am."

"No, it's okay. I just don't want you to choke or make yourself sick."

"I don't make myself sick," Elizabeth said sharply.

"Have all you want. I don't mind."

"I guess it's from being places like that," Elizabeth said, going back without explanation to her discussion of the foster home. "Places you had to fight for your food. Eat as fast as you could or whenever you had the opportunity, in case you didn't get the chance again for a while. I know I shouldn't do it, but sometimes it gets away from me, and I act a little... uncivilized."

Leo laughed. "That's okay," he said. "I can be uncivilized too!"

And to demonstrate, he knelt beside the pond—the one where dogs swam and people threw rocks and garbage—and pretended he was going to drink the water straight from the pond. He was sure she would stop him. Elizabeth looked startled.

"What's that?" she asked, pointing into the water.

Leo looked closely. Rocks, trash, bugs, maybe a fishing line. "What?"

"That, right there on the bottom, doesn't it look like—"

Leo peered down into the water and suddenly she pushed the back of his head, dunking him under the surface.

Leo immediately gasped instead of holding his breath.

He exploded out of the water, coughing and flailing his arms, trying to escape.

When he managed to settle down, to breathe in the warm, sweet air, and stop coughing, Elizabeth was staring at him, wide-eyed.

"I'm sorry," she said. "It was just a joke. I didn't mean to scare you."

Leo collapsed on the tablecloth, trying to clear his throat. He closed his eyes. "It's not you," he said. "It's..."

"Your dad."

Leo nodded. Again, his dad. He just couldn't escape the man, even when he was lying asleep or dead in the hospital. Everywhere he went, Leo still had to deal with what his father had done in the past.

"He could be... very cruel, calculating."

"And he tried to make you drink from the kiddie pond?" Elizabeth suggested lightly.

"I wish that was all it was. No. He would... when he didn't believe us, he would torture us, try to get us to talk."

"Like with the fingers," Elizabeth said.

"That was only for major punishments. But for smaller things. When he thought we were hiding something from him. Or the teacher called from the school. He would hold us down. Pour water over our faces. I would think I was going to drown. He would stop to let me get one breath of air and then he would start all over again. It felt like hours and I'd only get a few breaths. Sometimes I was sick from choking on too much water and would throw up. One day I was choking and throwing up so much, I was throwing up blood."

Elizabeth's eyes were huge, listening to the story. "That's horrible," she said softly.

"Yeah," said Leo. "So I kind of overreact to water on my face."

"I'm sorry. I was just playing around. Having some fun with you. I wasn't trying to be mean."

Leo nodded. He closed his eyes, trying to stem the flow of memories and calm the wild beating of his heart.

"I know. It's okay. I'm fine..."

Lyall gave Leo a look when he came in the door that set Leo's heart thumping.

What had he done to attract his father's attention?

Nothing was said and Leo continued on his way without a word, anxious, but unwilling to say anything in case it should set Lyall off. Leo hung up his jacket carefully, standing on his tip-toes to reach the hook.

He went to his room and stretched out on his bed, picking up a couple of action figures to play with while he waited for supper. Since Lyall was already in, there would be no TV for Leo tonight.

"Leo!" Margaret called impatiently from the kitchen. Leo got up guiltily, knowing he should have been doing chores or homework rather than playing.

"Mom?" he said, going to see what she wanted.

"Would you please take the girls? They're underfoot."

Leo motioned to Michelle and Joyce.

"Come on, girls, let's go play," he invited. They followed him eagerly to their bedroom and looked around for a toy or game to engage them with.

He was setting up dolls with them when Lyall came and stood in the doorway. The children all looked up nervously.

"What's this?" Lyall demanded, holding up the pack of gum that he had retrieved from Leo's jacket pocket.

Leo gulped, swallowing the piece of gum he had forgotten he was chewing.

"Um—my gum," he answered.

Lyall stepped into the room and hauled Leo up by one arm. "Your gum? Where did you get gum?" he demanded. "Where did you steal it from?"

Leo shook his head. "No, I didn't steal it! I got it at school!"

Still holding onto his arm so hard it hurt, Lyall stared fiercely into Leo's face, his eyes bloodshot. "Where at school? Who gave it to you?"

Leo hesitated. He knew that Lyall didn't like him working with professionals, with outsiders who might suspect that something was wrong and report them to Child Services.

"From… a friend," he lied weakly.

Lyall dragged him out of the bedroom and down the hall toward the bathroom.

"A friend?" he mocked. "What friend? You don't have any friends."

"Yes, I do!" Leo protested, stung. "A boy in my class. His name is… Mark," Leo invented wildly.

Sometimes Mark talked to him. They didn't play together or eat lunch together, but there was a boy named Mark, and he could have been Leo's friend in a different world.

"And Mark gave you a whole pack of gum?" Lyall demanded, throwing Leo ahead of him onto the floor of the bathroom. "Out of the kindness of his heart? Is that what you're trying to tell me?"

"He… I helped him with some schoolwork. And he wanted to thank me, so he gave me the gum. He's got lots. His mom buys cases of it at Costco."

Lyall started the water running in the tub. Leo's stomach heaved convulsively.

He inched away from Lyall, though he knew it was hopeless. Lyall, once focused on the task of worming the truth out of Leo, would not give up until he had what he wanted, and more.

"You helped him," Lyall laughed derisively. "You? Just how stupid is he, if you know more than he does?"

Leo's anger rose at the belittling. Tears burned his eyes.

The teachers told Leo he wasn't stupid. He just had learning disabilities. Leo *could* have helped Mark. He could have helped him with something.

"It was math," he retorted. "We started times-ing, and he was away that day, so I showed him how to do it."

Lyall grabbed Leo by the long hair at the back of his head, and pulled his head under the tap, so Leo was arched backward over the edge of the tub, and the water was pouring down over his face, into his nose.

Leo had taken a deep breath in preparation, but that didn't matter.

The cold water hit him with a shock, and although he managed not to inhale immediately, he couldn't hold his breath forever, and he struggled to reach the surface to get more oxygen.

Lyall held him firm, and Leo gasped, inhaling a mix of water and air. He coughed and choked, inhaling more water, struggling to turn his head to the side, out of the stream of water.

Lyall lifted his head and let him breathe. He waited for Leo to stop coughing and sputtering.

"You helped Mark with his times-ing?" Lyall mocked.

Leo coughed.

Lyall's grip on his hair tightened, threatening to pull him under again.

"No," Leo admitted hoarsely. "No, I didn't help him. I—" he coughed deeply, ejecting as much water as possible. "He's just my friend. He was just being nice."

Lyall pulled him under again.

Leo struggled to escape. He inhaled more water and flailed wildly.

Lyall brought him up for air.

"You don't have any friends," Lyall growled.

Leo shook his head weakly, gasping, his chest burning, his throat already raw.

"No friends," he agreed faintly.

"What?"

"No friends. I don't have—" he was interrupted by a coughing fit, gagging and almost vomiting up the water he had swallowed. "I don't have no friends."

"Then where…" Lyall held the package of gum right in front of his eyes. "Where did you get this?"

"From the school."

Lyall started to pull him down. Leo resisted, shaking his head in panic.

"The resource teacher," he said as fast as he could before Lyall could put him all the way under, "to help—"

Too late, he was under the water again, mid-speech. Leo closed his mouth and fought wildly to free his head.

He ended up smashing his forehead forward against the faucet and nearly blacked out.

When he went limp, Lyall pulled him out and shook him.

"Stop that," Lyall said irritably as if Leo was losing consciousness merely to annoy him.

"To help with my ADHD," Leo sobbed, trying to get the words out despite the coughing, despite the pain, despite the blackness threatening to envelope him.

Lyall paused, not pulling him under again immediately.

Leo tried to breathe deeply, tried to get enough oxygen into his body again.

"What ADHD?" Lyall demanded.

Leo swallowed.

"They say I have ADHD. And they say…" he coughed, his eyes streaming tears, "chewing gum helps. To focus better. On the work." The words came in short bursts, between gasps and gulps and sobs.

"*Who* says?" Lyall questioned.

"Resource room teacher. Where I go for extra help."

"I never approved any extra help. No resource room teacher. No stupid quack diagnoses."

"They said it's okay. That all the kids get it. There's no extra fee."

Lyall shoved Leo away. He fell into the tub and whacked the back of his head on the far edge.

Leo didn't care, he was just happy to be released. Relieved when Lyall turned the water off.

Lyall left him there, and went into the kitchen to talk to Margaret. Leo could hear him arguing with her, repeatedly insisting Margaret call the school and put a stop to any counseling or therapy or special attention they were giving Leo.

Leo climbed out of the tub and sat on the edge, coughing and trying to get his breath back.

Resting his head in his hands, he quickly realized his forehead was bleeding where he'd smashed it on the faucet. He pressed a rag to it, trying to stop the bleeding. The back of his head was also getting a bump and throbbing.

Leo went back to the girls' bedroom and sat down. The little girls looked at him, but made no comment on the interruption of their game, his soaked hair and shirt, or his bleeding head.

"Christie is going to have a party," Michelle announced, holding up one of the dolls. "They are going to have tea. And cookies. Choc'late chip ones."

"That's nice," Leo murmured. "How about the princess? Is she going to come?"

He pointed to one of the other dolls. He played with the little girls, still coughing up water, and waited for things to settle down and dinner to be announced.

Rascal squirmed over to Leo, belly on the ground and snuffled in his ear. Leo opened one eye and looked at him.

"I'm fine, Rascal. Don't worry," he told the animal.

Rascal promptly started to wash Leo's face.

Leo sat up, pushing him away. Elizabeth burst into peals of laughter. Leo had to chuckle a little himself.

"Well, if you're too afraid of water, Rascal can always wash your face," Elizabeth hiccupped, and they both sat there, trying to settle down and catch their breaths again.

Leo laughed. "Yeah, no kidding," he agreed. "Who's a good dog?" he asked in a baby voice and gave Rascal's ears a vigorous scratch.

Juleen woke up and started to cry again. Elizabeth groaned.

"I was just starting to relax," she complained.

"It's okay," Leo went over and picked Juleen up. He jiggled her around. "She just wants to see what all the noise is about. Don't you, Juleen?"

He got up with her and walked around until Juleen started to quiet and look around. Leo went back over to the picnic and sat down.

"There, she's okay now, aren't you Juleen?"

He put her down on a clear corner of the tablecloth, and Rascal got up and went over to sniff her. He laid down at her feet and panted happily.

CHAPTER THIRTEEN

L EO WATCHED THE BOXING match avidly, his eyes mostly on Heartbrake as he fought.

Leo wanted to pick up his moves, see where his weak spots were. Anything that might give Leo an edge in his upcoming fight.

During one break between rounds, Heartbrake looked at him and nodded slightly, eyes narrowed. Leo nodded back in acknowledgment.

It was a good match. The opponents were evenly matched. The fight went on for some time, with each giving and taking a little. Leo was glad it wasn't a one-punch fight. It was hard to learn someone's form and tricks with a one-punch fight.

Eventually, it was Heartbrake who triumphed, with a strong left uppercut that left King Smith flat on his back, out cold.

Heartbrake turned, found Leo in the crowd, and pointed at him. The meaning was obvious. 'You're next. That's gonna be you next week.'

Leo just smiled at him steadily. Never back down. Always show a confident face. Half of the battle was psychological. In a moment or two, Leo was lost in the crowd and could no longer see Heartbrake's face as the crowd swarmed around Leo.

The referee announced the winner, held up his arm, and announced Heartbrake's next fight—next week with Leo Bakerfield.

Several people nearby knew Leo and turned to him.

"You're fighting next week? Excellent. You gonna beat him?"

Leo shrugged at the fuss. "Heartbrake's good," he acknowledged. "I'm training hard and I'm going to do my best to do next week what he did tonight."

It was a good response, well-crafted, and they appreciated it.

Leo got lots of encouraging slaps on the back and 'good luck' cheers, and then people started to stream for the doors, and afterward, to the bars. Fighting was a thirsty business. Anyone who wasn't drinking before would surely be drinking now. Leo let himself be jostled along by the crowd.

As was often the case, there were flyers being handed out with coupons for bars, unofficial fights coming up during the week, new bands playing at nearby clubs, and any other advertisers who felt the fight crowd was a good target market. Leo accepted a few of the flyers and glanced through them to see if there was anything interesting going on. He looked at one for a new singer, an attractive girl he hadn't heard of before and tried to talk to the guy passing out the flyers.

"Do you know her? Is she good?"

"I don't know, buddy, I just hand out the flyers."

"I'm looking for an agent. Do you represent singers?"

"Not me. I just hand out the flyers. But you can call the office," he dug a business card out of the snug pocket of his skinny jeans. "They'll point you in the right direction."

"Great, thanks!"

Leo headed toward the door again. Maybe he'd stop and listen to this girl. See if she was any good. See if he could make any contacts for Stormy. He really wanted to get her singing somewhere more reputable.

"Here, take this. Good entertainment. Another fight," someone said, thrusting another flyer at him. Leo took it and glanced down to see if it was anyone he knew. Front and center on the page was a snarling dog. A black Rottweiler, sharp fangs. Bloody.

"Hey!" Leo tried to catch the guy who was handing out the flyers. "What is this?"

The guy looked at him. "If you're interested, text the number."

Leo looked down at the page. There was no time or location listed. Just a cell phone number. He wondered if he should go. Though it sickened him, he knew the underworld of illegal dog or cock fights existed. As an animal control officer, he handled the victims of these fights. Sometimes the victim, sometimes the victor, but always bloody, starved, hopeless creatures. They were driven crazy by their treatment, starved and beaten and only released to fight another animal to the death. It was a horrific scene.

Leo felt the lion inside his breast rise at the thought of the way the dogs were victimized.

Helpless creatures.

Creatures who wanted nothing more than to serve their masters, twisted and tortured into becoming killing machines. Disposable, never lasting for more than a few fights. There would be a new king for a while, a dog that managed to stay on the top for a few fights, and then he would be swallowed up by the machine, spit out, left on the road for Leo or his coworkers to find.

Leo pulled out his phone and texted the number indicated in the flyer. A time and place were returned within a few seconds. It must have been an auto responder.

Leo looked at the address, wondering what to do. He wandered out of the arena and into the street, following the stream of the crowd, not really deciding where to go, but just wandering with the bulk of them.

He could go see the singer and try to make a contact for Stormy. He could go to the dog fight and try to find a way to break up the dog-fighting ring.

Try to help his little sister out of her downward spiral or try to save helpless animals from certain death. What a choice. Would he be able to do anything about the fighting ring even if he tried?

Leo stepped off to the side, letting the crowd flow past him. He looked around quickly for the man who had been handing out flyers for the dog fight, but didn't see him.

He took a few steps down a quiet side street and turning his back on the crowd and leaning against the wall of an old brick building, he dialed the police.

It wasn't an emergency, really, so he wasn't sure about dialing the emergency number, but he never could remember the non-emergency number and they usually just shunted him back to the emergency queue anyway.

"Police, ambulance, or fire?" the chirpy voice of the emergency dispatcher inquired.

"Police," Leo told them.

"Police service, what's your emergency?" another dispatcher asked, sounding flat and bored.

"I—um—I got some information on an illegal dog fight," Leo explained.

"Illegal dog fight? Is this fight going on right now? Are you at it at the moment?" she queried.

"No. It's in an hour. I'm not there, but I've got an address."

"Where did you get this information?"

"A flyer at a boxing match."

"Is this a reliable source?"

"I don't know," Leo replied testily. "I've never gone to one of these fights."

"Give me the address listed and we'll see if we have a unit that can go over and take a look."

"Great, thanks," Leo approved. He read the address out to her.

She verified it back in a monotone. "Thank you for calling, sir," she told him and disconnected.

Leo stood there for a moment just holding the phone, unsure what to do now. Should he go to the fight location, see what was going on, see if the police managed to bust them? He would hear about it the next day at work, anyway…

Leo decided he'd better leave it alone. He didn't want to show up at the fight and manage to get arrested himself. Or make the police or the dog-fighting ring suspicious of him. Best to just stay away and let the police department pursue it.

Leo looked at the other flyer instead, the one with the singer on it. The club wasn't far away. He might as well take a look before turning in for the night.

The night was nice, cool but not cold. Refreshing. When he got there, there was no lineup at the door or bouncer taking names. Just a friendly little independent club. He entered and looked around.

The stage was small. There were no dancing girls. No strippers. That was good news. Not a huge audience, though. It looked like maybe they did karaoke or poetry readings other days of the week. Maybe a little comedy or improv. It wasn't really a nightclub, nor was it a theatre. Something in between, sort of an artsy, community type place.

Leo found a table and sat down. The waitress brought him a Diet Coke when he ordered it, with no commentary or flirting. Leo saw some of the other fight patrons talking to each other and finding seats, all clutching the light-blue flyer in their hands as they took in the view. The wait staff seemed to be used to this. They were neither annoyed nor rushing to serve everyone. Everything in its own due course.

It was only a few minutes before the girl came on. It looked like she was performing about every half hour, with a few other numbers in between, or just some background music playing that wasn't a radio station, while people talked and visited.

She was very nice looking and had a low, throaty voice. Leo enjoyed listening to her. His eyes scanned the room as he tried to figure out if she had an agent or manager there. Someone taking care of her, watching to see how she performed and how she was treated. No one stood out. She sang two numbers, was applauded noisily, and retreated backstage once more.

"Who is she?" Leo asked someone at the next table. "Have you heard of her before?"

"He has sung here before," the neighbor acknowledged.

Leo's confusion must have shown.

The man nodded. "Yeah, she's a he," he confirmed.

"Oh," Leo felt himself flushing red. He looked back down at the flyer, looking for clues. The singer's name was Stevie. Sure, it was a male name, but there were plenty of Stephanies that used it.

The name of the bar was The Closet, and now that Leo realized the singer was a transvestite, he suddenly understood the double entendre.

"Oh, I didn't know," he said weakly.

The man laughed. "Don't worry about it. Only half of the people who come here the first time do. But that's sort of the point. All genders and orientations welcome, just come and hang out in a friendly atmosphere. Doesn't matter if you're straight or queer or something else. It's about the art, not anything else."

Leo gulped the rest of his Coke as quickly as he could. He wanted out of there, and fast.

"Don't leave," his neighbor told him. "Stay a while. Check out the other acts. Maybe you'll see something you like."

"I liked her—him," Leo said. "I mean… not *that* way, but you know, as an artist he was good. But I… I have somewhere to go."

"There's nothing to be scared of. You don't need to run away," the man said with a chuckle.

Leo wasn't the only one who was running. Several of the other boxing patrons, their blue flyers in their hands or on the table, were getting up abruptly and heading for the door.

One man was shouting and making a scene on the other side of the room and bouncers were moving in to eject him before a fight started.

Leo tried not to look like he was running. He had no intention of offending anyone. But he wanted to get out of there before someone saw him and thought him part of the scene.

"Leo?"

Too late. Leo's heart dropped into his stomach. He looked around to see who had spotted him. Maybe one of the other fight patrons who had been caught by the clever marketing ploy and was leaving. They would share a laugh, and promise never to speak of it again.

It was a man behind the bar. Younger than Leo, with a bald, shaved head, a couple of big black earrings stretching out his earlobes, and tattoos on his neck and arms. It took Leo an instant to recognize his younger brother.

"Phil?" he asked in disbelief.

"What are you doing here, man?" Phil demanded, coming out from behind the bar, wiping his hands on a towel. "Good to see you!"

Leo was too slow to avoid the vigorous hug Phil bestowed upon him.

Just his luck. Not only was he being seen by other boxers or fans in a gay bar, or whatever you called this sort of place, but he was hugging another man. A very strange-looking man.

Leo gave Phil a quick hug-with-a-back-slap and pulled out of the embrace.

"How's it going, Phil?" Leo asked. He hadn't seen Phil in months. As close as the family had been when they were all living under one roof, trying to protect each other from the monster, none of them really stayed in contact any more. They were embarrassed by their past. They didn't want to talk about what had happened over the years. The injuries they had suffered, humiliations they had undergone, or why they had put up with it for so long.

"I'm really good, man," Phil said, smiling cheerfully. "Really good place to work, this. What do you think?"

"Umm—great. I came to hear Stevie. Didn't realize he was a… he. Got caught by your marketing, I guess."

Phil giggled. He threw his bar towel over his shoulder, and Leo saw, for a moment, Phil's long claw, before Phil tucked it behind his back, without even looking like he thought of it now, the movement was so automatic. Leo's eyes followed it.

"Oh," Phil said, and he pulled his hand out from behind his back, looking at it. "Yeah. I guess you've seen this before."

Phil was missing all but the thumb and forefinger of his left hand. He took it in stride, as they all did, just dealing with what he couldn't change. He'd told Leo once how grateful he was Lyall had left him with a thumb and index finger, so he could still manage everyday tasks. Not stuck without opposable thumbs. He was also missing the index finger on the other hand but used his middle finger to compensate for it. Leo displayed his own mangled hand, embarrassed but trying to share a moment of brotherhood and solidarity, with Phil.

"I'm sorry, I gotta go," he said. "Why don't you give me a call? We should get together for coffee sometime."

"Sure." Phil nodded, but Leo could see no intention to follow through in his eyes.

"Hey," Leo said, before turning and leaving, a thought striking him. "Do you ever have straight people in here singing?"

"Sure. Open to all genders and orientations. We don't discriminate. You want to come do a show?" Phil giggled to himself.

Leo felt himself flush red.

He took a deep breath, trying to force the animal in his breast to remain quiet and ignore the teasing. "No, not me. I wondered about Stormy. You know, she's trying to catch a break. Maybe she could sing here sometime."

Phil raised an eyebrow. "Sure, I could tell her about it. You got her number?"

Leo hated having to remain a minute longer, but this was what he had come for. To try to make a contact for Stormy. And it ended up being their own brother! He waited for Phil to get out his phone and key in Stormy's name, then gave him the number.

"Thanks, Leo," Phil said. "It was good to see ya again."

"Yeah. Good to see you… take care, okay?"

"Always do," Phil agreed.

Leo gave a small wave and walked out of the club.

Seeing Phil out of the blue made Leo dream about his brothers. Little things from the past he didn't even remember when conscious came back to him when sleeping.

Leo glanced at the clock and listened for his father in the living room. The TV was still going, but Leo hadn't heard him shout at the TV or get up for another beer for a while. He might be asleep now.

Leo sat up on the bed. He looked at the other two beds, at Phil and Lewis, for any movement or sign they were awake. Neither one stirred. Little Phil, dirty blonde hair cropped short, was curled in a tight ball with his thumb in his mouth.

Leo got silently to his feet and padded into the living room.

He stopped in the doorway, peeking around the corner, and watched for any movement.

Not a flicker.

"You awake, Dad?" he whispered.

Still nothing.

Leo tiptoed further into the room.

The TV flickered, throwing weird shapes and shadows on the walls. Leo bent around his father and looked him in the face. Eyes shut, mouth wide-open, face slack.

Definitely asleep now. And pretty far gone.

Leo watched him sleep for a few minutes, alert to any sound, any twitch that might indicate he was still too close to the surface and might reawaken.

No sign.

The house was quiet. There wasn't anything going on that might wake Lyall back up again.

Leo tried to control his breathing, which seemed to be rasping much more loudly than usual in the darkened room.

Leo assessed the position Lyall was sitting in. He tugged on the corner of Lyall's coat slightly. It was a blue-jean jacket, lined with fleece, nice and warm when he was doing work in the garage, and since the house wasn't much warmer at this point in the winter, he had kept it on when he came in from the garage to have his supper and unwind.

Leo checked the pocket.

Keys. No wallet.

He moved silently to the other side of the chair, and tugged out the other corner of the coat. Lyall groaned and shifted.

Leo froze, and waited.

One minute. Two.

Lyall didn't appear to be waking up. Leo took a couple of deep breaths and again tugged at the corner of the coat. He managed to free the pocket from between the chair and Lyall's body.

He stopped and looked at Lyall's face dimly lit by the TV. With another deep, controlled breath, he worked his fingers into the pocket and pulled out Lyall's wallet.

Thankfully, Lyall didn't trust banks, credit cards, and ATMs. That meant the wallet was full of cash, not plastic. Leo slid the money through his fingers, considering how much they would need. Feeding six children was not cheap. Lyall was stingy with the money and rarely gave Leo enough to feed them from one pay check to the next. They relied on the school lunch program and supplemented it in whatever way they could.

This time, that meant helping himself to the money in Lyall's wallet. It was the only way. The cupboards and fridge were practically empty, and Leo couldn't prepare a meal to keep Lyall happy and the kids' tummy's filled if there was no food to start with.

He slid a few worn bills from the wallet and tucked them into the pants of his sweat suit.

Then he closed the wallet and worked it back into the coat pocket, stopping again when Lyall shifted and scratched his chin.

Leo waited for Lyall to stop moving and waited for his breathing to regulate and get deeper again before finally pushing the wallet the rest of the way into the coat pocket and fleeing the scene of the crime.

He ducked into his room and stood just inside the door, breathing heavily, shaking all over.

If Lyall ever caught him stealing money from him…! Or if he even suspected Leo or one of the other kids was taking his money… Leo could only imagine the hell that would break loose.

Leo crept back to his bed and started to climb in.

"You okay?" Lewis asked.

Leo whipped around and looked at him. Lewis was propped on his elbow, watching him.

"Sheesh, Lewie. You scared the crap out of me."

"You're crazy, you know that?" Lewis said. "What if he woke up and caught you?"

Of course Lewis knew what Leo had been up to. Lewis always knew what was going on. That crippled body did not hold his brain back one bit.

Leo breathed out a puff of breath, trying to calm his heart down again.

"We gotta eat," he said reasonably. "Especially the little ones."

"Can't you just ask him for more? Sneaking around and stealing it! He would seriously kill you, bro."

"I know. And you know how many times I ask for more money. He just thinks I'm going to buy drugs or spend it on junk food. He thinks I just waste it; that I don't know how to shop."

"Show him the bills—"

"Show him the bills?" Leo repeated. "Are you listening to yourself? Who's the crazy one now? He can't read the bills."

Lewis was still, looking at him. "What do you mean, he can't read the bills?"

Leo frowned, looking at Lewis incredulously. "He can't read," he repeated.

"Sure he can."

Leo shook his head. He sat on the edge of his bed, pulling the blanket around his shivering legs. "Lewis... he can't read."

"Since when? Of course he can read. He reads his orders and maps for work, gets magazines on fixing up cars, pays the bills..."

Leo chuckled. "You mean I actually know something you don't?" he asked. "You're always teasing me for not knowing about stuff."

"You're just talking crazy. He reads all kinds of stuff."

Leo laid down on the bed. He put his hand into his pocket to make sure the money was still there, neatly folded, snug in the bottom of his pocket where it wouldn't fall out.

"You just watch him," Leo said. "He doesn't read the mechanic magazines. He looks at the pictures and diagrams. And he pays the bills to the teller at the bank."

"How would he do his job without being able to read?" Lewis demanded.

"I don't know. I haven't watched him at work. But he figures it out somehow."

Leo rolled over and closed his eyes to go to sleep.

CHAPTER FOURTEEN

LEO WAS RUNNING NEAR Elizabeth's apartment, so he stopped to see if she was around. She buzzed him up without saying anything. Leo didn't know if the intercom wasn't working and she didn't know who it was, or if she had answered and he hadn't heard her response. He went up to her apartment, but she hadn't opened her door. Leo hesitated for a moment before knocking.

She opened the door to let him in. Only it wasn't her. It was a young man with his hoodie pulled over his face, blond shaggy bangs shading his eyes as well. He grunted at first and didn't say anything.

Leo looked around for Elizabeth. Juleen was screaming in the other room, and Leo assumed Elizabeth was in with her, trying to put her down for a nap, or to settle her down.

"Hey. I'm Leo," he greeted his alternate host.

"Hey," the boy answered laconically.

"Umm… you're a friend of Elizabeth's?"

"Eli," he said curtly and offered Leo a fist bump by way of a handshake. Leo was puzzled but accepted this introduction. He sat down, turning his head and looking for Elizabeth to come back in.

"Juleen's having trouble today?" he asked.

"Stupid brat's always having trouble," Eli said gruffly. Leo was angered by the words and the attitude. He clenched his fists and bit his lip.

Who did this guy think he was? Hanging around like he owned the place, being rude about Juleen?

Elizabeth had never even mentioned him, and Leo couldn't place what position he might hold here. Brother? Boyfriend? Another soldier? He didn't seem old enough or strong enough to be a soldier, but if he was, he could even be Juleen's dad. Elizabeth had been pretty unclear about the details and had never mentioned any boyfriends.

"You been here for long?" Leo asked, pretending he knew who Eli was. 'Here' could have been the country, the city, or just Elizabeth's apartment. Eli could interpret it as he pleased.

"No. Not long," Eli said, giving nothing away.

Leo couldn't think of what else to say, how to bring Eli out and find out more about him. Eli was reticent about giving anything away, his answers curt and gruff. Dismissive.

Leo wished Elizabeth would finish up with Juleen or bring her out. He didn't want to be stuck with Mr. Communicative.

Deciding to ignore Eli, Leo pulled out his phone and checked his messages, e-mails, and texts. Nothing exciting.

There never was. Leo really didn't embrace technology.

He turned on something called Jewel Quest Stormy had insisted on downloading for him. He fiddled with it, popping jewels and trying to figure out what the object of the game was.

Eli sat there watching him though Leo couldn't see his face clearly under the hoodie. This went on for some time, and then Leo just couldn't stand it anymore.

Breathing heavily, the beast inside him pacing restlessly, just looking for a reason to attack, Leo got abruptly to his feet. Without a word to Eli, he went to find Elizabeth.

Obviously she needed some help with Juleen. She wouldn't be upset if he went looking for her.

Leo walked down the hall and knocked lightly on Juleen's door, then went in.

The room was dark and cold.

Leo felt a chill.

He turned the light on and looked around. The room was empty. Juleen was there in the crib, but no Elizabeth.

Juleen's cries hitched slightly and she looked through the bars, eyes squinting in the bright light, to see who was there. Leo went over and picked her up.

She was soaking wet.

Her skin was chilly. She wasn't dressed warmly enough for the cool room and had no blankets.

Leo held her against him for a minute until she started to calm down.

"Why don't we get you changed, huh Juleen?" Leo whispered. He put her down on the carpet beside packages of diapers and wipes and changed her into a dry diaper. He tossed the wet diaper in the pail and looked through the little shopping bags full of baby clothes until he found a sleeper with long sleeves.

After dressing Juleen, Leo held her close, speaking softly to her and calming her down. Juleen was calmer, but still crying. She squirmed against Leo, rooting for milk.

He kissed her forehead. "It's okay, baby. We'll find out what's going on here and get you taken care of, okay? I'll get you something to eat, and we'll find your mommy and get you taken care of."

Cuddling her close, he went back out to the front room where Eli was sitting, now with the TV on and his feet up on the coffee table.

"Where's Elizabeth?" Leo demanded.

"I'm Eli," the boy said, not looking up from the TV.

"Duh. You already told me. I want to know where Elizabeth is. Did she go out somewhere? Are you supposed to be babysitting Juleen?"

"I don't *do* babies."

"Oh, you don't do babies. So you'd rather just sit here, listening to her screaming in the other room than to help?"

Eli nodded, not looking up.

Leo struggled to keep the cat from emerging. "Where the hell is Elizabeth?" he shouted.

The boy turned toward him—bangs and hood still obscuring his face. "Elizabeth isn't here," he said. "Sometimes she needs a break, you know?"

It was Eli's longest answer yet. Something about it rang alarm bells for Leo.

What was going on? There was something about Eli's voice and way of speaking that didn't seem right.

His speech was similar to Elizabeth's and he wondered if they were related somehow. A half-brother or a cousin.

"Who are you? Are you her family?"

"We don't have any family."

"We?" Leo repeated. "So you are related to her."

Eli turned back toward the TV, face away from Leo, to avoid being trapped by Leo's logic.

"She's not here," he repeated. "I'm Eli."

Leo blew out his breath in exasperation. He went to the kitchenette and opened the fridge, hoping for some bottles of milk for Juleen. It was nearly empty. No milk.

He checked the freezer in case Elizabeth was freezing a supply of breast milk.

No such luck.

He searched all the cupboards for formula, and still, no luck. He couldn't find anything.

Leo cast his eyes around. He hadn't seen anything in the nursery, either. There were barely any baby supplies, and no formula for supplementing.

Leo didn't know how long Elizabeth had been gone, or how long she was going to be, but he figured he'd better do something.

"Do you know when Elizabeth is coming back?" he questioned the mercurial Eli.

"Maybe never," Eli snapped.

"And you don't know where she went? Or how to reach her?"

Eli didn't look at him, didn't answer him. Finally losing control, Leo grabbed him by the arm, pulling him around. In a fury, he grabbed the back of the hood and pulled it off to reveal the stranger's face.

At first, he just stared, stopped in his tracks, trying to process what he was seeing.

Eli was Elizabeth's twin.

His face was hard, his natural expression different from Elizabeth's. The hair was styled differently, maybe a slightly different color.

He wore boy clothes, but after his experience at The Closet, Leo wasn't going to be fooled by clothing.

Studying Eli, he looked for some sign of recognition.

"Elizabeth?"

"I told you, I'm Eli. Elizabeth isn't here," the boy said harshly, his voice low and angry.

Leo stared at him. Or her. There was definitely a figure hidden under that baggy hoodie. Eli pulled the hood back up around his head.

"You *are* Elizabeth," Leo insisted.

"No."

"Elizabeth. Come on. Quit messing around. Juleen needs to be fed. You're breastfeeding; you can't just pretend and ignore her needs."

"I'm Eli."

There was no hint of humor. No sign that she was teasing or understood he was onto her. Leo went cold.

"Oh, man. What's your doctor's phone number? Are you off your meds?"

"I don't need a doctor. I don't take any meds."

"Your doctor. Marvin. What's his number?"

"I don't know. I don't know who that is. I don't have any doctor."

"Elizabeth's doctor," Leo insisted.

"I don't keep track of her phone numbers."

Leo shook his head in frustration. He wanted to pound her until she listened. How could she be so stubborn? Her baby was suffering!

"Come *on!*"

It was obvious Eli wasn't going to back down. Having a baby in his arms prevented Leo from acting on his anger, but the cat continued to rage inside him.

Leo pulled out his phone and dialed for information. "I need a Doctor Marvin. Psychologist or psychiatrist."

The operator gave him a number and said she was connecting him.

Leo waited for an answer, tapping his foot and jiggling the crying baby.

Eventually, a nurse or receptionist picked up. "Dr. Marvin's office."

"I've kind of got an emergency here, with one of Doctor Marvin's patients."

"What's the patient's name?"

"Elizabeth Peterson. Um, or maybe Lisa on your records."

"One moment, please. Okay. What seems to be the problem?"

"Can I talk to the doctor? I really don't want to have to explain this twice. It's urgent. I don't know whether I should call the police, or ambulance, or what I should do!"

There was silence. Leo assumed the nurse was browsing through Elizabeth's record to decide how important it was.

"I'm going to have to put you on hold for a minute. Is that okay? Are you in any danger?"

"Yeah, I'm okay. I just need to talk to him."

Leo heard music begin to play. The notes grated on his last nerve.

Elizabeth continued to watch TV, ignoring Leo. Leo didn't understand how she could continue to play this game.

Continue to act as though she was someone else.

She could hear her baby crying. She knew Juleen needed her, and there was no other milk in the apartment for her.

But she just continued to pretend to be Eli, completely unattached and uncaring.

The minutes ticked by. Leo knew it seemed longer than it really was, but he was on pins and needles, wondering how long it was going to take to explain it to Dr. Marvin, or if he should just hang up and dial the police or the ambulance or Child Services instead.

There was a click, and then Dr. Marvin's voice. "Hello, how can I help you?"

"Umm, Dr. Marvin. My name is Leo. I came in with Elizabeth—Lisa—before."

"Yes, I remember you, Leo. What's wrong?"

"Something is weird with Elizabeth. She won't take care of Juleen. She says she's Eli, not Elizabeth, and she just… won't do anything. I don't know what's going on, or what I should do."

Dr. Marvin swore. "Is Juleen okay?" he asked.

"She's hungry and there's no formula. Elizabeth won't feed her. She was wet and cold, but I changed her. What should I do?"

"I'm going to send police and an ambulance for Lisa. She may get violent when the ambulance shows up, but if we're lucky, she'll just agree to go along with them. If not, we'll need the police there to take her into custody and then turn her over to the paramedics, so they can take her to the hospital to be treated."

"She said she doesn't take any meds. I guess that means she's off of them."

"I would guess she hasn't taken them for a day or two, anyway. How long since you saw her last?"

"Just yesterday or the day before."

"How was she?"

Leo thought back. "Anxious. Upset about Juleen being so colicky. We went for a walk and a picnic, that seemed to calm her down. I didn't know…"

"No, I wouldn't expect you to understand what's going on with Lisa. I wouldn't expect anyone to understand. She's a whole new unexplored country all by herself. I don't understand her and I'm supposed to be the expert in these matters."

"Is she… I guess you can't really talk about her case to me, but is she one of those people, like on TV? She has a split personality, or whatever?"

The doctor didn't answer directly. "I'm sure you've seen her behave very differently under different circumstances. This time is more obvious, more startling than the rest. But you can see she can be a very different person from one day to the next."

Leo shook his head. He was watching Eli, but the boy seemed unaware Leo was talking about him and watching him.

Leo had a hard time even thinking of this person as a girl, let alone as Elizabeth. Eli's behavior was completely foreign to him.

"When we went to the park, she said I should call her Lu," Leo said.

"Lu? Let me just write that one down. And today she's…"

"Eli."

"Oh, yes. I've met Eli before. Well, thanks for calling, Leo. I'd like you to stick around until the police get things under control, but don't confront her. Confrontation will not help in this situation."

"Okay. What do I do about Juleen?"

"The police can bring Child Services into it. But it may take a social worker some time to get there."

"Should I go out and get some formula to feed her? She seems really hungry. I don't know when was the last time she ate."

"Is there a store close by? You can't be running around town with her. The police and Child Services will need to know where she is and take custody as soon as they are able."

"There's a convenience store just at the corner. I bet they have some kind of formula," Leo suggested.

"Okay. Well, why don't you check it out? Is Lisa—Eli—calm and going to stay put if you leave?"

"I think so. He's—she's—just watching TV. I think if he doesn't know they're on their way or anything…"

"Right. Well, go ahead and try. I'll get the authorities there as quickly as possible."

"Okay," Leo agreed. "Thanks."

He hung up his phone and looked at Eli.

"You mind if I take Juleen away for a little while," Leo asked. "See if I can get her to stop crying?"

Eli didn't look in his direction. "Be my guest."

"Will you buzz me back in when I get back?"

"Sure."

Leo left, down the hall, down the elevator, and down the street to the convenience store. He passed Lady Housecoat pacing down on the street.

She stopped and looked at him shrewdly. "What are you doing with Elizabeth's baby?"

"Getting her some formula," Leo told her.

"Well, it better quiet her down, I keep getting complaints from the neighbors about her crying."

"Some babies just cry a lot," Leo placated. "People have to know that."

"Doesn't stop them from complaining."

"No, I guess not. Sorry, but I'm in kind of a hurry," Leo told her and continued on his way to the corner store. Rather than looking around once he got there, he just asked the girl behind the desk:

"Baby formula?"

"Aisle three, at the far end."

"Thanks."

Leo darted down the aisle and looked at the shelf. There were several different kinds of formula.

How was he supposed to know which one was best for Juleen? She'd only been breast fed until now.

Except when Elizabeth had been in hospital. Juleen must have been formula-fed during that time.

At least she should be accustomed to a bottle.

A bottle. Leo realized he was going to need one of those too. He looked around in a panic. He didn't want to have to go to the department store to look for bottles. But there were a few brightly-colored bottles on the shelf above the formula.

Leo took a bottle of formula off the shelf that said 'no mixing, ready to drink' on one side with a 'DHA for brain health' banner on it.

No mixing and ready to drink sounded good.

It had a screw-off top, so he didn't need a can opener to use it. He picked up a bottle and the formula and took them to the counter to pay.

The cashier looked at the purchases and looked at Juleen, sobbing in his arms.

"Is this your baby?" she asked suspiciously.

"No, my friend is sick and suddenly can't nurse her. So the poor thing's starving."

"Oh," she looked properly chastened. "I'm sorry. Well, let's get her something as soon as we can."

She rung the purchases up and Leo paid for them. As he finished punching his number into the PIN pad, he realized the cashier was disassembling the bottle, taking off the lid and the cardboard label.

Leo unscrewed the cap from the formula, hearing it pop as the vacuum released.

The cashier handed him the bottle and Leo filled it. He screwed the nipple back onto the bottle and put it to Juleen's mouth. She took the nipple without hesitation and started to suck. Leo breathed a sigh of relief.

The cashier screwed the top back on the formula, which Leo had only used half of. She handed him his receipts.

"That's better," she said with a smile.

"Yeah. Poor thing. Thanks for your help."

She nodded. Leo went back down the street to the apartment. Elizabeth/Eli did not buzz him in when he rang the apartment.

Leo swore and started hitting all the buttons on the board, ignoring the various annoyed squawks and queries. One of them buzzed the door, so he let himself in.

He'd had the foresight to leave the apartment door unlocked when he left, so he simply walked back into the apartment.

To his relief, Eli was still there, not having moved in the time Leo was gone. Leo glanced at the clock. He had been under five minutes.

In a few more minutes, there were sirens outside and Leo went over to the window and watched the ambulance and police car both pull up. The police and paramedics consulted with each other and then headed into the building. As soon as they buzzed, Leo hit the door release. He opened the apartment door and stepped into the hallway to await them.

"Are you Leo?" one of the police officers asked, approaching him.

Leo nodded. "Yeah. She's in there. She might not cooperate."

"Why don't you just stay out here for a moment, out of the way, and we'll see how it goes over," the cop advised.

Leo nodded.

"Okay."

The police entered the apartment, followed by the paramedics. Leo waited. There were angry shouts of protest, the repeated refrain of 'My name is Eli!' But in a few minutes, the paramedics came out with her. She wasn't in handcuffs and appeared to be going voluntarily. But she gave Leo a venomous look. One of the officers went with the paramedics and one stayed behind.

"Baby looks okay," the cop said, looking down at Juleen.

"Yeah. Just hungry right now, I think."

"It doesn't look like mom's in any shape to take care of her. Good thing you called."

"Yeah. Poor thing. She was just crying and crying. Elizabeth wasn't doing anything about it. Wouldn't even nurse her."

"Child Services will be here in a few minutes. They'll find someone to take care of her until mom is back on her feet."

"I don't know if they should give her back too soon…"

"No, probably not. But we'll just have to leave that to Child Services' judgment."

Leo shrugged his shoulders. He thought back to Elizabeth talking about her experiences with foster homes, and how the social workers had always failed Leo and his family, and he wasn't comforted. He wanted so much for Juleen to just be okay.

"Can I stay until they get here?"

"Yeah, of course," the cop agreed, looking surprised. "I'm not just going to snatch her out of your arms. You make yourself comfortable and wait until they get here."

Leo nodded gratefully. "Thanks."

He went back into the apartment and sat down on the easy chair, cuddling Juleen close.

"Yeah, that's better now, huh?" he said quietly. "You feel better now that you've got something in your tummy. All warm and dry and safe now."

Her face was relaxed now that she had been fed and taken care of. Her eyes were getting heavy, and the redness was fading from her face. Leo stroked her cheek.

"There, there. Go to sleep," he encouraged.

Before Child Services got there, Dr. Marvin showed up. He walked into the apartment and looked around. "Leo? Good to see you again."

"Oh, Dr. Marvin. Hi. I didn't know you were going to come."

"I didn't figure I'd be able to get here before the ambulance, but I thought I'd stop by, just to see how things went."

"They've been gone for a while."

"Did she go quietly?"

Leo nodded. "Pretty good, yeah. She wasn't happy about it. There was a lot of yelling, but they didn't have to sedate her, or put her in handcuffs or anything."

"Well, that's a blessing, anyway. Poor girl. And how's the little one?" he looked down at Juleen in Leo's arms and sat down across from him.

"Sleeping now," Leo stated the obvious. "She settled down after she'd eaten."

"Good. They'll put her somewhere safe until Elizabeth is stabilized again."

Leo was silent for a while, just rocking Juleen, then he brought up something that had been niggling at the back of his mind. "Do you do, you know, normal cases too? Or just ones like Elizabeth?"

Dr. Marvin chuckled at this. "Sure, I do some counseling with run-of-the-mill cases too. If everyone was as high needs as Lisa…"

"I guess that would be pretty tough to keep up with," Leo admitted.

"Yes. Not to mention, cases like Elizabeth's are pretty rare. You can't rely on them as your bread and butter. And the fees… they have to be paid by subsidy programs because… well, they aren't often able to hold down a job."

"So Elizabeth going into the army and serving overseas, that doesn't usually happen?"

Dr. Marvin shook his head. "No. I'm not sure how she managed to pass the army psych exam. Obviously, they never even pulled up her history."

"Yeah. I didn't think of that. I guess she can put on a pretty… normal… front sometimes? Make it seem like everything is okay?"

Dr. Marvin pursed his lips at this. "Well, you know I can't discuss a patient's personal history with you," he said, despite what he had already said. "But some patients are very good at putting on a normal front for long periods of time. Under the right circumstances and in the right environment, they can function for a year or two at a time without revealing any cracks in the facade. And then… there is a crisis and it all comes tumbling down."

"Like getting pregnant."

"Like getting pregnant. Being exposed to horrific violence. Being assaulted. Being under a great deal of stress. And anything, even things that might seem small to you or me, might trigger PTSD and flashbacks."

Leo nodded. "PTSD… that's what soldiers get, right?"

"Post-Traumatic Stress Disorder. Soldiers get it. Children with histories of abuse. Disaster survivors. A lot more people than you might think. And it can be disabling."

Leo nodded. "Yeah. I know some people… but they still manage to function okay."

"It can take years to come to a head… and years to recover. And with some people," he nodded to Elizabeth's front door. "We never know all that they have gone through. All the layers of trauma and abuse that have to be peeled back. But… I imagine you're not asking me this for your own entertainment. Are you looking for a therapist?"

Leo nodded awkwardly. "Well, maybe. I have… well… a bunch of problems I guess. I've had psychiatrists and stuff before, but I never really wanted any help. Now I'm thinking… maybe I should. Maybe it's time."

"Good for you. What all might be wrapped up in this 'bunch of problems,' do you think?"

"Well, they've said ADHD, bipolar, anxiety… I have learning disabilities and all…"

"And how much of this do you think is inherited? Tell me about your family history."

Leo squirmed.

"Yeah. Well… my mom… she disappeared when I was twelve. Left us kids. There were six of us. I was the oldest. Before that, she had been in and out of hospital and institutions since... I was seven, I guess. She wasn't in there all the time. Just..." Leo shrugged, "maybe once or twice a year, for a week or two."

"Yes, it certainly sounds like she had some problems. Do you have any idea what her diagnosis—or diagnoses—were? I realize you were pretty young at the time."

"I really don't know," Leo said, scratching the back of his head, trying to think of whether Margaret or Lyall had ever said what exactly it was that was wrong with her. But he didn't think so. Just that she wasn't feeling well, or was having problems again. "I don't think they ever told us."

"What about your dad? Is he still around? Could you ask him what she had?"

"No. He's... he's in a coma in the hospital. He was in an accident."

"Oh, I'm sorry to hear that. This must be a very difficult time for you. What about medical papers? Would there be files at his house that might say something? Would you have access?"

"No, he never liked having papers around."

Older now, Leo understood why Lyall had been so threatened by the written word. He couldn't read, so it was like being surrounded by a secret code... anyone could write anything about you, and you wouldn't know what it said. It could be used against you in some way, as a weapon.

And he was jealous all of them could read and he couldn't. Even Leo, with his dyslexia, could read enough to get by.

Lyall had been completely in the dark.

Until last year.

"I don't think we ever kept anything."

"Well then, maybe you could tell me about how your mother's problems manifest. Did she stay in bed all day?"

"No... not unless she had to... She would lose it... she would get upset and do stupid things... she would get confused really easily, and think things were real... when they weren't."

"Do you think she was schizophrenic?"

Leo shrugged. "I dunno. She could be."

"And what about your dad?"

"What?"

"How was his mental health? Did he have learning disabilities like you? ADHD? How were his mood and behavior? Normal?"

Leo pondered on the questions and thought through his answer.

Even with how open he was with Elizabeth about his history of abuse, he didn't feel comfortable revealing it to Dr. Marvin. He was an authority, and authority figures were always dangerous. Professionals and authorities had never helped them. They were always causing trouble rather than helping.

Leo had learned to keep it all quiet.

"Well... he just learned to read last year. So I guess he has learning disabilities like me. He never finished school. Dropped out and became a truck driver and a bit of a mechanic."

"Sounds like he did. What else?"

"He was an alcoholic. He had... moods."

"Depression?" Dr. Marvin asked.

"No... irritable. Angry."

"And one of your diagnoses is bipolar?"

Leo nodded. "Yeah. I don't know if I am, though. I don't get... you know, depressed, want to stay in bed all day..."

"How about the opposite? Antsy and unable to sleep, starting off on fabulous new projects, doing things you know you shouldn't, like going on shopping sprees when you don't have any money?"

"No. Not really."

"Do you take any meds for bipolar?"

"No. Went through some, but... the side effects were too bad. They never worked."

"So what is it you see yourself as needing help with? I can prescribe meds for ADHD, but if you've already tried that route, there's not much I can do for ADHD using cognitive therapy."

"I was wondering about... anger. I, um... have trouble controlling my temper, sometimes."

"Ah," Dr. Marvin nodded. "Yes, anger I can help you with."

"And..." Leo took a deep breath. "I just feel like my life is out of control all the time. It might overwhelm me. And I always have to help everyone else. I kind of ignore my own problems."

"A lot of us would rather take care of other people's problems than our own," Dr. Marvin chuckled. "How do you think someone ends up in my profession?" He waved a reassuring hand. "But I'm joking. Of course, it can be a problem if you let it take over your life and won't face your own problems. I can help you try to work through that."

Leo sighed, relieved to have gotten it out in the open. "Great," he said, "so I should set up an appointment with your office?"

"Yes, please do. I look forward to working with you."

CHAPTER FIFTEEN

TEN-YEAR-OLD LEO held Margaret's legs across his lap and very gently dabbed her chafed ankles with salve. In spite of his care, she still jerked and pulled away as he touched them.

"Sorry, Mom," Leo apologized, tears burning his eyes in his distress.

"It's okay, Leo. You're doing a good job. It just hurts."

"They're so scraped up!"

She just nodded. Leo moved down to her feet and rubbed them.

"Oh, that feels good."

Leo worked on them, trying to make her feel better. It wasn't fair that on top of her feet and ankles being swollen and sore from her pregnancy, she had to deal with the bite of the shackles and freezing floor of the basement dungeon as well.

Leo couldn't understand how Lyall could treat her that way. The woman who was carrying his baby. Who took care of his children. She cooked and cleaned and slaved for him and he treated her worse than an animal. Margaret rarely complained, even when Lyall was away on a trip and couldn't hear her. She just took it, like she thought she deserved it.

"Do you want me to make supper?" Leo offered. "I could make macaroni for you."

She closed her eyes while he continued to rub her swollen feet.

"Yes," she agreed. "Oh yes, that would be so nice. I should make salad and vegetables to go with it, but since your father's gone… maybe we'll just have macaroni."

Leo nodded.

"If you want, I could cut up carrots and celery too," he suggested, "then you can have vegetables."

"You're so thoughtful," Margaret said distantly. Her voice flat and expressionless as though simply reading lines.

Leo searched her face for some emotion, but her eyes were closed and her face was slack. He continued to rub her feet, frowning until she started to snore softly. Then he slipped her legs off his lap and onto the couch and covered her bare feet and legs with a blanket.

He went to the girl's bedroom and looked in the door. Michelle and Joyce had dressed Phil up like a girl and were having a quiet tea party with their dolls and teddy bears.

"Can we come out now?" Michelle demanded. "I want to see Mom."

Leo shook his head.

"She's sleeping now. Mom is sick, so you have to be quiet and let her sleep. Okay? You guys are doing great at keeping Phil quiet," Leo shook his head, chuckling over Phil's get-up. "Just play for a while longer, and I'll make some supper, okay?"

They nodded grudgingly. Phil hit a plate with a miniature spoon, crowing, and Michelle quickly grabbed his wrist.

"Shhh, Phil," she remonstrated. "You need to be quiet like a mouse. Hush so Mom can sleep."

He grabbed at the play tiara on Michelle's head, and she removed it and put it on his head. Phil primped and laughed happily.

<hr>

When the dinner was ready, Leo woke Margaret gently, shaking her arm.

"Mom. Mom, dinner's ready. Are you hungry?"

She opened her eyes and looked at him. She didn't smile or greet him, but when he encouraged her to get up, she walked woodenly to the table and sat down. Leo called to the others.

"Come on guys, dinner's on!"

The other children rushed into the room, the girls and Phil still dressed up for their tea party, though tiaras and earrings now hung askew. Lewis, quiet in his wheelchair, studied Margaret as seriously as one of his math problems.

Leo served Margaret, anxious for her to get some nourishment and to feel better.

"Mama!" Phil cheered, rushing up to give her a hug. Margaret accepted the hug limply, and after a moment patted Phil on the shoulder. Leo herded Phil back to his seat and motioned for Michelle to give him some macaroni.

"How are you feeling, Mom?" Lewis asked tentatively, his eyes moving over the stringy, tangled, dirty blond hair hanging limply around her face, the thin nightgown that did nothing to keep her warm, and the abrasions around her wrists where the manacles had worn the skin.

Margaret stirred the macaroni on her plate with a fork. "I'm feeling fine." She started to poke at the macaroni, looking for something hidden amidst the noodles. "Who made this?" she asked.

"I did, Mom," Leo volunteered. "Just the way you like it."

She laid down her fork and looked around the kitchen. It was dim but warm from the heat of the stove. Margaret's eyes darted back and forth quickly, agitated. Leo looked at Lewis, gulping.

"Have some food, Mom," he encouraged. "You must be hungry."

"It's poisoned," Margaret protested. "He poisoned it, didn't he?"

Leo shook his head. "Nobody poisoned it," he protested. "I made it myself. Nobody else touched it."

"Lyall. He was here."

"No. He left after he let you out. He wasn't around when I was cooking."

"He came back. And you let him poison it!"

"No! No, he hasn't been here. I wouldn't let him put anything in your food. I just made it from the box, like it says on the package. With a little bit of ketchup, the way you like it."

"He got in. Somehow he got back while you weren't looking and he poisoned it."

"No," Leo shook his head. "Why do you think it's poisoned? It's good! Look!"

Leo picked up her fork, and he took a big scoop of the macaroni and put it in his mouth. Margaret looked at him with wide-eyed horror. She shrieked and jumped to her feet, shoving the underside of the table to flip it on its side, all the dinner and dishes flying off. The three younger children started to cry. Leo saw Lewis' head snap back as the table was flipped. Margaret leapt back and took a couple of large steps back from the table.

"It's poisoned. It's all poisoned! You can't eat it! No one can eat it!"

Phil wailed in dismay and fear. The two girls, who had started to cry, stared at Margaret with their mouths open, tears still running down their cheeks, but voices silenced.

Leo stood there paralyzed, trying to figure out what to do next.

"Mom, it's not. It's okay. See, I'm okay."

"You just didn't get enough. Or it takes a while to work. He's trying to fool us, making it look okay. But it's poisoned."

"No," Leo protested faintly.

She withdrew, going to her bedroom, and opening and closing drawers.

Leo looked at the others. "You guys… have a bit, before she comes back out again," he whispered. "Just… eat something, okay?"

"It's poisoned," Michelle wailed in protest.

"It's not. Mom just thinks… she just thinks it is. But it isn't. Have something, before she comes back out."

Lewis nodded. He was pressing his hand to his forehead, trying to stem the flow of blood from an open gash where the table had hit him. "Yeah," he agreed. "Listen to Leo. Come on guys, get something in your bellies quick."

Leo nodded gratefully and left Lewis to deal with the children. He went to Margaret's and Lyall's bedroom, where Margaret was throwing clothes around. Some were ending up in the suitcase she had opened on her bed, but most of them were just ending up on the floor or around the room. She wrenched drawers out of the dresser, threw dresses from her closet onto the bed or suitcase, and raced wildly around the room.

"Mom, can I help you?" Leo offered. "What do you need me to do?"

"We have to get out of here. Get out while we still can. He might come back tonight. We can't take the chance."

"He won't be back tonight," Leo soothed. "It's a three day run, at least."

"That's what he wants you to think. He wants you to think you have all that time to get away! Away, lay, kay… It has to be tonight. We have to get away. Away, sway, lay…"

"It's okay, Mom. Calm down, okay? It will be all right. Really. Come and have something to eat. Take your pills. You'll feel better."

Margaret shook her head adamantly. She got a jacket from her closet and pulled it on over her nightgown.

"No. Whoa, whoa, whoa… no, it's all woe."

He gently helped her to straighten the jacket and zip it up.

"There, see? Nice and cozy," he said. "Why don't you lie down for a few minutes now?"

"No sleep. Can't sleep when you need to run. Come on. Pack everything up, lup, sup!"

Leo put a couple of things carefully into the open suitcase.

"Where are you going?" he asked. "Aunt Robin's? Aunt Robin said you could always go there if there was any trouble. Is that where you want to go?"

"So, no, go… Go to Robin's?" she shook her head. "No. No, he'll know to look there. We have to hide. Hide in the woods." She gestured to the window. "Hide like a bear."

"Mom… it's cold out… we can't hide in the woods," Leo protested. "Do you want to go into town? Maybe someone there could pick us up. We could find you some help. Try to get you fixed up, so you'd be safe."

"No, go, Leo! No, no, no."

Leo put a few things into the suitcase, trying to figure out what to do. "Where are we going in the woods?" he persisted. "Mom…"

She threw a few more pieces of clothing in the suitcase and zipped it closed. She headed out of the room and toward the door.

"Come on. Come on all of you," she ordered the other children.

Phil was still crying, his tiara gone, his face smeared with orange cheese. She snatched him up.

"Go, go, go," she ordered. "Have to be safe. We have to run. Come, come, come."

The other children looked at Leo for guidance. He shrugged widely. "Get your coats," he said helplessly. "Make sure you've got mittens, hats, lots of warm stuff."

"Where are we going, Leo?" Michelle demanded.

"I don't know… out there…"

"We don't have a car," Lewis protested.

"I know," Leo agreed, looking at Margaret and shaking his head. "I don't know what…"

"Come now," Margaret ordered, grabbing him tightly by the arm with an iron grip. Phil cried and squirmed in her grip on the other side, squashed between her body and arm as she gripped him against her, also holding the suitcase in her hand.

"Okay, okay, I'm coming, Mom, I just have to get my coat. And Phil needs a coat," Leo insisted. He tried to pull away from her, but she held on tightly. Leo twisted and pulled, trying to escape her grip. She was relentless.

"Give me Phil," Leo insisted, trying to pull Phil away from her. "I have to get him ready to go. He needs a coat. And… he needs to pee, don't you Phil?"

Phil just cried, shaking his head.

"Come on, Mom," pleaded Leo. "Please."

She let Phil go, then released her grip on Leo. "Everybody get ready," she insisted. "Before he comes back."

They all busied themselves with getting on their heavy winter coats and gear. They avoided looking at each other, not acknowledging how frightened they were. Phil made Leo take him to the bathroom like he had suggested. By the time they got out of the bathroom, Margaret was dragging the two girls out the front door. Phil ran after his mother, calling out to her. Leo looked at Lewis, wheeling himself determinedly toward the door.

"She said we're going in the woods, Lew," he said.

Lewis nodded.

"You can't get through there in your chair," Leo pointed out. "Do you want… should we leave you here or do you want…?"

"I'm coming," Lewis said.

Leo looked at Margaret and the children rapidly heading across the yard. "I'll piggyback you," he suggested.

Lewis nodded his agreement. "Yeah, okay," he said. Leo crouched in front of the wheelchair, one hand on it to hold it still, the other reaching out for Lewis. He felt Lewis push himself out of the wheelchair and grab hold of his neck. Leo grabbed his legs and hefted him up.

"That okay?" he asked, worried about squeezing Lewis's legs too hard and hurting him. "Are you all right?"

"Yeah," Lewis said breathlessly. "Let's go."

Leo hurried outside after the others, pulling the door shut behind them.

"What are we going to do?" Lewis whispered in his ear.

"Go with her," Leo said. "I don't know."

"What if she doesn't… come back again…"

"I don't know," Leo repeated.

For a while they were quiet, just trudging through the woods, following in Margaret's footsteps. The younger kids up ahead had stopped crying and fussing and were playing and talking as they walked through the woods like it was a nature walk instead of… whatever it was. Leo was glad they could relax and play and be happy picking up pine cones and sticks to show their mother, but he and Lewis were silent, trying to figure out what to do, what was going on.

The sun was going down quickly, and before long they were left in the twilight, getting colder. The children were quiet now as they stuck close to Margaret, whining occasionally to ask where they were going or if they were almost there.

Leo started thinking about wolves and coyotes and wildcats. And bears. They had all met wildlife rambling through the woods from time to time. Usually the animals avoided people and kept to themselves, but if it was dark, and they were hungry, and one of the little ones was lagging…

"Stay close," Leo ordered Phil, grabbing him by the hand. He couldn't pick the boy up. He already had Lewis's weight on his back. He was incredibly tired and sore but refused to say anything about it and make Lewis feel bad.

"Tired. Don't wanna," Phil complained, resisting.

"Come on. We're almost there," Leo promised.

Eventually, they reached a clearing.

Leo wondered if they were lost.

Or maybe they could turn around now, and go back to the house, and climb into their warm beds to go to sleep. The moonlight was dim, but Margaret must have known where they were going. She pushed her way through the bushes to the door of a cabin almost completely overgrown with vegetation and she turned the creaky handle and pushed the door open. The children and Leo followed her into the room.

It was pitch black, and although they were now sheltered from the brisk breeze, it wasn't any warmer inside than it was out.

"Mama, I don't like it. It's dark," Joyce protested.

"We'll turn on the lights," Margaret said, moving about in the darkness by instinct or memory. Margaret struck a match and lit a lamp, which emitted just enough light to see the general shape of the objects in the room. A bed in one corner. A small cook stove. A rocking chair. Piles of unidentifiable junk. Stiffly, Leo moved to the bed and with a sigh, sat down on the edge, and released Lewis's legs, letting him slide off Leo's back and onto the bed.

"I'm hungry," Michelle complained.

Leo shook his head at her. She shouldn't complain. None of them should say anything that might make Margaret upset.

Margaret moved around the cabin in a trance, lighting a couple of candles and opening the cook stove to see if there was any wood in it.

"Is there a woodpile outside?" Leo asked. "Should I light a fire for you, Mom?"

She made a vague gesture toward the door. Leo went back outside. Sticking close to the walls of the cabin, he searched around. There was some old wood in a pile in one corner. It wouldn't last them more than a day or two. But it was old and dry. Leo stripped what sticks and bark he could for kindling and took an armload into the cabin.

The children were now all on the bed with Lewis, while he tried to entertain them with a made-up game.

Leo bit his lip and busied himself with getting a fire going in the stove. He couldn't stop to worry about what Margaret was going to do next.

The wood was dry and didn't take long to light. Joyce came close and warmed her hands in front of the stove, taking a minute to sit on Leo's lap and rest her face against his chest.

"Nice fire," she murmured.

"Thanks, princess."

"We're hungry."

"I know you are. I'll see if there's anything to eat, okay?"

Margaret continued to pace around the cabin, looking through piles of junk, opening boxes, prowling about anxiously.

"We're safe here," Leo told her, hoping to talk her into calming down and coming back to herself. "Nobody can hurt us here."

She nodded absently.

"Is there anything to eat?" Leo asked. "You must be hungry. You need to eat for the baby. And the kids are hungry."

"Supplies," Margaret said, motioning around. "Flies, lies."

Leo started to investigate the boxes, pulling things out, seeing what was in their stores. He found a box of crackers and took it over to the bed.

"Have a few," he said. "Not too much, they'll make you thirsty."

"There's water," Lewis commented.

Leo glanced around the cabin but didn't see any jugs.

"No, there's not," he disagreed.

"The snow outside," Lewis pointed out. "We can melt it."

"Oh," Leo said, feeling stupid. "Yeah, I guess."

Lewis tore open the cracker box and started to distribute crackers to the kids. Leo held out his hand and Lewis gave him a few.

Leo went over to Margaret, offering them to her. "Mom, have some crackers. They'll be good for the baby."

She looked at his hand in horror like he had offered her a snake. "No!"

"Yes," Leo insisted. "It's a cracker. It's good. Please eat."

After a moment of blankness, her expression softened. She took the handful of crackers from Leo and nibbled at them, looking out the window into the blackness outside.

"It's safe here," she said, her voice lifting slightly in a questioning tone.

"Yes. It's safe here," Leo repeated.

He didn't like it. It was dark, and cold, and out where the wild animals were. It didn't feel safe to him at all, with Margaret teetering on the edge of sanity and the children all thrown into a jumble, frightened and anxious.

Leo didn't sleep. It was a long, restless night. The little ones cried, then finally slept. Lewis tried to stay awake, but he eventually gave in and dropped off as well.

Leo was afraid if he went to sleep, Margaret would wander off, start a fire, or something else he couldn't predict. So he sat there, or when he got too tired, got up and paced, watching her and trying to keep them all safe. When the morning came, she seemed a little better. She stopped muttering and slowed down, yawning and rubbing her temples tiredly.

"Why don't you lay down now, Mom," Leo encouraged her, shaking the younger kids awake and shooing them out of the bed. "Come, come lie down and have a little rest, Mom. You have to get some rest."

Margaret let him guide her toward the bed and laid down.

Leo sat on the edge of the bed and stroked her hair, trying to comfort her and to get her to relax to go to sleep. The little ones were starting to fuss. Lewis pushed himself over to the edge of the bed and slid himself off, bum-shuffling over to the stove and checking the fire, feeding a few more sticks into it.

"Come on guys," he said. "Come get warmed up. Come sit with me, Philly. Come on."

Phil ran over to Lewis on his short, toddler legs and sat in his lap. He chattered to Lewis cheerfully, holding his hands out toward the fire. The girls wandered over and joined Phil and Lewis on the floor.

Leo stayed on the side of the bed, stroking Margaret's hair, humming to her soothingly. "S'okay, Mama," he whispered. "Go to sleep."

After she had dropped off, they started looking through the boxes and piles of junk, seeing what supplies were there. They separated items into separate piles. Food. Blankets or clothes. Useful things. Bits of trash.

"When are we going to go home?" Michelle whined, getting bored with the game.

"I don't know," Leo said. "Maybe when Mom wakes up. We'll see how she feels, okay?"

"Can't we go home now?"

Leo shook his head.

Michelle didn't ask any more questions. She didn't ask what was wrong with Margaret. She didn't ask why they couldn't make any noise or what they were going to have for breakfast.

Leo looked over the small food rations they had sorted. It wouldn't last long. He couldn't stretch it out much. Joyce tugged on his sleeve.

Leo took a deep breath and looked down at her. "What is it, sweetie?"

"Hafta pee."

Leo laughed. "You get to go outside," he said like it was a special treat.

Joyce looked up at him, her forehead wrinkled. "Outside?" she repeated.

"In the snow," Leo told her.

She stared at him. "In the *snow*?"

Leo nodded. Joyce slipped her hand into his.

"You go with me," she said firmly.

Leo nodded. "Sure, Joy," he agreed with a smile. He looked at Lewis as he left with her.

"We won't use that snow for water," Lewis told him, straight faced.

Leo nodded in agreement, grinning.

"And Leo…?" Lewis said.

"Yeah?"

"I hafta pee too."

Leo raised his eyebrows. He nodded.

"Sure," he said after a second. "I'll take you out after Joy's done. Michelle, you gotta go?"

Michelle nodded and Leo jerked his head at her.

"Come on, then. Ladies first."

"And me!" Phil put in.

"No," Leo told Phil firmly. "You wait until after the girls. You go with me and Lewie. Okay?"

Phil grumbled about it, but he stayed with Lewis while Leo took the girls out behind the cabin to water the snow. Disgusted by the whole process, as befitted the little ladies they were, they went back into the cabin vowing not to go to the bathroom again until they got home.

Warning them to be quiet, Leo left the girls there with Margaret. With Lewis' permission, he picked Lewis up and took him and Phil out for their turn. Phil's reaction was completely different from the girls', with a boy's typical delight in marking his territory in the snow.

After returning Lewis to the cabin, Leo went back out for the remainder of the woodpile.

Margaret didn't sleep for long. She woke up and moved around restlessly.

"We have to block the door," she insisted. "Lock, clock, block it. Keep us safe. Safe inside."

Leo looked at the door, the only way in and out of the cabin.

"We're safe here, Mom," he assured her. "Nobody else is here. We're safe."

She shook her head. "We have to block it," she repeated. "Keep him away. Stay. Keep us safe."

There was no talking her out of it. Before long, the bed was blocking the door, and as many boxes and bits as they could fit on and around it.

There would be no more bathroom breaks.

No escape.

It was another three days before Lyall found them.

The firewood was all gone, and so was the small store of food.

They could feed the fire with scraps of boxes, paper, and wood, but there was nothing left to feed the little mouths.

Lyall had picked up a voicemail from the school inquiring as to why the children hadn't been in attendance and drove all night to get back home. He got to the house to find it empty, the table tipped over and their last dinner spread across the kitchen floor. The next morning, soon after sun-up, he was at the cabin in the woods, pounding on the door.

"Margaret! Margaret, open the door!" he shouted, trying to push it open.

"No! No more, Joe!" she argued, under her breath, too low for him to hear.

"Daddy!" Michelle shouted.

"Are you there?" Lyall demanded. "All of you?"

"Yes!" Michelle shouted back. "Mo—" her cry was cut short when Margaret grabbed her and jerked her back, putting her arm around Michelle's throat and squeezing tight.

"Shhh," she ordered. "Nobody talk. Everybody quiet."

The rest of them froze. No one tried to call out to Lyall. Leo looked back at Margaret, holding Michelle tightly across the throat, strangling her.

"Mom, let her go," he whispered urgently. "Mom, you're hurting Michelle!"

Margaret stared at him with a look full of malice.

Leo crawled toward her.

"Leo, don't," Lewis warned. "She'll hurt Michelle more."

"You try to get stuff away from the door," Leo whispered back to him. "So he can get in."

He reached Margaret. "Stop Mom," he pleaded. "You're hurting Michelle."

"Go away," she hissed at him. "Leave me alone!"

"Mama," he tried again, reaching for her arm. "Please, let go!"

Her grip was iron.

Leo couldn't budge her.

He tightened his grip, pulling harder. He pushed his knee against her for leverage, trying with all his might to release the pressure on Michelle's throat.

Michelle was turning red and purple, her eyes bulging, tears running down her cheeks.

Leo dug his nails in.

He could hear Lewis trying to drag the boxes and everything out of the way of the door. The younger children crying and trying to help him. Lyall ramming the door with his shoulder, trying to force his way in.

Margaret threw Leo across the room.

Leo's head hit the floor, and his teeth snapped shut, cutting the tip of his tongue.

Leo swallowed blood. He got up, head throbbing, and tried again, running at her this time, trying to knock her off balance so she would let go of Michelle.

"Leo," Lewis warned. "You're going to hurt her or the baby!"

"Michelle can't breathe!"

Leo grabbed Margaret's fingers and pulled them back as hard as he could. They bent back so far he was afraid he was going to break them. But Margaret showed no sign of pain, no sign of weakening.

Leo pulled with all his strength, tears running down his cheeks, blood from his cut tongue dribbling down his chin. Margaret struck out at him again, this time loosening her hold on Michelle to push Leo off of herself.

She let Michelle fall from her grip.

Another smash on the door, and this time Lyall broke through, throwing the bed and the rest of the boxes and junk several feet back. He cast his eyes around the small interior of the cabin, taking in Leo sprawled on the floor, bleeding, Michelle unconscious, and Margaret crouched there, wild-eyed and fierce.

"Margaret," he pounced on her, pulling her to her feet and hugging her close. "Margaret, what's wrong?"

"Let go of me!"

Margaret spit, pulling away from him wildly, scratching his arm, long red tracks cut into his skin.

Lyall held her more tightly, wrestling to get a good grip that would prevent her from escaping.

Leo slowly got up onto his hands and knees, crawling over to Michelle.

He tried to shut out the sounds of Lyall fighting with Margaret. The blows connecting. Her cries and his grunts. The curses of both of them as they fought tooth and nail.

Margaret hit the floor heavily, lay still for a minute, and then started to cry, the fight finally gone out of her.

Lyall bent back down and pulled her up to her feet again, and this time Margaret didn't fight him. She continued to weep. Lyall looked around at the children.

"Leo. You bring Michelle."

Leo patted Michelle's cheeks, trying to bring her around. "What about Lewis?" he asked.

Lyall looked at Lewis, frowning. "How did he get out here?"

"I carried him."

"All the way?"

Leo nodded.

Lyall scowled. "Is she okay?" He gestured at Michelle.

"I don't know," Leo said.

Lyall dropped Margaret onto the bed and gave her a fierce look to make sure she was going to stay.

He bent down beside Michelle, felt her mouth for her breath, and patted her cheek.

"She'll be okay," he said gruffly.

"Mom had her by the throat… really tight… "

"She's breathing. I'll take your mom back, then I'll come back here for you kids. You stay here."

Leo looked around at the others and nodded. "Okay."

"Dad," Lewis piped up.

Leo looked at him warningly.

Usually it was Leo saying things he shouldn't, getting in trouble for opening his mouth when Lewis tried to stop him.

Lyall looked at Lewis in irritation as he pulled Margaret back up to her feet. "What?" he snapped.

"When you come back… could you bring some food?"

Lyall scowled. "You can wait until you get back to the house to eat."

"But we've… there was hardly anything here… we had to ration it, and… I don't think Leo's eaten the whole time."

Lyall looked around the cabin, wrinkling his nose at the putrid smells. He shook his head and walked to the door out with Margaret holding her steady on her feet.

"When you've got a family," he said in an angry tone. "You gotta take care of yourself first. It's like they say on an airplane. You can't take care of anyone else if you're fainting from hunger yourself."

Mouth open, Leo watched Lyall go.

CHAPTER SIXTEEN

LEO WAS ANXIOUS AND antsy. He danced around on his toes, trying to burn off a little of the anxiety and get ready for his fight.

Work had stretched out interminably. Nothing exciting or interesting had happened all day. He'd barely seen an animal, let alone performed any daring rescues. Some days were just like that, but anticipating his fight tonight, the day had just dragged. The minutes seemed to take hours.

Now he was all ready to go, but it wasn't time for the fight yet. He could hear the sounds of the crowd gathered in the auditorium, the announcer making some general announcements and doing a countdown until the start of the fight. But Leo's wasn't even the first fight tonight. He had to wait through the first couple before they got to him.

"Just relax," Jaime advised him. "Have a water. Sit down for a while."

"Man, I wish I didn't have to wait! This is killing me!"

"You're going to have to deal with it. Best to just keep yourself calm and cool. You get too worked up, and you're going to be wound too tight for the fight and get injured. You know you have to stay loose."

"I know, I know," Leo agreed. But it wasn't going to be easy. He paced around the tiny dressing room and had half of a bottle of water. He tried to sit down, but that was no good. There was a knock on the door and Leo looked up to see Elizabeth.

"Hey!" Leo greeted, surprised. "I didn't think I'd see you here!"

She smiled. "Well, you left me a message and I didn't have anything better to do."

"Great. So… how are you feeling?"

Elizabeth shrugged. "Okay. I'm always a bit dopey after I get out of hospital. Until I really adjust to the new meds."

"Yeah. Did they change them around?"

"They always do. But it never really changes how I feel. Except for the side effects."

Leo nodded sympathetically. He'd never had much success with drug therapy either. Being zoned out didn't help with school or work. Nothing ever felt 'right' when he was on meds. He kept waiting for them to make him feel normal. To magically make him like everyone else. But that never happened.

Normal people were normal, and Leo was not.

"So have you got Juleen back?"

"Not yet." She hesitated. "I'm in no great hurry, to tell the truth. I know she's my responsibility, and all, but… it's hard to take care of somebody else when you can't even take care of yourself. Especially a screaming baby."

"Yeah. Maybe once you've been out for a while and had a chance to adjust."

Elizabeth nodded.

"So…" Leo wondered how to approach the question. Was it okay to ask people about their craziness? He knew the only people who'd ever asked him specific questions about what was going on in his head were therapists. Normal people avoided asking.

He often wished they would ask so he could explain what was going on. It would be a relief just to get it out there in the open. Not to have to avoid it or hide it. "I don't know if I should ask, but… these other names… Eli, for instance…?"

Elizabeth looked at him warily. "Yeah? What about him?"

"Do you… I mean, do they… do you know the others exist? Do you know about your other personalities…?"

Elizabeth glanced at Jaime, but he was reading a book and did not appear to be listening. Elizabeth walked over to where Leo was sitting, and sat close to him. She leaned forward slightly and kept her voice low.

"Yeah," she said, "Some of us know about the others… and some of us don't."

"Oh. Well, that complicates things, doesn't it?"

She nodded.

"Who are you right now?" Leo asked.

"Lisa. I'm… well, I'm usually Lisa when I get out of hospital."

"So that's your… stable personality? Do they have different roles, like on TV shows. A gatekeeper and all that?"

"It's not a game. It's not an act. It's just… different parts of me. They're all me."

Leo nodded. "So tell me about Lisa," he suggested.

"I'm strong… self-aware… try to help myself. I see the doctor and try to take my meds and stay on track."

"Okay," Leo said slowly. "So that's why the doctor's office has your name down as Lisa on their records."

"Yeah. I don't usually go there as anyone else."

"So Dr. Marvin, he doesn't usually get to meet your other personalities?"

"Sometimes. Sometimes he does regression or hypnosis or something to try to trigger one of the others. Different things can trigger them… getting upset about something… stress… things that trigger flashbacks."

"What things give you flashbacks?"

"I don't know. I can't always identify them. Things remind me of being a kid, sometimes they'll trigger a… less mature… personality."

"So who are some of the others? What about Eli?"

"Eli's kind of a jerk," Elizabeth said apologetically. "Sorry about the other day. I know you were trying to help out, and he didn't really care."

"It's okay," Leo assured her. "Why is Eli such a jerk?"

"Sometimes the world is just too much. I need someone who makes me feel strong. Someone who doesn't really care what the rest of the world thinks, so I can just be me."

"He kind of protects you from the rest of the world. When Juleen was crying and you couldn't handle her any more, he made you not care."

Elizabeth nodded. "Yeah. Sometimes you have to just let it all hang out, you know?"

"Sure… So was Eli there a lot in the army? Is he the one that took over all that stuff?"

"No," Elizabeth laughed. "He'd never serve in the army. Listening to orders, keeping a schedule, having to always be properly uniformed and all? No way!"

Leo could see that. He wouldn't like to be in the army either. It took a different kind of personality than he—or Eli—had.

"So who was in the army?" he asked.

"I don't know… I don't remember a lot of it. Lizzie a lot of the time, I think. Lizzie's used to having to take care of people, so being a soldier… that's kind of similar. Lots of discipline, learning how to do chores the right way, protecting other people."

"Wow." Leo thought about it. He didn't want to push too hard with any of his questions, but he found it fascinating. "Do you know who it was that put Juleen in the bag and locked her in the car? Did you ever remember that?"

Elizabeth shook her head. "No. I'm not sure who did that. That was pretty… ruthless. Could have been Eli, but I don't think he would bother. Someone who gets rid of problems and doesn't care how anyone else feels."

"What would you have done if I hadn't shown up, and Juleen suffocated to death?"

Elizabeth breathed in deeply. She rolled her eyes upward, blinking. "Some of us just aren't cut out to have kids," she said. "I should never have had Juleen. If I'd known I was pregnant, I could have had an abortion. I didn't understand what was going on."

"You don't have to take care of her," Leo reminded her. "If you can't take care of her, she's still young enough there'd be plenty of people who would like to adopt her. Don't you think?"

"I don't *like* adoption," Elizabeth said, an edge to her voice, "Adoption just… hurts people."

"It hurt you once," Leo said, "but it could be good for other people. Adopting older kids is hard, but babies? Juleen would be okay. She'd grow up with a family who loved her. They wouldn't… send her back."

"That's what you say. But you don't know."

"No, I guess I don't. But I think she'd be okay. Better than suffocating in a car."

"Listen, I didn't come here to have you tell me what to do," Elizabeth griped. "You said you were going to fight. I just came to watch."

"Yeah." Leo looked at the clock. "Won't be much longer now. I'm sorry about getting on your case. I just worry about Juleen."

"I don't have her right now, so you don't have to worry about it."

"I know. I'm sorry."

Leo fell silent. He looked over at Jaime, wishing he would interrupt with some sort of distraction. Leo could introduce Elizabeth to Jaime. Something.

"We can still talk," Elizabeth said after a few minutes of silence, her voice softer. "Just not about adoption, okay?"

"Okay. Sorry."

"Don't worry about it."

Leo nodded. He cast about for something else to say.

"So… something pretty bad must have happened, huh?" he asked. "From what I've heard, they say this happens with long-term abuse and that kind of thing. As a defense mechanism."

"That might be true for some people," Elizabeth acknowledged. "But not for everyone. I didn't have any big trauma or abuse. Just being with different foster families. Annoying, but not something that… makes you crazy. I guess I just inherited that."

"Do you know anything about your birth family?" Leo asked. "You've never said anything about your life before foster care. Do you remember?"

"I don't remember that far back. I was three or four when I went into foster care. I'm not sure."

"Did your parents die?"

"I don't know. Maybe. Or maybe they just didn't want me anymore. Maybe they were as crazy as I am and finally figured out they couldn't take care of me anymore."

"Didn't you ever ask, or look at your records?"

"Why would I want to? I don't want to know why. I don't want to know what happened. Would you?"

Leo considered.

He remembered everything about his life.

All the abuses. All the fights.

The torture, the harsh words, the criticisms.

He remembered all the stuff his parents had done, how he and his siblings suffered, how the social workers screwed up and the school teachers were ignorant and humiliated him.

What if he couldn't remember that? What if he just remembered general stuff, and what he got for his birthday, fun games he'd played with Lewis. What kind of a person would he be then?

"I don't know… I guess I'd be really different if I didn't remember everything," he said.

"Wouldn't you be happier?" Elizabeth suggested brightly. "Why remember the bad stuff? Why not just make good stuff happen for yourself and then you'll be happy all the time."

"Yeah… but that's not the way life works."

"Maybe it should. Maybe it can. Just choose not to remember all that garbage, all the pain. Just live in the present instead. Live in the moment. Have fun. Meet people. It would be really nice, wouldn't it?"

"It sounds like it. But stuff has a tendency to come back to you. You can't shake it off so easily."

"Well, you can at least try," Elizabeth said coyly. She stood up and started to walk around the room. "Is it soon?"

"Yeah, not much longer now."

"Should I go out there and wait? Find a seat?"

Leo looked at Jaime. "Is there enough room in the reserved seating for Elizabeth?"

"Assuming you haven't brought another ten people I don't know about," Jaime said dryly.

"No. I doubt there will be anyone else."

"Then there's plenty of space."

"You may as well stay here," Leo said. "You can go out when I do and Jaime can show you where to sit."

"So is Jaime your coach?" Elizabeth asked.

"Well… he kind of helps me with my training. I can't afford a professional coach or trainer. But he owns the gym I work out at and has the connections. He helps me to train and to set up fights."

Elizabeth nodded. "I'm Lisa," she introduced herself to Jaime.

He smiled and shook her hand. "I'm pleased to meet you. Leo never talks about his girlfriend."

"Well, I…" Leo protested weakly.

Jaime and Elizabeth just laughed at his awkwardness.

Leo heard the announcer relay the results of the last fight, and got to his feet, preparing himself.

"You'll do fine," Jaime told him again, one final time. "You just stay loose and fight the way you've trained. Don't get all freaked out about it."

Leo nodded. He shifted back and forth on his feet, trying to stay warmed up.

"All right, this way," Jaime instructed, and led Leo and Elizabeth out of the waiting room.

Leo was led up to the ring and climbed into his corner. The announcer made the requisite introductions and Leo watched Heartbrake on the other side of the ring. He looked fresh, ready to go.

Leo bounced around nervously.

He smiled, thinking about Billy and how he always got so jumpy at the beginning of a match.

He put up his gloves and waited for the bell to sound. They entered the middle of the ring and tapped gloves.

Leo watched Heartbrake and let his instinct and training take over.

This was it, the real deal.

He blocked punches and tried to strike whenever he could.

Heartbrake had powerful punches, and when they landed, they jarred Leo head to toe. Heartbrake was tougher than most of the guys Leo practiced sparring with.

Leo had to focus to try to avoid too many of those punches. Make Heartbrake move around more than he wanted to.

Try to wear him out so Leo could surprise him with a blow, try to take him by surprise.

It was obvious after the first few punches that Heartbrake was stronger and better skilled than Leo.

Leo held his own but didn't seem to be getting any closer to a win.

Heartbrake started to slow down, but so did Leo. He tried to stay just out of Heartbrake's long reach to avoid the full force of his punches. Leo had to conserve his energy if he wanted to come back in this match.

The bell rang and they took a break. Leo had a swig of water.

"You're tiring out," Jaime told him. "You've got to work harder. Draw on your reserves. This match isn't over."

Leo nodded.

He didn't point out how much better Heartbrake was than he. To do that was to admit defeat.

He had to do his best, hope to get a lucky punch in, or that Heartbrake's energy would flag.

Leo found himself being distracted.

He caught a glimpse of Elizabeth in the audience and flashed a smile at her.

He thought at one point he saw Stormy, but wasn't sure and couldn't take a longer look. He took a couple of powerful blows from Heartbrake and was suddenly reeling.

He heard the crowd gasp and groan. And some of them cheered.

Leo tried to regain his balance. He backed up, looking to rest for a second or two until he could get his bearings back. But Heartbrake followed him, a triumphant look on his face.

Leo danced away, but Heartbrake was inexorable. Leo wasn't about to concede it was over. But he couldn't even see straight to throw a punch.

Heartbrake drew back a powerful fist and slammed into Leo.

It hit Leo like a freight train. He felt himself flip over backward and hit the floor.

For a while it was quiet and Leo listened carefully for the ref's count.

If he rested a few seconds, maybe he'd be able to get back up to his feet before the end of the count.

But he couldn't hear the ref counting. Groaning, Leo opened his eyes and looked around.

There was no ref, no audience, no Heartbrake Kid.

Leo was no longer in the ring, but back in the waiting room, stretched out on the examining table. He groaned again and tried to force himself to get up.

"Just stay there," Jaime told him. "No getting up. Stay put."

"But—"

"No 'but.' Match is over. You need to rest for a few minutes."

"I'm fine."

"Sure. Doctor said your vitals were strong. But you're to stay here until he comes back and clears you. So don't be a hero. Just lay still. We don't want you having some kind of hemorrhage or something. He's got to check you out more thoroughly."

"Okay," Leo conceded.

Stormy and Elizabeth were both there.

Leo was surprised Stormy had come. She didn't often come out to see him. He didn't think she was squeamish about the boxing, but she didn't see the point in coming to watch him.

Maybe when he was better at it, she would come more often.

Leo made a motion between the two of them.

"Stormy, Elizabeth. Elizabeth, Stormy," he said, the words coming out a little slurred.

The ladies nodded to each other.

"I figured," Stormy commented.

"Nice to meet you," Elizabeth acknowledged.

Leo smiled, his head woozy. "Did you enjoy the match?"

"I didn't think it would be so bad," Elizabeth said. "I thought it would be okay and wouldn't bother me."

Leo could see it coming.

"But it was awful! What a barbarous sport! I can't believe it's even legal! Just let two guys beat each other senseless? Everybody cheering them on?" She shook her head in amazement. "I can't believe it. When you went down… I thought you were dead. You were so still!"

"Out cold," Stormy told Leo cheerfully. "Before you even hit the canvas." Leo saw something in her eyes that belied her careless demeanor. He had scared her too. But Stormy was strong. She would never admit it.

"I guess," Leo admitted. "I didn't do as well as I had hoped."

"How could two people do that to each other?" Elizabeth demanded. "Just try to beat each other up."

"People do it all the time," Leo commented. "Only difference is we've agreed to do it, with rules. Much more civilized than just trying to jump a guy in an alley."

"Civilized?" Elizabeth exclaimed. "Do you even hear yourself? This isn't civilized! This is the furthest thing from civilization! You participate in this willingly?"

"Yes—"

"I thought you had enough of getting beaten up by your dad. Why would you choose to do this? You didn't get enough as a kid?"

Leo's anger circled his belly, starting to get wound up. "This doesn't have anything to do with my dad," he growled. He was too tired and unsteady to fight anyone, but the cat didn't seem to know that.

"Oh no? That's not *him* out there, you know. What's the point in trying to beat him up over and over again? Even if you beat the guy out there, you haven't beaten your dad. You haven't beaten anyone *for* anything, just played a game at beating people up. I don't get it."

"What about you?" Leo snarled, hurt. "You're the soldier. You think you're going to get back at your parents and foster parents for what they did to you? You think shooting the enemy is going to make someone love you? How is what you are doing any better?"

"I became a soldier as a matter of survival! It was the only way for me to make a living, have a steady job and education."

"Yeah?" Leo challenged. "You don't think I'm trying to pull myself up? I don't exactly have the money for school either. All I've got is my body, and this is a way to make money. It's a sport. You should be impressed."

"Impressed?" Elizabeth spat. "Impressed you didn't get killed? Or just that you didn't land flat on your face? It's not a sport, Leo, it's barbaric!"

"So is war."

"Of course it is! But no one pretends it isn't. Nobody says 'it's just a sport' about war. We're honest about what it is we're trying to do. Kill the enemy. That's what it's all about."

Leo and Elizabeth stared at each other. Leo tried to sit up, but Stormy pushed him back down.

"You are supposed to be staying down. You promised your coach," she insisted when Leo tried to get up again. "If you don't listen, you're going to end up in the hospital instead of going home. Is that what you want?"

"No," Leo said morosely and settled back again.

"Maybe you should go," Stormy told Elizabeth. "He can't hang out with you tonight, and you guys aren't going to solve each other's mental problems by arguing. Just let it go."

Elizabeth stared at Stormy. "Fine," she said tightly.

She turned to go, flipping out her cell phone to text someone or check her messages. She missed the doorway, running straight into the wall and grunting with the force of it.

"Don't walk and text," Stormy warned, laughing.

Elizabeth gave her a look, then corrected her course and left the room. Stormy shook her head, laughing in delight. "All of those jokes about blondes," Stormy said. "They were about *her*, weren't they?"

Leo snickered. He didn't like Stormy being rude about his friend, but it *was* funny. Elizabeth *was* an airhead. Even though Leo understood why she had problems, it was still pretty funny.

"I don't know how she ever got into the army. Running like clockwork and staying on the schedule and all that."

"Well, maybe that's what works for her," Stormy said. "Maybe *not* having any structure is the problem."

One of her personalities probably thrived on it. Elizabeth had said it was Lizzie who had been there most of the time while she was in the army. Leo wondered if there were others too, some buried too deep for him to ever know about, others who knew exactly who was where, and when. Maybe there was even a personality directing it all, deciding who would show up.

Leo closed his eyes dizzily. His head was spinning. Thinking about Elizabeth's convoluted personalities wasn't helping at all.

CHAPTER SEVENTEEN

LEO TOSSED AND TURNED. He ached all over. The doctor said nothing was broken or ruptured. There was no internal bleeding, but he was a mass of bruises, some of them pretty deep.

Leo was used to being sore after a fight, but Heartbrake had really put him through the wringer. He felt more like he'd been run over by a truck—a couple of times—than just through a boxing match.

He took painkillers before bed, but they didn't seem to be doing anything. Staying still was uncomfortable, but moving was an agony and he couldn't seem to settle down to go to sleep.

Leo rubbed the scars on his arm, trying to calm himself down. It was a nervous gesture. Left over from when he had first been burned. They didn't hurt him like they used to; they just ached sometimes. But today everything hurt. Old or new, it didn't matter. Everything hurt.

He felt feverish.

Hot and sweating one minute, then chilled and pulling the blankets up.

He couldn't seem to get comfortable.

Leo must have fallen into a fitful sleep because he started to dream. Started to dream about that day. He rubbed the scars on his arm, remembering.

Lyall had come to the school to pick them up.

He was in a fury over something, but Leo was too young to understand what. Lyall kept yelling, threatening, screaming about how he couldn't trust them. How they had all betrayed him, that the two babies had been taken away, and it wasn't worth it anymore. He was just going to end it all, for all of them.

Leo and Rachel were both pulled out of their classrooms by scared-looking teachers and administrators and handed over to their parents.

Leo and Rachel climbed into the back seat of the car, frightened, exchanging worried glances. Rachel's face was almost as white as her snow-blonde hair. Lewis was buckled into his car seat between them.

Lewis hated the car seat and tried to unbuckle himself, but Lyall had fixed it so he couldn't. Leo tried to play with Lewis to distract him, but Lewis just kept pushing Leo's hand away in irritation and fussing loudly about the car seat.

Lyall drove home. Margaret kept giving little shrieks of panic when he passed a car on the double solid or rounded a corner going too fast. She kept looking back at the children, her dark eyes wide and ringed with white all around the pupil. They got back home, far from neighbors who might snoop. Lyall pulled into the driveway in a skid and jumped out of the car.

"Stay there," he ordered his family.

He ran into the house. Everybody sat there, straining their ears to listen. They could hear him crashing around the house, yelling at no one, or at the whole world. Leo knew Lyall had been drinking. He'd been drinking and he was on the warpath. Maybe if they were really lucky, Lyall would pass out in the house, and they'd be safe for tonight.

Leo and Rachel sat quietly, making no attempt to get out of the car.

"It's okay," Margaret said to the two of them, looking over her shoulder at them. "It will be all right. Just stay right there. It will be all right."

Leo didn't believe it. He looked at Rachel. She didn't believe it either.

They both knew how this was going to end. In beatings, torture, and tears. There was no escaping it. Even if they ran away, there was nowhere to go.

They were too far from help.

Margaret got out of the car. Leo watched her, panic rising in his chest.

What was she doing? She was supposed to stay in the car. She was going to get them all in worse trouble.

Why was she out of the car?

Margaret disappeared into the garage. Leo turned to Rachel, wanting to know what she was going to do. Her expression reflected what he felt—stark terror.

"Where's she going?" Rachel cried, looking in panic at the house, then back at the garage.

How could she just abandon them?

When Lyall came out of the house and she wasn't sitting obediently in the car, he would kill them all.

"I dunno. I dunno, should I get her?" Leo asked.

Like he, a seven-year-old, was in charge of his wayward mother and needed to parent her. Rachel shook her head.

"No," she told him. "No, no, no!"

Leo swallowed and looked around again. At the house. Where was Lyall?

Was he passed out? Drinking more?

Dreaming up some new torture to try on them?

He looked back at the garage.

Where was their mother?

What was she doing? Why had she left them alone there?

Margaret came out of the garage and Leo breathed a sigh of relief. She was coming back. In her hand was a gas can. The one they used for filling the lawn mower and other small machinery.

What was she going to do with it? Mow the lawn? It didn't make any sense.

Leo mouthed the word 'Mom?' but no sound came out. He couldn't get her attention. Margaret started to walk around the car.

"It's okay," she said. "It is all going to be okay. It's okay, children."

Leo watched her circuiting the car. Tipping the gas can so it dribbled out on the car and the dry ground. The sharp smell of gasoline rose to Leo's nostrils, making him feel nauseated.

"Mom?" he croaked, "Mom, what are you doing?"

He wasn't loud enough for her to hear him. She just kept walking around the car, making calm, sane, soothing noises. Telling them not to worry, she would keep them safe. Everything was going to be okay.

Then she lit the match.

Leo could have counted to about three before the conflagration. Then they were suddenly surrounded by fire.

It crackled and burned and seared his lungs instantly.

The smoke made his eyes water, or would have if he hadn't already been crying.

Leo couldn't see his mother any longer. Was she on fire too or was she okay?

Rachel started to scream. Lewis was struggling to get out of his car seat.

Leo searched outside for his mother.

Where was she?

Then he made her out on the other side of the wall of flames. She was laughing and crying hysterically.

"You'll be okay now," she shrieked. "Nothing will happen to you now!"

Lyall came racing outside. For once, Leo wasn't frightened at his approach. He was even a little bit glad.

"What are you doing?" he screamed at Margaret. "What have you done, you crazy woman?"

Rachel was screaming. Lewis was screaming.

Leo might have been screaming as well.

Lyall jumped at the flames, tried to get into the car. The interior was starting to smoke and burn.

"Leo!" Lyall yelled. "Leo, open the door! Get out of there!"

Leo stayed where he was, frozen.

His father's words worked their way into Leo's brain, slowly being translated there, trying to worm their way into his non-functioning consciousness.

Open the door.

Get out.

Leo reached for the door handle.

It was too hot. His flesh seared on it. He jerked his hand back.

"Leo! Rachel! Help Lewis! Pass him out the window!"

Leo grabbed at his baby brother.

It was no use, he was still buckled into the seat, and Lyall had tied him in to make sure he couldn't get himself out. Leo felt for the straps and bungees tying Lewis down, working at them, trying to get them loose to get Lewis out.

He could hardly breathe. He couldn't see a thing.

One of the straps came free.

Leo worked desperately at the next. The fire roared in his ears, drowning out Leo's own sobs.

His fingers worked at the straps.

Pulled at the ropes.

Worked on the knots and hooks.

Finally, the other strap came free.

Leo forced Lewis' arms through the straps, even as Lewis struggled and held himself rigid, fighting back. Leo dragged the small boy across him and pushed him out the window.

"Dad, take him!"

"I got him," Lyall shouted back. Leo felt the boy's weight lifted from his arms.

"Get yourself out," Lyall told him. "Just get out the window."

Leo reached around the car seat, trying to grab his sister.

"Rachel," he shouted. "You go out the window too!"

"It's too hot!" she screamed back. "I can't get it open!"

"Come out mine!"

Leo pulled on her arm, dragging her behind him. She was heavy, but he pulled as hard as he could, trying to get her out.

He couldn't push her through ahead of him, she was too big, too heavy.

He climbed out the window himself, trying to pull her through behind him.

The flames were all around him.

His clothing was on fire.

Leo pulled on Rachel, trying to drag her through the window. She was resisting or caught on something.

Hands closed around Leo, strong hands, lifting him up, out of the flames, into safety.

He tried to hang onto Rachel, to pull her to safety behind him. But the hands pulling on him pulled too hard and Leo lost his grip.

"Rachel!" he screamed, trying to catch hold of her again. "No!"

He was thrown violently to the ground, and Lyall was hitting him, beating him all over, punishing him for not rescuing his sister.

Leo was in agony.

The bite of the flames.

His father's hands punishing him.
Until it was too much and he passed out.

Leo awoke with a gasp, tears streaming down his face.

He sat up and turned on the light, trying to reassure himself with the familiar settings, to reassure himself he was safe, and the fire was long ago.

Over the intervening years, he had come to realize his father hadn't been beating him in punishment but was beating out the flames.

When Leo awoke after the fire, he knew Rachel was dead. She never made it out of the car after he let go.

Lewis had survived, but his legs were very badly burned.

The newspapers picked up the story and published a picture of Leo, the hero. Leo was sitting at Lewis's bedside, his head down on the pillow next to Lewis's, his bandaged hand protectively around Lewis's shoulder.

Margaret said she didn't know how the fire started, and none of them contradicted her.

'Just a freak accident,' they all said.

CHAPTER EIGHTEEN

LEO DRAGGED HIMSELF OUT of bed for work. He really didn't want to go. The best thing would just be to soak in a nice warm tub for the rest of the day to let his muscles and bruises heal up a little bit before being required to go out and rescue the furries.

But he knew if he failed to show up at work after a fight—and they certainly would know he had been in the ring by his bruises the following day—he would be forced to either give up boxing, or be fired from his job. So he buckled down and went in. With any luck, it would be a quiet day, he'd spend most of it just sitting in his truck downing coffee and Ibuprofen. Then he could go home and try to catch up on his sleep.

A couple of dog-at-large calls. One about a skunk under a porch, which Leo skipped over. Let someone else get sprayed.

His eyes settled on another call. Kitten in a drainpipe. He'd taken a couple of cat-in-a-tree calls before. Usually, the cat was out of the tree by the time he got there. Sometimes he had to prod it out or use the loop. It was rare they had to actually climb to get one, or get the fire department or city workers over with a cherry picker. Cats were perverse animals and could usually get out of a tree if they wanted to. They just had to want to, and preferred climbing down the rescuer's face or back to climbing down the tree.

Kitten in drainpipe sounded interesting, though. Leo responded to the call and programmed his GPS.

Leo was expecting to find the cat cornered in a culvert or storm drain, not wanting to come out because of the people trying to persuade it. A cat would just keep backing up, squeezing itself into a tighter and tighter space. It would refuse to come out until the people had dispersed and it was left to its own devices.

When he got there, though, the unhappy householder took him to the corner of the house, to the downspout connected to the eaves.

"It's in there," she said, pointing.

Leo looked dubiously at the narrow drainpipe. He'd seen cats squeeze themselves into some pretty tight places. Leo tapped the drainpipe and the kitten set up to wailing. The sound put it about halfway up the side of the house.

"How'd it get in there?" Leo asked.

"I don't know, it just got stuck."

Surveying the length of the drainpipe, Leo clarified. "I mean did it go down from the top or up from the bottom?"

"Down from the top, we think."

"How'd it get up there?" Leo looked at the height of the roof. Difficult for a little kitten to get up there. Was it an adult or a wee one? It made a difference.

"The tree," the man pointed to a big elm next to the house. "The neighbors have had the cats in the shed. But they were out and a dog chased a couple of them up the tree. This one must have been chased up and dropped onto the roof. No one saw it happen."

"How long has it been in there? Have you tried to get it out, or left it to find its own way?"

"I just left it for the most part. I figured if it could get in there, it could get itself back out, once it figured the dog was gone. But it's been crying for hours."

"How big?"

The man held his fingers out in estimation, then shook his head. "I really don't know. The others are next door. You can see."

Leo nodded and the neighbor led the way over to the house next door. The cats had apparently been taken into the house instead of remaining in the shed. Leo was conducted to the new nest where the mama cat was nursing the remaining kittens. He looked down at them. They were pretty small. Big enough to explore and get into trouble, but still nurslings. They could squeeze anywhere a hamster could. And that was pretty small. There should be lots of room for it to get through the downspout unless it had run into an obstruction.

The mama cat looked up at him and uttered a mournful cry. Leo bent over and scratched her ears for a moment.

"Have you tried letting her call him out?" Leo asked.

They all nodded. One of the children was hovering nearby, tear tracks down her face. "She called him and called him," she sobbed, "and he just kept crying and didn't come out."

"Okay. I'll see what I can do."

Leo went back out and confronted the problem. It was going to be a tricky rescue. He took the extensions off of the drainpipe until he had just the piece that went straight up, attached to the house. Because of the elbow connector at the bottom, he couldn't see into it. He went back to his truck and brought out a TV camera with a light, pencil thin, on a bendy gooseneck. He threaded it up the bottom portion of the drainpipe and looked at the monitor.

"There is something blocking the pipe," he pointed out.

"The kitten," the householder said.

"No. Something else. Debris from the eaves, maybe."

"Maybe… but would that hold the kitten's weight?"

"Might be something bigger."

"Can you go in from the top?"

There was no way Leo was climbing up on top of the house. He shook his head.

"No. It's too far down. Almost halfway, I'd say."

They both stared at the house.

"We're going to have to detach the drainpipe. Take it off, disassemble it, maybe even cut it, depending on where the kitten is in relation to the joins. Then you'll have to reinstall it again after."

The man sighed, nodding. "Okay."

Leo was fine as long as he didn't think about the height as he put his ladder against the house. Just focus on what he was doing. There were several brackets that had to be unscrewed. He tapped the drainpipe a few times to figure out where the kitten was and locate the nearest join. The kitten appeared to be right at the join, which meant taking the whole kit and caboodle down. If he pulled off the bottom half and the kitten fell out the top half, it would be curtains for kitty. Too risky.

Leo proceeded to unscrew all of the brackets and then moved to detach the top.

"Can you hold onto the bottom?" he called to the homeowner. "I don't want it to fall when I get the top unhitched."

The man took hold of the bottom and braced the drainpipe as high as he could reach, trying to keep it all straight and safe. Leo detached the top of the drainpipe and looked briefly at the hole the kitten had gone through to get into the drainpipe.

Holding the top end of the pipe, he slowly backed down the ladder, gradually leveling out the pipe as he held the top and the man held the bottom. When the drainpipe reached about a forty-five degree angle, the kitten started to skitter and scratch, making his way back uphill. When it reached level, the kitten stopped moving altogether, probably frightened or disoriented. Leo looked into his end as he reached the ground.

"Still right in the middle there," he observed.

"Should we try to shake it out?"

"No, I don't think so. Let me just figure out where he is in relation to this join."

Leo made his way down to the middle and tapped around, trying to figure out where the kitten was. It seemed to be right above the join, so they carefully took the two pieces apart. He heard it try to skitter up higher. There was a bunch of debris jammed in the bottom half that they removed. Taking a sight up the drainpipe, it seemed to be clear other than the kitten now. Leo tipped it at a higher angle until the poor thing started to slide down again, and then there it was. It blinked in the sunlight at them, mewling softly, wet and bedraggled. Leo laughed at it and picked it up, holding it against his body to warm up.

"All right!" the man said. "Great job! Thank you so much for your help!"

"So what was blocking it?" Leo asked, looking at the remaining piece of drainpipe.

The man examined it and pulled out the blockage, shaking his head, and showing a nest of leaves clustered around a tennis ball.

"The neighbor kids probably threw it on the roof to start out with!" he said.

"Kids."

"Yeah."

Leo walked back over to the neighbor's house, where the children were watching excitedly out the window, obviously having been told to stay inside out of the way. They let him into the house and Leo let them have a quick peek at the kitten before taking it back to its mother.

The mama cat sniffed the little fellow thoroughly before dragging him back to the rest of the litter and setting him between her paws, where she started to clean him. Both mama and kitten purred loudly.

Leo chuckled. "There you go. A happy ending."

"Thank you, mister. Thank you so much for saving Patches!"

"You're welcome. Now, are you going to keep these guys inside where it's safe, so this doesn't happen again?"

They all nodded. The children's mother sighed. Taking in the mama cat probably hadn't been her idea. Probably a stray that picked out their shed to have her babies in without any input from the owners.

"And don't throw balls onto the neighbor's roof," Leo told the children sternly.

"What?"

"How did you know that?"

Leo raised an eyebrow. "Just don't do it again," he told them.

"Okay, mister, we won't. It was an accident…"

Leo said goodbye and went back to the truck, checking in with the dispatcher to report his success and to see what other calls were still outstanding. Happily, someone else had been called to deal with the skunk call. Skunk calls never ended well. The best resolution was if you got there and the animal was gone. Someone else's problem.

There were no more interesting calls, but Leo was satisfied. He hadn't felt like coming in to work, but he was glad he had. You didn't get those tender reunions often enough.

Leo checked his truck back in at the end of the day.

"Nice job with the stuck kitten," Melanie commented with a smile.

"It was great," Leo agreed. He turned to go, and then paused. "Say, last week I heard something about dog fights. Was there a bust?"

She looked at him, puzzled. "Dog fights?" she repeated. "No, nothing. Where did you hear that?"

"I don't even remember. There was something in the paper? Or maybe it was on the internet."

"Maybe not local," Melanie said, a little puzzled. "Are you sure it was in the city?"

"I don't know," Leo fumbled. "I guess I wasn't paying enough attention."

"Hmm. Well, let me know if you hear anything else. But we certainly didn't have any dogs come in from dog fights in the last few days."

"Okay," Leo said. "Thanks. I must have misheard."

CHAPTER NINETEEN

LEO LOOKED INTO THE hospital room. Shayla was sitting by the bed reading a book and looked up when he came in.

"Hi Leo! Oh, what happened to you?"

Leo indicated his black eye, shrugging. "This? Nothing. Boxing match."

"Oh, that's right. I forgot you do that. I don't understand why anyone would want to risk being crippled or killed…"

Leo hoped she wasn't going to go off on him like Elizabeth. "Yeah, I know," he said. "A lot of people don't get it."

She accepted this and didn't pursue it any further. Leo sat on the edge of the bed, looking Lyall over. Every day, he seemed a little more distant, a little more remote. When Leo looked at him now, he didn't see his father. He could not see any of the force that had been his father in the empty shell.

He was starting to understand that what the doctors said was true. His father wasn't there anymore. He was gone forever, vacated, leaving the house empty.

"Does he look different today?" Leo asked.

Shayla looked at Leo, then at Lyall. "Not really, I don't think. Why? Do you think he looks better?"

"Not better, no. Just… different."

"Oh," Shayla's face fell, disappointed. "The nurse said there seemed to be some fluid on his chest. He's got a little bit of a fever."

Leo looked back at his father, then at her. "That doesn't sound good. Does that mean pneumonia?"

"I don't know. She said she'd talk to the doctor about it. I haven't seen anyone yet."

"If it is pneumonia, what do you want to do?"

"What do you mean?" she asked naively.

"Do you want… do you want them to try to save him?"

"Of course!"

Leo sighed. He had thought maybe this was the beginning of the end. But if Shayla wasn't ready to give up yet… he couldn't hurt her. She had always been so nice to him. Naive about everything his father had done and what sort of person he was, but nice to Leo. Shayla hadn't thought Leo a monster because of his attitude toward his father. She just acted understanding and gentle toward him.

"What was he like?" Leo asked. "When you met him, and were together, what was he like to you?"

Shayla smiled. "He was such a gentleman, Leo. Always so kind to me. I know he was… unpolished, rough around the edges, but he was charming."

"And he treated you right? He never hurt you?"

"No, not at all. Always a gentleman. I know he did things when you were younger that he shouldn't have. He told me about the drinking, and he was ashamed of the way he treated you kids when you were growing up. He was ashamed of having been an alcoholic and hurting you."

"He should be," Leo agreed.

"Well, I guess so," Shayla agreed reluctantly. "But everyone deserves a second chance. You know how he turned his life around, quitting drinking and learning to read. It opened up a whole new world for him."

"But he was still the same person. I mean… he could go for a while without showing his true colors, but he was still the same person inside. People don't change that much."

"Maybe he *didn't* change that much inside. Maybe it was just the outside that changed."

"What do you mean by that?" Leo asked, frowning.

"Maybe what you saw was just the outside, just a mask to cover up what he was inside. Maybe he was always scared and vulnerable, and didn't know what to do. Maybe the… anger… was just a cover up, not who he really was. And giving up drinking and learning to read, that allowed him to show who he really was."

Leo closed his eyes. "So you think inside he cared. But he decided to cover that up by beating the crap out of us. So we wouldn't know what was on the inside."

"Well… yes. But I don't think he really…"

"Yes, he did. Don't try to cover up what he did!" Leo insisted.

"No… I'm not trying to."

"He might have told you he didn't treat us right, but he didn't have the honesty to tell you how it really was. What he did to us. We're not just talking a smack on the butt with a newspaper, you know. You don't want me to tell you how it was and I don't want to hurt your sensibilities. Just trust me that saying he 'wasn't a very good dad' and 'didn't always treat us right' is sort of like saying 'Mount Everest is a pretty big hill'. He wasn't being honest with you, he was covering it up."

"Well, to his credit," Shayla said, "I didn't want him to tell me the details. You're right, it hurts my sensibilities. I like you, Leo. And I love Lyall. If there was something I could do to change your past, to make everything okay between you guys, I would. But me hearing all the details, that's not going to make anything better. Especially not now, when he's… so far away." There was a catch in her voice.

"It just makes me mad," he said. "Hearing how he lied to you about it. If he was going to lie about it anyway, why didn't he just say it never happened?" The cat inside of Leo uncoiled and started to pace. Leo shifted uncomfortably, his chest getting tight. "Why didn't he just say we made it up and he never did anything? Say that we hate him because that's how our mother told us we should feel? I mean, why admit to some of the truth, and then cover it up?"

"I don't know."

They both sat in silence for a while.

"What was your mother like, Leo?" Shayla asked. "You don't ever talk about her."

Leo thought about it. "She wasn't like he was," he said slowly. "But she didn't protect us from him. Didn't keep him from hurting us. So in a way, that's just as bad, isn't it?"

"Yes, I guess… they say battered women can't help it, though, it's not their fault."

Leo nodded. "It's a good excuse, anyway. I still tried to help protect the other kids, even though I was abused. She could have done something."

"What?"

Leo thought about her dousing the car with gasoline. She'd thought of a way out. It didn't work, but she'd tried at least once to free them from their prison.

"She was mentally ill," he admitted after thinking about it for a while. "I don't know what she was like in the beginning. Before she had to deal with him. But from the time I was little, she was… not well. She did what he wanted her to do, even if it meant she had to hurt us. And when she did try to get us out of there, to protect us…" he shook his head. "She hurt us even worse."

"I'm sorry, Leo," Shayla said softly.

Leo nodded.

"What happened to her?" Shayla asked. "How did she die?"

"I don't really know. I don't know whether she killed herself, or he killed her, or if she just took off one day. I don't even know if she's dead, or if she's living somewhere else, having forgotten all about us."

"Lyall said she was dead," Shayla said, surprised.

"Well then, maybe she is. I don't know. We never had a funeral. She was just gone."

"Maybe he couldn't stand to admit she was really dead," Shayla said. "Maybe it was just too hard for him."

"Or maybe he buried her in the back yard," Leo said darkly.

Shayla's eyes got big. "Leo!" she rebuked.

Leo rolled his eyes, chuckling to himself. "Always bury the bodies," he repeated to himself, "or the body parts. It's an important lesson to learn, Shayla. We can't go digging up the past."

"Well, no," she agreed, frowning in confusion. "But I—"

"You don't know what happened to her. Unless you're lying to me."

"No. I'm not lying. I don't know what happened. I'm sorry, I shouldn't have brought it up."

Leo stared out the window.

He turned and looked at Lyall's body, at his face. Was it Leo's imagination or was Lyall paler? Slipping away from them?

"He saved my life once," Leo said. "Did you know that?"

"He did?" Shayla's expression brightened, pleased. "What happened?"

"He pulled me out of a burning car."

Shayla's eyes widened. "Whoa. He never told me about that."

"I was about seven. Lewis was two or three. Rachel was nine."

"Rachel?" Shayla didn't know the name.

"She didn't make it. She couldn't get out. I couldn't get her out." There was a lump in Leo's throat. It was a long time ago. But the dream had brought it all back. He'd never talked about it. It was one of those things they all knew not to bring up. Rachel's name had never been mentioned after the funeral.

"Oh, I'm sorry, Leo. That must have been so hard. Maybe that was what made your mother… ill. It must be awful to lose a child."

"She was sick before that."

He didn't tell Shayla Margaret had lit the fire. That was one of those things Shayla just wouldn't want to know. Leo and his siblings and mother had learned to keep quiet and not tell their stories because that was what Lyall had forced them to do.

Shayla chose to turn away and hide from it. She could have asked him, Leo would have told her. But she didn't want to know. And that was different than being forced to be quiet.

"I'm glad you told me about that," Shayla said. "About how he saved your life."

Leo nodded. That, she'd heard. She wanted to think of Lyall as a hero. He'd always been a hero to her, somebody who had overcome addiction and disability. Now she had something else to admire him for too. Leo wasn't sure why he'd even told Shayla. It seemed right at the time, but he was irritated now by her hero worship.

"I've got to head out," Leo said, looking at his watch. "Sorry."

"It's okay," Shayla said. "I'm glad you came today."

Sweating, Leo took a swig of water from his bottle. "I want you guys to practice these exercises at least once a day before the next lesson, okay?"

The boys muttered and nodded. He wondered how many of them really would. Or if they would forget as soon as they walked out the door.

"Good. Chase, stay after."

"What?" Chase protested. "What did I do?"

"I just want to talk to you. The rest of you, scatter. Go home."

The boys obeyed, looking at each other and at Chase, as they left him behind. Chase danced nervously from foot to foot, looking at Leo to see if he was in trouble.

"No," Leo said. "You didn't do anything. I just want to talk to you. Let's take a walk."

"Umm, okay, Coach. Where?"

Leo took him out the back door so they wouldn't have to walk past the other boys who had just been dismissed and could have some privacy.

"Chase…"

"Yeah, Coach?"

"Things are getting pretty bad."

"What're you talking about?"

Leo brushed Chase's hair back from his face, searching his eyes. He hooked a finger over Chase's t-shirt and pulled it down, baring part of his chest, revealing a couple of round, angry red burn marks. Chase pushed Leo's hand away.

"Coach, don't!"

"Who is it?"

"No one. I just hurt myself."

Leo held his forearm in front of Chase's face, pointing to a couple of round, pale, puckered scars.

"Yeah, just like *I* hurt myself," he said.

Chase raised his eyes to Leo's face, looking astounded. "You?"

"Yeah. Me too. And lots of other kids. You're not alone. But we can't let him keep hurting you. So tell me who it is."

Chase pursed his lips and scratched his head. Leo understood. How many times had he tried to screw up the courage to tell someone? But after being hurt so many times, disbelieved, blocked when he tried to get help, Leo had stopped.

"Chase. I'll help you. Let me."

Chase bit his lip. "Coach… it's okay, really. I'm all right. And he said… he said he won't do it again, he's sorry."

"And do you think that's true?" Leo said. "You think he's going to stop?"

Chase shook his head gloomily. He knew better. It likely wasn't the first time he'd heard that line.

"Your dad?" Leo asked.

"My dad's gone."

"Who is it, then?"

"My… my step-dad," Chase admitted. "John."

They kept walking while Leo considered this.

"Is he home?" Leo asked. "I need to talk to him."

Chase was having second thoughts about letting Leo get involved. "No, Coach. Really, I think he'll stop now. I don't want you to talk to him, he'll just get mad. It'll get me in more trouble."

"No. Keeping quiet just means he can keep hurting you. I'm not going to cause more trouble for you. I'm going to help you."

"What're you going to do?"

"I'm going to get him to leave."

"Get him to leave?" Chase echoed. His voice lifted slightly, hopeful.

"That's right," Leo said.

Chase hesitated.

"Let's go," Leo said.

Chase nodded. He led Leo down the street and they walked in silence until Chase stopped in front of a tiny pink house with a dead lawn.

Chase gestured at the house. "Here we are."

"Let's go in," Leo said. While he was trying to show a strong, confident front to Chase, inside his heart was pounding hard and anxiety was tearing at his insides. He was nervous about facing down Chase's abuser. What if he was a huge, strong guy, and Leo couldn't intimidate him?

What if Leo couldn't do what he promised?

Chase led the way reluctantly. He went up the stairs and opened the front door and Leo followed him in. Leo looked around. The scene was a familiar one. Mom in the kitchen making supper or cleaning up dishes. Step-dad John in the easy chair in the front room, dirty and stinking of sweat, drinking his beer, watching his TV.

They always thought they deserved to rest at the end of the day. That everybody else should serve them. Men who could hurt and intimidate everyone else into doing what they wanted. The man looked up at Chase's entry, a scowl on his face. When he saw Leo, he modified his expression slightly.

"Who are you?" he demanded.

Chase's mom, a thin, severe looking woman, looked out of the kitchen at this unexpected question. She wiped her hands on a towel, frowning.

"I'm Chase's Coach," Leo said.

"What do you want?"

"I came to talk to you about him," Leo explained, stepping further into the room, approaching the sacred chair.

"What's he done now?" John said irritably. "The boy needs a good whipping. He's in trouble all the time!"

"I want you to *stop* whipping him," Leo said, heat rising in his chest. "Stop whipping him, and burning him, and hitting him. Just leave the boy alone."

"Who's gonna make me?" John sneered.

"If you don't leave him alone—not just leave him alone, but leave town —I'm going to have the cops on you."

"Where's your proof? What's gonna make the cops believe you?"

Leo stepped closer to John, hands clenching into fists. "He's got scars and burn marks. I'll tell them you admitted it to me when you were drunk. I'll say his mom cried to me about it when she picked him up from boxing. I'll say whatever I have to, and I'll get you thrown behind bars, whatever it takes."

John looked uncertain. "Why would you do that? Why do *you* care?"

"Why do I care? Everybody should care! I want you out of here."

The man just sat there, staring at him.

"Get up," Leo ordered. "I want you out of here now."

"Now?" John repeated stupidly.

"Yeah. Now!" Leo shouted. He kicked the chair, clenching his teeth and trying to keep the cat from bursting out all at once. "Get up and get out!"

"You can't kick me out of my own house!"

"Can't I?" Leo demanded, reaching into his pocket and pulling out his phone. "I'll just call the cops then, shall I? And we'll see if you stay or leave."

"No," John said nervously. "Don't do that."

"Then get out."

John looked at Chase's mom, trying to figure out if she was going to support him or not. She stood frozen, paralyzed by indecision.

"Now!" Leo shouted.

He grabbed John's arm and pulled him out of the chair.

The man tried to throw a punch at him, and Leo blocked it and returned a right cross to his chin.

John just about fell back into his chair, staggered.

"You can't come into my house, threaten me, hit me, try to kick me out!" John protested in outrage.

"No?" Leo challenged. "I can still call the cops. You could tell them about it."

John steadied himself on the chair, trying to get his bearings. He flashed an angry look at Chase's mom and at Chase.

"Stinkin' house anyway," he said venomously. "Who'd want to stick around here? Not me, that's for sure! I was gonna hit the road anyway."

Leo gestured to the door. "Be my guest."

John pushed past Leo, struck out at Chase and missed, and stopped in the doorway.

"Git," Leo said, "and don't come back."

John went down the steps and into the night. Leo watched him get into his car and pull out with a screech.

He turned back to Chase, who was looking at him anxiously.

"He left! But are you sure he'll stay away? For real?"

Leo shrugged. "If he comes back, we'll call the police. If he's smart, he'll stay away."

"Why did you do that?" Chase's mom asked suddenly. She'd had no voice for the whole encounter, but now her strident tones filled Leo's ears. "Why would you do that?"

Leo looked at her in amazement. "He was hurting Chase! You didn't want him to keep doing that, did you?"

"No… but it wasn't so bad. He said he wouldn't do it anymore."

"He lied!" Leo said. "He wasn't going to stop. They never stop. How could you just stand by and let him hurt Chase?"

"John was a good provider," she said. "What am I supposed to do now? How am I supposed to support us?"

Leo glowered. "Get a job. Get assistance. It's better than being beaten!"

She shook her head, her face white and pinched. "I needed him."

"You don't need anyone who's going to hurt you or Chase. Anything is better than that."

"How would *you* know? You don't know what it's like."

Leo shook his head in disbelief. "If he comes back," he told Chase. "You tell me. If she's not going to keep him away, we'll find you somewhere else to stay. Okay? Somewhere safe, where you're not going to get hurt."

Chase nodded. Glancing at his mother, he shrugged a little sadly. "She tries," he said apologetically.

Leo headed for the door. He patted Chase on the shoulder; gently, in case Chase had other burns or injuries Leo didn't know about. Chase offered a fist bump and Leo obliged.

"Thanks, Coach," Chase said.

"Take care of yourself. Don't forget those exercises. I'll see you Tuesday."

Was it the encounter with Chase's mother that took him back? In his dreams, Leo went back to that day. Another day that had changed their lives forever.

Leo and the others got home from school. Leo led Phil off the bus by the hand. He got into the house and found Stormy in the living room crying. Leo let go of Phil's hand and picked Stormy up.

"Hey, what's up, princess? What's wrong?"

Stormy buried her face in his neck, sobbing and holding him tightly. Leo looked around at the kitchen and his mother's bedroom.

"Mom? Where are you?" he called, looking around for her. He couldn't see her. He looked out the window. She could be outside. Could be in the garage helping Lyall with something.

But Leo had an uneasy feeling something was wrong.

The chill in the house took on an added coldness.

Like it had been sitting empty all day.

"You guys get to your homework and chores," Leo told the younger kids.

"I don't have homework," Phil informed him.

"No. Preschoolers don't get homework. Why don't you set the table?"

"Okay," Phil agreed cheerfully and went to work.

The older kids looked at Leo and didn't say anything. They went to their bedrooms, knowing better than to ask questions.

With Stormy on his hip, Leo went outside.

"Mom? Mom, are you out here?" he called, looking around.

Margaret was nowhere to be found.

Leo went to the garage and found Lyall under the truck, working on his engine. Stormy clung to Leo, pressing her face so hard against him he felt her teeth grate on his collarbone. He jiggled her, trying to calm her.

"Uh, Dad?"

There was a bang and Lyall swore. He slid out from under the truck, looking peeved and holding his hand to his head. "What're you doing, sneaking in here?"

"Sorry. I thought you heard me come in."

"What do you want? Don't you have homework and chores to do?"

Leo nodded. "Yeah, I will. I just wondered… where mom is."

"Quit fussing about your mother and just get to work."

Leo frowned. "I just… is she home? Is she… downstairs or something?"

Lyall looked at him with narrowed eyes. "You are not allowed to go downstairs without permission," he growled.

"I know. That's why I asked. I didn't go downstairs, so I don't know."

"Your mother went away. Deal with it."

Leo stood there frozen, staring at him. *She went away?*

How could she go away when they only had one vehicle, and Lyall was working on it? Leo felt a knot in his stomach, swelling up to nausea.

"Went away?" he repeated. "Went away where? For good? I don't get it!"

"Never were too bright, were you?" Lyall mocked. "She's gone. She's not coming back. Go take care of the kids."

Stormy was sobbing. Leo just stood there looking at his father. Lyall slid back under the car and continued to work without further comment to Leo.

Dragging his feet in the dust, Leo slowly walked back out of the garage and to the house.

"What happened, Stormy?" he asked. "Did you see what happened?"

She looked at him, her eyes big dark hollows. She shook her head and pressed herself against him.

Leo swallowed.

What had happened? How could Margaret just be gone?

Had someone come to pick her up? Had Lyall taken her away somewhere?

Was she hurt?

Was she in the basement and Lyall was just lying to him?

He went into the bedroom where Lewis was sitting with his school-books out, staring into space, not doing anything.

"Lew?"

Lewis focused on him. He looked grim. Lewis was younger, but he usually figured things out before Leo did.

The school kept telling Leo he wasn't stupid, he just had learning disabilities, but Leo knew Lewis was tons smarter than he was. Maybe just because Lewis didn't have learning disabilities. Or maybe Lewis was smart and Leo was stupid.

"Did you find her?" Lewis asked hollowly.

"No."

"What did he say?"

"He said… she's gone and isn't coming back."

Lewis's face went sheet white. He gripped the handles of his wheelchair tightly, sitting rigidly, staring at Leo in horror. That was how Leo felt on the inside and he was secretly glad to see he wasn't the only one feeling that way.

"You have to check downstairs," Lewis told him.

Leo swallowed and nodded. "I know," he agreed. "Here," he handed Stormy to Lew. "Sit with Lewie a while, Stormy."

"I would help…" Lewis said bleakly.

Leo nodded again. "I know. You can't go down the stairs. You can help by looking after Stormy for a few minutes."

Lewis smiled weakly, knowing this was inadequate. He wasn't really helping. He wasn't facing what Leo was.

Leo took a few deep breaths and felt lightheaded.

There were some things he just couldn't bear. He started his feet walking.

He couldn't think about it. He had to just go ahead and do it. If he thought about it, he would delay and he wouldn't be able to do it. Before opening the door to the stairs, he looked outside, making sure Lyall wasn't coming back to the house. Leo opened the board door, turned on the light switch, and walked slowly down the steep stairs.

Through the moldy-smelling storage room lined with dusty old shelves of jars and other various junk none of them ever used. To the door in the dark corner.

He pulled the bolts and turned the door handle. Groped inside for the light switch, holding his breath.

The dim bulb lit up, and Leo took a quick glance around the room.

Margaret was not there.

The thin cot in the corner was empty. The shackles were unlocked and lying loose on the floor.

Alert for any sound from upstairs, Leo slipped into the bare concrete room searching for any clue as to what had happened. He shifted the shackles slightly with his foot. Moved the thin blankets on the bed looking for any sign of fresh blood. Nothing had been touched in the last few days.

The room was cold, dank, and airless.

Leo breathed a sigh of relief and walked out of the room, shutting the light switch back off.

He closed the door and locked the bolts. He went back upstairs to his room. Lewis was holding Stormy in his lap, cradling her like a baby.

"No," Leo said. "It's empty."

Lewis didn't look relieved.

Leo stood looking at him, feeling he had missed something. "What?" he asked.

"Then where is she?" Lewis said.

Leo's heart dropped. "I—don't know…" he said slowly.

Lewis looked bleak. "What did He say?"

"He said… she's not coming back."

The both just looked at each other, the time ticking away. Leo shook his head, understanding dawning on him. "No," he said.

Lewis didn't say anything.

"No," Leo insisted. "She's not gone. She can't be gone."

"Did he say where she went?"

"No. He just said she was gone. But she could be at the hospital. Or out shopping. Maybe Aunt Robin came and got her."

"You know what he did," Lewis said bleakly.

"No. No, no, no," Leo protested, a lump in his throat. "She went to the hospital. To the institution. Somewhere better than here. She just couldn't take it anymore."

They all knew she was fragile. Her mental health was tenuous at the best of times. Since the advent of the fire, things had never been the same.

She couldn't be trusted to make safe decisions. She would go off, lose touch with reality for days at a time.

Sometimes when Lyall got home from a trip, he would take her to the institution until they could get her stabilized.

Maybe he had just given up. Had decided she was too unstable to be at home any more.

Or maybe her sister had come to rescue her. Had finally convinced Margaret to abandon her family and go somewhere safe, back to her own family where she could be loved and cared for.

That was where she had gone. Not… whatever Lewis was thinking and feared to put into words.

Lewis rocked Stormy, kissing the top of her curly head. "You'd better get dinner on," he warned.

Leo walked mechanically back to the kitchen. He started moving around pots and pans and rifling the fridge, looking for something that would make an acceptable supper.

She was gone.

She was gone and she was never coming back.

How were they going to manage without her?

CHAPTER TWENTY

LEO AWOKE FROM A dream, gasping for breath. His head was pounding. No, someone was pounding on the neighbor's door. No… was someone pounding on his door? Leo looked at his alarm clock. Three in the morning. Some drunk, probably. If Leo ignored it, he would go away. Leo rolled over and closed his eyes, covered his head with the pillow, trying to shut out the noise and find sleep again.

Rascal got up and started whining, pacing restlessly from Leo's bed to the door and back.

Leo growled at him. "Lay down, Rascal! Stay!"

The dog lay down but continued to whine, a high-pitched, grating sound. The obnoxious drunk wasn't getting the idea and continued to knock on the door. Leo gave up and pulled the pillow off his head.

Muttering under his breath, he got up to go see who it was.

"Stupid drunk, just go home and sleep it off, will you?" he muttered to himself.

As he got closer to the door, he could hear a voice. A female voice. Leo looked out the peephole. Elizabeth! Leo unlocked and opened the door.

"Elizabeth? What are you doing here?"

"I just came for a visit," Elizabeth said dreamily.

"A visit? It's three o'clock in the morning!"

"What's going on?" Elizabeth asked. "Aren't we going to have a party?"

Leo stared at her in consternation. A party? What was she talking about? Elizabeth's eyes were far away. She stared past him, not even seeing him. Leo shook his head. "A party? We're not having a party."

"I *like* parties," Elizabeth said excitedly, looking around.

"I'm sure you do. But… there's no party here."

"Is it a surprise?" Elizabeth queried.

"Who are you today?" Leo asked with a frown. Certainly not Lizzie. Not Eli or another boy.

Elizabeth seemed unperturbed by the question. "Lisbet," she said.

She went into his kitchen and started going through the cupboards and fridge, pulling out random foods. "How about eggs?" she asked, bringing out the carton and putting it on the counter.

"Are you hungry?"

"Well, you can't have a party without food," Elizabeth pointed out.

"Well, no, I guess not. I don't think I want any eggs, though. I ate before I went to bed…"

Elizabeth didn't get the hint. She turned on the stove and put a frying pan on the element. Leo watched her move around, perfectly at home. It was nice she felt comfortable, but it was a little out of Leo's comfort zone.

She continued to move around, throwing random foods onto plates, cooking the eggs, and chattering away.

Leo went back to the bedroom. Rascal was still obediently laying where Leo had told him to 'stay'. When Leo walked in, Rascal looked up at him, eyes wide, ears back, whining.

"Come on, Rascal. You can come say hi," Leo told him.

Rascal leapt to his feet, and after stopping for a conciliatory scratch from Leo, he bounded over to Elizabeth. She shrieked, surprised, and pulled back.

Rascal fell back, flinching away.

"Hey," Leo said. "It's okay. It's just Rascal."

Elizabeth looked at him with wild eyes. She looked at Rascal, then looked around at the house, bewildered.

"Shh," Leo said. "It's okay."

"What—what are you doing here?"

"This is where I live," Leo said dryly.

Elizabeth looked around again. "This is your house?" she repeated, her eyes scanning back and forth.

"Yeah, well…"

"How did I get here?"

"You were pounding on my door. You said you were here for the party."

Elizabeth looked around at the plates of food, and at the eggs on the stove, which were turned up too high and starting to smoke.

"You're having a party?" she asked in a bewildered tone.

"No. But I guess *you* were."

Elizabeth stared at him like he was crazy. Leo started to laugh.

"What's so funny?"

"You are. You come over here, practically break down my door, insist we're having a party, and start to cook…" He went over and stirred the eggs and turned the element down. "I hope you're hungry! You're looking at me like I'm out of my mind, but I'm the one in pajamas in my own house. You're the one showing up out of the blue and making dinner."

Elizabeth looked at the food on the counters around her with a frown. "Well, I could eat the eggs, but I don't think I can eat all of this…"

Leo chuckled. He took the frying pan off of the burner, and moved some crackers onto the same plate as some pickles, then used the plate they had been on for the eggs.

"What do you like on your eggs?" he asked. "Pickles? Crackers? Cheese?"

"No… just salt and pepper…"

"Ketchup? Sausages?" Leo looked at the other food spread out on the counters.

"Maybe some ketchup," Elizabeth conceded, scowling at him.

"So who are you now?" Leo asked. She had obviously changed personalities when Rascal had startled her.

She looked at him slightly suspiciously.

"Lisa," she said. "But when I was sleepwalking…?"

"Lisbet. Were you sleepwalking? Or were you just Lisbet and don't remember?"

"No. Lisbet doesn't hide anything. But sometimes I do things in my sleep."

"Yeah? Like throwing a party?"

Elizabeth shook her head at the various dishes. "If I'm Lisbet!"

She salted and peppered the eggs, got out a fork, and took her food to the table. Leo sat down with her and watched her eat.

"Tell me more about Lisbet," he suggested.

"Well, she likes people. Likes a party. She's fun to be around."

"She seems a little flighty," Leo observed.

"Yeah… more so if I'm asleep. If I'm awake, you can't always tell."

"Do you do this a lot?"

"I don't know… I don't usually remember after."

"Does your doctor know?"

"Yeah, I do it at the hospital too. Though I don't get to have parties there!" Elizabeth laughed.

"I guess not. Did you have parties before the army? Assuming you didn't have any when you were in the army."

"Not many, no," Elizabeth agreed. "Before, when I was with my foster families, I guess I had some. I was never popular at school, but I tried to get people to like me. Tried to invite them over and have parties like the popular kids did. But somehow, it never really worked out the way it did for the popular kids. It doesn't help to pretend you are popular. Everyone still knows you're not like them. Once a freak, always a freak."

Leo nodded. He'd had his own experiences with stereotypes and being unpopular. He was an outcast himself. A freak. Even if you were a little boy who had saved your brother from a fire, it didn't make you popular. He wondered sometimes if having his picture in the newspaper had made the other kids jealous of him. Made them notice all the ways he was different.

"How were *you* a freak?" he asked.

"I was always the new kid. Not something I'd recommend. Starting at a new school halfway through the year. You have to make all new friends."

"But at least you got a fresh start. People didn't have a preconceived notion of you, know anything about your past."

"Part of your past always travels with you. And kids… they can sense these things. They don't need to know you were unpopular at your last school. They know it as soon as they look at you. Being a foster kid, you have worn out clothes, stuff that's not fashionable. You never have the latest toys or games. You don't have a car. No money to buy things. You bring a bag lunch from home, a sandwich, and an apple. Water from the fountain, not from a bottle. No pop or fancy energy drinks."

Leo thought back to his own school experience. How often he had wished he had somewhere else to go, somewhere he could start fresh, where people didn't know him already. But he supposed it would have been the same for him. They would still have known. He would have had the stink of failure on him from an early age.

"Is that why you went by so many different names?" Leo asked. "Because you wanted a fresh start?"

"I wanted to wipe out the past, forget about it, start over again. I hated them calling me by a name I'd used before, bringing old memories back to the surface. I wanted to be a new person."

"Yeah. Well… at least we grew up," he said, watching Elizabeth slowly eat the eggs. "I'm glad I'm not in school any more. The whole 'real world' experience is much better for me."

"I'm still waiting to grow up," Elizabeth said wistfully.

Leo grinned at this. But he supposed it was true. She had made an attempt to be a grown up. She had joined the army and tried to support herself somehow. Even had a baby. But she still hadn't really grown up. All these personalities… most of them were still children. Little fractured pieces of herself that had never progressed beyond their formation. All stuck in the past.

"What do you plan to do next?" Leo asked tentatively. It was always good to have a plan. Grown-ups had plans.

"I don't know. I've failed at everything I've tried. I don't think I'm cut out for… being a responsible adult."

"Well, when you get Juleen back, you'll need—"

"Juleen!" The fork dropped from her hand. Elizabeth's eyes bugged out.

Leo swallowed, a knot of anxiety forming in his stomach. The cat stirred. "What?"

"Where's Juleen?"

"Isn't she still in foster care?"

"No, I got her back. Where is she?"

"You didn't bring her with you. Is she back at your apartment?"

"Oh man. I sure hope so!"

"How could you forget her?" Leo demanded, outrage growing even though he knew it wasn't her fault.

How could Child Services have even considered giving Juleen back to her yet? She'd been out of hospital and stable for what, three days?

Stupid, stupid people.

"I don't know!" Elizabeth defended herself. "I was asleep!"

"Do you want me to take you back to your apartment?" Leo asked, getting up and patting his pockets for keys before realizing he was in his pajamas and his keys were beside the bed with his wallet and other pocket contents.

"Did I bring my car?"

"How do I know? You just came to my door. I didn't see whether you walked or drove. You can't drive in your sleep, can you?"

"I can do anything in my sleep," Elizabeth retorted.

"Do you want me to come with you?"

She hesitated.

Leo jumped in. "I'll come with you," he asserted. "I don't want you to… get sidetracked. You might need help with Juleen."

Elizabeth nodded. "Okay. You want to drive with me, or in your own car?"

"I'll bring mine. If you're okay to drive."

"Well, if I can drive it while I'm asleep, I can sure as heck drive while I'm awake."

"Okay. Let me just get my stuff and I'll be right along."

"Yeah. I'll go find my car."

When he pulled out into the street, Leo saw Elizabeth's car as she waited for him. At least she'd found it. It hadn't gotten towed away. He followed her back to her apartment and went up with her.

Elizabeth had left the door wide-open. Leo tried to keep the panicked feelings down.

Anyone could have wandered into the apartment while she was gone. Juleen was not safe!

He followed Elizabeth into the apartment. She went straight to Juleen's crib.

"She's okay," Elizabeth told him, relieved. "She's right here and she's still asleep."

Leo bent over the crib, looking the baby over for any sign of harm. She was dressed warmly enough. She was asleep. No tear tracks on her face. Her clothes were not obviously wet or soiled.

All safe and well.

"Good," he breathed. "That could have been really bad."

"Where would she go?" Elizabeth dismissed. "Of course she's fine. She can't walk away."

"You can't take the chance of leaving her alone. Anything could happen. What if someone had come in here?"

"Looking for a baby to steal? More power to them."

"Elizabeth… if you don't want to take care of Juleen, or if you can't, you have to tell Child Services. You can't just keep taking her back and then forgetting about her or refusing to take care of her."

"I don't want Child Services to take her. She's my baby. I always wanted a family and now I've got one of my own. She's mine. I'm the one that's going to take care of her."

"Well then, what are you going to do to keep her from getting hurt? How are you going to make sure you can't just walk out of the apartment and forget about her? Maybe… we could put a chain on the door, high up."

"You think I can drive a car, but I can't take a chain off the door?"

"I don't know, then," Leo said. "A loud motion alarm that will wake you up? We have to do something, to protect Juleen."

"We?" Elizabeth repeated. "I told you, she's *my* baby. Not yours. I don't know why you think you're in charge of me. Or in charge of her. She's my baby. Just mine."

CHAPTER TWENTY-ONE

WHEN HE AWOKE TO THE phone ringing, Leo had barely fallen back asleep. Groaning, he turned over and looked at the time.

Six o'clock. Who would be calling him so early?

He picked up the phone and looked at the caller ID. Shayla.

Leo pressed 'talk.' "Hi. Shayla?"

"Leo. I'm sorry to call so early. I didn't want to miss you before you went to work."

"No, it's okay. What's wrong?"

"He's worse. They said he's really bad. I need you to come."

Leo rubbed his eyes. If there was one day he wanted to just go back to sleep, it was today. Why did Lyall have to get sick today?

It was like he was still trying to wreck Leo's life. Like he knew today was the worst day for Leo to have to get up and take care of Shayla.

"Okay. I'll be there as soon as I can," Leo promised.

"Thanks, Leo. Thank you."

"See you soon. Bye."

Leo hung up. For a few minutes, he just sat there on the bed, face in his hands, trying to get his internal engine revved up enough to go to the hospital and see what was going on with Lyall. And if he got there and the only problem was that Lyall had a slight fever or was 'looking' worse, Leo was going to be some ticked off.

He was too tired even to be angry.

Maybe *that* was the solution to his anger problem. Sleep deprivation. Make himself too tired to react to anything.

Leo got to his feet and walked to the bathroom. He stripped down, hoping a hot shower would get the blood flowing and help him to face the day. That and a couple of cups of hot coffee.

At the hospital, one of the nurses at the nursing station looked up at his approach and motioned him over. That was unusual. Usually, they ignored him as much as possible. With dread, Leo approached her.

"How is he?" Leo asked.

"He's taken a downturn," she informed him. "He has pneumonia. He's having a hard time getting enough oxygen. We've turned his mixture up, but his levels are still really low. I… don't think he has much longer."

It was a relief for Leo, but Shayla was not going to take it well. If Lyall would just die, then Leo could move on, forget about him, and carry on with his life. But Shayla would be upset. She would insist they do everything they could for him.

"Is there anything else you can do?"

"He's already on a vent. His lungs are full of fluid. We just can't get him enough oxygen for survival."

"What about antibiotics?" Leo suggested. Didn't they give antibiotics for pneumonia?

"We can try," the nurse said disapprovingly. "But heroic measures at this point… Don't you think it's time to just let nature take its course?"

"I don't know," Leo said.

She continued to look disapproving. Leo withdrew and went into the hospital room, braced for the worst.

Shayla sat by the bed, holding Lyall's hand. She hovered over him watching closely for the minutest change. She looked up when Leo came in.

She let go of Lyall's hand and went to Leo. She gave him a tight hug. "Oh, Leo! Thank you for coming!"

"How bad is it?" Leo asked.

She held onto him even after he tried to pull away. "Listen to him try to breathe. It's horrible. And he's so pale and gray. What are we going to do, Leo?"

"Maybe it's time."

"No. No, it can't be. We need to try, we need to make him better."

Leo looked down at the corpse of his father, feeling empty. "When an animal comes to the shelter that is really sick or hurt," he said, "we don't let them keep suffering. It's more humane to let them go peacefully."

"No! This is your father, Leo. We're not talking about someone's unwanted cat. We're talking about a human being. A human being who raised you, who took care of you, who saved your life once."

"Then how could I let him suffer?" Leo countered.

"You're not going to pull the plug on him. I know you won't. We've talked about this."

"I know. And I haven't done anything. But I don't know if there's anything we can do now. They say his brain is dead. His body can't take much more. I think you need to be prepared."

"I know, and I am, but I can't… I can't bear to think of losing him. We've been so happy together."

"Yeah. He was happy too," Leo said, thinking back to the day of the hunting accident.

Lyall had been happy. Very happy. It had seemed almost ominous to Leo.

What kind of person feels that something is wrong when someone else is happy? Why couldn't he be happy for his father, instead of worried about what was to come? If Lyall was happy, then he wouldn't hurt anyone.

But it was the calm before the storm. An eerie calm. He didn't trust it.

Lyall had talked about Shayla. How compatible they were. How he had missed having a partner. He felt whole. Shayla had completed him. All the time he talked, Leo's anxiety grew and grew.

He knew he had made the right choice. The only choice.

Poor Shayla.

"He was happy," Shayla agreed.

Leo sat down in one of the visitor chairs, watching his father's chest rise and fall as the machine pumped and pumped for him. The machine was rhythmic, but the sounds of Lyall's respirations were painful. He didn't cough or choke, but the breathing sounded strangled, and every now and then the respirations stopped while the machine went through an automatic suctioning cycle, trying to clear the mucus away. While it suctioned, Lyall grew grayer, more cadaverous.

There wasn't much longer now. He probably wouldn't last through the day.

———

Leo didn't realize he had fallen asleep in the chair. His late-night party with Elizabeth and the early-morning wakeup by Shayla and sitting vigil had caught up with him. He awoke with a start to the doctor talking to Shayla.

"It's time to let him go," Dr. Becker was saying.

"No," Shayla insisted. "Not yet."

"It's too late to donate his organs," Dr. Becker said angrily. "You should have done that while his body was still healthy, before infection set in."

"We don't *want* to donate his organs," Shayla said fiercely. "You can't have them!"

"Don't want them now," the doctor growled.

Leo shifted and stood up. They both turned and looked at him.

"You're his conservator," Dr. Becker said. "Not her. So tell me, what do you want to do now?"

"Just let nature take its course," Leo said gently.

Shayla started to cry.

"Do you want me to take him off the machines?" the doctor asked. "You can see him without all of the apparatus one last time and say goodbye."

Leo looked at Shayla. She shook her head.

Leo wouldn't force her. What difference did it make now? She didn't want to say goodbye. Neither did he, but for completely different reasons.

"Fine," the doctor said. "Let the nurses know if there are any changes or you need anything."

Leo nodded. Shayla looked like she would say something. The doctor shook his head and left. Leo looked at Shayla. She smiled weakly at him.

"Thank you, Leo."

"You don't need to keep thanking me."

"I'm just so glad you're here. I don't know how I would do this myself."

Pretty much the same. Leo wasn't doing anything except sitting with her. She went back over and sat on the edge of the bed, holding Lyall's hand. They both watched and waited.

And waited.

The day wore on. Leo watched Lyall slip away. Eventually, the heart monitor stuttered and stalled.

Shayla gasped. "Oh, no. No, Lyall!"

She clung to Lyall's hand, kissing it, holding it to her face as if to keep it warm. The nails were dark and dusky. Leo got up and stood by Shayla awkwardly.

"I'm sorry, Shay."

A nurse came in, quietly, with no urgency. She moved slowly in beside them and shut off each of the machines.

The room was deathly quiet.

It had been quiet before, but there had been the noise of the machines in the background. Pumping, beeping, hissing.

Now it was dead, as silent as the grave.

Leo was walking past the gym. It was late. He had called Jaime earlier in the day to explain why he couldn't take the program that afternoon. Jaime had promised to cover the class for him, so the boys would still be looked after and have something to do.

It was quiet. Everyone had gone home. Jaime was probably cleaning up, getting ready to close for the night. Leo stopped, watching a slim form bouncing a ball in the dark, taking a couple of shots at a hoop barely illuminated by the light inside the gym. The closest streetlights were out, and the neighborhood was dark. Leo stopped and watched for a moment. Then he walked into the compound.

The boy tensed and whirled around to face him. Then he saw who it was and relief flooded over his features.

"Coach!"

"What up, Bubblegum?"

Billy smiled fleetingly. He dribbled the basketball, not answering. Leo motioned for a pass and tried the shot. He was way off. They alternated shots for a few minutes. Neither of them was on their game.

"What's wrong, Billy?" Leo finally asked.

"Nothin', Coach. Just shooting some hoops."

"Why aren't you at home? It's late."

"Just wai—just hanging around, man. Sometimes things aren't so good at home, I don't want to go back right away. You know how it is."

"I do know," Leo said. "But I don't think you're telling me the truth."

He watched the boy's body language. The way he kept looking around. How jumpy he was.

"Why, Coach? I'm telling the truth!"

"Who are you waiting for?"

"No one," he lied.

"Billy."

"Watch this!" Billy tried to distract Leo with a three point shot, but it didn't go in.

Leo looked around. Someone came out of the gym.

Hakim.

"Hey, man," Leo greeted.

"Hey. Missed you today. You forget about your babysitting duties?"

"No, I was at the hospital. My dad died."

"Oh!" Hakim looked shocked. "I'm sorry. I didn't know."

"Me neither, Coach," said Billy. "I'm sorry about that. Was he sick?"

"He got shot a few weeks ago," Leo said. "His body just couldn't hold out any more."

"Oh," Billy said, eyes wide. "Oh wow."

Leo looked at Billy and Hakim and bit his lip, shaking his head. His suspicions coalesced with their nervous glances at each other.

"You two…" he said. "You're selling drugs?"

Billy and Hakim both looked guilty. Both launched into denials. But Leo could tell.

Those looks that had passed between them lately.

The little 'tells' that had given them both away the last couple of weeks.

Neither of them was really cut out for it. They didn't have the mercenary attitude it took. Neither had acquired the skill of not caring about people.

"You stay away from Billy," Leo told Hakim fiercely. "If I see you around here again, I'll call the cops."

Hakim's hands clenched into fists and he brought them up near his chin. Leo knew Hakim was a good fighter. But for once Leo was so drained he just didn't want a fight. He just wanted to go home to bed.

"You really want to go there?" he asked Hakim. "Just get lost and don't come back. I'm not turning you in, just telling you to get lost. Find someone else to do your dirty work for you. Not kids. Especially not *my* kids."

Hakim glanced over at Billy. "Kids are too unreliable," he said with a shrug. He started to walk away. "I never wanted to do this," he explained, "but a man has to make a living somehow. I've got a family to support."

"And you really think they want to see you behind bars? How would that help them?"

"You don't understand," Hakim said. He disappeared into the darkness.

Leo looked at Billy.

The boy's relief was obvious. His face relaxed and he blew out a 'whew' sound as they stood there. Leo wasn't sure what to do next.

"You okay?" he asked, with a bit of a shrug.

"Coach!" Billy threw himself at Leo, hugging him tightly, his voice muffled against Leo's chest. "Thank you! I didn't know what to do. I didn't want to keep doing it. Not after getting caught. But he kept… he said there was no way out."

Leo hugged him and patted him on the back. "It's okay, Billy," he soothed. "You're out now. He comes around here again, I'll report him. Same with if he shows up at school and tries to convince you. You just tell me and I'll take care of it. Okay?"

Billy nodded, sobbing.

The lights in the gym went off and Jaime came out of the building, turning to lock the door behind him. He had a security flashlight he swept through the playground.

"Who's there?" he demanded.

Leo let go of Billy, whose face was streaked with tears. He patted him on the back again. They were caught in the glow of the flashlight. Leo covered his eyes, squinting.

"Jaime, it's me. Leo. And Billy's still here."

"Billy? Go home. You can't hang around here in the dark."

Leo stepped toward Jaime. "Hakim's been dealing drugs on your property," Leo told him. "I told him to get lost and not come back."

Jaime didn't look surprised. He nodded heavily. "I've been watching that one. He's been too… too jumpy lately. Too secretive."

Leo nodded. "You won't let him back, then?"

"Of course not." Jaime looked at Billy. "You stay away from him. Got it, Bubblegum?"

Billy nodded. "Yeah, I will," he said. "Thanks."

"I'll walk you home," Leo offered.

"Aw, Coach, you don't gotta do that."

"It's late. I want to make sure you get home safe."

Billy shrugged and didn't protest as Leo tagged along with him. He lived in a single wide in a trailer park nearby with his grandma. Leo didn't know his whole story, but he had a pretty good idea how things worked. Kids never had both parents around. Sometimes they didn't have any. They all struggled, like Leo had, with poverty, abuse, mental illness, and crazy circumstances no one should have to go through. Not fair. They were too young, it was too much of a burden on them.

But their parents were the same way. Some of them Leo had known as a kid, older kids he had gone to school with. He'd envied them back then, but now, seeing how their own kids struggled, he had to wonder how many had been fighting their own demons back then too.

He'd been so caught up in his own troubles, he'd never once stopped to wonder about the others around him. What their lives were really like, what secrets they covered up.

"Thanks, Coach," Billy said, as he left Leo's side and mounted the steps to the trailer.

"No problem. Stay out of trouble, okay?"

"Yeah. I will."

CHAPTER TWENTY-TWO

LEO STARED AT THE TV, but he had no idea what was even on. The noise just washed over him. In his mind, he had gone back in time.

The ride in had been a long one. As Leo started to unpack their gear from the truck, Lyall embraced the whole of outdoors with a big stretch and yawn, and a satisfied grunt.

"The big ol' outdoors," Lyall said, with a grin. "Nothin' beats it, does it, boy?"

"No, sir," Leo agreed. He continued to pull their gear out of the car.

He was not enjoying the brisk morning breeze, the birds chirping in the trees, or the bright spring sunshine.

He was here for one reason, and one reason alone, and that wasn't to enjoy himself. It was not a pleasure trip.

"You should wear an orange vest," he prodded his father, pulling on his own.

Lyall shook his head, grimacing. "You look like a clown in that thing. All the animals are gonna fall down laughing at you."

"Well then, they should be easier to shoot."

"Anything is going to see you coming for a mile. That's not how I taught you to hunt."

"No, sir," Leo agreed. In spite of the fact he knew what was coming, and that it didn't matter what his dad said to him anymore, it still nettled. Lyall knew the right way to do anything, and his way was the only way. "But you don't want a hunter to mistake you for a deer."

"Nobody else out here. Just you and me. This is our own special place."

"There could still be others around," Leo said. "There could still be an accident."

Lyall laughed at him. "Quit being such a pansy, boy. Be a man, for once. Show some brass."

Leo shrugged. He loaded up a pack and picked up his firearm. As he ran through a quick safety checklist, Lyall picked up the other pack and his weapon. He didn't bother with a safety check.

"I'm glad you wanted to come hunting today," Lyall said in a more conciliatory voice. "We don't really do anything together. It's nice to get out with my boy and enjoy nature."

The only thing Lyall enjoyed about nature was shooting its guts out. Lyall didn't ask Leo what had made him change his mind. What had made him go from a bleeding-heart dog catcher to someone who wanted to hang out with dad and shoot some critters.

"I had something I wanted to talk to you about today," Lyall added.

Leo shrugged. He motioned for Lyall to go ahead. Lyall led the way down the familiar trail, quiet before introducing the topic of conversation. They didn't normally talk on hunting trips—not that they'd gone on any since Leo was able to get out of the house.

Usually, Lyall just told anyone who dared peep to shut up and quit scaring the game away. Why he'd ever bothered to take them on hunting trips, Leo would never know. The kids had always been too noisy and careless for Lyall to bag anything good. They spent the whole time trying to be quiet, with Lyall hollering at them and berating them for being so loud and clumsy.

Lyall probably scared more wildlife away with his temper than the kids did with their carelessness. Hunting trips were not something Leo looked back on with any degree of fondness.

"It's about Shayla," Lyall said finally.

"What about her?" Leo asked.

"She's… a nice girl. We really get along well together."

"Yeah. Good for you. That's nice."

"I've been lonely since your mom left," Lyall said. "Shayla's the first one who's really filled that hole."

Not that he had ever gone long without women. No one had stepped in to fill the place as their mother, but there had been plenty of girlfriends. Most short-term. Most on the road, not at home. Mostly loud, loose women who had no use for kids.

Shayla was a different kind of girl. Not much older than Leo, kind and gentle, she saw something in Lyall's heart nobody else did.

Even the news reporters who had made such a fuss over his story, over how he had overcome illiteracy, had not seen him as a kind, gentle man. They knew he was a gruff old codger; that was part of the charm of the story. Curmudgeon overcomes all odds to learn how to read. New vistas open up. Too bad it hadn't happened when he was a young man and could really have changed his life around.

But Shayla was something else. Preacher's daughter, raised by parents who sheltered her from the real world, she had a sort of innocence he really didn't see much. She saw something in Lyall, some sort of goodness and vulnerability. Leo didn't understand it. He thought she must just be naive. But she really did love Lyall.

"You thinking of moving in together?" Leo asked, to fill the silence.

"We already have," Lyall laughed.

Leo hadn't known that part. They were moving even faster than Leo had thought. "Oh. Well, congratulations."

"We were thinking of taking the next step."

"Is she going to be my new mommy?" Leo said sarcastically.

Lyall whirled around, fury lighting his eyes. Leo cringed back, looking for an escape, for a way to defend himself.

"I can still take you, boy. Don't think you can disrespect your mama and Shayla that way! This is no joke. I don't need your approval or blessing. I just thought… you should know."

"Yes, sir," Leo agreed, frozen, watching for the opportunity to strike or flee.

His father stood there looking at him for a moment.

His knuckles were white as he held the gun tightly.

In days gone by, there would have been dire consequences for a smart aleck comment. Now that Lyall was no longer drinking and was mellowing out in his life with Shayla, the rage wasn't quite as close to the surface anymore.

But Leo could still see it there, bubbling under Lyall's eyes, just like the cat that lurked in Leo's gut. They had both become better at hiding their anger, but it was still there.

Anyone who thought Leo had changed from the angry, uncontrollable delinquent that had fought everybody all through school, kids and administration alike, was wrong. He was still the same person. Just with a bit better veneer. Just hiding the rage a little bit better.

Lyall too was still the same person he had always been.

Eventually, Lyall relaxed his hold on the gun and turned back around, walking down the path. Leo followed him.

Why? Why was he putting himself in a position of vulnerability?

He had forced himself to come on this trip. He was doing what he had to, not what he wanted to.

What he wanted to do was to run away, to escape back to where he was safe.

He followed behind Lyall in silence.

"Shayla is a special girl," Lyall tried again. "She makes me feel… like a kid again. Like I am whole for once."

For once. Leo noticed he didn't say whole again. But whole for once. He hadn't felt that way with Margaret. This was the first time.

The lion within Leo growled.

He had told himself time and time again that he didn't care about Shayla, she could never replace his mother, she was just another woman passing through Lyall's life, the same as a hundred other women. And even if she was special, why would that matter to Leo? Why would he care? She wasn't going to be his mother. He was all grown up. She wasn't going to be anything to him. She wasn't going to be part of his life at all.

"That's good, Dad," Leo said.

"Yeah. Yeah, it's good," Lyall agreed.

He abandoned the subject. Abandoned the attempt to bring Leo into his life, to tell him about his feelings, whatever they were. They had never shared feelings before, why start now?

They moved through the woods together in silence. It was Lyall who spotted the deer in the valley down below them. He pointed them out.

"You stay here," he ordered. "I'm going to go around, to the right flank, and back behind them. I'm going to move them toward you if I can't get a clear shot. Got it?"

Leo nodded. "Yeah, I got it," he agreed softly.

He stood there and watched Lyall disappear into the trees. He kept watching the trees to the right and behind the deer. Every now and then he got a glimpse of Lyall, even though he was wearing camouflage.

Leo waited.

Hunting was all about waiting.

The deer's heads suddenly went up, and Leo knew Lyall was close to them. He raised his rifle and looked through the sights, trying to spot his father in the trees behind them.

The deer leapt toward Leo and Lyall moved out of the trees.

Leo centered the sights, breathed in, held his breath, and squeezed the trigger.

Everything seemed to happen in slow motion. The gun roared in Leo's ear, and Lyall jerked and hit the ground.

Leo breathed out.

Why did Lyall have to get together with Shayla? Why did he have to threaten to start another family? Other innocent children.

Why couldn't he just have carried on as he started? Independent, a loner, not caring about anyone anymore?

Why did he have to ruin it by bringing more children into the mix?

Leo pondered all this morosely as he picked his way down the slope toward the clearing where his father had fallen.

All there was left to do was to discover he had accidentally shot his father and to report it to the police.

They would transfer the body to the morgue.

And it would all be over. Clean and clear.

CHAPTER TWENTY-THREE

L EO WATCHED THE FIGHT in the ring, feeling himself getting drawn into it. When Dr. Marvin had asked him about why he boxed, Leo told him what he told everyone—it was a great workout, a sport that required lots of fitness and skill. It was the challenge that attracted him to it.

But deep down inside, he knew—and he figured Dr. Marvin knew—those things really had nothing to do with why he boxed.

Leo could remember a time when he was younger. A time when he didn't carry the anger with him that he did now. He dealt with the abuse in a different way. He remembered being scared. Hypervigilant. Watching and listening for Lyall and his mother, all the time. He was always ready to run and hide. He'd squeeze himself into a closet, under the bed, run into the dark woods, and freeze, hardly even breathing, waiting for the danger to pass.

He had lived a life of fear, and that was different from what it was now. He still had fear and anxiety, but it was different. Not because he was bigger and stronger, but because the anger had taken over. As he grew from a child to a teenager, things started to change. He wondered now how much of it was puberty, just the increased testosterone levels, that made him more competitive and angry, trying to fight for dominance in the family, to find his alpha level.

He saw other boys around him becoming more competitive, putting on attitude, acting defiant toward teachers and other authorities. But Leo had always pushed it even further. Who else would have pushed Lyall so hard, knowing how strong and dangerous he was?

Leo liked boxing because of the fitness level? The challenge? No.

Leo *had* to fight.

He really had no choice. It was part of his make-up. He was just like Lyall.

Before he had found a legitimate outlet for his fighting—boxing in a ring—things had been pretty bad.

Leo got off of the bus and flowed with the crowd into the school and to his locker. His stomach was growling and he wondered if he could sneak down to the cafeteria without a bunch of people seeing him. The little guys went there almost automatically, but they didn't get teased for participating in the free breakfast or lunch programs. Or if they did, they didn't tell him about it. And they didn't get into fights over it like he did. Leo rubbed his stomach as it growled, so painful it felt like his stomach was going to eat itself if he didn't get something into it.

Giving up on trying to figure out what books he needed or what his first class was, Leo slammed his locker shut and hurried toward the lunchroom. He didn't see anyone in the hallway approaching the cafeteria, so he darted in and waited impatiently in line. He could smell the muffins, even through the plastic wrap.

"Morning Leo," one of the lunch ladies greeted cheerfully.

Leo scowled at her. He didn't want anyone drawing attention to him. He gestured to a carton of chocolate milk, and she handed it to him.

All set with his muffin and chocolate milk, Leo slipped out of the lunchroom, even though he was supposed to stay in there to eat. He snuck out a side door to the parking lot to wolf down the breakfast before anyone could see him. Bad luck for him, he was standing close to Aubrum's parking space. The boy roared into the parking lot in his Mustang and pulled into the parking space with screeching tires.

Leo turned away from him, chewing and swallowing such a big bite he nearly choked. It hurt all the way going down.

The bigger boy got out of his car and slouched toward Leo. "Yo, Leo! You're gonna get caught smoking out here!" he warned.

Leo nodded, keeping his face turned away. He washed the last couple of huge bites of muffin down with the chocolate milk, dribbling some down his face, which he wiped with the back of his hand as Aubrum got close enough to see what he was really doing.

"What? No smoke?" Aubrum asked.

Leo shook his head. "Just… havin' a bite before class," he said, headed back for the building.

Aubrum looked at him, his raised eyebrows disappearing into his shock of red hair. "You use the free lunch program?" he asked incredulously.

"No," Leo protested. "It's from home."

Aubrum started to laugh. "No, it's not! Poor Leo. Why didn't you tell me you were poor? I coulda brought you a sandwich!"

Leo felt his face get hot. The lion rose. "Go to hell," he growled and reached for the door handle to go back inside the school.

"You use food stamps too?" Aubrum demanded. "Oh yeah, I forgot you got no mama!"

The cat exploded inside him.

Leo threw himself at the older boy. Half the kids in the school had no mother or had multiple step parents, but that didn't matter. It was still a shot below the belt and Leo wasn't going to allow himself to be pushed around.

He grabbed Aubrum and threw him to the pavement.

Leo dropped on him and started smashing his face as hard and fast as he could.

Aubrum was taken by surprise, but he threw Leo off and tussled with him in the gravel.

They exchanged a few blows, but neither one could get the upper hand. It wasn't long before they were pulled apart by a couple of teachers.

Leo had a split lip, Aubrum a bloody nose.

"You boys know better!" Mr. Klass reamed them out. "There's no fighting on school grounds! You're behaving like a couple of animals! Detention for both of you."

Leo dabbed at his lip with his shirt. "I gotta catch the bus after school," he said. "Can't get home no other way."

"Then you can serve detention over lunch," Klass snapped back.

Leo shrugged. Not like he had anything to do over lunch anyway. Just hanging out smoking or trying to get a free lunch and eat it without anyone noticing. Maybe if he was in detention, he could eat without anyone seeing him…

Leo studied Aubrum covertly, trying to gauge who had come out of the fight better. He was pretty sure he had, and he was a couple of years younger and a good fifty pounds lighter than Aub.

Secretly, Leo exulted over his success. He was getting to be a better and better fighter. One day, he would be big enough, strong enough, and brave enough to fight Lyall.

To fight him and take him down.

But he knew it wasn't weakness that kept him from fighting Lyall. It wouldn't have mattered if it was just Leo. It was the younger kids and what would happen to them that kept him from challenging Lyall every time he saw him. He couldn't avoid every fight; sometimes the cat just came bursting out of him; but he tried. He tried to keep calm and not defy Lyall to his face, for the sake of the kids.

Klass and the other teacher took the boys to the office to write them up and get a lecture from the principal.

Leo sat in a hard chair while Aubrum talked to the principal, then Aub was escorted out, giving Leo a dirty look, and it was Leo's turn. He walked into the principal's office. He didn't wait to be invited to sit down, he just slumped into a chair and looked at Principal Henry, his jaw set, and his eyes challenging. Mr. Henry, middle aged, overweight, and balding, always seemed slightly uncomfortable in his suit and jacket. He pulled on his tie and straightened his lapel fussily.

"Why don't you tell me what happened, Leo?" Mr. Henry asked, looking Leo over with sad basset-hound eyes.

Leo shrugged. "Aub was buggin' me. He wanted a fight, so I gave him one."

"You know our policy on fighting. This isn't exactly your first time. What are we going to do with you?"

Leo shrugged again. There wasn't anything they could do. There was no other school to send him to, so they couldn't expel him. He had no parent at home most of the time, there was no point in suspending him. An in-school suspension would just mean he was sitting around the office when he should be in class learning, and he couldn't afford to miss classes. Not with his marks.

"Who threw the first punch?" Mr. Henry questioned.

"I did," Leo offered proudly.

"If he's bothering you, why don't you get a teacher? You can't just start pummeling anyone who tries to get a rise out of you."

"Maybe it'll teach them to stop," Leo retorted. "You think a detention is gonna stop him next time? No; but maybe if I can beat the crap out of him, he won't do it again."

"Violence is not the solution. No matter what."

Leo just folded his arms and waited. They could strap him, but he'd been strapped before and it hadn't made any difference. Why would it?

"Leo, I want you to talk to someone."

"I don't need to talk to no one."

"You do. You need to start working through these issues before they ruin your life. I don't think you understand how negatively this could affect your future. You need an education. You need to learn how to control yourself. You need to learn… how to be happy."

Leo looked at Mr. Henry, one eyebrow raised. Since when did they care if he was happy? He rolled his eyes to the ceiling and said nothing. Mr. Henry stared into his soul.

Leo shifted uncomfortably.

"If you want me to see someone, I can't really do anything about it, can I?" Leo snapped. "But I've seen my guidance counselor. I've seen the resource teacher. They haven't done me any good. Who else is it going to be?"

"Well, we could try a psychiatrist. Maybe try out some medications to see if they will help you."

"Drugs; good idea," Leo laughed.

"I'm serious, Leo. I don't think you've ever tried this route, have you? What if there was something that could make you feel better? To focus on your work, keep you from acting so impulsively, improve your mood. Wouldn't that be worth it?"

"I can't stop you," Leo said with a shrug. He wasn't about to show weakness. Make Mr. Henry think he had something Leo wanted? He had to show no weakness, no pain. Just keep on an impassive mask.

Mr. Henry nodded. "What about your dad? He'd have to agree to medical treatment, whatever we manage to arrange."

Leo shrugged. "Give me a permission slip. I'll get it signed." Getting a permission slip signed wasn't a problem as long as they didn't follow up with a phone call to make sure the signature was legitimate. And why would they?

Mr. Henry looked pleased. Leo wondered if he'd been too cooperative.

"I'll do that, Leo. And I'll let you know when we arrange for you to see the doctor, okay?"

"Yeah, whatever."

<hr>

He'd always thought psychiatrists spent the whole time talking about feelings. But Dr. Skelton, a thin, severe looking woman, didn't press him. She asked him vague questions about his family and about the things he generally got in trouble for and made the occasional note in the file in front of her.

At the end of their session, she got out a prescription pad and wrote on it.

"I think we'll start with a stimulant," she said, "for ADHD. You've never been on one before?"

"No."

"We'll see how it goes. I think you'll notice a big difference in your ability to concentrate on your work and keep your emotions and impulses under better control."

Leo took the prescription from her and looked down at it. "I don't know if we've got money for drugs," he said. This hadn't occurred to him before. He had forged the signature on the permission form but how was he going to get his hands on the prescription? He knew these drugs could be expensive and they didn't have any kind of medical plan that would cover it.

"There's a program at the school to cover it," she assured him. "Just show it to the secretary and she'll give you a voucher."

"Yeah? Okay. Thanks."

Leo headed back to school.

His heart lifted for the first time in a long time. What if it worked? What if the drugs made it so he could do his work just like the other kids?

Could he keep the lion buried so he could act like the others? Keep his temper and not always make people think there was something wrong with him?

Maybe he could be just like any other kid.

He hardly dared to hope.

The next morning, Leo caught Phil's expression and laughed. "What's the matter, Philly?"

"You're actin' funny," Phil said, puzzled. "Why're you actin' so funny?"

"I'm not acting funny," Leo said, tossing his books into his backpack. "I'm just happy. You all ready for school?"

"Happy?" Phil repeated as if he'd never heard the word before. He frowned at Leo and didn't move.

"Yeah. Can't a guy be in a good mood for once?" Leo teased.

Phil gave him a half-smile. "Okaaaay," he agreed hesitantly.

The girls were packing their bags. "You are acting funny, you know," Michelle said. "What're you so… hyper about?"

"I dunno," Leo laughed. "I guess I just got a good sleep or something. I feel like I could take on the world today!"

He started singing a silly song and held his hands out to Stormy to dance. She danced for a minute holding his hands, her eyes wide with surprise. Leo swooped down and picked her up and continued to whirl around the room with her.

"No!" Stormy protested, pushing on his chest and squirming. "Put me down! Let go!" She kicked hard and Leo let her slide to the floor.

"Hey, princess, what's the matter? I'm not hurting you."

She hung back from him, her hands held out to keep him back. "Don't grab me!" Stormy insisted, tears leaking from her eyes.

"Okay… I'm sorry," Leo said, taken aback. He hadn't meant to startle her.

"Do me! Do me now!" Joyce shouted, holding her hands out to Leo.

Leaving Stormy alone, Leo grabbed Joyce's hands and danced her around the room, and then at her insistence, picked her up and twirled her around. Joyce squealed and laughed happily.

"Bus is here!" Lewis shouted from the porch. "Where are you guys?"

Leo put Joyce down, and everyone hurriedly grabbed their schoolbags. Leo put his hand out to Stormy.

"Come on, Storm. Walk me to the bus."

She held back and shook her head sullenly. Leo shrugged and raced for the bus, beating everyone else there. He jumped up the steps, laughing and calling back, 'Come on, slowpokes!' He looked at the kids on the bus who were picked up before the Bakerfields.

They all stared at him as if he'd grown a second head.

Leo grinned. "Hello, people!" he greeted. He grabbed a seat and sat down. He caught the face of the bus driver looking at him in the mirror in surprise. The other Bakerfields trooped onto the bus, and the bus driver lowered the ramp for Lewis to get on last. Lewis pulled his wheelchair over to the side where a bench had been removed to make space for him and put on his brakes.

"Why does everyone keep looking at me?" Leo demanded, amused by their reactions.

"Maybe cause no one's ever seen you smile before," said Shannon, a girl from the next farm over, who was a year younger than Leo. "You win the lottery?"

Leo giggled. "Can't win the lottery if you don't buy tickets," he pointed out. "No, I'm just feelin' good!"

He started to sing to himself under his breath, watching out the window.

***

Leo was pulled out of his first class only five minutes in, told to go down to the office and talk to his guidance counselor. Leo shrugged, picked up his books, and exited. The halls were empty, and he ran down them for no reason, just feeling exhilarated and energized. He laughed with delight. He entered the office and knocked on Mr. Teller's door. At the 'come in,' he opened the door and entered.

"Ah, Leo," Mr. Teller greeted. "Good to see you. Thank you for coming down."

"You got it, boss!"

Leo paced across the office, too hyped up to sit in the guest chair. Mr. Teller watched him for a moment with shrewd eyes. He had dark hair and eyes and was pretty young-looking. He wore polo shirts instead of a suit to make himself seem more accessible to the students. Leo found his chumminess to be fake; too forced and awkward.

"Leo," Teller said slowly, "someone has expressed concerns there is something going on with you this morning. Can you think why that might be?"

Leo shook his head.

"I'm doing great this morning," he said. "I don't know why everyone keeps saying I'm being weird. Isn't a guy allowed to be happy now and then?"

"Happy is good," Mr. Teller agreed. "As long as it isn't at the expense of your health. If, for instance, you had something to drink or… er… eat that made you feel happy."

"I haven't had anything to eat or drink this morning," Leo replied naively. "And you know what?" He gave a little bounce on his heels. "I'm not even hungry!"

"Oh. Well, you should always go to the lunchroom for breakfast if you haven't had anything to eat before school," he advised. "So this mood of yours… It's not due to, say, taking drugs?"

Leo paced around the room, touching Mr. Teller's books and belongings, wanting to feel and experience everything.

"No, I'm not taking drugs, man," he said. "Not like that. But I got some meds. Meds from the feds! Doctor-prescribed and everything."

"What are they?" Mr. Teller asked, frowning.

"I dunno. Flippin' Ritalin or something. ADHD stimulants," he took a plaque down from Mr. Teller's shelf to examine it. "Very stimulatin' stuff. Man, if I can take this stuff all day, and not crash, I am gonna—be—flyin'—high!"

"Yes," Mr. Teller agreed dryly. "How much did you take, Leo? Did you take the right dose on the bottle?"

"Sure thing, boss. Just one pill. Mighty strong little buggers!"

"So I see. Is there anyone at home, Leo? Someone we could call to pick you up?"

Leo shook his head. "Pick me up? Why? I'm not sick. I'm just happy. You suspending people for happy these days?"

"No. I just think… your behavior might be a little distracting to the other students today. I think you need some time to calm down. Maybe hang out here for a while."

"No!" Leo protested, "I want to go to class. This is supposed to help me learn. I want go to class and see if it all makes sense now!"

"I don't think that's exactly the way it works, Leo," Mr. Teller started.

"But it's so clear! Everything is so crisp and clear, and shiny! I want to just open my books and have it all make sense! Like other kids!"

"It's not going to change your understanding," Mr. Teller said. "It just helps you to focus a bit better… though I'm not sure how you're going to concentrate on anything today. Maybe tomorrow you could try a half dose."

"No way. I like this stuff. So, long as you're not suspending me or something, I'm going back to class," Leo informed him.

Mr. Teller just sat there and watched him go, looking thoroughly baffled. Leo went back upstairs and into the classroom and sat in an empty seat. The teacher stopped lecturing for a moment and frowned at him.

"What are you doing?" he questioned.

"Just here to learn," Leo sang out cheerfully.

"You're not in this class."

Leo looked around at the faces of younger students who were clearly not in his grade. He bust out laughing.

"Whoops! Well, I guess I'd better go find out what room my class is in, huh?" he said. Picking up his bag once again, he exited the room, calling out, "Two plus two is four, kids! Remember that for the test! Life is a test! Life is the final test of your mortality!"

There were giggles and murmurs from the class as he left.

Leo wandered around a bit more before he managed to find a class that was his, and sat down. The teacher glanced at him but didn't say anything. A few students turned around in their seats as he sat down, then turned back around and didn't say anything. Soothing signs he was in the right place. Leo bounced his heels on the floor, examining the work on the board. He put up his hand. In astonishment, Mr. Fitch stopped mid-word.

"Uh—Leo?"

"I don't think that's right," Leo said, gesturing at the board.

"Don't think what is right?" Fitch asked.

Leo got up and walked toward the board.

"Have you lost your mind?" one of the other students growled at him as he walked up the aisle.

"Not that I've noticed," Leo said cheerfully. He approached the teacher.

"I think you made a mistake, man. See it all makes sense, now!" Leo made an expansive gesture. "Now I get it!"

"Well, I'm glad you're picking it up, but—"

"This isn't right," Leo said, grabbing a marker and eraser and starting to wipe out Fitch's example. Fitch grabbed at him.

"Cut it out! Leave that alone! Hey!"

Fitch pushed Leo away angrily, wrenching the eraser away from him. Leo stared at him, astonished.

"But it's wrong!" he protested. "What're you pushing me around for?"

"Go sit in your seat, Mr. Bakerfield. Or leave the room. This kind of… bizarre… behavior will not be tolerated!"

Leo pulled the cap off of the pen and started to sketch out a primitive house where he had erased Fitch's work.

"No, you see, you gotta think bigger," he insisted. "You're doing it all wrong!"

Someone in the class laughed. Everyone else was still watching the drama unfold in stunned silence. Fitch grabbed the pen and shoved Leo violently away.

"Keep the hell away from my board!" he shouted, incensed.

Leo planted a hand on his chest and shoved him back. A gasp went up from the class, and someone dashed out the back door to fetch help.

"You just aren't doing it right," Leo said, his face uncomfortably close to Mr. Fitch's. "If you're going to teach the class, you should do—it—right!" He poked his finger into Mr. Fitch's chest with each word to emphasize his point. "You should do it my way!"

Mr. Fitch socked him. Socked him right in the nose with a closed fist, knocking him clean over. Leo lay on the floor and groaned, confused. One of the classmates came back with a couple of teachers, who hurried up to the front of the room and surveyed the scene.

Leo felt his nose, groaning. "Damn," he moaned. "How come nobody else can see it?"

"Let's get you up and to the nurse's," one of the rescuers suggested. He and the other teacher both bent over and each grabbed an arm, pulling Leo to his feet.

Leo swayed slightly but kept his feet. "Maybe I could tell *you* about it," he suggested.

"Yeah. Why don't you tell us about it while we take you down to the nurse's."

Leo went along compliantly, rubbing his face and bubbling on again about the big picture.

He bounced around the nurse's office, holding an ice pack over his nose while she tried to talk to him and get him to sit still to examine him.

"Leo. Just sit down!" she said in exasperation.

"No, no, I'm okay. It's all right. What do you think? Do you think this is working?"

"I don't know what you're talking about."

Leo laughed. "It's all just so great," he gushed. "I could do this forever!"

"Sit down. Come on. Come over here and try to settle down."

"I can't. I can't. I can't sit, I can't be quiet. Why does everybody keep telling me that?"

"Because you're not acting like yourself. This medication you took is really affecting you."

He shook his head, smiling at her in amusement.

They did their best to keep Leo contained during the rest of the day. Away from the teachers and other students where he might do harm or get into trouble. Keeping him from hurting himself doing something silly like trying to fly out a window.

He was starting to feel more like himself when it was time to go home. The nurse walked him to the bus to make sure he got on and was going to be all right.

"Now you're going to have to just sit down," the nurse told him sternly. "Leave the driver alone and don't mess around with the other kids. Just sit quietly until you get home, okay?"

Leo shrugged. "I'm okay," he said, a little embarrassed by the attention. "It's wearing off. Really."

"I don't want to hear you've caused more trouble."

"I didn't really cause any trouble," Leo protested. "I was just... I was okay, it was the teacher that hit me."

"I know. Get on."

Leo got into the bus and sat in his accustomed seat. There was a lot of whispering going on toward the back of the bus.

"Are you okay?" Lewis asked in a low voice as he settled in. "I heard Mr. Fitch beat you up!"

Leo shook his head. "Just hit me once," he said, rolling his eyes. "It wasn't anything. Ended up missing all my classes because the nurse wouldn't let me go back."

"You're complaining about missing classes?" Lewis said incredulously. "Man, you really are high."

Leo giggled slightly. "I wanted to go," he said. "I was feeling so clear, I felt like I'd be able to understand everything today."

Lewis shook his head. "Trust me, you might have thought you'd understand it. You wouldn't. It's a drug, not magic."

Leo sighed. "I just felt so... I felt like I could do anything."

Lewis nodded. "Well, just relax now. You'll be all normal again tomorrow."

"I'm going to take another one tomorrow," Leo asserted.

"Oh no, you're not," Lewis told him.

Leo looked sideways at him. "You can't stop me."

At home, Leo tried to get some supper together. But he just stood in the kitchen looking at the empty pots and pans, his brain gradually grinding to a halt. Joyce and Michelle came in, giggling to each other. Leo turned and looked at them.

"What's wrong with *you?*" Michelle asked, looking him over and tossing her hair.

"I just... can't..."

"Are you sick?" Michelle asked.

Leo rubbed his temples. His head was pounding something awful. He couldn't focus on anything. The world had gone fuzzy.

"I dunno... do you think you could do something for me?" Leo asked, motioning at the kitchen, "Just... sandwiches, or KD or anything?"

"Okay," Michelle agreed with a pained sigh. "If you can't do it."

Leo nodded and left the kitchen. He went to the bathroom and opened the medicine cabinet to find an aspirin. As he shook a handful of them into his palm, his eyes fell on his prescription bottle on the side of the sink.

If he took another one, maybe he could get his head working again.

They were only supposed to be one a day, but what harm would it do to take one now that the morning dose had worn off?

He grabbed the pill bottle and stared at it.

It was empty.

He'd only taken one pill! How could it be empty?

Leo stalked into the bedroom, where Lewis was working hard on his homework and brandished the empty pill bottle.

"Did you take them?" he demanded.

"You can't use them, Leo. Not with the way you reacted."

"Mr. Teller said to try a half dose next time. I can still take them!"

Lewis shook his head. "Go back to the doctor and get something else. This stuff messes you up."

Leo growled in frustration, the lion inside him snarling furiously. He looked over at Lewis's bedside table and grabbed his narcotic painkillers.

"Well, why don't I just hang onto *these*, then, huh? I'll hold your pills until you give me back mine."

Lewis blanched. "I need those!"

"I need mine," Leo countered.

Lewis licked his lips. "Come on, give them back, Leo."

"Give me mine."

"I can't!"

"What do you mean, you can't?" Leo demanded.

"I—I flushed them," Lewis confessed.

Leo stared at him, the blood rushing to his face and roaring in his ears. "What?"

"Take it easy, Leo," Lewis said nervously. He released the brakes on his wheels, looking around for an escape route.

Leo went back to the bathroom, panicking. He lifted the lid of the toilet for any sign of the pills. He looked around the floor and garbage can in case any had spilled.

Gone!

All gone!

"No!" Leo punched the wall furiously. "No, no, no!"

No one came rushing in to see what was the matter. They all knew well enough to stay away or to hide when someone was angry.

Leo punched the wall again, screaming, trying to get himself under control.

He went back to the bedroom. Lewis held up his hands defensively. There were tears on his cheeks, and his eyes were wide with fear.

"Leo," he pleaded.

Leo couldn't hurt Lewis. The sight of his tears stopped Leo cold.

He put Lewis's pills down on the table again and flopped down into his bed, burying his face.

Lewis was silent for a few minutes. Then Leo heard him creaking closer to the bed.

"Are you okay?" he asked softly.

"Just lemme alone," Leo snapped.

"I'm sorry. I'm really sorry," Lewis sniffled.

Leo scrubbed at his eyes, not looking up. "You did the right thing," he growled. "But I don't have to like it."

Lewis made a noise halfway between a sob and a laugh. "Can I help you?" he asked penitently. "Do you want me to get you something? I guess the girls are making supper."

"No," Leo said. "I'll just try to sleep. I feel so… awful."

Lewis rubbed his shoulder. "You'll feel better in the morning," he promised. "You're just crashing from the pills."

Leo moaned. "How can people take meds if that's how it makes them feel?"

"Well… It's not supposed to make you feel like that," Lewis said. "Plenty of kids in my class take them, and it hardly affects them at all. Just makes it easier to sit still and be quiet."

"That's the last thing I felt like doing at school today," Leo said, pulling his face out of the pillow and turning it toward Lewis.

"Yeah, that's what I hear," Lewis said dryly.

Leo snorted and put his hand over his eyes. "I think I'm just gonna go to sleep," he said. "My head's killing me and my brain is going in circles…"

Lewis nodded. "Okay," he agreed. He wheeled around and headed out of the room, turning off the light.

Leo rested his forearm across his eyes and tried to sleep.

Dr. Skelton saw him a few days later, and with several reports from the school in hand, agreed stimulants were not for Leo.

"I'm sorry it didn't work out, Leo," she said. "But we don't always hit on the right medication the first time."

"I felt great," Leo said. "It didn't help me focus on the schoolwork, and I still got in a fight and got punched in the face by a teacher. But I felt *great!*" He laughed sadly, rolling his eyes.

She cocked her head to the side, shaking it slightly. "That shouldn't have happened. We'll go another direction instead. I'm wondering if maybe the issue isn't ADHD at all. Different things can mimic it. I don't really know anything about your family history. Your parents, other near relatives… any signs of… oh, depression… mood swings… unexpected anger, or anxiety…?"

Leo gulped. "Yeah, maybe," he agreed.

"Sometimes alcoholism or other addictions are signs of bipolar too," she suggested.

Leo nodded, not giving any details away, but encouraging her to go on.

"Yes, I definitely think we're dealing with something more than just ADHD here," she said, warming up to the idea. "How about you, Leo? Do you have periods of sadness or anger? Ones that last a long time, more than just passing emotions."

"Yeah, sure," Leo agreed. "But I thought… with my, you know, learning disabilities, I thought that was all ADHD. What's bipolar? Does that cause learning problems too?"

"Oh, for sure," Dr. Skelton said cheerfully. "Bipolar is often co-morbid with learning disabilities." She saw Leo's blank look. "They go together. One difference in the brain's wiring can have all kinds of impacts on mood, behavior, attention, information processing, executive function…"

"Oh," Leo nodded. "Okay. So I'm… like… brain damaged? Is it because I got hit in the head or something?"

"No, no, it's probably something you inherited. These things run in families. You've had it since you were born, but it becomes more difficult as you get older. Especially as a teenager. A lot of mental illness starts to appear in teens."

"Mental illness," Leo repeated.

"It's a broad term, Leo. It doesn't mean you are schizophrenic or belong in an institution. A lot of people battle with mental illness and the people around them have no idea. Your dad could be mentally ill and you don't even know it."

Yeah. Right.

They knew he was crazy.

Call it bipolar, or mental illness, or whatever you liked. It hadn't escaped their notice.

"We'll try something else this time," Dr. Skelton said, pulling out her prescription pad. "See if this works any better."

CHAPTER TWENTY-FOUR

THE AFTER-SCHOOL BOYS had their heads together in a tight group. Leo's stomach clenched into a tight knot. He tried to school his breathing.

Something was wrong.

They should have been playing basketball, laughing, fooling around. Something had happened.

A couple of them looked up at his approach and they all fell silent. Leo looked around at the pale, somber faces.

"What is it? What happened?"

They exchanged looks, no one eager to tell him.

"It's Bubblegum," Reggie finally said in a strangled voice.

"Bubblegum. He didn't get arrested again, did he?" Leo's thoughts went to Hakim. If he was still using Billy to courier his drugs, Leo would kill him! It had been a mistake to just let him walk away.

"He's in hospital."

"Why? What happened?"

"He got beat up. It's real bad."

Leo searched their faces. "He got in a fight at school? Who beat him up?"

They looked at each other and no one answered.

"Who? Did he get in a fight?"

"It wasn't no fight," Reggie muttered.

A couple of the others made warning noises at him. Reggie stared down at the asphalt, pressing his lips together.

Leo scowled at the other boys. "What's going on? Tell me what happened to Billy!"

There was no answer.

Leo focused on Chase, meeting his eyes and not letting him look away. "Chase. How did Bubblegum get hurt?"

Chase scuffed at the pavement with the toe of his shoe. "I don't know for sure. Just things I've heard…"

"What did you hear?"

"There's this goon at the high school. Works for some real bad dudes. Muscle, you know, for if kids step out of line."

Leo stared at him. "And he beat up Billy?"

Chase nodded. There were small nods from the other boys as well. Leo looked from one to the other.

"Because he said he didn't want to deal drugs anymore," Leo finally surmised.

"You knew about that?" Reggie demanded, his voice overly loud in his surprise.

The other boys winced and looked around cautiously.

"Let's go inside," Leo suggested.

"No, man," Chase said, alarmed. "People will hear!"

"Hakim isn't there. He's not allowed back."

They exchanged uncertain glances with each other, but with Leo's encouragement, they went into the gym. Leo sat them on the floor in a corner where they were blocked from view from the rest of the room by the boxing ring.

"How long have you guys known about Billy and Hakim dealing drugs?" Leo asked. "You should have told me."

"Just today," Reggie asserted. "None of us knew nothing, Bubblegum never said a word. Not until today, when we heard what happened. That's when it started to leak out."

"How bad is he hurt?"

"Real bad, Coach. Real bad."

"What's this guy's name? At the high school?"

Reggie spluttered. "You think I'm gonna tell you? You think I want to end up in hospital next? Or dead?"

"We can't get these creeps off the street if you won't talk about it." Leo looked over their somber, scared faces. "Come on, guys. For Bubblegum. Billy. And the rest of the kids that this enforcer might hurt."

They all shook their heads and looked away from him.

"Can't do it, boss," Chase murmured. "We just can't."

Leo hadn't expected to be back at the hospital again so soon after Lyall's death. It was a weird feeling to be there to see someone other than Lyall.

"He's in ICU," the receptionist who looked up Billy's name on the computer advised. "Family only."

Leo nodded. "Thanks."

He knew where ICU was.

"Are you family?" the nurse who guarded the portals to ICU demanded.

"Yes," Leo lied. He didn't give any explanation of how he was related. She looked him over suspiciously, then nodded and pointed toward the curtained area Billy was in.

Billy's grandmother sat beside the bed. She looked small and shrunken next to the tall hospital bed. Leo had met her a couple of times in connection with the after-school program. Her face, lined with worry, smoothed a little when she looked up and saw Leo.

"Coach! I'm so glad you came."

She moved to get up, but Leo stepped forward, motioning for her to stay. He took her hand, not shaking it, but clasping it in both of his for a moment, trying to communicate his concern to her.

"How is he?"

They looked at the small form in the hospital bed.

Both of Bubblegum's eyes were black. His nose had been set. His face and neck were battered and bruised. Leo wasn't sure what kind of damage the hospital gown and sheets hid, but there were several tubes snaking under the covers.

Billy's grandmother dabbed at her eyes with a crushed tissue, sniffling.

"They're keeping him under to give him a chance to heal. He has swelling in his brain. He might lose a kidney."

She held her hand over both eyes, forehead wrinkled.

"He's breathing on his own," Leo observed.

"Yes." She sniffed and looked up. "They said that's a good sign."

"Do they… do the police know what happened?"

"They just keep asking me questions… Was he involved in drugs? Was he involved in organized crime? Was he in a gang? They searched his room." She shook her head. "I don't understand it, Coach. How could this happen? Billy is a good boy!"

"I guess… maybe he got in over his head… maybe he got into something without understanding…"

"What? What did he get into?" Her eyebrows drew down. "Do you know?"

"I… there is a man at the gym. Or he *was* at the gym. I'm sorry, I didn't know he was dealing drugs or that he got Billy involved…" Leo swallowed.

His hands clenched into fists.

There must have been something else that he could have done. Some way that he could have protected Bubblegum.

Billy's grandmother's eyes were daggers, cutting into him. Leo's face burned. He wanted to fight back. To defend himself.

"We signed him up for the after-school program to keep him *out* of trouble. How could you let that go on right under your nose? How long have you known about this?"

"I didn't know. Not until this week. I told him to stay away from the gym and away from Billy."

The words sounded lame in Leo's own ears. He put his hands over his face.

"I never thought Billy was in any danger. I thought…" He shook his head.

"Why didn't you tell me? You didn't call the police?"

"I… didn't want to get Billy in trouble."

"Would getting in trouble have been worse than this?" She gestured at Billy lying in the bed.

"No. I never thought anything would happen. I thought if I got rid of Hakim, Billy would be fine. I never thought… I never saw this coming."

She shook her head and turned her face away from him. Leo swallowed.

He stood there for a minute, looking for something to say. Then he turned and fled from the room.

The beast raged inside him.

He had to get home before he blew.

Get home so he could let go and hit something.

CHAPTER TWENTY-FIVE

AFTER WATCHING THE LATEST boxing match, Leo glanced around at the various hucksters passing out flyers and trying to sell their wares. He wondered if the dog fight guys would be passing out flyers again. Last time, he had tried to get the police to bust them, and they hadn't.

What else should he do? Could he do it himself? Could he make the police believe him and check it out? He understood dog fights were not at the top of the police's list, but Leo couldn't bear to think of these dogs being hurt and killed without at least trying to stop them.

For him, it *was* the top of the list. At least today.

He collected flyers from various hucksters handing them out around him and got another dog fight flyer.

Leo walked out of the building with the crowd, trying to look casual. He texted the number on the flyer. Not the same number as last time, so it was a good thing he had come to get another flyer. The old one probably wouldn't work. Maybe it would even make them suspicious of cops. He immediately got an address and time texted back. He headed over to the address.

There were a few people who headed in the same direction. None of them looked at each other. They pretended the others didn't exist. Nobody wanted to be identified. When Leo got to the address on his phone, it didn't look right. He was expecting a warehouse, a place that could be used as a temporary ring for the fight. But there wasn't anything there. Just an empty street, with closed bodegas.

There was a man on the corner, his hand in his pocket, looking around.

Leo hung back. It just didn't make sense to him.

One of the other men who had walked there from the boxing match looked around, then approached the waiting man. He got close, talked to him for a minute, and then walked away. Leo wondered if he should just follow him. But that might be a dangerous proposition. Trying to follow someone to an illegal fight sounded like a good way to get shot.

The second man who had walked over from the fight approached the one standing on the corner. He spoke for a moment and then he walked away, but in a different direction.

Leo stood there, wondering. The waiting man looked around and focused in on him. With a jerk of his head, he motioned Leo over. Leo hesitated, then finally steeled himself and approached him. He was a big man, black, wearing jeans and a white t-shirt with a black jacket and sunglasses.

Really, sunglasses at night?

Arms crossed over his chest, the man looked him over. "Are you a cop?"

Leo shook his head. "No, not a cop," he said, taken aback.

"You look like you could be a cop. What are you here for?"

Leo looked down. He considered backing away and leaving. "I'm…" he fluttered the dog fight flyer he was still holding, "I was just looking for this."

"Dog fight?" the man asked. "What do you want with that?"

Leo shrugged. "I'm… I'm a boxer. I guess I just… like fights."

The man stared at his face, shifting slightly from one side to the other. "You've broken your nose before," he hazarded.

Leo touched it self-consciously. "Yeah, a few times," he agreed. "What boxer hasn't?"

"Well, I guess you're all right, then."

The man gave him another address. "Go east down Main to get there," he ordered. "We don't want everyone taking the same route. Keep an eye out for anyone suspicious, any cops. If something looks hinky, don't stick around. Take off. Come another night instead."

Leo nodded. "Okay. Thanks."

He looked around to orient himself and the man gestured. "That way."

"Right."

Leo walked away at a quick clip, glancing over his shoulder once or twice to make sure nobody was following him.

These guys were well-organized. Cautious. If the police had shown up after Leo's call, they would not have found a fight. Only a single sentry, who would quickly make them for what they were, even if they were in plainclothes. And it was easy for one person to disappear. There would be no more visitors to the fight that night, but the ring would survive to fight another day.

He wasn't sure what to do once he was at the building, which was, as he had expected, an old warehouse.

Should he go in?

Should he get more details, or take off?

He didn't actually want to be part of this, but how was he to save the animals without being sure? Leo swallowed and knocked on the door.

Someone opened the door a crack and muttered, "What is it?"

Leo flashed the flyer. The door opened further. "Come in, then," he said gruffly.

Leo entered the dark, noisy, smoky room. He worked his way through the bustle and noise to the makeshift ring. He could smell animals. Not just dogs, but fowl too, probably cocks. And rats, but they might have been the local residents rather than animals brought in to fight. There were beer and other refreshments for sale. Leo recognized a few people from the boxing fights. Players, managers, and regular attendees. But there were lots of people he didn't know too.

Leo looked around. He didn't want to be there.

He didn't actually want to see the fight.

"What's up, man?" a tall, beanpole of a man beside him asked.

"Huh? Nothing. Just looking to see who is here," Leo said.

"You been here before?"

"No. First time."

"You a cop?"

Leo shook his head. "No, a boxer," he insisted.

The man looked him over, and like the sentry on the street, Leo saw his eyes focus on Leo's nose, convincingly a boxer's nose. And he had plenty of other scars. Obviously someone who enjoyed a good fight.

"Cool," he said. "I'm Slim."

Leo cracked a smile. "Yes, you are," he agreed.

"No, my name. Slim."

Leo nodded. "Leo," he introduced himself.

Slim held out a fist to pound and Leo obliged. They both looked around the room again.

"Starting before long," Slim promised.

"Yeah? So you've been here before, huh?"

"Sure, plenty of times. Good entertainment."

"Who runs it? Are they here?"

Slim scrutinized him again, eyes squinted half-shut. "What are you asking questions for?"

Leo shrugged and inched away from Slim slightly, feeling anxious and crowded. The place was getting noisier, hotter, and smelled of sour sweat. Leo liked a good audience when he fought, but he didn't enjoy being in a crowd.

"I just wondered. I got the flyer at a boxing match, and I wondered if they had, you know, boxing connections. Maybe it's a manager or trainer I already know."

"If they knew you, wouldn't you have heard about it before now?"

"Maybe. I dunno."

Slim looked away from him, not answering the question. Leo shrugged it off and looked back at the ring.

"It's a dog fight?" he asked. "I smell other animals too."

"You can smell other animals?" Slim questioned suspiciously.

"Well, sure… can't you?"

"Animals all smell the same."

Leo raised his eyebrows. "Not even close," he laughed. "You ever been in a house with a lot of cats? It doesn't smell like dog!"

"No cats here," Slim muttered.

"No. Smells like chickens and rats. Is there a cock fight too?"

"Yeah, maybe. Sometimes. Don't know if there's one tonight. But I don't know anyone who fights rats."

Leo nodded. "They probably just live here."

Slim suddenly looked nervous. He looked down at the floor, up at the dark ceilings. He shuddered.

"I hate rats. You think there's rats in here?"

Leo nodded. "I know there are. I can smell them."

"Well… maybe it's just a couple of lawyers," Slim joked feebly.

Leo laughed. Not likely. He'd never seen a lawyer's nest that smelled like that.

Suddenly a loudspeaker cut in, announcing the fight. Leo looked around to see who was talking and spotted the man with the mike; a short man, dark greased back hair, a small mustache like a junior high kid sports to show off their manliness when he develops faster than everyone else. He looked small, and sweaty, and insignificant.

Leo looked at the people standing close to the announcer. Were the owners here, the people who had organized the fight? They'd have to be, wouldn't they? It was their enterprise, they'd want to be watching over it in person. They presumably enjoyed the bloodshed and the violence of it.

Leo shuddered himself. Rats didn't bother him so much. It was the people who bothered him. Why anyone would want to put innocent animals through this, he couldn't understand.

A couple of snarling dogs were brought into the ring.

One, a boxer maybe, on leash and tugging, snarling, trying to get in on the action.

His opponent, in a cage, set in the opposite corner. Leo couldn't tell the breed for sure. Maybe just a mutt. Maybe a husky cross.

They put the cage down and one person prepared to open the cage, as the man with the boxer put his hand on the collar, ready to release the leash.

On a three count, both released their dogs. Leo cringed, readying himself for the violence.

The dog in the cage did not exit.

The boxer menaced him, barking and growling, trying to get at him. The man with the mutt jabbed something into the cage to prod the dog out, and he rocketed out like he'd been stung.

Leo tried to see what the man he had. Some kind of electrical weapon. A cattle prod. Barbaric.

The fight was on. The husky cross kept trying to get out of the ring, leaping at the walls and yelping. The boxer pursued him, hot on his heels.

Leo's hands clenched into fists. How could anyone allow this to go on? How could they let these animals hurt each other?

He watched anxiously as the mutt was forced to turn and fight. They faced each other, circled, growling savagely.

The dogs lunged at each other and went down in a fury of fur and motion.

Leo jumped forward, trying to see, but more than that, his instinct to protect was so strong it was overwhelming.

He had to get in there.

He had to stop this.

Hands grabbed him, other spectators protesting, holding him back.

Leo's eyes were riveted on the scene. The battle ceased, the boxer stood over the mutt, growling.

It was over too fast. The crowd booed and complained. The dogs were quickly removed from the ring.

Slim looked at Leo. "Exciting, huh? Don't get carried away!"

"I just… I don't know."

"Hey, it's cool. But you gotta stay put, or people can't see around you. And the bosses don't like people getting too close to the ring, so just stay back where you are."

"Yeah," Leo agreed, trying not to give away his anger.

What he would give to be able to just start clearing everyone out of here.

Just take them all down, because this wasn't right.

He couldn't stand to see the blood. To stand by while innocent animals were slaughtered.

Acrid smells filled the air and Leo felt nauseated. Overwhelmed by the crowd and the sensations.

"I gotta get some air," he muttered and headed for the door.

There was a bouncer at the door who stopped him. "Where are you going?"

"Gotta get some air," Leo shouted. "I'm gonna be sick!"

The man stepped back to let him through the door. He'd probably encountered enough such scenes to know to avoid getting vomit on his designer shoes.

Leo darted out into the cooler night air and took a few long, deep breaths, trying to calm himself, to settle his stomach down.

He stood with his hands on his knees, hunched over slightly, gulping. The cat was raging crazily inside him, demanding to be let out, to rip, to tear. To administer some justice.

"Hey, man," there was a hand on his shoulder and Leo whipped around.

The bouncer quickly fell back a step. He didn't want any trouble.

"Just checking to see if you're okay," the man soothed.

"Yeah. I'll be fine," Leo growled, keeping his distance, needing space.

"You never been to a fight before?"

"No. Not like that. I've been to fights before. Human fights."

The bouncer looked him over and nodded. "It's a little different in here," he observed. "Wilder. More primal."

Leo nodded his agreement. He straightened up, still breathing deeply.

"You gonna come back in?" the bouncer asked.

"No, I don't think so. Not this time."

"You get right back in, it will be easier next time. If you avoid it, you just get more squeamish. You gotta face it, you know? Head on."

Leo nodded. "Yeah. I know. I just… I'm fighting a stomach bug or something tonight. Too queasy. You wouldn't want me losing it right in the middle of the crowd."

The bouncer grimaced and nodded. "Prefer you didn't," he agreed. "You'll come back again, though?"

Leo nodded, not wanting to make him suspicious. "Yeah," he agreed. "Next time." He looked down at the flyer still clutched in his hand. "Is there, like, a hotline or something? A way to find out where and when the next fight is without having to track down a flyer?"

The bouncer nodded. "What's your cell number?" he asked, pulling out a small coil notebook.

Leo hesitated. Now he was going to be on the hotlist of the fight ring? He wasn't so sure he wanted to commit. What if there was a police sting and he was caught?

The bouncer seemed to understand his concern.

"We're careful," he said. "You've seen that. If you don't want to give me your number, then you'll have to track us down like you did today. It's easier if we can reach you. We don't give your number to anyone. It's secure."

Leo relented and gave his number.

The bouncer nodded. "Great," he said. "I'm K-Bob. I'll see you next time."

Leo bumped fists with him and then retreated into the night.

When he got home, he scrubbed his hands, but still felt filthy.

He showered. A long, hot shower until the hot water ran out.

He still felt that dog's blood on his hands, together with all the other smells and secretions that had seeped into his flesh in the warehouse.

CHAPTER TWENTY-SIX

LEO PRESSED ELIZABETH'S BUZZER. He had initially been a bit hesitant. They hadn't exactly ended up on a positive note the last time he had seen her. He wanted to check on Juleen, but without seeming to be checking up on them.

But Elizabeth had called him on his way to work, inviting him to come by for supper and to watch a movie. It was a pleasant surprise, and Leo was happy for the diversion from Lyall's death and the dog fights. Things hadn't been exactly happy lately.

Elizabeth buzzed him in without answering. Leo went up to the apartment and she was waiting at her open door.

"Hi!" she said brightly. "I'm glad you could come!"

Leo smiled. "Thanks for inviting me," he said. "It was just what I needed."

"I don't know a lot of people," Elizabeth said. "So it's nice to have someone I can call when I don't feel like being alone."

"Well… you're not alone," Leo said. "Where's Juleen?"

"She's sleeping. Don't wake her up, I want her to sleep."

"Sure, okay."

"And having a baby around is not the same as having adults around. People you can talk to. You can have a hundred babies and still be lonely."

"I guess," Leo agreed.

He'd never felt particularly lonely with his siblings around. But they hadn't all been babies, either.

Time with just his siblings had been nice. It was the adults who had always wrecked things for him.

"So, what are you making?" Leo asked, taking a glance in the kitchenette.

"Nothing big. Actually," she giggled, "I'm just warming up frozen stuff and opening a bag of salad. But it will still make a nice meal! Shh, just don't tell anyone!"

"Sounds good to me. I'm easy to please. Anything I don't have to make myself is a treat."

Elizabeth nodded agreement. "Better get busy, Lizzie," she said to herself. She looked at Leo with laughing eyes. "Except I'm not Lizzie. I'm Lizard! Lizard the gizzard!"

Leo raised his eyebrows. "Lizard the gizzard," he repeated. "Sounds like a schoolyard name."

Elizabeth nodded. "Everybody always got called names on the school grounds, didn't they? But even with bullying and teasing, it was still a safe place. There were always supervisors around, places to play."

"Uh-huh," Leo agreed.

Assuming you were a girl playing on the climbers or hopscotch and not a boy fighting in the parking lot to defend your honor or that of your siblings. He'd never found school to be a particularly safe place. It *was* better than home, though.

"So is Lizard a school girl? Just a kid? Should I be trusting her to make me dinner?"

Elizabeth laughed. "I told you, I'm just warming it up," she reminded him.

"But maybe you shouldn't be allowed to use the stove."

"Oh, I've always been old enough to cook. I was born with a frying pan in my hand!"

"Who has always been old enough to cook? Lizard or Elizabeth?"

Elizabeth looked at him quizzically. "Lizard's always been old enough to cook," she said slowly, working it out. "But she wasn't really born with a frying pan in her hand. That's just a funny thing to say." She chuckled a little uncertainly.

"Yes, it is," Leo agreed.

Elizabeth relaxed, her forehead smoothing out and shoulders dipping down slightly. "People are always saying funny things," she said. "I like the expressions people make up. Driving me bananas. Duller than a sack of hammers. Elevator doesn't go to the top floor. It's funny, isn't it?"

"Sure. I feel sorry for people just learning English. We have such strange sayings sometimes."

"Lizard the gizzard," Elizabeth sang softly, as she fluttered around the kitchen, taking bowls out of the microwave and the fridge, assembling the pre-made food on plates. "Lizard the gizzard is silly, silly, silly. A silly Willy!"

"Willy willy silly," Leo contributed.

Elizabeth laughed.

"Willy, willy, willy," she singsonged.

She handed plates to Leo and he put them on the table. Elizabeth whipped back and forth, putting cutlery on the table, making a hundred trips to put everything on the table when it should only have taken one or two.

Leo watched her, analyzing this new persona.

She was dressed in an immature style. Blue jeans with a wispy blouse that wasn't tucked in. Bare feet. A gauzy scarf that didn't match anything, inexpertly tied around her neck.

"Are we ready?" he asked, looking at everything scattered across the table.

"Yup, ready Freddy!" Elizabeth agreed.

But in spite of her words, she still danced around a bit more, collecting things to put on the table. A bowl of nuts. A cut flower without a vase. A jug of water, even though they had glasses already filled with wine. Leo grabbed another glass to take advantage of the water instead of the wine. He made a dramatic gesture, pulling Elizabeth's chair out for her and holding it.

"Oooh, what a gentleman," Elizabeth trilled. She sat down and adjusted the seat.

"It all looks so good," Leo commented, sitting himself down and glancing over the table.

Elizabeth started picking at her food and he watched her while he took a few bites.

"Mmm, tastes good. Thanks very much."

Elizabeth nodded. She jumped up from the table and put on some music. Louder than necessary if they wanted to have a conversation, but Leo shrugged it off. Lizard was young. Kids tended to like their music loud.

He wondered how long Lizard had been at the forefront and how she was managing Juleen. He would have to stay long enough for Juleen to wake up, so he could check in on her and make sure she was okay.

"So, anything interesting at your work today?" Elizabeth asked.

"Not very. I did manage to net an old lady's parakeet that had gotten away from her."

"Awww," Elizabeth crooned. "I love parakeets!"

"They're not my favorite animal, but I'm glad I caught it for her. Animals like parakeets get out in nature... you don't know how they're going to survive, or if they'll do too well and impact the ecosystem. You know, like the snakes in Florida."

"Aren't there snakes in Florida?" she asked.

"Well, yeah. But some snakes aren't supposed to be there, like boas, they take over and eat all of the snakes that are supposed to be there, and it upsets the balance of things."

"Oh. I don't like snakes. They're too... slimy."

"They're not actually slimy. They're smooth and dry. Not like earthworms. No mucus."

"I still don't like them." She shuddered.

"That's okay. A lot of people don't."

"Do you think snakes really tempted Eve?" Elizabeth asked. "I don't think that really happened."

Leo raised his eyebrows. "Well... a lot of people don't believe the Bible literally," he said. "I think they would agree with you."

"But what do *you* think?" she persisted.

"I think... You're probably right. I don't think they are literally true stories. Just fables. Old stories with morals."

"Yeah. Just fables," Elizabeth agreed. "Fables on the tables... tables on the... hmm, on the floor. No food on the floor, just on the table."

Leo ate in silence, trying for a minute to sort this out. He shrugged it off uneasily.

Elizabeth wasn't making sense. She acted drunk. He had thought this persona was just being silly at first, playful.

But her repeated rhyming and disorganized speech made him nervous. Was she breaking down?

"You want to go out and dance after we eat?" Elizabeth asked.

"No, we can't go out and dance. You said we could watch a movie. We can't just leave Juleen here and go out dancing."

"Oh, we could take her with us."

"I don't think a dance club would be a good atmosphere to put her in. Babies need things to be quiet, predictable. She'd get overstimulated at a club, even if there wasn't any smoke or really loud music or anything."

"Babies are annoooy-ing!" Elizabeth announced in a dramatically bored voice.

"Yeah, I know. But she's your baby, so we have to think about things like that."

"You want to go somewhere else?"

"Why don't we just stay in and watch a movie?" Leo persisted.

"We could go out dancing."

Talking her out of it obviously wasn't working. Leo switched tactics. It wasn't for nothing he'd raised five siblings.

"Where did you get this chicken?" he asked. "It's really nice. Like that stuff you get at the restaurant."

"It's just out of a box, at the grocery store," Elizabeth said, fluttering her eyelashes at him flirtatiously.

"Yeah? Well, it's really nice. I saw there was a movie on tonight that was really good, but I can't remember what it was."

Elizabeth bounced out of her seat, grabbing a couple of remotes and bringing up the current movie showings on the screen of the TV. Leo scanned them to see what movie might appeal to her.

"Hey, it's that new Disney," he commented. "You don't mind watching a kid's show, do you? I've heard it's really good."

Elizabeth nodded. "Yeah, I've been wanting to see that," she agreed.

"Good. We can turn it on after we're finished eating."

Elizabeth started flipping channels at high speed. Leo had to look away, the rapidly changing images making him dizzy.

He smiled at her. Sooner or later, she would settle on something, and that's what they were going to watch. It didn't really matter. The point was just to spend some time with her, but not to go out. Leo wondered if he should try to find Elizabeth a babysitter so she could go out sometimes without Juleen. Escape from being a mother for a while. Maybe that would help to sort out the problems of keeping Juleen safe.

Elizabeth continued to flip channels, her eyes unfocused and her expression going blank. Leo watched her. "You okay?" he asked.

She stared at the screen, not paying any attention to him.

Leo touched her on the hand. "Elizabeth," he prodded.

She looked away from the screen, focusing on him. "Leo," she said suddenly.

"Hey," Leo said softly. Had she just shifted? Or was she still Lizard?

"This looks really good," Elizabeth said, sitting back down at the table and looking at her plate with wide eyes. She left the TV on a sports news station, and Leo didn't try to switch it to anything else.

"Everything all right?" he asked, as Elizabeth ate in silence.

"Yeah, it's really good, thanks," Elizabeth said.

"You made, it, not me."

"Yeah, but you came. I'm glad you came over."

"I am too. But are you all right? Everything going okay?"

"Sure. Of course."

The rest of the meal was pretty quiet. When they were finished, Elizabeth got up and looked in the fridge and freezer for a few minutes.

"I've got this frozen tiramisu cake," Elizabeth said. "How does that sound?"

"Wow, sounds really rich. Do you want to split a piece?"

"No! I want my own piece," Elizabeth snapped.

"Well, of course. Sure you can have your own," Leo agreed quickly. "I just meant the dinner filled me up pretty well. I wasn't sure if I could eat a full piece, but I can try."

"Good," Elizabeth said. She pulled it out of the fridge and squinted at the directions on the side of the box.

A thin cry rose from the bedroom and Leo just about tipped over his chair in his haste to get Juleen.

"I'll grab her," he told Elizabeth. "You get the cake out and I'll just check in on her and see how she's doing."

Elizabeth nodded. "Okay, thanks," she agreed.

Leo walked at a normal pace to Juleen's room, even though he wanted to get there as quickly as he could.

He opened the door and peeked in at her. "Hey, sweetie," Leo greeted softly. "How's it going, honey?"

She quieted down, maybe recognizing his voice. Leo picked her up. She was wet but otherwise seemed to be fine. Leo changed her into a dry diaper and carried her out to the front room. Without asking, he went to the fridge and found the formula he had bought and prepared Juleen a bottle. This didn't seem to bother Elizabeth one bit. Juleen sucked on the nipple greedily.

Leo couldn't help wondering how long it had been since she'd been fed last. She was looking less and less a bouncy baby girl these days. Too thin, too old in the face. Leo didn't like the changes he was seeing. Elizabeth was doing more than just forgetting a feeding now and then. It was becoming a real problem.

After Lyall's memorial, Stormy, Phil, and Leo were all huddled at a table to themselves off in one corner of the church cultural hall, trying to remain inconspicuous and avoid people offering their condolences. They drank their coffees and ate desserts the church ladies had prepared and kept their backs to the rest of the room.

Shayla came over. "I'm so glad you guys came," she said.

"Sure," Leo said. "Sorry I couldn't get the others."

"I'm glad to get any of you," Shayla said. "I wasn't sure if…" Her eyes glistened with tears.

"We're here," Leo said quickly, not wanting her to get emotional over the connections—or lack of such—between Lyall and his children. "We're here to support you."

"Yes. I sure appreciate it. And Lyall would be happy to know you are here too," Shayla said sincerely.

They all made agreeable noises.

"You've done a nice job," Leo said.

"I hardly did anything. Just called the committee at church. They pulled everything together."

"It's a good thing you have them," Leo said.

They exchanged a few more pleasantries and Shayla withdrew to circulate around the room.

"Lyall would be glad to know we're here," Stormy grumbled sarcastically. "Lyall would be sorry it's a dry party. What's a wake without whiskey?"

"He was on the wagon," Leo protested. "At least—he was when he died. He wouldn't want there to be booze, I don't think. Do you?"

"I don't think this is his kind of party," Phil said, siding with Stormy. "I think he'd be asking when the hell the good stuff was going to start. What he'd like at a wake would be booze, and plenty of it, strippers, loud music, and to go out with a bang. This little… Sunday School… is not his kind of thing."

"Well," Leo shrugged. "It's not really for him anyway. He's not here. It's for Shayla, and this *is* her kind of wake."

Stormy glanced across the room at Shayla. "So what is Shayla like?" she asked. "Is she as dopey as she seems?"

"She's nice," Leo protested. "And she loved him. So what does it matter?"

Stormy shook her head. "I can't see him with a flighty little thing like her. And as far as him being off the bottle…"

"Well, he was for the two weeks or whatever before he died," Phil said phlegmatically. "Seeing as he was brain dead at the time."

"Being brain dead never stopped him drinking before," Stormy offered, laughing uproariously. She quickly desisted when she saw all of the eyes turning toward her. "Yipes. No jokes allowed. I don't know why you stayed around at the hospital, Leo," Stormy said. "But it was nice of you to be there for Shayla."

Leo shrugged. "She's a nice girl. I couldn't just abandon her."

"You always have to be Prince Charming."

None of them said anything for a few minutes. Leo sipped at his coffee and nibbled another shortbread cookie.

"So," Stormy started up again, unable to keep still and quiet. "You promise to help me to make a break, find an agent or someone who is interested in me, and this is who you find?" She gestured at Phil. "My own brother?"

Leo laughed, embarrassed. "I know, Stormy. But it was just… meant to be. If it's… you know, you're worried about the kind of place it is… I didn't think you'd mind… They said they didn't care about the people in the acts, they didn't have to be… you know, oriented in any particular direction."

Stormy and Phil both laughed at Leo's awkwardness. He felt his face flush red.

"No, it's okay," Stormy said with a mischievous giggle. "It actually looks like a really good opportunity. I'm just yanking your chain."

"Oh. Okay," Leo said, relieved. He wiped his forehead. "Good, then. Are you going to sing there? Should I come and listen to you?"

"We're still getting her scheduled," Phil said. "One of us will let you know."

"Okay. Don't forget."

"You actually don't mind coming?" Phil asked. "You didn't seem too comfortable last time you were there." He snickered.

Leo looked at Stormy. "If this is Stormy's big break, I want to be there," he said. "No matter what."

Elizabeth called Leo in a state of excitement. "You have to come up," she said. "I have something I want to show you. You have to come today, okay?"

Leo wondered what was going on. "Sure," he agreed. "I've got the after-school program today, but I'll come over after that."

"So what time will that be?"

Leo considered. He would have to cut his own workout, but if he worked harder with the kids, that could count as his workout. And if his job kept him active instead of just sitting in the truck all day, it might not harm his training.

"Five-thirty is about the earliest I can manage," Leo said cautiously.

"Five-thirty!" Elizabeth sounded crestfallen. "You can't come before that?"

"No, sorry," Leo said. "I've got work and then the school program. I can't get there any earlier." He thought he'd been pushing it with five-thirty. He wasn't sure he could even get there by then.

"Fine," she said irritably. "Be here at five-thirty."

She hung up the phone before Leo could say anything further. He sighed and stared at the phone, trying to decide whether to call her back to try to calm her down. He decided he didn't have the time, and it probably wouldn't make any difference. She would still be upset he couldn't get there any earlier.

The day went slowly, and Leo was too inactive for his liking. He wanted to be able to get part of his workout during the day, but that just wasn't happening.

He found the boys grumpy and difficult to deal with. He left the gym feeling restless and out of sorts.

Leo needed a run. He needed supper. He needed to just go home and chill with Rascal, who also needed a run.

But Leo sucked it up and went to see Elizabeth and her surprise.

"Come on," Elizabeth encouraged him at the door. "Come in and see!"

Leo followed her into the apartment, intrigued.

"Come on, come on," Elizabeth said. She grabbed his hand and towed him into the front room and pointed at the couch. Leo looked at the pile of cushions and looked at Elizabeth. She looked at him expectantly. Leo looked back at the couch.

A few cushions, like always. A blanket draped. A cat curled up in the corner. A *cat?* Leo looked at Elizabeth in disbelief.

"You got a cat?" he demanded. "A *cat?*"

She nodded happily. "I got it at the Humane Society," she told him delightedly. "Where you work."

"How the *hell* could you get a cat?" Leo snarled. "You can't take care of your baby! You can't take care of yourself! How could you adopt a cat?"

Elizabeth looked indignant. "I can take care of myself! You're supposed to be happy! I rescued an animal. Like you do!"

Leo shook his head in amazement. "I'm happy when people rescue animals when they're going to take good care of them. But you can't. You'll forget you even have one and let it out in the street. Or you'll starve it. Come on, Lizzie…"

"Don't call me Lizzie," Elizabeth snapped, her face darkening.

Leo had used it as a pet name, to try to connect with her, forgetting in his shock that each name meant something different to Elizabeth. Not just *something* different, but *someone* different.

"Sorry, I didn't mean—"

"You think you can just call Lizzie, and she'll take care of everything?" Elizabeth demanded. "Because she's so responsible, she'll just overrule everyone else?"

"No, it was a slip. I didn't mean Lizzie. I just meant Elizabeth. I'm sorry."

"Why don't you just get out of here?" Elizabeth demanded, her voice deepening, her expression hard and dark.

Leo froze. He didn't think it was Eli, but by the voice and stance, this was a male personality. And male might mean aggressive. Placating, Leo took a step back, holding his hands up .

"If you don't want me here, Elizabeth, I'll leave," he said soothingly.

She still looked angry.

Leo looked at the cat on the couch and took a chance. "Hey! You got a cat!" he said enthusiastically. "Can I see? Will it let me pet it?"

Confusion crossed over Elizabeth's face. She blinked a few times. Leo advanced toward the cat and sat down next to it. It was a gorgeous little tabby, long and lithe and unmarked silver-gray. She looked young; not a kitten, but not yet full-grown either.

"Well, hello there, little miss," Leo crooned to her, ignoring Elizabeth. "Aren't you just beautiful?"

The cat looked at him and stretched, elongating and showing her belly, looking at him upside down. Leo laughed.

"She's very friendly, isn't she? A people-cat."

"You like my kitty?" Elizabeth asked in a childish voice.

"Who could not like this little girl?"

"I've always wanted a cat," Elizabeth said tentatively, stepping toward him.

"Did you ever have a pet before?"

"No. I move around too much. People don't keep me for long. They don't think I'm responsible enough to have a pet. But I am!"

"You'll take good care of her? What's her name?"

"Silver."

"Very appropriate. She really shines, doesn't she?"

"I thought you'd like her because you're the dog catcher. You protect animals. I want to protect them too."

"Good for you. I'm glad you want to help animals."

Elizabeth approached and sat on the couch, starting to pet Silver. Her face was childlike and serene. Leo watched her while patting and playing with the cat.

He'd never seen her cycle through personalities so fast. Was that a warning sign? Was she a danger to Juleen, or the cat, or even to Leo himself?

He hadn't liked the change that came over her when she felt threatened.

Sure, Leo was a trained fighter, but he knew from experience how psychosis could endow a person with incredible strength and make them impervious to pain.

You didn't want to be fighting someone like that.

Especially not someone you didn't want to hurt.

"Are you remembering to take your meds?" he asked. "To keep you healthy and strong?"

She looked at him through her top lashes. "I don't need any medicine," she said. "Only Lisa takes medicine."

"And has she been taking it?"

Elizabeth nodded. Leo sighed with relief. Hopefully, that meant Lisa was taking the pills regularly. It wouldn't be good if Lisa only showed up once a week.

"Will I see Lisa sometime soon?" he asked.

"I don't know. She's out right now."

"Does she know you got a cat?"

"It's okay. Pets are good for kids. They make you feel good and teach responsibility." She picked Silver up and held the cat against her face, breathing in her fur.

"Good," Leo observed. "You take good care of her, okay?"

"Of course," Elizabeth agreed.

CHAPTER TWENTY-SEVEN

LEO WAITED NERVOUSLY IN the police conference room, eager to talk to someone about the dog fights, or to get out of there.

Waiting was the worst part.

He'd been around enough police conference and interrogation rooms in his time. Acting out at school, underage drinking, vandalism, assault, all of that.

And then, after him, his siblings… Leo drifted back to one day he went to the police station to pick up teenage Michelle.

Leo explained who he was at the front desk and was taken to a conference room to talk to one of the arresting officers. A cop brought Michelle in with him.

She looked pretty messed up. Her dark hair was disheveled, her eyes bloodshot. She moved with a sloppy sway that said she'd had a lot to drink. Leo shook his head. Stupid of her. She should know better.

The officer deposited her in one of the chairs at the table. He was probably pushing retirement; tired, overweight, and world-weary.

"Who are you?" he asked, looking Leo over.

"Her brother."

"Where are your parents?"

"Our mom left us years ago. Dad's a truck driver, he's not going to be home for a few days. I'm nineteen," he said, anticipating the cop's question.

"Well, she's obviously not going to get any discipline from you. I should just put her in juvenile care until your dad can pick her up."

Leo looked at Michelle. She glared back, putting on a cold, uncaring front. An attitude to mask what she was really feeling.

"What happened?" Leo asked the cop.

"We had to break up a party. Disturbing the peace. There were illegal drugs, underage drinking. This one," he gestured at Michelle, his eyes flicking over to her, "waaaay too much to drink. Does she party like that often?"

Leo shook his head. "This is the first time she's been picked up," he said. "Usually she's at home, not out with friends. I'll keep her at the house. She won't be going out anywhere else."

"What's stopping her?"

"I am. There's only one car, and that's mine. She won't be taking it."

"How did she get to this party, then? You took her there?"

"A friend at school. School just let out for spring break today. She won't be going back to school or seeing any of those friends for another week." He shot a look at Michelle. "She'll be in her room."

Michelle made a face at him, her nose wrinkled in a sneer.

The cop shook his head and pressed his lips together. "She's a wild one. She's not going to stay home just because you tell her to."

"We're out in the sticks. None of her friends are going to be sober enough to drive out and get her."

The cop looked Michelle over. "You sobered up enough to talk for yourself now?" he questioned.

Michelle inclined her head slightly, which threw her off balance and she rocked in her seat, catching herself.

"If I release you, are you going to stay home?" he demanded.

"Yeah. Leo won't let me go anywhere," she grumbled.

The cop looked at Leo, frowning. "Do I know you from somewhere?" he asked uncertainly.

"Yeah, probably. We've lived around here my whole life. I've… gotten into some trouble of my own. When I was younger," this was aimed at Michelle, "and stupid."

The cop chuckled at this, but his eyes were searchlights, trying to figure out where he knew Leo from.

Leo sighed. He pulled out one of the other chairs and sat down around the corner of the table from Michelle.

"Are you okay?" he asked, studying her. She'd obviously had a ton to drink. And from her rumpled look, he assumed she'd been messing around with the boys. She was only fourteen; he didn't like her pretending she was all grown up. If she ended up pregnant at fourteen, an alcoholic, or dead… she just didn't understand the dangers. Leo did. He pushed her mussed hair back from her face, over one ear, looking into her eyes. "Is everything okay?"

She shook her hair back down so it covered her mutilated earlobes.

"Yeah," she said sarcastically. "Everything is just peachy keen."

She folded her arms across her chest, giving Leo a defiant look. Leo turned to look at the cop, to see if he could talk the man into releasing Michelle. Taking the trouble to send Michelle to juvie meant paperwork, transportation out there, and all of it again in reverse when Lyall got back to claim her—just for being drunk at a spring break party… He was sure the cop would rather not deal with all that.

The cop was looking, not at Michelle, but at Leo, his brows drawn down in consternation. Leo followed the cop's gaze to Leo's hand, with one finger missing and one mangled. Leo closed his hand and slid both hands into his pockets. He gave Michelle a significant look.

"What?" she demanded. Then she caught on, and she slid one of her hands into her jacket pocket too, with an exaggeratedly cautious air that drew attention to her missing fingers. Leo rolled his eyes. Expecting her to be subtle when she was drunk… not a bright idea.

"Are you going to release her?" Leo asked the police officer briskly.

"I do know you," the cop said slowly. "Leo."

"Yeah. Leo. That's what I said. And I'm Michelle's brother. I'll keep an eye on her if you'll just turn her over to me…"

"I was called out to your house once," the officer said.

Leo's mouth went dry as he also recognized the cop.

He didn't recognize Leo from seeing him around town, from some scrape Leo had gotten into. He knew Leo because he'd been one of the cops who had taken the call when Leo reported Lyall to Child Services for cutting off his finger.

Now Leo understood the expression on the cop's face. Horror. Guilt. Panic. He'd seen Leo's hand. Before she, oh-so-subtly, slid it into her pocket, he'd seen Michelle's too. He knew he'd screwed up by not taking Leo's complaint seriously. He had chewed Leo out and not bothered to verify his story. He hadn't taken the simple expedient of examining Leo's bandaged hand.

"If you've been out there, then you know she's not just going to run back to town," Leo said reasonably, trying to deflect the cop's thoughts back to Michelle and their immediate problem. "You know we're far enough out she's not going to just call a friend and get a ride to the next party."

The cop nodded woodenly, expressionless. "And your dad... he's out of town, you say?"

"Yeah. He's away a lot. I look after Michelle and the other kids. I take care of them."

"I'll release her to you."

The officer walked over to Michelle and indicated she should stand. Leo got up as well and put his arm around Michelle to keep her on her feet, guiding her back to the car. The cop walked with him in silence out to the front reception area.

"I'm sorry," he muttered, as they stopped in the reception area.

Leo shrugged. "Just doing your job," he said lightly. "Don't worry about it. I'll keep an eye on her."

He escorted Michelle out.

But the police station had always been a safe place for Leo too. Somewhere to cool off, to get help, to get his feet back on the ground again. Lyall couldn't reach him there. Being picked up by the police had never been a deterrent for Leo. At least he knew what to expect from the cops.

Waiting to talk to them about the dog fights, though, Leo wasn't so sure. He knew he was doing the right thing. He just wasn't sure how they were going to react. Would they take him seriously? Would they care? Would they decide he was one of the guilty parties? A cop came in and sat down across the table from Leo. He was broad, his hair dark. He had a brass name badge that said 'Ledger.'

"So you have some information for us," he said.

"About illegal dog fights," Leo agreed. He laid the flyer on the table. Ledger looked down at it and pulled it over in front of him. His eyes flicked over it.

"So how do you know where and when?" he asked.

"You text them and they text you the back time and place. But it's not the time and place of the fight. It's a halfway point, this guy gives you the real information, once he checks you out."

Ledger frowned. "Everybody who wants to go to the fight has to go through this one point of contact?" He tapped the paper with the pads of two fingers.

"Yeah," Leo insisted. Then he thought about it. Maybe different flyers led you to different locations. Or maybe the texts that came back gave various different locations to check in at. They wouldn't have to all give the same location. "I don't know. Maybe there's more than one contact point. I only got one. But I gave them my cell number to send me texts about future fights," Leo said.

"Good. So you don't have to rely on getting a flyer. Maybe our guys can intercept those texts so we can get right onto any new fights."

Leo nodded eagerly. "Yeah, that would be good."

"Do you text a lot? Would we get a lot of junk if we intercepted your texts?"

Leo had to stop and think about that. Intercept all his texts? If he actually had friends he conversed with via text, it could be rather intrusive and embarrassing. But the fact was, he couldn't remember the last text he had received, other than the ones with the dog fight addresses.

"No, I don't think so. I don't text a lot," Leo said reluctantly, a bit embarrassed.

"Oh good," Ledger said with relief. "Some of the kids these days… hundreds of texts a day. It would be a nightmare."

"I prefer face to face," Leo said.

"Me too. You don't want too much floating out there in cyberspace. And it doesn't have quite the same human touch, you know?"

Leo nodded in agreement.

"So what did you see, once you got there?" Ledger questioned.

Leo outlined the situation to him. The location, the people he had seen or talked to. As little about the actual fight as he could.

"I love animals," he excused himself. "I couldn't really watch it."

"Understandable," Ledger said gruffly. "Senseless violence. Some of the guys that are into it are as twisted as pedophiles. You don't want to be one of them."

"I'm a boxer," Leo said, "but I still can't understand it. Two people, deciding to fight for sport, with rules and a referee, that's one thing. But helpless animals, scared, fighting to the death… I just can't fathom that."

Ledger nodded. He looked over his brief, illegible notes. "The two gentlemen who made contact with you. Slim and…"

"K-Bob," Leo said with a grin.

"How did you feel about them? How deep do you think they are in the organization?"

Leo thought about it. He hadn't really considered they were part of the group that had set it up. K-Bob was just a bouncer, like an employee at a bar. That didn't make him part of the brains of the operation. And Slim, he'd just been there in the audience, the same as Leo.

Was it possible he was involved more deeply?

"Well… K-Bob, he did take my phone number. He knew how the system worked. I guess he's involved somehow. He didn't say he didn't know, or I should talk to management."

"Right," Ledger agreed. "Chances are, he wasn't just told to take numbers. Everyone you dealt with had to decide whether you are trustworthy, or whether you might be a cop. You don't put just anyone on your mailing list. Not when you're trying to keep the operation underground."

Leo nodded thoughtfully. Then he thought about Slim. It had just been a chance encounter, hadn't it? Slim had been suspicious of him at first. Keeping a lookout? Making sure of any unfamiliar faces? He had definitely been familiar with the fights, with this particular ring. He hadn't acted like management, but he might know things.

"I don't think Slim was involved. It never occurred to me at the time. But… he did want to be sure of me. So maybe…"

Ledger nodded. "Most people aren't going to get involved with an unfamiliar face at a scene like that. They stick with who they know, who they trust. He could have just been a social guy, thought you had a likely face, but… he was probably a spotter. A spy, just keeping an eye on things. A little extra security."

Leo shuddered, a chill running down his spine.

Ledger smiled in amusement. "Always someone watching the watchers. These guys are good. They're careful."

CHAPTER TWENTY-EIGHT

ELIZABETH'S APARTMENT WAS COLD. She paced, seeming restless and worried. Leo had passed Lady Bathrobe on the way up, and the woman had warned her about Elizabeth.

"There's something wrong with that girl. You keep an eye on her. Look out... something's brewing."

From one crazy person about another.

"I don't know," Elizabeth said when he persisted in asking how she was. "Sometimes I just wish I was normal. That I could think straight and behave like everyone else. I get tired of the drama. The confusion over who I really am, deep down. Forgetting things I want to remember... not being able to be a really good mom to Juleen... it looks so much easier for everyone else! Is it really, or does it just look that way?"

Leo thought about it. Was it easier to remember or to forget? Was it easier to be one person, dealing with all your problems, or to shift between personalities to deal with them individually? It was just as hard for him to imagine living inside of Elizabeth's head as it was for her to imagine living inside of his.

"I don't know," he said. "It's not easy. But I'd rather know what I was facing. What really happened in my past, what the problems are now. That doesn't mean it's easy. I hate having to deal with my problems... I'd rather solve other people's. Rescue animals. Facing my own demons is... hard."

Elizabeth nodded. "You remember about your past," she said, "but sometimes I think you're running just as hard as I am."

"I know," Leo agreed. "But at least I know who I am, where I'm coming from."

"Dr. Marvin says I can remember if I really want to. That I'm in charge, and I can tell my subconscious, all the parts of me, to open the doors. When I'm ready."

Leo stared out the window, down at the street. "And are you ready?"

If he could just help her to do this… her life would be so much easier if she didn't keep relinquishing control to other personalities. And he could help her with Juleen. He could rescue Juleen and Elizabeth.

But he knew it had to come from Elizabeth. Like Dr. Marvin said, she had to want to. She had to be ready.

Elizabeth rolled her eyes upward, trying to control her emotion. She didn't succeed and her eyes started to leak. "I don't even know who I am," she sobbed. "I just want to know that. Who I really really am. Which one is me. I can't be someone different every time I walk out the door."

"So who do you think you are?" Leo asked. "Is there one personality that is you, or is the whole mixture you? Or have you buried yourself?"

"Will you help me?" Elizabeth asked.

Leo braced himself. He had a feeling this would be a bumpy ride. "Of course," he agreed, masking his uneasiness. "What can I do?"

"Just… I don't know… keep reminding me I want to know. That I want out."

"Okay," Leo said cautiously. "Right now? Are you going to try right now?"

It was a little like an exorcism. He shivered in anticipation.

It could be that nothing would happen. He was no expert, but certainly Elizabeth could just 'try' and not have any kind of breakthrough. How long had she been working with therapists before now? None of them had managed to break through all the personalities and find the 'true' Elizabeth, to 'cure' her of this malady.

Wasn't it more likely to be a long process, taking years, than to be a one-hour solution?

"Yes," Elizabeth said resolutely. "I want to know. I want to know and I'm telling myself that I want to know. It's time. It's time to stop locking it all away."

"Okay," said Leo. "So… what do you remember? What is the earliest thing?"

Elizabeth looked around vaguely. "I remember when I moved here and started seeing Doctor Marvin," she said.

That hadn't been very long ago. Only a few months or a few years, however long she'd lived there before going into the army.

"You remember before that," he prompted. "You remember the old lady whose husband died. What was her name?"

Elizabeth frowned. "Lots of people have husbands that died," she said. "What are you talking about?"

"The one who kept the corpse in the living room. Who didn't want to give him up."

"That doesn't…" Elizabeth's face changed perceptibly. "Oh. I remember her. Mrs. Ogilvy."

"Right," Leo agreed. "And how old were you then?"

"I was… I don't know… seven?"

"You were Lizzie," Leo suggested. "She called you Lizzie, right?"

Elizabeth nodded. "I'm Lizzie," she agreed placidly.

"So how about before that? Where were you before that?"

"Lots of places. I don't know. It doesn't matter."

"You wanted to remember," Leo prompted her.

"No. It's okay. I was just a kid. People can't remember that far back."

"People can remember before they were seven," Leo assured her. "I remember when I was three or four."

"I don't remember further back than that," Elizabeth said certainly.

"Well, who does? One of you remembers further back than that."

"No. I don't think so."

Leo looked at Elizabeth's open, wide-eyed, childlike face.

"What were you called before Mrs. Ogilvy nicknamed you Lizzie?" he asked.

"I don't know." Elizabeth lounged across the easy chair, one leg up on the arm, swinging her foot. "I've had lots of nicknames. I think Elizabeth has more nicknames than any other name in the world."

"I think you're right," Leo agreed. "What have some of the other ones been?"

Elizabeth considered. "The boys used to call me Lizard," she said.

"That's cute," Leo said. "What boys?"

"All kinds of boys. It's just one of those instincts. Elizabeth—Lizzie—Lizard. They all get there sooner or later."

"I suppose so," Leo said. "Did they tease you a lot at school? Or were these boys your foster brothers? Or what?"

"Mostly boys at school," Elizabeth said vaguely. "They did it to bug me, but I really didn't care."

"You like lizards?" Leo asked, wondering if it brought any specific images to mind for her.

"Oh yeah," Elizabeth agreed earnestly. "They're so cool. The way they can walk up walls. They like to lay in the sun, getting all warm and nice."

"Nice," Leo echoed. He liked lizards too. He didn't see a lot of them as an animal control officer, but he liked them nonetheless. Especially in the wild, as Elizabeth said, out basking in the sun.

"I laid out in the sun sometimes," Elizabeth said in a small, giggly voice.

"You did, did you?" Leo asked, at a loss as to where this was going.

"Naked," Elizabeth giggled, snorting at his surprised expression. "It's so nice, lying in the sun."

Leo shifted uncomfortably. Elizabeth put her head back and closed her eyes, stretching languorously, basking in the sun.

"Did you get in trouble?"

"No… nothing wrong with a lizard lying in the sun," she told him.

"How old were you? Was this before Lizzie?"

"I did it at school sometimes… back behind, where we weren't supposed to go."

"By… yourself…?"

"No! They wanted to watch and to touch. Not by myself."

"They shouldn't have done that," Leo said flatly. "Nobody should have hurt you."

"It didn't hurt," she said in a sing-songy voice. "Just lying in the sun, little Lizard…"

"What happened before that?" Leo asked, hoping to get away from this memory, further back to the roots of her problems. "Before you were a lizard in the sun?"

"That's far enough," she said, still singsong.

Leo shook his head. "You wanted to remember, Elizabeth. You asked me to help you."

"I remembered. That's far enough."

"How about before that? Where did you live before that? With your mom and dad?"

"I don't have a mom and dad," she snapped, coming quickly out of the Lizard personality, "I never had a mom and dad."

"You did sometime. A long time ago. Do you remember?"

"No, I never had a mom and dad," her voice was hard and angry, her denial flat.

"What about your birth mom? Do you remember her?"

"I don't have a birth mom."

"Then where did you come from?"

"I'm an alien," Elizabeth claimed. "I was just left here. No mom. No dad."

Leo chuckled. "Really. I think you're telling me stories."

"Who do you think you are? You don't know what happened to me! You don't know who I am or where I came from!" Her voice rose to an angry yell.

"Then why don't you tell me? What happened to you?"

"Nothing happened to me!" she insisted.

"Where did you come from?" Leo demanded, anger and frustration in his voice.

"You don't know anything!" she shrieked.

Leo took a few deep breaths, trying to keep his own alter-ego at bay.

The wildcat didn't like screaming. It didn't like arguing.

It didn't like having brick walls thrown up every time he tried to investigate further. It especially didn't like these shifting personalities.

It felt threatened.

Exposed.

Leo breathed, trying to slow his heartbeat. Thinking of green trees, purring cats, running paths, other peaceful images to try to settle his anxious innards back down again.

"Why don't you tell me?" Leo questioned with forced calm. "You said you wanted to know. So tell me about it."

"I'm not telling you anything! Why don't you just take a hike? I don't like you!"

"You want to know, Elizabeth. You asked me to help."

"You're not helping me! You just want to get into my brain. You don't know me!"

"You wanted to know."

"Lisa wanted to know! Lisa's not allowed here!" The voice was hoarse, angry, furious.

"Lisa needs to know. She wants to get help. She wants to live a normal life."

"Lisa can't know. She can only be Lisa if she doesn't know."

This baffled Leo. She could only be Lisa if she didn't know?

He thought over what he knew about Lisa. Not a lot, except she was the one who took the medication. The one who went to the doctor. The one who wanted help. Did the rest of them not want help?

Was Lisa the only one? If so, why did she want help and the rest didn't?

"Who am I talking to?" he asked.

"Elijah."

A boy. He had half-guessed it from the voice. Was a boy automatically a protector? Someone to keep her from being hurt? Why was it necessary for her to change genders all of the sudden? Had he made her more vulnerable by going too far back?

"Elijah. Not Eli?"

"No," Elizabeth said, sounding annoyed. "Not Eli. What a stupid name."

"Elijah's a good name," Leo suggested.

"Elijah's the best name. Right out of the Bible. It's a strong name."

"Because you're strong," Leo said. "And you're good."

Elizabeth lifted her chin proudly.

"What happened before Lizard?" Leo said. "Was that when you were with your birth mom?"

"No. And I don't want to go back any farther. Just back off."

"Elizabeth wants to know," Leo repeated.

"Lisa wants to know," Elizabeth countered.

"Why can't Lisa know? How can she help you if she doesn't know?"

"Nobody can help. I have to take care of myself."

Leo cast his mind back, trying to think of anything else that might help Elizabeth get past this barrier.

What had happened before? Before Elizabeth was Lizard… He guessed Lizard was five or six, sunning herself back behind the school, exhibiting herself to the boys.

"Lisa has to be strong," Elizabeth offered in a growl. "She can't be strong if she goes back too far."

"I think she's stronger than you think. I think you're afraid she's going to make you disappear."

Elizabeth scowled at him. "She can't make me disappear."

"No, I don't think she can. I think you'll always be there. But I think *you're* afraid she can make you disappear. You're scared to let her find out more."

"I'm never scared."

"Well, that's lucky. So you come out when the others are scared? You know everybody gets scared sometimes. So even if you don't think you do… I think you're still scared inside. You're just trying to hide it."

"Others aren't like me. Others can't just make the fear disappear."

"That would be handy," Leo said. He thought back to his own life. All the times when he wished he hadn't had to be so scared. Times when it would have served him well to just be able to shut off the fear. But…

"There's a reason for fear," Leo said. "Fear helps to protect us too. It tells us where the danger is. Tells us to be cautious. Not having any fear isn't good, it's dangerous."

"I'm strong. Danger doesn't matter."

"I think it does. I think you're scared, but you're trying to prove you're strong."

The answer was a few moments in coming. Elizabeth's expression softened. "I am strong."

Her voice was suddenly quieter.

Elijah the protector had merely dropped away when confronted. Unmasked, he faded into the background. It was, Leo thought, too easy.

Elijah had retreated too fast, had perhaps fallen back to another position.

"You're not Elijah anymore," he said. She was cycling so fast, it worried him.

He wasn't sure who was coming next or if his amateur tinkering could end up causing her irreversible harm.

What if she had a complete psychotic break?

What if he forced her to go too far and her brain or psyche just couldn't take it?

But he had to do it. It was the only way to help her.

"Who are you?" he pressed.

"Lu."

Leo felt a chill. He knew what happened when Elizabeth had become Lu before. He knew it meant she was destabilizing. "Hi Lu," he said gently.

Her eyes were wary, and yet… tender. She shifted her position, curling into herself. Protecting her body, yet staying alert to him. Careful, defensive, watchful.

"Hi."

"Are you going to tell me what happened?" he asked. "Before Lizard?"

"She was hurt," Elizabeth said sharply. "Those awful people hurt her bad."

Leo felt a wave of compassion for her. After all Elizabeth had already revealed, there was still worse to come. Her story was almost as bad as his own. Or perhaps it was worse and that was why she was so badly damaged.

"Who hurt her?"

"Those people who adopted her. Those mom and dad."

Leo nodded slowly. "The adoption that went wrong," he said. "What happened that hurt her so much?"

"Lots of crying," Elizabeth informed him. "Lots of hurt. They said keep her forever. They said take care of her forever. Never go hungry. Never be hurt. No more be afraid anymore. They lied!" she barked.

"They thought they could take care of her," Leo surmised, "but it didn't work out. They gave up on her."

"They promised! They promised *forever!* Over and over. We promise! You never hurt no more! You never scared no more! They promised!" Elizabeth's words were short and clipped, harsh and bare. "You safe! We love! *Forever!*"

But that wasn't how it had ended up.

Mama stood with Liza at the airport gate. Liza looked around anxiously. This was all new to her and made her nervous. She didn't know who any of these people were or why Mama had brought her here. She shuffled closer to Mama, standing on top of her feet to squeeze herself as close to Mama's legs as she could.

"Liza!" Mama said irritably. "Get off my feet! That hurts! How many times have I told you not to do that?"

Liza didn't get off until Mama shook her loose and pried her away from her legs.

"Don't touch me! That hurts!" Liza pouted.

"Oh, enough of that already. You know how to behave, I expect you to do it. Now go sit on one of those chairs and be quiet and still."

Liza looked at the chairs, far away by the windows. She would be very far away from Mama. The windows looked out onto the enormous runway, a wide-open space that made Liza feel small inside. It was a long way down to the ground if she fell.

"No!" She grabbed onto Mama's jacket, twisting it in her fist.

Mama tried to pull it out of her grip. "Liza! You heard me! Be a good girl and go sit over there."

Liza shook her head. Mama took her hand tightly and marched her over to the black chairs. She lifted Liza onto one. Liza clung to the arms of the chair, worried she might slide down the slippery material onto the floor.

"There. Just stay there," Mama ordered. She went back over to the gate and was talking to the ticket lady.

Liza stared out the window as a big plane moved slowly down the runway, gathering speed until it was right next to the window, filling the room with noise and vibrating the glass. Liza hung onto her seat for dear life, her whole body clenched in terror. The plane moved past the window and raced down the runway, suddenly rising into the air and disappearing beyond the view of the window.

"Oh, wow!" a boy watching out the window with his father exclaimed. "That was cool!"

"Oh, wow," Liza echoed.

The boy turned and looked at her. His father looked at her too and smiled. "Do you like planes?" he asked.

Liza shook her head no.

He chuckled. "You sounded like you enjoyed it," he pointed out.

Liza sucked her thumb.

The boy looked down his nose at her. "Are you a baby?" he demanded. "Only babies suck their thumbs!"

"Ben, that's not nice," his father chided. "We don't say things like that."

"She looks like a baby."

The father smiled apologetically and they moved on. Liza took her thumb out of her mouth and instead grabbed a lock of hair, winding it around her finger. Mama came over and looked down at her.

"Were you talking to that man?" she demanded. "You know not to talk to strangers."

Liza shook her head.

Mama looked at the clock. "They're going to start pre-boarding in a few minutes," she said. "And since you're little, you get to get on the plane first. Won't that be exciting?"

Liza shook her head. "Don't want to go," she whined. "I wanna go home."

"You're not going home. You're going to a new place now."

"No," Liza wheedled. "Liza go home, Mama."

"Come on, you need to get ready." Mama picked her up to stand her on the floor and let go quickly. "You're wet!" she exclaimed, her face getting red. "Did you wet your pants?"

Liza danced from one foot to the other. The urine was stinging her legs uncomfortably. "Scared," she said. "The plane comed right up here!"

"Liza! You're a big girl now. No wetting your pants! Now I'm going to have to change you, and you're supposed to be boarding soon!"

Mama looked around for a bathroom and hauled Liza toward it, pulling her by the arm while taking big strides that Liza had to run to keep up with.

"Don't have to pee," Liza insisted, trying to pull away. "Don't have to go bafroom."

"You have to change into dry clothes. Now come on. Quit pulling and just behave."

Liza started to shriek, angry and afraid and wanting to get in control of the situation. She wrenched herself away from Mama and threw herself on the floor, screaming. Mama had to pick her up and carry her into the bathroom.

Once there, she laid Liza roughly down on the floor so Liza bumped her head on the cold tiles.

Mama started pulling her clothes off. Liza shrieked and tried to hold onto them.

Mama ignored her cries, continuing to undress her by force until Liza was rolling around naked on the cold, hard floor. Mama let her go to dig fresh clothes out of the diaper bag.

"You're not a baby," she groused. "You know how to go to the bathroom and how to ask when you need to go. You don't just pee your pants!"

"Wanna be baby," Liza moaned, holding her body, trying to cover her goose-bumped skin, terrified by her nakedness and vulnerability. "Mama's baby."

"You're not a baby. Now help me get you dressed. Come on."

Mama threaded her legs through panties and stood her up on her feet impatiently. Liza stood there limply, not helping as Mama pulled the dry clothes on.

She tried to hug Mama. "Sorry, Mama. Sorry I pee."

"Enough," Mama pushed her away. "Come on, now. It's time to get on the plane."

She pulled Liza back out of the bathroom, back across the open space, to the place where the ticket lady stood by the microphone.

"Sorry, I had to go get her ready. Are you pre-boarding yet?"

"Yes, we just made the announcement," the ticket lady smiled.

"Okay. Liza's ready to get on the plane, now."

"She's going by herself?"

Mama nodded. "I made arrangements. They said it wouldn't be a problem."

"Certainly. If you'll just wait for a moment. We'll get her all fixed up."

She tapped more information into her computer. Mama bent down to talk to Liza face to face. Her eyes were piercing.

Liza looked away, uncomfortable, feeling her safe space invaded.

Mama grabbed her face and turned it back with both hands, forcing Liza to hold her gaze.

"Now listen to me, Liza," she said firmly. "Here is your letter. When you get off the plane, then you give it to them, okay? Not until you get off the plane."

"No," Liza whined.

"Yes. You listen to me. You be a good girl on the plane. You don't talk to anyone, you don't pee your pants, and you sit nice and quiet and look at a book."

She pressed a small backpack into Liza's hand, making her take it. Liza grabbed her stuffed puppy out through the gaping zipper and held it to her face.

"Just play with Lulu," Mama approved.

She put the letter into Liza's jacket pocket.

"Now be good," she repeated again. She kissed Liza firmly on the cheek.

Liza pulled back and pushed her away. "No kiss," she growled, wiping her face.

Mama shook her head and gave Liza a tight hug, her eyes glistening with tears. "Be a good girl," she whispered again.

"Okay," said the ticket lady brightly. "We're going to put this necklace on Liza." She put a lanyard with papers in a plastic pouch around Liza's neck. "And then you can get onto the plane. Okay, sweetie?"

Liza was looking at Mama's teary eyes, a knot growing in her stomach. The ticket taker grabbed her hand and Liza started to wail.

"Mama!" she yelled. "No—no go! I be good!"

Mama turned away from her. The ticket lady led her into a big white hallway. The floor bounced in a funny way when they walked on it and Liza clutched the woman's hand more tightly, anxious about falling.

"It's okay," the ticket lady encouraged. "You're going to have a really fun time. Oh, it's so beautiful up there in the sky, above the clouds."

Liza walked beside her, clinging to her hand. She didn't continue to cry once out of Mama's sight. She looked around the long white hallway, eyes wide, her whole body cold.

She knew she would never see Mama again.

That life was over.

The ticket lady stroked her hair. "There, that's better, isn't it?" she said. "Everything is going to be okay." She led Liza through a doorway into a long room with windows. "Now we're in the plane. Do you want to see the pilot in the cockpit?"

Liza shook her head, but the woman took her in anyway. Liza gazed around the cockpit with all of its buttons and switches and displays.

The pilot turned to look at her and smiled. "Is this my new copilot?" he asked.

They both chattered at her. Liza looked around at all the controls. She reached out and started flipping switches and touching indicator lights curiously.

"Whoops, none of that!" The lady reprimanded and grabbed her hand.

"We can't touch anything in here. Let's go find your seat and get you settled."

Liza let herself be led into the body of the plane, where she looked out the windows and down at the ground far below, her stomach feeling sloshy and sick.

"Okay! Here's a seat for you. It's on the aisle so you can call the flight attendant if you need anything. We'll just sit you here and put your bag up in the compartment."

Liza grabbed for her bag.

"Want hold it," she whined, not liking it disappearing from view. It was her only tie to Mama and home now. "Mine bag!"

"You can have it once we're in the air," the woman promised.

Liza hugged Lulu to her tightly, afraid of losing her puppy too.

"When we're taking off, you'll need to put your teddy in the seat pocket here. Just until they say it's okay. All right?"

"Lulu," Liza told her.

"What?"

"This Lulu," Liza explained, pointing to the threadbare stuffed dog.

"Oh, she's very nice, sweetie. Now here's one of the flight attendants." The ticket lady motioned to a stewardess approaching from the back of the plane. "This is Josie. She'll help you with anything you need during the flight, okay? You just call her if you need anything."

Liza looked at the new caregiver. "Josie," she repeated.

"That's right," Josie said with a smile. She was a tall redhead with a big, bright red smile like a clown. "What's your name, honey?"

Liza didn't answer.

"This is Liza," the ticket taker told her. "Now I'd better get back and see if there's anyone else who wants to pre-board. Then we'll get everyone else going. Okay? I'll see you, Liza. It was nice meeting you."

Liza waved her fingers as the woman turned and retreated. Josie continued to smile down at her. "Have you ever been on a plane before, Liza?"

Liza shook her head. Josie pointed out the various controls above her for air and light and calling for help. But they were all way beyond Liza's reach. So she just sat, hugging Lulu, looking around her anxiously.

When the regular passengers started to board, they put a man beside Liza. Josie introduced Liza to him and asked him to let them know if Liza needed anything. The man's name was Mr. Michaels. Liza gazed at him suspiciously, watching him for any threatening movement.

"Is this your first time flying by yourself?" Mr. Michaels asked.

Liza nodded.

"You'll have a great time. It's nice your parents let you come by yourself. Are you going to grandma's?"

Liza shook her head. "I dunno."

He considered her for a minute. "That's a nice dog you got there. Does your doggie have a name?"

"Lulu," Liza contributed, holding Lulu toward him slightly so he could see her face.

"Well, she's very nice. She seems very well-behaved."

Liza made a face at him, thinking him silly for playing a game that Lulu was real. She missed the *real* Lulu. Liza made barking and growling noises, shaking the toy dog at Mr. Michaels.

"Lulu bites," she warned.

"Oh, I'll have to be careful then, won't I? Why would she bite me? Isn't she trained?"

"Lulu 'tect me."

"Oh, I see. Well, I'm not going to do anything to you. Lulu doesn't need to worry."

Liza put Lulu down in her lap. In a few minutes, the flight attendants were talking, waving seat belts around and pointing to the doors. At the word 'emergency,' Liza looked with alarm at the doors, tightening her grip on the stuffed toy. Then Josie was putting Liza's seatbelt on and pulling it tightly around her hips. Liza squirmed.

"No," she protested. "Too tight! Let go!"

"You have to have your seat belt on, honey. Just like in the car. It will only be a few minutes, and then you'll be allowed to take it off again. Okay? Now puppy needs to go here," she tore Lulu out of Liza's grip and stuffed her into the back-of-the-seat pocket, out of Liza's reach, "until we're in flight. Then you can have her again."

Liza shrieked, trying to reach her toy, trying to figure out how to unbuckle the seat belt so she could get it.

Josie pushed her back against the seat. "You'll be all right. In a few minutes, we'll be in the air and you'll be fine."

Josie moved on, briskly dealing with other passengers, helping them to get all their items stowed, making sure belts were tightened, and chivvying everyone along. Liza screamed and kicked her feet, panic-stricken and frustrated. Mr. Michaels patted her on the arm.

"It's okay, Liza. Won't be but a few minutes," he comforted.

Liza struck out at him, keeping him away from touching her, scowling at his attempts to quiet her. He tried to distract her, pointing out the window. Liza saw with increasing alarm that they were moving, gliding along down the tarmac, gaining speed, getting into position.

"No!" she screamed. "Mama!"

As the engine wound up and the plane started moving faster, Liza flailed, trying to escape, scratching the man's arm and her own skin as he tried to settle her down. She screeched at the top of her lungs. Finally, Mr. Michaels plucked Lulu back out of the pocket and handed her to Liza.

"Here, here's Lulu," he said. "Hold her."

Liza hugged Lulu to her tightly. She stopped screaming and kicking but was still frightened. As she held the dog and watched out the window, the plane lifted off, making Liza's stomach feel like she was in an elevator. Her ears hurt and the sound was muffled. She cried, leaning her face against Mr. Michaels' arm. He put one arm around her and rubbed her back soothingly.

"It's okay," he comforted. "Just relax. You'll get used to it in a minute."

Liza gulped between sobs. Her ears popped, making the sound go back to normal. She strained to see out the window, unable to see the ground any longer. She could only see fluffy white clouds. There was nothing holding the plane up.

"See, it's okay," said Mr. Michaels. "Everything's fine. We're up above the clouds now. We'll just stay up here until it's time to land."

Josie came by and unlocked Liza's belt. "Everything okay now?" she said brightly.

"Mine bag?" Liza asked, reaching upward.

"Do you have a bag in here?" she asked, opening up the overhead compartment. "Oh, I'll bet this one is yours."

She pulled Liza's backpack down and handed it to her. Liza hugged the bag. She'd been sure she was never going to get it back again.

"We're going to bring a snack around in a minute," Josie said. "Do you want a cookie?"

Liza nodded. Josie moved in, talking with other passengers and making sure everyone was comfortable. Liza looked in her bag. She didn't want anything out of it, she just didn't want to let it go. Mr. Michaels smiled at her.

"Feeling better now?"

Liza nodded. She gazed out the window for a moment, still uncertain about being above the clouds. She sat there and hugged Lulu to her. She alternated between looking at the window and watching Josie move the food cart down the aisle. The airplane lurched and Liza grabbed the arms of her chair in panic.

"It's all right," Mr. Michaels reassured her. "It's just turbulence. Like bumps in the road."

"Bumps in clouds?" Liza said doubtfully.

The plane bounced again and her stomach lurched. Liza held her hands over her mouth.

"Uh-oh!" Mr. Michaels waved for one of the flight attendants and punched the call button. He grabbed a paper bag from the seat pocket and opened it up, trying to hand it to Liza. She looked at it, uncomprehending.

"If you need to throw up, you throw up in there," Mr. Michaels told her.

Liza looked at the bag queasily. She shook her head. Josie came by with the snack cart.

"Is everything okay?" she asked.

"I think she's going to be sick," Mr. Michaels warned.

"Just use the bag, honey," Josie encouraged, holding it toward Liza. Liza shook her head resolutely. "Do you want to go to the bathroom? It's at the back of the plane." Josie gestured.

Liza looked back. It was a long way away. She shook her head.

"Are you going to be okay? If you're going to be airsick, you need to use the bag."

Liza nodded.

"Okay. Do you want a cookie or ginger ale?"

Liza pointed to the cookies and Josie handed a package over.

"And you, sir?" Josie asked Mr. Michaels.

"Beer, please."

She poured it for him and handed it across Liza. Liza moved suddenly, jogging Josie's arm, and the beer spilled on Liza and Mr. Michaels.

"Oh! I'm sorry!" Josie grabbed a couple of napkins and tried to help Mr. Michaels blot the spilled beer off of his clothes. She looked at Liza, scowling. "You did that on purpose!"

"No," Liza responded quickly, distressed. "No, no, no!"

"It sure looked like it! What were you doing?"

Liza indicated her puppy. "Lulu," she explained. "Was Lulu."

"Well, Lulu had better behave herself and not do that again. Or I'll have to put her away."

Liza sank down in her seat, hugging Lulu close. Josie topped off the glass and handed it carefully across to Mr. Michaels, watching Liza for any movement. The drink safely delivered, she moved up to the next row of passengers and continued her service.

Liza watched Mr. Michaels drink his beer, holding one hand over her stomach as it continued to lurch and roil with the movements of the plane.

She nibbled on the cookies, which helped her stomach a little. The flight was long, and she eventually laid her head on Mr. Michaels' shoulder and went to sleep.

Liza awoke as the plane started its descent. She clutched at the arms of her chair and Mr. Michaels' arm tightly.

"It's okay," he reassured.

Liza held onto him until they landed. Liza let out a deep sigh, relieved to be back on the ground again. The plane taxied to the airport building and when it stopped, Josie came and undid Liza's seat belt, which had been buckled while she was asleep.

"Okay, duckie. This is the end of your trip."

She picked Liza up, and then frowning, put Liza down on her feet quickly and wiped her hands. She didn't make any comment about Liza's soaking wet pants. Liza put her thumb in her mouth, hanging onto her dog tightly. Josie guided her down the aisle and into another long white hallway that led to the inside of the airport. When she got to the waiting area, she looked around.

"Who is meeting you here, Liza?"

Liza looked up at her and said nothing.

"Liza? Do you know who is meeting you here?"

Liza took the paper out of her pocket and handed it to Josie. Josie raised her brows and unfolded it slowly. Her eyes moved across the page, widening.

Josie swore under her breath and looked at Liza.

"Why don't you just sit down here, honey?" She gestured to the chairs.

Liza looked at the chairs and did not sit down. Josie went over to a ticket taker at a nearby counter and spoke to her, then picked up the phone and dialed a number. Liza looked around, feeling lost in the wide-open area. She followed Josie and grabbed her around the leg, holding onto her tightly.

"It's okay," Josie told her. "Someone will be coming to pick you up."

But it wasn't Mama.

She wasn't coming back.

Leo reached out to Elizabeth reassuringly, wanting to comfort her.

She drew back from his hand, growling in the back of her throat.

Leo withdrew, backing up so he was out of her comfort zone again, trying to remain nonthreatening.

"I'm sorry," he said softly, his eyes burning. "That must have been so hard."

"Went to court," Elizabeth explained. "Tried to make them. No good! Bad girl! Devil child! Can't love her! Bad girl!"

Leo's throat was tight with emotion. "You weren't bad," he told her. "They just didn't know how to take care of you."

"Bad girl," Elizabeth insisted. "Pee in closet. Hide food in bed. Run around naked. Hurt the babies. Kill the cat. Hitting, hiding, biting, stealing!"

Leo tried to swallow the lump swelling in his throat.

He recognized some of those behaviors as survival techniques. Ways Elizabeth had coped with trusted loved ones not taking care of her. Stormy's therapist called it Reactive Attachment Disorder. He said Stormy was 'RAD, not bad.' She hadn't been able to attach to anyone, with all she had gone through. She couldn't feel or show love like a normal child. She had to be independent and push everyone away because that was the only way to be safe.

The only way to survive from one day to the next.

And Stormy hadn't been the only one.

"You weren't bad," he repeated to Elizabeth. "They didn't understand."

She looked at him with a hopeful light in her eyes. "Bad," she repeated mournfully.

"No." Leo reached out for her again. "Just trying to survive."

She snarled and withdrew.

Leo backed off again. He had to keep a tight rein on his emotions.

He wanted to show her love, to comfort her, to help her to get through this. But her rage, that bit of her that kept her safe, wouldn't let him approach.

Maybe she didn't have a lion inside her, but she had something. A watchdog, maybe. It slunk in the shadows when Elizabeth seemed safe, but it came out and bared its teeth if she was threatened.

Wiping her eyes, Elizabeth went on to tell the story of the court case.

"We're here to dispense with the matter of Elizabeth Peterson and her adoptive parents, Marge and Edward Peterson. The parents are charged with abandonment and have applied to the court for dissolution of the adoption." He looked at the Petersons over the top of his glasses. "We don't *do* that."

They both looked down in shame. They said nothing. Their lawyer spoke up.

"I think once Your Honor has heard the evidence, you'll see the situation was untenable. No one could be expected to raise a child like this long term. Elizabeth needs an institutional, therapeutic setting. Her parents cannot afford to put her in such a place."

"We'll see." The judge looked at Elizabeth, sitting at the other table on display.

She had her threadbare, stained stuffed dog on the table in front of her. She used it as a pillow, resting her head on it. She did not look like a child whose behavior was out of control.

Elizabeth sat there for the whole hearing, mostly with her head on the table, her far away.

When Mrs. Peterson sat on the stand, Elizabeth put her chin in her hand, leaning her elbow on the table, and watched her with half-closed eyes.

"I don't even know where to start," Mrs. Peterson said. "The whole thing just became a nightmare…"

"What made you decide to adopt Elizabeth?" one of the lawyers questioned. "Obviously, you didn't feel this way from the start."

"No," Mrs. Peterson admitted. "In the beginning, things were just fine… she was very affectionate, eager to please, she fit in with our family right away."

"You had interviews with your social worker about her?"

"Yes, of course."

"Did they ever use the term 'honeymoon period' with you?"

"Yes… and we knew things weren't going to be perfect, but we weren't prepared for how she turned out."

"Did they warn you about her past? Talk with you about bonding issues?"

"Yes. We thought she had bonded with us. We learned all about it in our foster parent training. They talked a lot about abused and neglected kids and how they might behave. How you needed to be consistent and accepting and show physical affection. And it didn't seem like there was a problem. She was so sweet and tried so hard that the little accidents didn't matter."

"Little accidents?" the lawyer repeated.

"Wetting the bed, breaking things, making messes… it all seemed like normal kid stuff."

"Yes, it sounds normal to me."

"But after the adoption was finalized… it started to seem like her behavior was deliberate. Whenever we had a nice moment with her… she would do something to sabotage it. Our son was having nightmares and started wetting the bed. We thought it was just the disruption of having another child in the family. Things would settle down after a little while. Once he understood there was enough love for all of them."

"So this is about your son's behavior too."

"No. We took him to the therapist, to help him work through his feelings. And that's when we found out… Elizabeth was…" Mrs. Peterson's voice dropped, and she looked uncomfortably at Elizabeth, and then over at the judge. The judge nodded encouragingly. "Elizabeth was abusing him… molesting him…"

"Wasn't Elizabeth younger than your son?"

"Yes. But she was persuasive and she convinced him not to tell us about it…"

"That must have been quite a shock to you."

"Yes. We were very upset. And talking to Elizabeth about it… well, she's only four and she completely denied it. It's hard to explain to someone so young… we knew she was probably acting out on abuse she had suffered herself… but it meant we always had to be watching either her or Jacob, all the time. And at night, we had to put a motion alarm on her door and on Jacob's door, so we would hear if she woke up and was sneaking around."

"That would be a difficult situation."

"But that wasn't the end of it. Even if we were watching them, if they were in the same room, and we just looked away or turned your back, she would be over there. It's hard when you can't let kids play together, or roughhouse, or show affection toward each other. Jacob didn't understand it. He felt guilty, thought it was his fault."

"But you knew it was because of Elizabeth's past, not because she was trying to be mean or abusive."

"Well, it seemed… it seemed like she *did* want to be mean. Wanted to hurt him. Her behavior was very sneaky, and she would look delighted when she got caught. She was happy for you to see how malicious she was. How she could do something and we couldn't stop her."

"How old is Elizabeth?"

"She's four. But you don't know how it was. What she was like."

The lawyer turned around and looked at Elizabeth, sitting at the table, the puppy cuddled close to her. Her eyes were distant and pathetic. He sighed, and turned back to Mrs. Peterson to continue the questions.

"So the accidents and the abuse of your son; was that the extent of the problems?"

"No. The way she was acting before the adoption, that completely changed. She wasn't being obedient or trying to please us anymore. She was defiant and disobedient. Anything we asked her to do, she would refuse, throw a fit. If she thought we wanted her to do something, she would do the opposite. When we got mad or upset, she would suddenly be all affectionate, try to hug and kiss us. But if we showed her affection or had a nice time with her, she would… retaliate."

"Retaliate how?"

"She would wet or mess her pants intentionally. Smear… smear her poop on the walls, on everything. Break things, destroy the thing she thought was the most important to you," Mrs. Peterson shook her head, tears glistening in her eyes, "Not just precious things, crystal and china, but sentimental things—family pictures and scrapbooks, Jacob's artwork or school assignments… or she would try to hurt the baby, the younger children… she actually killed the cat, and I was so afraid…"

"And *that* was the final straw," the lawyer divined.

"No. The worst was… she would hurt herself. If we told her no when she wanted something, got after her for doing something wrong… she would hit herself, bang her head… it got worse… she would grab a knife, cut herself. Stab herself. Doctors kept reporting us to Child Services; they didn't understand what had happened. Living under constant suspicion… being accused over and over of abusing her when she was hurting herself and we were doing our best to take care of her… molesting our son, endangering the baby… destroying our possessions, our memories, being hateful toward us… we just… couldn't."

She had avoided looking at Elizabeth but looked at her now, pleadingly.

"I'm so sorry Liza," she apologized in anguish. "But we just couldn't."

"Liza not here," Elizabeth murmured. "Liza devil girl."

She turned her face away.

"It's okay, Elizabeth," Leo soothed. "It's hard to remember, but it's okay. It won't hurt you to remember. It will help."

"No more," she moaned.

Because she said 'no more,' he knew there was.

This still wasn't the beginning of her story, the beginning of the hurt. Life hadn't started at four or five years old when she was rejected by her adoptive family.

It hadn't started when she was first placed with them. There was still another family. At least one more. The family had wrecked her chances of bonding in the first place. Maybe her birth family. Maybe another foster family.

"Where were you before that?" Leo asked. "Before the adoptive family? Did they hurt you?"

"Leave her alone," a harsh voice growled. Looking at Elizabeth's face, Leo saw the shadow of Elijah there again.

"I'm not hurting her," Leo said, trying to keep his voice calm and soothing. "Elizabeth wants to know what happened. She wants to know so she can start to heal again."

"No. No more," she insisted angrily. "That's the end. There is no more."

"There is. Elizabeth didn't just fall out of the sky. She came from somewhere."

"Nowhere special. You just leave her alone!"

Her expression was dark and menacing. He could see the threat there, as he'd seen it on his father's face so many times.

"Elijah. I know you're scared," Leo soothed. "And it's okay. You're protecting Elizabeth. That's good. But I'm not going to hurt her."

"Everyone hurts her! Leave her alone."

"Elizabeth wants to know. That's what she said. She said she wants to know the truth now. She's ready."

"She's not ready."

"That's for Elizabeth to decide. Not you."

"It's just Lisa," Elizabeth said in Elijah's voice, with a disgusted shake of the head. "Only Lisa wants to know. Keep her out."

"Elizabeth decided. She said yes. She said she's ready to know."

Elizabeth shook her head adamantly, face tight. "No more!" she screamed. "It's time for you to go home!"

"Why don't I get a drink," Leo said, standing up and going to the kitchen to run the faucet and get a cold drink of water.

He was just trying to take some of the pressure off of Elizabeth. Give her some space to feel safe and relaxed. Some time for her to settle down and get control again, If she could.

And also to give himself some space to calm down and regain his perspective.

His chest was tight.

His stomach roiled as the cat clawed to be released.

He was barely keeping a handle on himself. He really wished he could drink alcohol.

He filled a glass of water and turned around to look at Elizabeth as he drank it. He was surprised by the look on her face. Mouth half open, tongue protruding slightly. Like she was dying of thirst, staring at the glass in his hand.

"Do you want something?" he asked. "Do you want me to pour you a drink?" Leo looked at the alcohol cabinet off to the side. Maybe a drink would help her to loosen up.

But her eyes didn't deviate to the cabinet when he motioned to it.

Her eyes stayed fastened on his glass.

Leo lifted his glass slightly in invitation. "You want some?"

She didn't answer. Her breath was coming faster, panting as she stared at his glass.

Leo got another glass out of the cupboard and filled it up for her. He took it over to her without a word. Elizabeth took the glass in two hands, careful not to spill a drop of the precious liquid.

She brought it up to her mouth and drank it down in a few starved gulps.

Leo looked at the glass. He took it back from her and she wiped her chin with the back of her hand, still watching Leo avidly as he went back to the sink and filled it a second time.

Again, she drained it in a few gulps. Leo decided he'd better slow down. She'd either end up throwing up or in hospital with water intoxication.

"Is that better?" he asked. "You were really thirsty, huh?"

She looked back at him, eyes wide and round, and spoke in the tiniest, softest voice ever, with a hint of a lisp. "Where's my doggie? Why you take her away?" she asked.

Her voice was full of pain and despair. She flinched every time Leo moved.

She lay across the arms of the chair, and unlike Lizard basking in the sun, or Elijah lounging with all his attitude and anger, she now seemed sick and weak, barely able to move. He saw a small child reflected in her eyes. A tiny wee one who could barely speak.

"Are you okay?" he asked softly.

"Her name is Lulu," Elizabeth whispered. "He kicked her and he whipped her."

"Your dog's name is Lulu?"

She nodded.

"Who kicked her and whipped her?"

"*He* did."

Elizabeth's eyes were glazed, feverish, dry.

"Why did he hurt her?" Leo wiped at his own eyes to prevent tears from escaping.

"She protect me."

"Lulu protected you?"

She nodded wordlessly.

"From the man?" Leo pressed.

"Yes."

"Did the man try to hurt you?"

Elizabeth shivered. "Cold outside," she moaned. "Hungry. Firsty. Gots owies. Nobody… just Lulu."

"You were outside?"

"Long time."

Elizabeth clutched her clothes around her, like they were rags that barely covered her body.

She shivered and hugged herself, her face drawn. "No go in no more. No more food. Just… whipping. Kicking. Hurting inside." She ended with a sob or a hiccup.

What kind of hideous beast had abused her?

Leo longed to take her in his arms and comfort her.

A baby, beaten, forced to lived outside, starving and cold, only a dog for company. No affection. Only hurt.

"And Lulu protected you when he tried to hurt you."

Elizabeth nodded slightly. "Where my Lulu?" she asked, looking around feebly.

"Lulu is still here," he told her.

Lu. The personality protecting the baby, right to the end.

"Don't tell her that," a harsh voice said. "Lulu is dead. Lulu is not coming back."

Elijah again? He was a persistent one. Elizabeth was sitting up straighter, looking at Leo with an expression of pure loathing.

"Lulu is still in your heart," Leo said. "She'll always be there."

The muscles in Elizabeth's face were hard. Her eyes were filled with fury.

She looked like she wanted to punch Leo in the nose. "Lulu was a stupid dog who let the baby eat her food and water and who tried to keep him away," Elizabeth growled. "Lulu died! Because she protected Bitsy instead of herself! You have to protect yourself."

"Why are you afraid to remember what happened?" Leo asked. "You don't need to be afraid."

Elizabeth jumped to her feet. After her weakness and frailty of only moments before, Leo was startled by the sudden show of energy.

Elizabeth closed in on him, getting right up in his face.

Leo jumped back and clenched his fists automatically. Ready to fight. Ready to defend himself.

"I would kill you," Elizabeth said in a deep, harsh voice. "If you weren't the dog man."

The dog man? Leo was momentarily confused.

Did Elizabeth mean because he was an animal control officer?

What did that have to do with it?

But he slowly processed the connections. Lulu had protected Elizabeth. The 'dog man' had taken Lulu away, but Elizabeth had survived. The animal control officer must have been called in on an animal abuse call. And he had unexpectedly found a tiny child, beaten, starving, and half-naked in the yard, protected by the dying animal.

"Elizabeth wants to know the truth now," Leo told her. "It's okay. It doesn't mean you have to go away. You've helped protect her, like Lu. But it's time for her to understand."

"You don't know anything!" Elijah's voice screamed, and with one more confrontational look at Leo, Elizabeth suddenly retreated, running to her room and slamming the door.

Leo stood there for a moment, drained, trying to figure out what to do. He walked quietly down the hall and listened at Elizabeth's door for a moment.

She was crying. He couldn't leave her; he had pushed her as far as she could go. He couldn't ask anything else of her.

Leo peeked in on Juleen. He was amazed she hadn't wakened at the slammed door. She slept peacefully, but Leo was uncomfortable looking at her.

She was so small and getting so thin.

He thought of the expression on Elizabeth's face when she had been the neglected baby Bitsy.

He couldn't let Juleen be hurt too. Not anymore.

With a hard, sick knot in his stomach, Leo retreated to the front room. He had one more glass of water before calling Dr. Marvin.

Elizabeth had to be sedated when Dr. Marvin got there and evaluated her. Once he'd managed to tranquilize her, he had the paramedics remove her to have her admitted to the hospital.

He looked at Leo grimly. "This is a dangerous game you're playing, Leo."

"She asked for my help. She wanted to remember."

"Then why didn't you call me? Set it up where you could be supervised? What would you have done if she got violent and tried to hurt you or herself? Or the baby? You can't just mess around in people's minds."

Leo shrugged, embarrassed.

The doctor was right, of course; Leo shouldn't have done this on his own.

But he was also proud. He had done something big, something important. Something nobody else had been able to do. Not even Dr. Marvin. And she had asked for Leo's help. She had needed *him*.

"I'm sorry," he apologized, looking down.

"I hope so," Dr. Marvin said gruffly. He looked at Juleen, who had woken up a few minutes earlier and was now nestled in Leo's arms. "She doesn't look very good," Dr. Marvin observed.

"No. I don't think Elizabeth can manage."

Dr. Marvin nodded. "She has a hard enough time just taking care of herself."

Leo stroked Juleen's head. "I'm going to miss her. But I want her to be safe."

"Well," the doctor motioned to the couch and chair. "Since we're going to be here for a little while waiting for Child Services, why don't you tell me what you found out."

Leo sat down. He moved Silver to the side a little.

Dr. Marvin frowned. "A cat?"

Leo nodded.

Dr. Marvin shook his head.

"I'll take the cat," Leo said. "I like animals."

CHAPTER TWENTY-NINE

LEO HAD FALLEN ASLEEP in front of the TV. Wrung out after the session with Elizabeth and the equally arduous debriefing with Dr. Martin. Weird images flickered through his dreams. Elizabeth singing. Boys and girls that he had never met, all claiming to be Elizabeth. Dr. Martin trying to teach Leo to knit. He said knitting would be better for Leo's anger than boxing.

He awoke with a gasp, nearly falling out of the couch. Someone was hammering on Leo's door. At first he thought it was Elizabeth, having come over for another party. But then he remembered Elizabeth had gone to the hospital. They wouldn't have let her out again so soon.

Leo tried to shake off the disorientation the dreams had left him with. He got up, rubbing his eyes and went over to the door to see what was going on.

Had the police finally come to arrest him for shooting Lyall?

The pounding on the door continued. He could hear a voice, but couldn't sort it out, again thinking of Elizabeth and the other kids in his dream. Leo squinted through the peephole and saw Chase.

He hurried to slide the chain and the bolt and to open the door. He glanced at his watch as he swung it open. What was Chase doing at Leo's house in the middle of the night?

Chase stumbled into the room when the door opened.

"Coach! Coach, you gotta come." Chase was gulping, sobbing, barely able to get the words out. "He came back. He's beating her up. You gotta come and make him stop!"

"He came back. Your stepfather?"

Chase nodded. His face was streaked with tears. He had a black eye and a busted nose. Blood ran from his nose to his chin.

"He's beating on my mom. You gotta stop him!"

Leo reached for his phone. "I'll call the police—"

"No, they won't do anything! *You* gotta come and stop him."

Leo's previous attempt in that area had obviously failed.

He tapped nine-one-one into his keypad. "The cops can get there faster. We'll go, but they can get there before us."

"No." Chase grabbed at Leo's sleeve, blubbering. "I want you! You can stop him! You can beat him up. The cops will just let him go tomorrow and he'll be back again!"

Leo felt helpless. He knew it was true. And Chase's mom would never issue a restraining order against John. She wanted him back. She had probably called him and asked him to come home again.

The cell phone emergency dispatcher answered and Leo had her put him through to the police emergency line.

Chase swung around and punched the wall in frustration, leaving a big dent. Not the first fist to dent Leo's walls. "No! No, *you* come and stop him."

"We'll go. Just let me talk to the police, then we'll drive over."

Chase had gone a long way on foot to fetch Leo. Even if he had run the whole way, the fight might be over by now. The police might already be there, called by a concerned neighbor.

Leo hated to disappoint Chase. But John probably hadn't dared return without a weapon to defend himself. And he would use it against anyone who got in the way of his drunken rage.

Leo filled in the police dispatcher and persuaded Chase to give him his address. He got off the call as quickly as he could, sliding shoes over his bare feet, and led Chase to the car.

Chase didn't say anything on the drive back to his house. He just sniffled and sobbed, staring out his window into the black night.

Leo was right about the police being able to get there faster. Chase's street was lit up with the flashing lights of two police cars and an ambulance.

"My mom!" Chase exclaimed, throwing open the car door and jumping out before Leo could even come to a complete stop. Leo followed as closely behind Chase as he could.

"Chase, be careful—"

He didn't want Chase to get in the middle of the fight or an armed confrontation with the police. But Chase paid him no attention, running into the melée to find his mother.

Leo's heart was pumping as fast as a piston as he followed. But the altercation was over. John was sitting handcuffed in a police car. Chase's mother refused medical attention from the paramedics. She pushed away all helping hands and headed back into the house.

Chase hurried after her. "Mom! Mom, are you okay? I thought he was going to kill you!"

Chase's mother turned around to look back at her son. Her face was a mess. Her nightgown was torn, falling off her shoulder, spattered with blood.

"Mom!"

She grabbed something off of the side table as Chase approached her. As he reached toward her for comfort, she lashed it down on him. Leo was stunned by the whip-like crack. For several long seconds, Leo could do nothing, unable to process what was going on.

Chase's mom held the loop of an extension cord in her hand and flogged Chase with it over and over again, screaming something incomprehensible at him.

Leo rushed forward to stop the brutal whipping. The woman saw him coming and tried to beat him off.

Leo barely even felt the pain of the cord making contact. He was too focused on stopping her. He ripped the electrical cord out of her hand and threw it behind him.

Grabbing Chase's mother in a bear hug, Leo attempted to pin her arms to her sides to stop her. She struggled wildly, using her elbows and head to try to fight her way out of his grasp.

Leo took her to the floor, still squeezing her, still trying to force her to submit.

Other hands grasped Leo and tried to pull the woman out of his arms. There was yelling. Chase was somewhere nearby, crying and screaming.

"You're hurting her, Coach! Stop! Let her go!"

It was only with a huge effort that Leo overcame the raging cat within himself.

The murderous red cleared from Leo's brain and he released her into the hands of the cops who had also rushed to Chase's aid. They escorted her out of the house yelling and protesting the whole way.

Leo got slowly to his feet. One of the officers kept an iron grip on his arm. The man's steely blue eyes drilled into Leo.

"Are you okay, sir?"

His voice and expression warned Leo that he was in danger of being arrested himself if he wasn't careful. He forced a sheepish smile onto his face. Relaxed his muscles.

"Sorry. I should have just let the police handle it. But I was closer... I just reacted."

The cop's hand released its grip on Leo's arm. "It's best for civilians not to interfere in an incident. I know it's hard, but we are the professionals."

Leo nodded.

"Are you injured? She got you too."

Leo lifted up his ratty, worn t-shirt to look at the stripe that the cord had left behind. The vivid red mark burned when he touched it, and also pulsed with an ache that he knew meant it would be a deep bruise.

"Yeah. It will heal. Man, she was whipping him!" Leo focused on his young friend. "Are you okay, Chase?"

Chase nodded. Tears were still streaming down his face and snot ran down from his nose. There were angry red welts across his face and Leo had seen her strike his body several times too.

"Chase, come over to the ambulance." Leo took the sobbing boy by the arm and led him to the paramedics.

Chase leaned sideways, putting his arm around Leo and burying his snotty face in Leo's side for a moment.

"It will be okay, Chase. We'll take care of it."

He rubbed Chase's back and turned him over to the paramedics. Leo looked for the cop who had spoken to him.

"You have to call Child Services. Get him out of here."

"They're on their way. We couldn't leave him here by himself with both parents going to jail tonight."

"You'll tell them about her beating him? They can't just put him back here in three days."

The officer shrugged. "I'll tell them."

His tone was flat. He wasn't making any promises about the way Child Services would handle the case. He knew as well as Leo did that foster care was overcrowded. There was nowhere else for older kids to go. A young teen like Chase, already getting into trouble, already hurt and angry, wasn't likely to find a family that would take him long term.

Child Services would make his mother take a parenting course and shunt Chase back home again when she was done.

Leo shook his head. He watched the paramedics tending to Chase's injuries, hopeless and helpless.

CHAPTER THIRTY

LEO WAS STILL FEELING hopeless and depressed when he arrived at the bar. He looked around The Closet anxiously as he entered. It was harder this time, knowing what kind of place he was walking into.

Would there be people there who recognized him? Who thought he was something he wasn't? As much as they professed tolerance for all, Leo had a pretty good idea that not many of the patrons were actually straight.

He looked for a corner to sit in, where he wouldn't be easy to see but where he could still see the stage when Stormy came on.

"Leo! Leo!"

Leo looked around to see who was calling him. He was startled to see Michelle waving wildly at him. Leo hurried up to her.

"Michelle? What are you doing here?"

The woman next to Michelle turned around and Leo saw it was Joyce. He hugged both of them fiercely.

"I'm so glad to see you! You came to see Stormy?"

"Of course!"

Leo looked at them in wonder. He had seen so little of them the last few years. He called every now and then but usually couldn't reach them. They didn't really keep in touch.

"I'm so glad you're here!" Leo said. "Did Stormy see you?"

"Not yet. It will be a surprise for her."

Leo's heart was pumping hard, like he'd just been running.

But there was a smile stretching the muscles of his face, not the usual grimace or scowl. It was nice to see his family again. To see they were still a family, even after the silence and distance of years.

"That's so great. She'll just be tickled to see you."

Joyce shrugged. "We see her every now and then. Have a girls' night out."

"Do you? That's good. I'm glad."

Phil came over from the bar, throwing a towel over his shoulder, and gave Leo a hug and slap on the back. "Thanks for coming, man."

"Of course. I wouldn't miss it."

Phil smiled knowingly at him, chuckling. "With how fast you scooted out of here the other day, it couldn't have been easy. You take good care of your sister, man."

"I wish I could do more," Leo said. He looked up at the stage mistily, even though Stormy wasn't there yet. "I wish she'd let me."

Phil shrugged. "You know how it is. We all learned to protect ourselves. Not to rely on anyone else."

Leo nodded. "Now if only Lew—"

"If only this big ape would get out of the way, I'd be able to get to the table," a familiar voice growled.

Leo looked around Phil to the young man in the wheelchair on the other side.

"Lewis!" he exclaimed. "Oh, I can't believe you're here—we're all here! We haven't all been together since..." He trailed off and shook his head. "I don't know the last time."

"The band of fifty-one reunited! Come down here," Lewis ordered, reaching up for a hug.

Leo bent over and hugged him roughly, slapping him on the back. He turned and pushed chairs aside so Lewis could get his wheelchair up to the table.

"How are you?" Leo demanded. "How is everybody?" He looked around at them all.

Everyone talked at once and Leo could only pick up bits and pieces of what each one said, but as he sat down at the table, he was happy. His whole family together. All the children, the brood he had fought so hard to protect and take care of.

They had all run away. Each of them, as soon as he or she could manage, escaped the house. Leo stayed behind, looking after the younger ones. Until only he and Stormy were left, and one night, he took her and they too left the house, never to return.

Leo and Child Services had done all they could to help Stormy, but Stormy refused; sleeping in homeless shelters, in youth shelters, on the street, wherever she could. Leo tried to get legal custody, to give her a better home those last few years; but although she'd stay with him for a few days or a week at a time, it didn't take much to set her off running again.

They had all instinctively migrated to the city. Away from the place they had called home, but toward each other. And now, now they were all here. All the Bakerfields in one place. Family again.

"When is she up?" Lewis asked Phil, glancing at the stage.

Phil looked at his watch. "In a minute or two. Any time now."

Leo looked around the table at his siblings chattering happily.

Like they were just normal people with no past, no anger, no lion inside. He wondered whether they all felt the same way inside as he did. Or if they buried the feelings deep away, like Elizabeth. Or whether they dealt with it some other way.

Leo looked from face to face, the faces he loved. His eyes traced the scars of abuse. They all had scars on their faces. The hands around the table were deformed by the loss of fingers. But they talked and gestured unself-consciously, picking up glasses, making motions in the air, touching each other on the arm or shoulder to get the other's attention. And poor Lewis, who, of course, hated any kind of pity, his legs so badly scarred from the fire he could not stand. His face and arms, like Leo's, scarred from the fire. But he pulled it all off with dramatic aplomb. He wore fedoras and pork pie hats and he was loud and demanding rather than shy and quiet like you might expect from someone so visibly damaged.

Michelle caught Leo's eyes on her. "What?" she asked.

Leo blinked. "Your ears," he said. "I—like them."

Michelle smiled. She touched her perfect pink-white earlobes. "Thanks. They look pretty good, huh?"

"I didn't know… they could fix them."

"They can do anything, with the right plastic surgeon and enough money. This was the thing that bothered me the most, so that's what I started with."

"Where did you get that kind of money?"

"Jimmy," she said simply, with a smile.

"Who's Jimmy?"

"Boyfriend."

"Ah." Trust Michelle to find a rich boyfriend to pay for her plastic surgery.

The stage lights came up and the room quieted. Leo looked up to see Stormy in the spotlight. Stormy started to sing. Quiet and soothing at first, then her voice rising in a crescendo until it echoed around the room. Everyone's eyes were fastened on her. There was a smattering of applause and murmured approval.

Leo was entranced. He knew Stormy had talent. He would have helped her even if she didn't, but he knew she had talent and he just had to put her in front of the right people for her to succeed.

But even he was blown away. This was nothing like her numbers at the strip club. This was real. Engaging. Heartrending.

When she finished, there was absolute silence for a few seconds, then thunderous applause. Stormy bowed graciously, smiling at the crowd, and left the stage.

"Wow!" Joyce exclaimed. "That was absolutely incredible. Who knew she had a set of pipes like that?"

"She's fantastic," Lewis agreed. "Hard to believe that's my baby sister."

Leo nodded and agreed. They all exclaimed over her performance. Five minutes later, Stormy made her way over to their table, pushing through the crowd. A few of the audience noticed her and praised her number. Stormy smiled and nodded and finally reached their table.

"What's all this?" she asked with delight. "Don't tell me I dragged all of you out here! What if I'd sucked?"

"We'd still love you," Lewis declared.

Stormy laughed. She circled the table, thanking each of them individually, smiling and chattering gaily. She stopped at Leo and looked steadily into his eyes.

"Thanks, big brother," she said. "This was a really good idea. I really enjoyed it."

Leo nodded, blinking. "You did such a great job," he said.

"Thanks."

"So… where's the girlfriend?" she demanded.

Leo felt his face get hot and ducked his head. The others were looking at him questioningly.

"Leo has a girlfriend?" Lewis asked incredulously.

"Finally?" from Joyce.

"I thought maybe you were here because you finally came out!" Phil teased.

Leo rubbed his forehead, looking away from them in embarrassment. "She's not my girlfriend," he asserted. "Just a friend, someone I've been helping out… And well, she couldn't be here. She's in hospital."

"Oh, sorry," Stormy apologized. "Is everything okay?"

Leo nodded and didn't fill them in on the details.

And then Stormy was off again, talking to the others, eventually sitting down and ordering a drink. She hadn't been sitting for long when a man leaned over her shoulder.

"Stormy? Could I talk to you in private for a few minutes?"

Stormy raised her eyebrows, then shrugged. Leo watched them walk away from the table. He caught Phil's eye.

"A friend?" he asked.

Phil shook his head. Leo wasn't sure if that meant 'no' or 'I don't know,' but the conversation at the table was too busy to inquire.

"Leo," Lewis said. "What're you looking so worried about? Loosen up. Enjoy yourself."

Leo forced a smile he didn't feel. He looked around at their faces, all looking cheerful, peaceful. He hated to ruin it. "Since we're all here," he said. "Do you mind if I ask a question…?"

"Go ahead."

Leo looked around at them slowly. "It's about Dad," he said.

They rolled their eyes and looked away, expressions darkening.

"Don't ruin the party," Phil said. "We're all here having a good time, what good will dredging up the past do?"

"It's not about the past. It's about the future."

"Well, since he's dead," Lewis said, "he doesn't really have a future, does he?"

"Not his future," Leo said. "Yours. Ours. He had a life insurance policy. The truck. The house."

"So?" Michelle asked. "It all goes to Shayla."

Leo shook his head. "No. They weren't married. It goes to his children."

"Count me out," Phil said. "I don't want anything of his."

Everyone shook their heads and growled pretty much the same thing. None of them wanted anything to do with it.

"He owes you something," Leo said.

"What he owed us he could never give us," Lewis said. "Not in a million years. Money would be an insult. After everything else… we don't need his money."

"What about Stormy?" Leo asked. "I could set up a trust for her, so she'd be looked after."

"She won't want it either," Phil said flatly. "Go ahead and ask her, but she'll shoot you down. Any of us would rather be sleeping on the street than on *his* dime."

"Then what should I do?" Leo questioned.

"Whatever you want to. If you want it, take it. You put up with him for longer than any of us did. Even sat with him at the hospital. None of us bothered. And none of us…" Phil looked around at the others and dropped his voice. "None of us went hunting with him," he murmured.

Leo swallowed. He looked around at them. All were quiet and somber now, all eyes on him. Their eyes told him more than any number of words would have.

They knew.

They all knew.

They had known it right from the moment they heard.

"I…" Leo started.

"Don't say anything, man," Phil said. "We know. Our Leo out hunting? We know the only animals you hunt end up at the Humane Society, not on someone's wall."

"He and Shayla… they were going to… they were starting a family," Leo choked out. His eyes were hot and wet. He rolled them up toward the ceiling, trying to keep his emotions under control.

The cat within him growled.

Wanted to vent its feelings.

Phil nodded. "We get it, Leo," he said firmly. "I would never have had the guts. But you knew. You put a stop to it."

They were all silent. Leo couldn't think what to say, or what to do. Should he leave now? He couldn't face the emotional silence, the black hole.

"Hey!" Stormy was coming back to the table, her whole face lit up, smiling like she just found out it was her birthday. "Hey, what's wrong? I leave the table and you all stop talking?" Her eyes sought out Leo. "What did you say?"

"Nothing," Leo protested. "So who was your friend? You look…"

"Not a friend," Stormy said. "An agent! No guarantees, but he's got some places he wants me to sing!"

There were happy squeals from the girls and everyone was all smiles again. There were congratulations all around.

"I'd get up," Lewis joked, reaching out for her. "But I think I've had a bit too much to drink!"

Stormy laughed and gave him a hug. Lewis pulled her down into his lap and gave her a big kiss on the cheek before releasing her.

"That's great," he said. "It'll work out. I know it will!"

CHAPTER THIRTY-ONE

"MORNING," LEO GREETED AS he walked into the Humane Society. "Anything interesting?"

"You're chipper this morning," Melanie observed.

Leo found himself smiling. "I guess. Feeling pretty good."

"You have a good date or something?" she teased.

"No. Just… some good news for my sister."

"That's nice… I didn't know you had any family."

Leo nodded. Funny, he'd never talked about his family at work. He was kind of a loner and didn't talk about himself. Not like he did when he was with Elizabeth. He reached for the work orders from Melanie.

"We had a big influx last night," Melanie said. "There will probably be a lot of extra calls today. Keep you guys busy."

"Oh? What happened?"

"Big dog-fighting ring," she said.

Leo raised his eyebrows. "Really? They did it? They got them?"

Leo had forgotten he had received a text last night. He had been busy with Stormy's performance and hadn't paid any attention to it. But the police must have intercepted it and busted them.

"Yeah." Melanie was pleased too. "But some of the animals brought in last night are in pretty bad shape. Poor babies. Hopefully, the rest that get brought in today will be in better condition."

Leo nodded. "Hopefully we've saved some," he said.

She handed him his work orders.

"See you later, Melanie."

He could tell from his list that some of the calls were from busting the fighting ring. There were a few marked as police orders, calls where the police had made an arrest and there were animals to be picked up. Leo started at the top of the list.

There was a police car sitting in front of the first house. The officer got out, stretching tiredly.

"Some inside and a few in the back yard," he advised Leo.

"Okay, you want to let me in, then you can clear out? I'll lock back up."

"Yeah, thanks."

He let Leo into the house. Leo wandered around, taking a look around and casing the situation out before beginning. The dogs were individually kenneled. Aside from needing to be taken for a walk, they seemed to be in pretty good shape. It was probably easiest to just take them out in their own kennels. It was heavy work, but he had all of the necessary equipment.

After the inside was done and he'd taken a walk around to make sure he'd gotten all of the dogs, Leo went outside to collect the last of the animals. Here was where the cocks were kept, with a small fenced area for them to scratch in occasionally. For now they were caged, so he didn't have to catch them either, just take then out to the truck. He saw a thin waif of a dog slinking around the back of the yard.

"Good boy," he murmured, trying to keep it calm and not scare it. When he took the chickens out he was careful of the gate to make sure the dog couldn't get out. He probably just should have caught it first so he didn't have to worry about it, but he had focused on the roosters first and he didn't want to be distracted from his original goal.

When the cages were in the truck, he went back for the last dog.

"Here, boy," he called softly. "Come here, boy."

The dog was skittish, avoiding him, slinking through the trees at the back of the yard. Leo stood still and watched. There was a dilapidated shed with a dog door in it. Outside it, a couple of dishes. But both of them were empty. Leo went and picked the less grimy one up and took it over to the faucet at the side of the house. He carefully washed it out, scrubbing it with his fingers, then he filled it and turned around. The dog was a shadow behind him, watching intently. Leo put the water dish down on the ground.

"Come in, then, boy. You're thirsty, aren't you?"

The dog licked its lips but didn't move. Leo backed away from the bowl, giving it more room.

"Come on. It's okay. Have a drink."

He waited. The dog watched Leo for a while, then started to creep forward on its belly, cringing, ears back. Leo just waited. Eventually, the dog reached the bowl. It sniffed at the bowl, looked at Leo, rolling its eyes back in fear. Leo didn't even whisper.

The dog lapped once, then cringed back.

Another quick lick.

It sat back, studying Leo, watching him with less fear now.

"That's a boy. Aren't you hungry? I can give you food too."

The dog retreated abruptly. Leo waited. Had he spoken too loudly? Too soon? The dog stopped and looked back at him. Leo was surprised. He didn't move. The dog took another step and looked back at him again. It whined slightly. Leo hesitated.

"You want me to come? You sure?"

He took a step forward. The dog took two more steps toward the shed. Looked back again. Leo followed slowly, quietly, trying not to do anything to frighten it. The dog pushed in through the dog door. Leo touched the doorknob of the shed. He tried it and was relieved to find it unlocked. The door creaked as he pushed it open, but the dog, caught for a moment in the shaft of light from outside, didn't run away.

Leo stepped into the shed. It was in shadows, his eyes still dazzled from the light outside. He waited for them to adjust.

There was a dark shape in the corner. Leo flashed back to Elizabeth's story, and in his mind's eye he saw tiny Bitsy, protected by Lulu, the dog. The shape in the corner assumed that of a child, curled up in the hot shed, thirsty, starving, helpless. The noble dog guarding her, fighting off the man who hurt her. Letting Bitsy eat Lulu's own food.

He moved quickly to the corner where the dog led him. The blanket was not wrapped around a little girl. It sheltered a nest of puppies.

"Ooh, it's not boy, is it? It's girl. Mama."

Leo put his hand in the nest to stir the puppies. They cried, moving sluggishly. Mama dog pushed her snout into the nest in concern and looked up at Leo pleadingly. Leo moved slowly and scratched her head.

She allowed his touch. He moved one of her forelegs to look at her belly. Red, raw teats. The pups nursed in vain. She had no milk. She was so thin it was a wonder she had carried and delivered the pups at all.

"Aww, sweetie," he murmured.

She pushed her nose into his hand. Leo scratched her ears again. Then he reached for the four tiny pups and carefully tucked them behind one arm.

"Come on, Mama," he told her.

She padded along beside him as he took the pups to the truck. She wasn't going anywhere without them. Leo made them as comfortable as he could in an empty kennel with a scrap of blanket. He bent over, face to face with the mama.

"Ready to come in here?" he asked.

She looked up at him trustingly. Leo gently picked her up. She was light as a bird, nothing but skin and bones. He gently put her into the kennel with the pups, and she nosed them all against her, where the pups tried weakly to nurse. Rubbing his eyes, Leo closed up the cage and got back behind the wheel.

He carried the cage into the shelter. Melanie was surprised to see him back already. Leo nodded at her.

"I've got a full truck. Needs to be unloaded."

"And what have you got there?" she asked.

Leo allowed her a peek in the kennel.

"Oh, the poor things," Melanie crooned. "Let's try Bertie. She's only got one kitten right now."

Leo followed her with the cage. They carefully transferred the puppies to the cage of Bertie, a cocker spaniel who happily nursed babies of any species they gave her. Bertie guided the weak pups to her teats, where they started to nurse, mewling softly. The lone kitten awoke and joined them.

"And now you," Melanie said. She gathered the emaciated mama dog up into her arms and cuddled her gently. "You need to get some nourishment too if you're going to get better and take over again once you're stronger." She put the dog in a separate cage beside Bertie's and put a bowl of soft food in beside the bowl of water already waiting. The mama dog took a bite and looked into the neighboring cage at her pups, whining.

"It's okay, you need to eat up, and so do they. We'll put you back together later. You eat up."

The dog ate a little, paced restlessly in the tiny space, and laid down, nose poked forlornly through the bars at her puppies. Melanie sighed.

"We'll need a name for her if we are going to try to save her. Do you want the honors?"

Leo looked at the noble little dog and nodded. "How about… Lulu?" he suggested.

CHAPTER THIRTY-TWO

LEO STOPPED AT THE nurse's desk. Or security desk, or whatever it was.

"Um, I'm here to see Elizabeth Peterson," he said awkwardly. "My name is Leo—Dr. Marvin said it was okay if I brought…" he gestured at Rascal, "if I brought him."

The nurse looked down at the dog but was unperturbed. "Sign the check-in sheet," she gestured to the clipboard in front of him. "Elizabeth is down the hall to your right, room seven twenty. I'm pretty sure she's in there right now."

Leo filled out the check-in sheet. "Thanks," he told the nurse. He walked down the hall, looking at the room numbers. At seven twenty, he stopped and took a deep breath to settle the anxiety about this visit, and he knocked on the door, then opened it partway.

"Elizabeth?" he called. "You decent?"

"Come on in," she called back, laughing slightly. Leo walked in the door, pushed past the curtain, and saw Elizabeth curled up on her bed, the sunlight streaming through the big window, reading a book. She looked up at him.

"Leo! I'm so glad you came!"

"I brought another visitor too," Leo said and pulled Rascal through the curtain behind him.

"Oh, Rascal! Come here, boy!" Elizabeth patted the bed beside her and Rascal obligingly jumped up beside her, squirming happily under her kisses, scratches, and hugs. Leo watched them, thinking about Elizabeth and Lulu. He was glad the sight of another dog didn't cause her pain. He wondered how Elizabeth felt about dogs, generally. Or did all of her personalities feel differently? Did dogs make her feel happy and safe? Protected? Or did she feel sadness for her lost doggie? Anger at the people who separated them? Elizabeth didn't seem to be sad as she hugged Rascal. She was smiling, like usual.

"So how are you doing?" Leo asked.

"I'm pretty good," Elizabeth said. "I'm… going to be staying here. For a while, anyway. Voluntarily."

"Good for you," Leo said. "I want you to take care of yourself. Get better."

Elizabeth nodded. "I don't know if I'll ever get better," she sighed. "But trying to make it out there… isn't working. I really tried. I tried to take care of Juleen, and myself, and to be a grown up, but…"

"You're still a grown up," Leo told her. "Some things are just harder for some of us. Everybody has trouble with something."

"A lot of me isn't grown up," Elizabeth admitted. "A lot of me is still… back there. Refusing to move on."

"Mmm-hmm…" Leo nodded. "You need to acknowledge it before you can move on."

"That's just a lot of mumbo-jumbo. I can't change who I am. They don't change just because I know who they are."

"Okay… so did it help at all? Us talking? Remembering the past?"

Elizabeth stroked Rascal, who settled up against her, cuddling close. "I guess," she agreed. "I couldn't remember all of that stuff before. It was really confusing. I didn't understand why there were so many blanks. Now I know… what happened, and who was there… I get a little bit more about why I'm so… damaged."

"I'm sorry they hurt you. I wish there was a way to keep children away from abusive adults. It's great to have Child Services and all, but it seems like… it fails too often. You. Me and my family. The kids I coach at wrestling. Where are they when kids are being hurt?"

"Sometimes they help," Elizabeth said. "They took me out of some places. But if someone really wants to hurt a kid… they will."

"I guess."

Elizabeth scratched Rascal's ears. "Dr. Marvin says it's a good thing you were the one who was with me," she said. "When I remembered about Lulu and Bitsy."

Leo grinned. "Elijah got pretty angry," he agreed.

Elizabeth nodded, laughing. "Yeah. Nobody's ever been able to get past him before. That made him really mad. But you were a dog catcher. A dog catcher helped Lulu and the baby. He couldn't do anything to you."

"What would he have done if I hadn't been animal control?" Leo asked.

Elizabeth's laughter stopped. She shook her head grimly. "Elijah's good at protecting me," she said slowly. "He would have hurt you."

It should have been funny, this little blond woman, talking about hurting him, except Leo knew it was true. He'd seen how strong a crazy person could be. If Elizabeth said Elijah would have hurt him, he had no doubt it was true. She had undoubtedly seen what Elijah could do in the past.

"I remember once when Elijah came out," Elizabeth said tentatively.

"What happened?"

"A family threatened to adopt me," Elizabeth explained.

Leo smiled wryly. "Threatened to adopt you?"

"Yeah." She didn't get his ironic tone. "I was… I don't know… ten or eleven, maybe. I'd been with this family. The Jensens. For a year or two. A long time. I'd been good. They decided to adopt me. Said they wanted me to be their daughter, forever."

"That didn't make you feel good?" Leo said. "You didn't want to be part of a family?"

"No." Elizabeth shook her head adamantly. "I'd done that once before… it wasn't good."

"Because they relinquished," Leo said. "They dissolved the adoption."

Elizabeth nodded. "We couldn't ever let that happen again."

"So what did you do?" Leo asked.

"Not me. Elijah."

"Right," Leo said, "Elijah. He had to protect you."

"That's why he's there," Elizabeth confirmed. "To keep anyone from getting too close. To keep everyone from getting too close. From hurting me again."

"So what did Elijah do when the Jensens threatened to adopt you?"

Elizabeth related her story.

"Bessie, why don't you sit down for a minute?" Mrs. Jensen told her.

Elizabeth hovered near the couch. "What did I do?" she asked anxiously.

"You haven't done anything. Just have a seat and let's talk."

Elizabeth forced herself to sit down. She looked around the room anxiously, wondering what was going on. She hadn't seen any sign of a social worker or packed bag. If they were sending her away, they hadn't sent out any of the usual warning signals. And there hadn't been any big problems lately. The usual school stuff. Problems when she didn't get her chores done or got home too late, but nothing big. Nothing that would account for a serious lecture or having to leave.

"I didn't do anything."

"No, it's okay. Bessie… we want to talk about adopting you."

Elizabeth's jaw dropped. She looked from Mrs. Jensen to her husband and back again. She couldn't draw breath. She was smothering. Mrs. Jensen giggled nervously.

"Are you okay?" she asked. "I didn't mean it to be such a shock."

"You want to adopt me?" Elizabeth demanded, her voice rising, the air filling her lungs with a whoosh that made her dizzy.

"Yes. You've been with us for a couple of years now and we've been talking it over the last few months… we want you to be part of our family permanently."

"Why?" Elizabeth asked, unable to fathom it.

Adoption? What had she done to give them the idea she wanted to be adopted? She hadn't gotten close to them. There were still plenty of arguments at home. She still got in trouble at school. Why would they want to adopt her?

"You sound upset," Mr. Jensen said with a chuckle. "You want to be part of our family, don't you?"

"Yes," Elizabeth forced the lie through her teeth. It wouldn't do to argue. She had to figure out what to do, had to sort it all out, but she couldn't tell them no. That would expose her too much.

"Well, I'm sorry if it was a shock," Mrs. Jensen said. "But I just wanted to let you know… We're talking to your social worker, getting the papers drawn up… we had to make sure we'd be allowed to first, before telling you anything. We didn't want to suggest it, and then find out they wouldn't let us have you."

Elizabeth nodded. "Thank you," she said woodenly. "Can I go to my room now?"

They both looked at her for a moment, disappointed. Elizabeth forced a smile, tried to look bright and natural.

"That's really cool," she said. "I just have to… think about it for a while. I'm really surprised."

"Okay," Mrs. Jensen said softly. "You go ahead and have some private time to think it through."

Elizabeth nodded and headed toward the stairs to go up to her room.

"And Bessie," Mrs. Jensen called to her.

"Yeah?" Elizabeth looked back to see what was up.

"You can call us Mom and Dad now."

Elizabeth gulped, and ran to her room, shutting the door solidly behind her.

She told them she was sick at suppertime. She couldn't look at them. Couldn't sit there and be forced to call them Mom and Dad.

She couldn't believe they would do this.

She was a long-term foster child. They knew that when she was placed with them.

She wasn't adoptable.

They couldn't just turn things on their head. They couldn't just change the rules all of the sudden.

"Bessie? Are you in bed already?" Mrs. Jensen queried from the hallway, outside her door.

"Yeah. I'm not feeling very well."

"Do you need anything? Medicine? A cold cloth? A bucket?"

"No, I don't need anything from you," Elizabeth insisted. She could hear Mrs. Jensen standing there, listening, for a few more minutes before she finally sighed and went away, leaving Elizabeth alone.

Elizabeth just sat there on the side of her bed, listening to Mrs. Jensen's retreat, her brain refusing to function.

Every time she started to think about being adopted, about if it could be a good thing, then her brain shut down. She would wake up an hour later and wonder where her consciousness had gone in the meantime. These were not the first blackouts she had ever had. She just ignored them.

Eventually, Mr. and Mrs. Jensen went to bed. They didn't knock on her door again. Elizabeth sat there in the dark, waiting. After some time, she figured they were probably asleep, and she got up.

It was Elijah who went down the hall with Mrs. Jensen's sewing shears, which had been secreted under the mattress for some time. Mrs. Jensen had already given up on finding them and bought a new pair.

Elijah liked the way the sewing shears could be taken apart at the pivot, to act as two knives. In the dark, he unhooked them, holding one in each hand. He went into the Jensen's bedroom, walking silently on the deep carpet. He went to Mr. Jensen's side of the bed first. He was stronger, the bigger threat. The man was always the bigger threat.

Holding a blade in either hand, Elijah started stabbing Mr. Jensen in the chest, neck, and stomach. There was an initial reaction, a groan, the arms flailed out uncontrollably, but the deed was done pretty quietly.

Elijah went around to Mrs. Jensen's side of the bed. Mrs. Jensen had started to wake up at the sound of her husband's attack, at the movements on his side of the bed. She opened her eyes as Elijah approached.

"Bessie? Are you okay? Did you get sick?" she asked drowsily.

"You leave her alone," Elijah snapped.

He let the blades fall, striking Mrs. Jensen again and again, causing her to fall quickly silent, to stop threatening Elizabeth.

He stood there for a few minutes at the bedside, looking over both of them, stains darkening on the sheets. Making sure there was no more movement.

They couldn't hurt Elizabeth anymore.

Then he turned and walked away.

When the police got there, Elijah was long gone. He packed a few things in a backpack and hit the streets. Flitting from shadow to shadow, he stayed out of sight, making sure no one driving by saw him, ducked into alleys if he saw someone walking toward him. Held a blade tightly in his hand and watched for anyone who might try to detain or hurt him.

Elijah was wary, resourceful, and very smart. Not book smart, maybe, but he knew his way around. Knew how to protect himself and all the girls.

He slept on the streets. Ate from garbage cans. No way he was going to ask anyone for food. Or go to a homeless shelter or soup kitchen. They would ask questions. They would call the cops. He knew better.

Stay out of sight.

Don't be seen walking at night.

Always be hidden in an alley, garbage bin, or box by the time night fell. Be seen only during the day, and even then, only briefly as he was forced to go from one place to another.

Talk to no one. No begging, no pickpocketing, nothing that would attract anyone's attention.

He sometimes caught the eyes of other street people on him. Bums, shopping cart women, buskers, young drug addicts. He held his blade in his hand in his pocket, ready for anything. They, in turn, saw the demon light in his eyes and stayed away from him. He was too strong for them. They knew he was dangerous. They knew he was the protector.

In the end, he was stupid. He got too greedy, too confident in his own abilities. Hungry for something other than dumpster food, he had been shoplifting in a corner store and the owner caught him. An angry, elderly immigrant, one of those tough old birds that wouldn't be put off by the eyes of a boy with a blade. He'd been through his own form of hell before scraping up the money to start this store, to pour his life blood into it. He wasn't going to let a kid with a hard face steal from him. He wasn't afraid.

Elijah was grabbed from behind, didn't even see or hear the old man coming. He struggled, tried to reach his blade, but the man was wiry and tough, and he kept an iron grip on Elijah.

There wasn't even an opportunity to run away when he called the cops, because he didn't release one of Elijah's arms to pick up the phone; he hustled Elijah out the front door, bells ringing wildly, and shouted for a cop, who happened to be patrolling down the street, writing traffic tickets and shooing drug addicts and bums out of the area.

"Here, you! Officer! Come here! Come get this boy! He is stealing from me!"

The cop came purposefully down the street toward them. Elijah struggled frantically to escape the hold of the store owner, to get away and run before the cop could lay hands on him. The man's grip was unrelenting. He waited until the cop got there and held Elijah out toward him.

"Careful. He's strong; don't let him go."

"I think I know my job, Phillipe."

"You watch him," Phillipe repeated, transferring his grip on Elijah.

Elijah tried one last time to wrench away, but they both held onto him tightly. The cop muttered to him irritably and closed a pair of handcuffs over his thin wrists. There was a short chain between them, not allowing much room for movement.

Elijah still tried to run away, but the cop held him and patted his pockets, coming up with the double blades of the scissors.

"Oh ho," he said. "What's all this? You could hurt someone with these, son."

"I'm not your son," Elijah spat.

"Take it easy, there. What's going on here? What's your name?"

"Elijah."

"Elijah what?"

"Elijah up yours!"

The cop chuckled, not the least bit offended by Elijah's venom. "Oh, you think you're a little man, huh? How old are you? You live around here? Runaway?"

"No."

"No what?"

"I'm not a runaway. I got no family. I just live where I want."

"Uh-huh. Well, we'll have to see about that, won't we? I'll take you to the station, get you fingerprinted, get Child Services in… We'll sort it all out."

"And charge him with shoplifting," Phillippe reminded him.

"Don't you worry about that. I have a feeling this one probably has a lot more on his record than a little bit of shoplifting. We'll take care of him."

The store owner nodded sourly, and the cop dragged Elijah to his police car and shoved him in the back.

"Behave yourself back there," he ordered.

Exactly what was Elijah going to get into, chained up in the back seat, bars on the windows, door locked? He sat sullenly, watching the scenery whip by, saying nothing.

At the police station, he was put in a bare room with a table and a couple of chairs. Concrete floors. Concrete walls. A small window in the heavy door.

They asked him questions, which he didn't feel like answering, and they discussed him like he wasn't even there.

"He's not showing up on the runaway list?" Earhart asked.

"Nope. We've been over it multiple times. No one knows him. Beat cops, nothing. No missing persons. No runaway. Fingerprints didn't show up, he doesn't have a record."

"How old do you think he is?"

"Twelve. Thirteen. No older than that. Where do we look next?"

"Leave it to Child Services. They can try to track down his family, put him in the Children's Center until they sort it all out. We've got a charge of shoplifting, but no name to go with it yet. You can put him in as a John Doe, I guess."

Conner nodded. "All right. Now… what about the scissors?"

Earhart pursed his lips. He turned to Elijah. "You hurt someone with those blades, kid?"

"No."

"Had to defend yourself against someone, maybe? You can tell me."

"No."

"Where did you get them?"

Elijah shrugged. "In a dumpster. Where I get everything."

He was certainly grubby enough for that to be true. The Children's Center was going to fuss over getting him cleaned up properly. And Conner was going to have to air out his car for a while. But, he'd probably had worse smelling bums in his squad car before.

"Well," Earhart said, "see if you can find any mention of them matching up to a recent crime, but there's not much we can do at this point."

"There is blood on them."

"I know. But we don't have a way to search weapons on the system. And we don't know if his story might be true and he just found them that way."

"Okay. Well, Child Services is on their way. I'm going to hit my beat again. So you'll just keep him on ice here until they show up?"

"Yeah," Earhart agreed. "We'll keep an eye on him."

Child Services never was very prompt. Elijah sat in the cold, empty room for hours, waiting, but he was tough and he didn't complain or squirm. The social worker finally showed up. Earhart filled her in, and she went into the room to talk to Elijah.

"Hi there, Elijah," she greeted.

"Hi."

"I'm Mrs. Wright. I'm here to take care of you. Tonight we'll take you to the Children's Center, and then we'll work on getting you a foster family. Okay?"

Elijah looked at her thoughtfully. "Yeah. Sure," he said.

"You could use a bath and a good meal."

He wiped his nose with the back of his hand. "I don't need anyone's help."

"Oh, I see. Well, unfortunately for you, we can't leave you to your own devices. We'll need to find someone to take care of you."

He shrugged.

"Well, come on then," Mrs. Wright invited, motioning for him to stand.

Elijah got up and sized her up. She shook her head.

"Just take it easy. No one is going to hurt you. This is your best chance for a comfortable night anyway. Take it."

He kept his face a mask. She led him out of the room.

"Why don't you tell me about yourself?" she prompted, as they walked out to her car.

"Nothin' to tell."

"They said your name is Elijah."

"Yeah. That's right."

"Elijah what?"

"Nothin'. Just Elijah."

"And where did you come from? How did you end up getting picked up by the police today?"

Elijah sat in the car and looked out the window, saying nothing. Mrs. Wright glanced at him a couple of times while they drove, but when it became obvious he wasn't going to talk, she turned on the radio and didn't disturb him anymore.

At the Children's Center, they took him to the showers first thing. Elijah flushed and tried to preserve his privacy, but the staff was uncooperative. One of the matrons saw to getting him dressed, then led him to a small meeting room, and the matron called in the social worker, and then they again called the police, putting Earhart on the speakerphone.

"You have some information for me?" Earhart asked, sounding interested.

"Your twelve-year-old boy is not a twelve-year-old boy," the matron said.

"What?"

"A girl. I'd put her closer to ten."

Elijah looked at the matron angrily. "What are you telling him that for? I'm a boy!"

"Nice try. Your birthday suit says otherwise. Now, what's your real name?"

"Elijah."

The matron snorted.

"Does this help you with identification?" Mrs. Wright asked Earhart.

"Certainly, we'll check the missing persons reports again. Gender definitely makes a difference in these things!"

The matron got an odd look on her face. She looked at Elijah, touching his hair, hacked short by handfuls with Mrs. Jensen's scissors.

"Long blond hair," she said slowly. "Pretty girl."

Mrs. Wright looked questioning. "Do you know her?"

"Yes. But I can't remember the name. There was a family—do you remember the story a couple of weeks ago? Parents stabbed. Their foster child missing."

"Jensens," Mrs. Wright said immediately. She tried to remember the report that had been sent out. "The child was… Elizabeth."

They could hear Earhart typing quickly on his computer.

"Give me a second… Elizabeth Peterson. Well, say hi, Elizabeth."

She sat back in her seat, Elijah's scowl disappearing from her face to be replaced by a friendly smile.

"Hi!" she greeted pleasantly.

Leo shook his head in amazement.

"So what happened to you then? What about… killing your foster parents?"

"That wasn't me. That was Elijah," Elizabeth said firmly. "And they weren't dead. Only stabbed. They survived. But they didn't want her back," she said with satisfaction. "Didn't want that little girl anymore."

Leo breathed out slowly, his stomach tight. They didn't want her after she stabbed them and ran away. How amazing.

This was the same Elijah Leo had faced only days before, totally unsuspecting.

With no protection.

And the only thing that had kept him safe was the happy coincidence that he was a dog catcher.

CHAPTER THIRTY-THREE

LEO LOOKED AWKWARDLY AROUND Shayla's house. It was weird, seeing things from his father's house here. It was all Shayla's style, and then there were things of his father's just thrown into the mix. There was a picture on the wall of an English springer spaniel that had been in Leo's mother's kitchen in the early years.

"Have a seat," Shayla invited.

Leo sat down on the edge of the couch. "How are you doing?" he asked.

"Oh, well, as well as could be expected. It was really nice of you to come and check up on me."

Leo nodded. "Listen… I don't know how you're set… but Lyall had an insurance policy."

Shayla shrugged. "I know. The police mentioned it. You kids are the beneficiaries."

"Yeah. But we don't want it, Shay. We agreed you should get something."

"We weren't married, so I don't have any right."

"We're not talking about legalities. I'm the trustee, and everybody else has signed waivers, so it's mine to do with as I please. And… you were good to Dad. He really cared about you, and I know you really cared about him too."

"I wasn't in it for the money."

"Good thing, because he never had any. This policy… he must have gotten it way back when Mom was around. It's more than he ever had when he was alive."

Shayla looked confused. "Well, that's nice of you, Leo."

Leo reached into his pocket and pulled out a check. He handed it to her. Shayla looked down at it, her eyebrows going way up. "Leo! Are you sure? It's so much!"

"You deserve it. Really."

"You should have given it to someone else, to someone that means something to you."

"That's not all of it," Leo said. "I've split it up between a few charities too."

"Oh, good." Shayla breathed out in a whistle. "Wow, Leo, this is really nice. Thank you so much. What are the charities you picked?"

Leo hesitated. "I… I didn't pick the charities Dad would have," Leo warned.

"I don't even know what he would have picked," Shayla laughed. "Hungry truckers? Literacy maybe?"

Leo chuckled. "There are three of them," he said. "One is the after-school program I volunteer for. It helps keep kids out of trouble and in school. So that's sort of literacy."

"Sure. He'd like that. He was always proud of how you were helping kids."

Leo squirmed uncomfortably. As far as he could tell, Lyall had never been proud of him for anything.

"And the Humane Society, for animal rescue."

Shayla nodded. "I should have guessed. Of course."

Leo swallowed, breathed deeply for a minute, and tried to calm the lion.

His anxiety was unfounded, ridiculous.

What was Shayla going to do? Attack him? Even if she didn't like his choice, she wasn't going to do anything about it.

He wasn't in any danger.

But the cat wanted out. Wanted to fight, to defend his choice before she could argue about it.

"The other one?" Shayla prompted.

"It's, umm, a program for abused kids," he said. "Counseling, helping them to be independent when they leave home or get out of foster care."

Shayla didn't explode. She didn't get angry. Leo waited for her to change the subject, to avoid the issue. To deny their pain. Shayla looked at him, her eyes sad. "I wish I could have shown you how he had changed, Leo," she said. "I wish I could have shown you that things were going to be different from when you were kids and he was so tough on you. We just ran out of time."

"Things were more than 'tough for us,' Shay. I know you don't want to listen to me, but hear me out."

She opened her mouth to object, then closed it and nodded.

"You've met most of us," Leo said. He held up his deformed hand. "Do you really believe we all have a genetic disease that did this?"

Shayla didn't answer.

"He cut them off, Shayla!" He wanted to shock her, to force her to understand. "You think someone like that could change, become a good father?" He pointed to the long scar down his face, by his left ear. "He hit me across the face with a pry bar. You know what it was like living with someone like that? Living with someone who would come after you for no reason? Punish you for the slightest infraction? Torture you because of some crazy suspicion in his mind?"

"That's when he was an alcoholic," Shayla protested, covering her eyes. "That's different. But when he wasn't drinking any more, he was a different person."

"But he was the *same* person. You can't just wipe out everything, pretend it didn't happen. We still remember. We're still suffering for it. Look at Stormy. Kids who went through stuff like that… they need help. They need someone looking out for them."

Shayla nodded. "Leo—it's okay. I… I never knew that Lyall. It doesn't mean I don't believe you. I just knew a different person. And I do think—abused—kids need help. All of the Stormys, and the Phils, and even the Leos. You give the money to who you want to. And you don't have to give me anything. Really." She held the check back toward him.

"I want you to have something too," Leo said. "It's the right thing to do." He nodded at the check in her hand. "I took him away from you… you keep it."

"Okay. Thank you. And… I'm sorry for how he treated you guys. I really am." She looked down at his mutilated hand. "It's hard for me to even imagine what it was like for you. It's so incomprehensible to me. But I wish it had been different."

Leo nodded. "Yeah. Me too."

Shayla looked around the room. "I want… I want to give you something, Leo. You've been so good to me and gave me this money when it was rightfully yours, and your brothers' and sisters'. Isn't there something I can do for you?"

Leo shook his head. "No. Just… find somebody else. Find a way to be happy and have your own family… I took that chance away from you."

"I don't know if I'll ever find someone who means as much to me as Lyall did. It's going to be a while before I even want to look. He really meant a lot to me."

"I know," Leo agreed.

He stood up in preparation to leave. Shayla stood and cast her eyes around. "I mean it, though, I want you to have something…" Her eyes alighted on the setter painting on the wall Leo had noticed coming in. "What about this? It was Lyall's. It always makes me think of you when I see it. Would you take it?" She removed it from the nail on the wall and held it toward him.

Leo looked down at it. "It was my mother's," he said. "She said she had an English springer when she was a little girl. It used to be in our kitchen."

"Take it," Shayla encouraged, pushing it into Leo's hands.

He received it hesitantly. "Thanks, Shay. This is… this is really special."

Shayla nodded, pleased. "I'm so glad."

Leo swallowed. He started to head for the door. "You remember how you said I should forgive him?" Leo asked. "It would only hurt me otherwise?"

Shayla nodded, taking his arm gently as they walked to the entryway. "Yes… I'm sorry. I know I can't understand what you went through…"

"No, you were right. And I do. I forgive him."

Shayla met his eyes, surprised. "You do?" she said.

Leo nodded. "Yeah. I don't want to keep holding on to the past forever."

"Good for you," she approved and gave him a peck on the cheek. "And that's the best present you could ever have given me. Better than the check."

Leo nodded, and after giving her hand a little squeeze, he left. He got into his car, and he just sat in the car for a few minutes, breathing, looking at the picture, evaluating how he felt.

He was telling the truth. He *had* forgiven Lyall.

Leo hadn't killed Lyall in anger.

It hadn't been the wildcat. He hadn't killed Lyall because of the fear, and bitterness, and anger inside of him.

He had started the forgiveness process when he had pulled the trigger, putting Lyall out of his misery, just like they would put a mad dog down at the Humane Society.

Just like they had put down most of the dogs from the fighting ring; dogs that had been tortured to the point of madness, cruelly trained to become vicious killers.

What sort of cruel fate had made Lyall the twisted piece of humanity he was? Was it genetics? Bipolar Disorder? Alcoholism? Had he been tortured and cruelly conditioned by his own father or someone else?

Whatever had produced the evil and madness in Lyall, there had only been one way to stop it. Leo had sped the bullet on its way with a whispered prayer. He couldn't blame Lyall for his violence any more than he did the dogs.

But you couldn't let a mad dog live.

Leo was sitting in front of the TV, Silver on his lap and Rascal on his feet.

It had been a long week and he was tired, but he felt good. The picture of the Springer Spaniel was on the wall and he felt peaceful for the first time in a long time.

He wasn't getting so wrapped up in everyone else's problems.

The wildcat slept more often.

Leo was able to go to sleep at night—most nights—without dreaming of his childhood.

Leo woke suddenly, not realizing he had drifted off. His phone was ringing. Leo glanced at the caller ID and pressed talk.

"Jaime."

"Hi Leo. How's it going?"

"Good," Leo said, yawning and stretching. "What's up?"

"Pretty good week with the boys, huh?"

Leo considered. "I still have to get Reggie straightened out. That boy…" he trailed off.

"Yeah," Jaime chuckled. "He's just about as bad as you."

Leo grunted. "Well, I'm almost reformed now," he joked.

"Your training is coming along pretty good," Jaime said, changing the subject rather abruptly.

Leo nodded to himself. "Yeah. I think my endurance is really improving. And I've been working a bit more on strength-building, get those power punches up to snuff."

"I've got a potential match for you."

Leo wasn't excited about it. Usually, he was excited when he had the chance at a fight. But today he didn't feel anything. "Um—okay, who is it?" he asked.

"Donaldo," Jaime said.

Donaldo. He was good.

Was Leo really good enough to fight him? After the disaster with Heartbrake, he wasn't sure he wanted to take on Donaldo.

"Well?" Jaime said expectantly.

"I don't know."

"I thought you'd be excited. This is a big opportunity."

"I know… I know, it's a great opportunity. I appreciate it. But do you really think I'm ready?"

"Sure," Jaime said. "I wouldn't set it up if I didn't think you were ready."

"I'm just not sure," Leo said.

"I've never known you to turn down a fight before."

"Yeah… I know…"

"So what's going on?"

"Let me think about it. I'll get back to you," Leo told him.

"Okay… Don't wait too long. I can't keep Donaldo's agent waiting."

"Sure. Thanks."

Leo hung up the phone. He remembered what Jaime had said to him before. That they were not animals. They were men. They didn't have to fight. They could choose.

Did Leo really want to fight Donaldo? He could choose not to fight. He could choose not to be a fighter anymore.

Dr. Marvin had challenged him to think about his choices. To find other ways to deal with his anger.

Leo always told the after-school boys to hold onto their anger until the right time, until they could fight in a match. Then they could let go. But Leo had been doing that as long as he could remember, and it didn't make the anger go away.

It didn't make it any less.

It was still there, he just kept a tighter grip on it. Waited until the next run or the next fight when he could release it, like the valve on a pressure cooker.

Until it built up again.

Maybe he wouldn't fight. Maybe this time, he would choose to be a man.

Leo the man, instead of Leo the lion.

Maybe.

Did you enjoy this book? Reviews and recommendations are vital to making a book successful.

Please leave a review at your favorite book store or review site and share it with your friends.

Don't miss the following bonus material:
Sign up for mailing list to get a free ebook
Read a sneak preview chapter
Other books by P.D. Workman
Learn more about the author

Sign up for my mailing list at pdworkman.com and get Gluten-Free Murder for free!

PREVIEW OF SHE WORE MOURNING

CHAPTER ONE

Zachary Goldman stared down the telephoto lens at the subjects before him. It was one of those days that left tourists gaping over the gorgeous scenery. Dark trees against crisp white snow, with the mountains as a backdrop. Like the picture on a Christmas card.

The thought made Zachary feel sick.

But he wasn't looking at the scenery. He was looking at the man and the woman in a passionate embrace. The pretty young woman's cheeks were flushed pink, more likely with her excitement than the cold, since she had barely stepped out of her car to greet the man. He had a swarthier complexion and a thin black beard, and was currently turned away from Zachary's camera.

Zachary wasn't much to look at himself. Average height, black hair cut too short, his own three-day growth of beard not hiding how pinched and pale his face was. He'd never considered himself a good catch.

He waited patiently for them to move, to look around at their surroundings so that he could get a good picture of their faces.

They thought they were alone; that no one could see them without being seen. They hadn't counted on the fact that Zachary had been surveilling them for a couple of weeks and had known where they would go. They gave him lots of warning so that he could park his car out of sight, camouflage himself in the trees, and settle in to wait for their appearance.

He was no amateur; he'd been a private investigator since she had been choosing wedding dresses for her Barbie dolls.

He held down the shutter button to take a series of shots as they came up for air and looked around at the magnificent surroundings, smiling at each other, eyes shining.

All the while, he was trying to keep the negative thoughts at bay. Why had he fallen into private detection? It was one of the few ways he could make a living using his skill with a camera. He could have chosen another profession. He didn't need to spend his whole life following other people, taking pictures of their most private moments. What was the real point of his job? He destroyed lives, something he'd had his fill of long ago. When was the last time he'd brought a smile to a client's face? A real, genuine smile? He had wanted to make a difference in people's lives; to exonerate the innocent.

Zachary's phone started to buzz in his pocket. He lowered the camera and turned around, walking farther into the grove of trees. He had the pictures he needed. Anything else would be overkill.

He pulled out his phone and looked at it. Not recognizing the number, he swiped the screen to answer the call.

"Goldman Investigations."

"Uh… yes… Is this Mr. Goldman?" a voice inquired. Older, female, with a tentative quaver.

"Yes, this is Zachary," he confirmed, subtly nudging her away from the 'mister.'

"Mr. Goldman, my name is Molly Hildebrandt."

He hoped she wasn't calling her about her sixty-something-year-old husband and his renewed interest in sex. If it was another infidelity case, he was going to have to turn it down for his own sanity. He would even take a lost dog or wedding ring. As long as the ring wasn't on someone else's finger now.

"Mrs. Hildebrandt. How can Goldman Investigations help you?"

Of course, she had probably already guessed that Goldman Investigations consisted of only one employee. Most people seemed to sense that from the size of his advertisements. From the fact that he listed a post office box number instead of a business suite downtown or in one of the newer commercial areas. It wasn't really a secret.

"I don't know whether you have been following the news at all about Declan Bond, the little boy who drowned…?"

Zachary frowned. He trudged back toward his car.

"I'm familiar with the basics," he hedged. A four- or five-year-old boy whose round face and feathery dark hair had been pasted all over the news after a search for a missing child had ended tragically.

"They announced a few weeks ago that it was determined to be an accident."

Zachary ground his teeth. "Yes…?"

"Mr. Goldman, I was Declan's grandma." Her voice cracked. Zachary waited, listening to her sniffles and sobs as she tried to get herself under control. "I'm sorry. This has been very difficult for me. For everyone."

"Yes."

"Mr. Goldman, I don't believe that it was an accident. I'm looking for someone who would investigate the matter privately."

Zachary breathed out. A homicide investigation? Of a child? He'd told himself that he would take anything that wasn't infidelity, but if there was one thing that was more depressing than couples cheating on each other, it was the death of a child.

"I'm sure there are private investigators that would be more qualified for a homicide case than I am, Mrs. Hildebrandt. My schedule is pretty full right now."

Which, of course, was a lie. He had the usual infidelities, insurance investigations, liabilities, and odd requests. The dregs of the private investigation business. Nothing substantial like a homicide. It was a high-profile case. A lot of volunteers had shown up to help, expecting to find a child who had wandered out of his own yard, expecting to find him dirty and crying, not floating face down in a pond. A lot of people had mourned the death of a child they hadn't even known existed before his disappearance.

"I need your help, Mr. Goldman. Zachary. I can't afford a big name, but you've got good references. You've investigated deaths before. Can't you help me?"

He wondered who she had talked to. It wasn't like there were a lot of people who would give him a bad reference. He was competent and usually got the job done, but he wasn't a big name.

"I could meet with you," he finally conceded. "The first consultation is free. We'll see what kind of a case you have and whether I want to take it.

I'm not making any promises at this point. Like I said, my schedule is pretty full already."

She gave a little half-sob. "Thank you. When are you able to come?"

After he had hung up, Zachary climbed into his car, putting his camera down on the floor in front of the passenger seat where it couldn't fall, and started the car. For a while, he sat there, staring out the front windshield at the magical, sparkling, Christmas-card scene. Every year, he told himself it would be better. He would get over it and be able to move on and to enjoy the holiday season like everyone else. Who cared about his crappy childhood experiences? People moved on.

And when he had married Bridget, he had thought he was going to achieve it. They would have a fairy-tale Christmas. They would have hot chocolate after skating at the public rink. They would wander down Main Street looking at the lights and the crèche in front of the church. They would open special, meaningful presents from each other.

But they'd fought over Christmas. Maybe it was Zachary's fault. Maybe he had sabotaged it with his gloom. The season brought with it so much baggage. There had been no skating rink. No hot chocolate, only hot tempers. No walks looking at the lights or the nativity. They had practically thrown their gifts at each other, flouncing off to their respective corners to lick their wounds and pout away the holiday.

He'd still cherished the thought that perhaps the next year there would be a baby. What could be more perfect than Christmas with a baby? It would unite them. Make them a real family. Just like Zachary had longed for since he'd lost his own family. He and Bridget and a baby. Maybe even twins. Their own little family in their own little happy bubble.

But despite a positive pregnancy test, things had gone horribly wrong.

Zachary stared at the bright white scenery and blinked hard, trying to shake off the shadows of the past. The past was past. Over and done. This year he was back to baching it for Christmas. Just him and a beer and *It's a Wonderful Life* on TV.

He put the car in reverse and didn't look into the rear-view mirror as he backed up, even knowing about the precipice behind him. He'd deliberately parked where he'd have to back up toward the cliff when he was done. There was a guardrail, but if he backed up too quickly, the car would go right through it, and who could say whether it had been accidental or deliberate? He had been cold-stone sober and had been out on a job. Mrs. Hildebrandt could testify that he had been calm and sober during their call. It would be ruled an accident.

But his bumper didn't even touch the guardrail before he shifted into drive and pulled forward onto the road.

He'd meet with the grandmother. Then, assuming he did not take the case, there would always be another opportunity.

Life was full of opportunities.

CHAPTER TWO

Molly Hildebrandt was much as Zachary expected her to be. A woman in her sixties who looked ten or twenty years older with the stress of the high-profile death of her grandchild. Gray, curling hair. Pale, wrinkled skin. She wasn't hunched over, though. She sat up straight and tall as if she'd gone to a finishing school where she'd been forced to walk and sit with an encyclopedia on her head. Did they still do that? Had they ever done it?

"Mr. Goldman, thank you for seeing me so quickly," she greeted formally, holding her hand out for him to shake when he arrived at her door.

"Please, call me Zachary, ma'am. I'm not really comfortable with Mr. Goldman."

Telling her that he wasn't comfortable with it meant that she would be a bad hostess if she continued to address him that way, instead of her seeing it as a way of showing him respect. He hadn't done anything to deserve respect and was much happier if she would talk to him like the gardener or her next-door neighbor.

Not that there was any gardener. Molly lived in a small apartment in an old, dark brick building that was sturdy enough, but had been around longer than Zachary had been alive. The interior, when she invited him in, was bright and cozy. She had made coffee, and he breathed in the aroma in the air appreciatively. It wasn't hot chocolate after skating, but he could use a cup or two of coffee to warm him up after his surveillance. Standing around in the snow for a couple of hours had chilled him, even though he'd dressed for the weather.

Molly escorted him to the tiny living room.

"And you must call me Molly," she insisted.

She eyed the big camera case as he put it down. Zachary gave a grimace.

"Sorry. I didn't come to take your picture; I just don't like to leave expensive equipment in the car."

"Oh," she nodded politely. She didn't ask him who he had been taking pictures of. That wouldn't be gracious. She would have to imagine instead, and she would probably be correct in her guess.

They fussed for a few minutes with their coffees. Zachary wrapped his fingers around his mug, waiting for the coffee to cool and his fingers to warm. It felt good. Comforting. He waited for Molly to begin her story.

"You probably think that I'm just being a fussy old lady," she said. "Imagining something sinister when it was just an accident."

"Not at all. Why don't you tell me why you don't think it was an accident?"

"I'm not *sure* at all," she clarified. "Maybe they're right. Maybe it was an accident. It isn't that I doubt their findings…" she trailed off. "Not really. I know they had to do an autopsy and all that. We waited for months for them to come back with the manner of death. I thought that once they ruled, everyone would feel better."

"But you still have doubts?"

"I'm worried for my daughter."

Zachary blinked at her and waited for more.

"She's not well. I had hoped that once they released the body… and after the memorial… and after the manner of death was announced… each milestone, I thought, it would get better. It would be easier for her, but…" Molly shook her head. "She's getting worse and worse. Time isn't helping."

"Your daughter was Declan's mother."

"Yes. Of course."

"What's her name?"

"Isabella Hildebrandt," Molly said, her brows drawn down like he should have known that. "You know. *The Happy Artist.*"

Zachary had heard of *The Happy Artist.* She was on TV and was popular among the locals. Zachary didn't know whether she was syndicated nationally or just on one of the local stations. She had a painting instruction show every Sunday morning, and people awaited her next show like a popular soap. Most of the people Zachary knew who watched the show didn't paint and never intended to take it up. She was an institution.

"Oh, yes," Zachary agreed. "Of course, I know *The Happy Artist*. I didn't put the names together."

"When it was in the news, they said who she was. They said it was *The Happy Artist's* child."

"Sure. Of course," Zachary agreed. He rubbed the dark stubble along his jaw. He should have gone home to shave and clean up before meeting with Molly. He looked like he'd been on a three-day stakeout. He *had* been on a three-day stakeout. "I'm sorry. I didn't follow the story very closely. That's good for you; it means I don't have a lot of preconceived ideas about the case."

She looked at him for a minute, frowning. Reconsidering whether she really wanted to hire him? That wouldn't hurt his feelings.

"You were going to tell me about your daughter?" Zachary prompted. "I can understand how devastated she must be by her son's death."

"No. I don't think you can," Molly said flatly.

Zachary was taken aback. He shrugged and nodded, and waited for her to go on.

"Isabella has a history of… mental health issues. She was the one supervising Declan when he disappeared, and the guilt has been overwhelming for her."

That made perfect sense. Zachary sipped at his coffee, which had cooled enough not to scald him.

Molly went on. "I think… as horrible as it may sound… that it would be a relief for her if it turned out that Declan was taken from the yard, instead of just having wandered away."

"That may be, but how likely is that? Surely the police must have considered the possibility, and I can't manufacture evidence for your daughter, even if it would ease her mind."

"No… I realize that. I'm not expecting you to do anything dishonest. Just to investigate it. Read over the police reports. Interview witnesses again. Just see… if there's any possibility that there was… foul play. A third-party interfering, even if it was nothing malicious."

"I assume you know most of the details surrounding the case."

"Yes, of course."

"How likely do you think it is that the police missed something? Did they seem sloppy or like they didn't care? Did you think there were signs of foul play that they brushed off?"

"No." Molly gave a little shrug. "They seemed perfectly competent."

Zachary was silent. It wouldn't be difficult to read over the police reports and talk to the family. Was there any point?

"The only thing is…" Molly trailed off.

As impatient as Zachary was to get out of there, he knew it was no good pushing Molly to give it up any faster. She already knew she sounded crazy for asking him to reinvestigate a case where he wasn't going to be able to turn up anything new. For no reason, other than that it might help her daughter to come to terms with the child's death. He looked around the room. There were no pictures of Molly's husband, even old ones. There was no sign she had raised Isabella or any other children there. There were several pictures of a couple with a little child. Declan and Isabella and whatever the father's name was. There was one picture of Declan himself, occupying its own space, a little memorial to her lost grandson. There were no pictures of anyone else, so Zachary could only assume Isabella was an only child and Declan the only grandchild.

"Declan was afraid of water."

Zachary turned his eyes back to her. He considered. It wasn't totally inconceivable that a child afraid of the water would drown. He wouldn't know how to swim. If he fell in, he would panic, flail, and swallow water, rather than staying calm enough to float. Molly wiped at a tear.

"How afraid of the water was he?" Zachary asked.

"He wouldn't go near the water. He was terrified. He wouldn't have gone to the pond by himself."

"How tall was he?"

Molly gave a little shrug. "He was almost five years old. Three feet?"

"How steep were the banks of the pond and what was the terrain and foliage like?" He knew he would have to look at it for himself.

"I don't know what you want to know… there wasn't any shore to speak of. Just the pond. There were bulrushes. Cattails. Some trees. The ground is… uneven, but not hilly."

Zachary tried to visualize it. A child wouldn't be able to see the pond as far away as an adult would because of his short stature. If his view were further screened by the plant life, the banks steep and crumbly, he might not be able to see it until he was right on top of it. Or in it.

"It's not a lot to go on," he said. "The fact that he was afraid of water."

"I know." Molly used both hands to wipe her eyes. "I know that." She looked around the apartment, swallowing hard to get control of her emotions. "I just want the best for my baby. A parent always wants what's best. Growing up… I wasn't able to give her that. She didn't have an easy life. I wonder if…" She didn't have to finish the sentence this time. Zachary already knew what she was going to say. She wondered if that rough upbringing had caused Isabella's mental fragility. Whether things would have turned out differently if she'd been able to provide a stable environment. Molly sniffled. "Do you have children, Mr.—Zachary?"

Zachary felt that familiar pain in his chest. Like she'd plunged a knife into it. He cleared his throat and shook his head. "No. My marriage just recently ended. We didn't have any children."

"Oh." Her eyes searched his for the truth. Zachary looked away. "I'm sorry. I guess we all have our losses."

Although hers, the death of her grandson, was clearly more permanent than any relationship issues Zachary might have.

In the end, he agreed to do the preliminaries. Get the police reports. Walk the area around the house and pond. Talk to the parents. He gave her his lowest hourly fee. She clearly couldn't afford more. He wasn't even sure she'd be able to pay on receipt of his invoice. He might have to allow her a payment plan, something he normally didn't do, but something about the frail woman had gotten to him.

He put in an appearance at the police station, requesting a copy of the information available to the public, and handing over Molly Hildebrandt's request that he be provided as much information as possible for an independent evaluation.

"You got a new case?" Bowman grunted as he tapped through a few computer screens, getting a feel for how many files there were on the Declan Bond accident investigation file and how much of it he would be able to provide to Zachary.

"Yes," Zachary agreed. Obviously. He didn't encourage small talk; he really didn't want Bowman to start asking personal questions. They weren't friends, but they were friendly. Bowman had helped Zachary track down missing documents before. He knew the right people to ask for permission and the best way to ask.

Bowman dug into his pocket and pulled out a pack of gum. He unwrapped a piece and popped it into his mouth, then offered one to Zachary as an afterthought.

"No, I'm good."

Bowman chewed vigorously as he studied each screen. He was a middle-aged man, with a middle-age spread, his belly sagging over his belt. His hairline had started receding, and occasionally he put on a pair of glasses for a moment and then took them off again, jamming them into his breast pocket.

"How's Bridget?" he asked.

Zachary swallowed. He took a deep breath and steeled himself for the conversation. Bowman looked away from his screen and at Zachary's face, eyebrows up.

"She's good. In remission."

"Good to hear." Bowman looked back at his computer again. "Good to hear. It's been a tough time for the two of you." His eyes flicked back to Zachary, and he backtracked. "I mean it's been tough for her. And for you."

"Yeah," Zachary agreed. He waved away any further fumbling explanation from Bowman. "So, what have we got? On the Bond case?"

"Right!" Bowman looked back at his screen. "I've got press releases and public statements for you. medical examiner's report. The cop in charge of the file was Eugene. He likes red."

Zachary blinked at Bowman, more baffled than usual by his abbreviated language. "What?"

"Eugene Taft. I know, it's a preposterous name, but he's never had a nickname that stuck. Eugene Taft."

"And he likes red."

"Wine," Bowman said as if Zachary was dense. "He likes red wine. You know, if you want to help things along, have a better chance of getting a look at the rest of that file, the officers' notes and all the background and interviews. If you have to apply some leverage."

"And for Eugene Taft, it's red wine."

"Has to be red," Bowman confirmed.

"Okay." Zachary looked at his watch. "Can you start that stuff printing for me? Is there anyone downstairs?" He knew he would have to run down to the basement to order a copy of the medical examiner's report. Just one of those bureaucratic things.

"Sure. Kenzie should be down there still."

Zachary paused. "Kenzie. Not Bradley?"

"Kenzie," Bowman confirmed. "She's new."

"How new?"

"I don't know." Bowman gave a heavy shrug. "How long since you were down there last? Less than that."

Zachary snorted and went down the hall to the elevator.

As he waited for it, Joshua Campbell, an officer he'd worked with on an insurance fraud case several months previous, approached and hit the up button. He did a double-take, looking at Zachary.

"Zach Goldman! How are you, man? Haven't seen you around here lately."

"Good." Zachary shook hands with him. Joshua's hands were hard and rough like he'd grown up working on a farm instead of in the city. Zachary wondered what he did in his spare time that left them so rough and scarred. He wasn't boxing after work; Zachary would have been able to tell that by his knuckles. "Hey, how's Bridget doing? Did everything turn out okay…?" He trailed off and shifted uncomfortably.

"Yeah, great. She's in remission."

"Oh, good. That's great, Zach. Good to hear."

Zachary nodded politely. His elevator arrived with a ding and a flashing down indicator. Zachary sketched a quick goodbye to Joshua and jumped on. He was starting to regret agreeing to look into the Bond case.

The girl at the desk had dark, curly hair, red-lipsticked lips, and a tight, slim form. She was working through some forms, those red lips pursed in concentration, and she didn't look up at him.

"Hang on," she said. "Just let me finish this part up, before I lose my train of thought."

Zachary stood there as patiently as possible, which wasn't too hard with a pretty girl to look at. She finally filled in the last space and looked up at him. She raised an eyebrow.

"You must be Kenzie," Zachary said.

"I don't know if I must be, but I am. Kenzie Kirsch. And you are?"

"Zachary Goldman. From Goldman Investigations."

"A private investigator?"

"Yes."

He didn't usually introduce himself that way because it gave people funny ideas about the kind of life he lived and how he spent his time. Most people did not think about mounds of paperwork or painstaking accident scene reconstructions when they thought about private investigation. They thought about Dick Tracy and Phillip Marlowe and all the old hardboiled detectives. When really most of a private investigator's life was mind-numbingly boring, and he didn't need to carry a gun.

"And what can I do for you today, Mr. Private Investigator?"

"Zachary."

"Zachary," she repeated, losing the teasing tone and giving him a warm smile. "What can I do for you?"

"I need to order a copy of a medical examiner's report. Declan Bond."

"Bond. That's the boy? The drowning victim?"

"That's the one."

She looked at him, shaking her head slightly. "Why do you need that one? It's closed. A determination was made that it was an accident."

"I know. The family would like someone else to look at it. Just to set their minds at ease."

"You're not going to find anything. It's an open-and-shut case."

"That's fine. They just want someone to take a look. It's not a reflection on the medical examiner. You know how families are. They need to be able to move on. They're not quite ready to let it go yet. One last attempt to understand…"

Kenzie gave a little shrug. "Okay, then… there's a form…" She bent over and searched through a drawer full of files to find the right one. Zachary had filled them out before. Usually, he could manage to do an end-run and Bradley would just pull the file for him. Officially, he was supposed to fill one out. He didn't want to end up in hot water with the new administrator, so he leaned on the counter and filled the form out carefully.

She went on with her own forms and filing, not trying to fill the silence with small talk. Which Zachary thought was nice. When he was finished, he put the pen back in its holder and handed the form to Kenzie. To the side of the work she was doing. Not right in front of her face. She again ignored him while she finished the section she was on, then picked it up to look it over.

"You have nice printing," she observed, her voice going up slightly. She laughed at herself. "No reason why you shouldn't," she said quickly. "It's just that the majority of the forms that get submitted here are… well, to say they were chicken scratch would be insulting to chickens."

Zachary chuckled. "That's the difference between a cop and a private investigator."

"Neat handwriting?"

"Yeah. Cops have to fill out so many forms, they don't care. You can just call them if you need something clarified. Me… I know if I don't fill it out right, it's just going to go in the circular file." He nodded in the direction of the garbage can.

"I wouldn't throw it out," she protested.

"If you couldn't read it? What else would you do?"

"I would at least try to call you."

Zachary indicated the form. "That's why I printed my phone number so neatly."

Kenzie smiled and nodded. "It's very clear," she approved.

"You'll call me?"

"I'll let you know when it's ready to be picked up."

Zachary hovered there for an extra few seconds. He was enjoying the give-and-take of his conversation with her but didn't want her to accuse him of being creepy. He wasn't the type who asked a girl out the first time he saw her.

He gave her another smile and walked away from the desk. Maybe next time.

She Wore Mourning, Book #1 of the Zachary Goldman Mysteries series by P.D. Workman can be purchased at pdworkman.com

www.ingramcontent.com/pod-product-compliance
Lightning Source LLC
Chambersburg PA
CBHW070822190726
48292CB00006B/2083